PENGUIN BOOKS

OCEAN OF STORY

Christina Stead was born on 17 July 1902 in Sydney. She worked in educational psychology in NSW before sailing for England in 1928 where she worked as a clerk. A novel, *Seven Poor Men of Sydney,* and a book of short stories, *The Salzburg Tales,* were published in 1934 while she was working in Paris.

She and her American husband, William Blake, went to live in the USA in 1937 and remained there during the War. During this period *The Man Who Loved Children, For Love Alone* and *Letty Fox* were published. In the late 1940s and early 1950s the Blakes lived in the Netherlands, France and Switzerland. They moved to England and settled in London until William Blake's death in 1968. This period saw the publication of *A Little Tea A Little Chat, The People with the Dogs, Cotters' England (Dark Places of the Heart)* and *The Puzzleheaded Girl.*

In 1969 Christina Stead visited her homeland for the first time in forty years on a Visiting Fellowship to the Australian National University and returned to live in Australia in 1974. In that year she received the Patrick White Award for Australian writers and in 1982 was elected to Honorary Membership of the American Academy and Institute of Arts and Letters. She died on 31 March 1983.

OCEAN OF STORY

The uncollected stories of Christina Stead

CHRISTINA STEAD

PENGUIN BOOKS

Penguin Books Australia Ltd,
487 Maroondah Highway, P.O. Box 257
Ringwood, Victoria, 3134, Australia
Penguin Books Ltd,
Harmondsworth, Middlesex, England
40 West 23rd Street, New York, N.Y. 10010, U.S.A.
Penguin Books (Canada) Limited,
2801 John Street, Markham, Ontario, Canada L3R 1B4
Penguin Books (N.Z.) Ltd,
182-190 Wairau Road, Auckland 10, New Zealand

First published 1985 by Viking
Published in Penguin, 1986

Offset from the Viking edition
Made and printed in Australia by The Dominion Press Hedges & Bell

CIP

Stead, Christina, 1902-1983.
    Ocean of story.
    Bibliography.
    ISBN 0 14 010021 0.
    I. Geering, R.G. (Ronald George). II. Title.
A823'.2

CONTENTS

Introduction

1 *The Early Years – Australia*

2 *Apprentice Writer*

7 *Biographical and Autobiographical*

Introduction

Ocean of Story

I love *Ocean of Story,* the name of an Indian treasury of story; that is the way I think of the short story and what is part of it, the sketch, anecdote, jokes cunning, philosophical, and biting, legends and fragments. Where do they come from? Who invents them? Everyone perhaps. Who remembers them so that they pass endlessly across city life? I know some of those marvellous rememberers who pass on their daily earnings in story; and then they are forgotten to become fragments, mysterious indications. Any treasury of story is a residue of the past and a record of the day; as in Grimm, we have ancient folklore and church-inspired moralities and some tales to shiver at which are quite clearly frightening local events.

What is unique about the short story is that we all can tell one, live one, even write one down; that story is steeped in our view and emotion. The passerby who looks up and wonders why one window is lighted in a town at 3:00 in the morning and the invalid looking down who wonders why that woman comes out of the doorway so late, followed by a man more like a jailer than a lover. The short story is what everyone has and so is ever new and irrepressible.

I am not going to run down any sort of short story, even the mangled trash which appears on TV and the shiny stuff tailored for the smart papers (though you see I am doing so); and an able writer will make something (just for a short run) out of it even if hard luck strikes him and he feels he has to write such stuff to pay the rent (we never believe this particular plot, though).

There is another reason why this name appeals so to me. I was born into the ocean of story, or on its shores. I was the first child of a lively young scientist who loved his country and his zoology. My mother died – he mothered me. I went to bed early and with the light falling from the streetlamp through the open slats of the venetian blind he, with one foot on the rather strange bed I had, told his tales. He meant to talk me to sleep; he talked me awake. A younger child, fatherless, had come to take my cot; and my bed was made up on a large packing case in which were my father's specimens, a naturalist's toys, things from the oceans around us and from the north, Indonesia, China, Japan. There was the crocodile head with a bullet hole over the left eye, the whale tooth, splendid ivory with an ivory growth in the root canal, the giant spider-crab, the dried human heads, shrunk, painted and with coconut fiber hair, a plate-sized bony disc picked up on a near beach, the kneecap of some monster extinct millions of years before, a snake's beautiful skeleton. 'What is in the packing case?' I would tell and, what I forgot, he told.

Then came stories of the outback, the life of the black people whose land it was, though even they were comparative newcomers, come from no one knew where, brave canoe-sailors, men washed away by wind and current; and then, events in geological time ('we are an old old country, even the mountains have been blown away to little hills and rocks; and the extinct volcanoes no longer bother us, while they blow their heads off across the trench in New Zealand'); and even a few historic events, mostly connected with the life of Captain James Cook: my father, when young, resembled him. I must leave out all the stories of those many nights, a thousand, between two and four and a half, which formed my views – an interest in men and nature, a feeling that all were equal, the extinct monster, the coral insect, the black man and us, the birds and the fish; and another curious feeling still with me, of terrestrial eternity, a sun that never set. This was because he bore hard upon the weathered and withered and red-yellow look of our sunburned land and perhaps because of the glittering seas: and, also, a total lack of any feeling of death. During millions of years, all these creatures had lived and died, the coral-insects, architects of the reef, the ancient leaves and saurians that had left only a small imprint in the kerosene shale; and I knew that death was necessary 'for evolution to take place.' But there was their frail print, they had been there. Chekhov has in a story a boring father who took his unlucky daughter for long walks, pointing out to her the magnitude of the starry distances and our infinitesimal life, and was vain about it and liked to frighten her. Perhaps that is what happens in a dreary northern land, where one knows extreme cold, the feeling of death: but that was no experience of mine. I rejoiced in it; it was like a grand cloak covering me, and allowing me to see unseen; 'the cloak of darkness.'

And it went on and on, night after night, for more than two years, until the young man remarried and had other children to think about. His speciality was fish. He had a lecture called 'Giants and Pigmies of the Deep.' I knew this lecture. There was more. There was the bunyip, the blackfellows' legendary bugaboo – every country has one: what was it but 'treetrunks rolled in the floods,' and its voice the voice of the blackfellows' bull roarer or even the bittern among the reeds.

When, in those nights, he left me and went to talk to his sister, a happy, talking man with a happy woman, I at once heard other voices; another sort of animates began to relate their lives; and curiously enough, unlike the extinct monsters and the infinitesimal ocean creatures, who had all had to die, these animates complained. In our house, a husband lost and a wife lost, no one ever complained. It must have been my own viewpoint: these creatures complained. The chest of drawers usually began, 'I am so heavy, full of old clothes, the drawers squeak in and out and they sandpaper me, I'm dusty . . .' And the floorboards, 'What about us? We have your weight, you're crushing us and there's the packing case, too . . .' They were a morose, selfish, grumpy lot. It must have been their own natures.

When the father remarried, I was past four, and soon I was looking after a younger child and then younger and then I became the cradle rocker and message runner and the one who sang the sleep and told tales. But I don't know what they were.

The story is magical. In mixed company let someone say, 'I'll sing a song,' and who cares? (Perhaps in Wales or Russia they care.) But let someone say, 'Here's a story; it happened to me'; and everyone will listen. It's the passion that made the bazar reciter and enthralls the folklorist and keeps us looking at the inferior, twisted, cramped, and sterile stories on TV. It is the hope of recognising and having explained our own experience. Give writers a chance, start magazines, open columns (and by writers, I mean everyone, not professionals, I mean anyone with a poignant urge to tell something that happened to him once), and there will be no end to stories and what stories carry that make them vital – genuine experience and a personal viewpoint. It isn't necessary that these stories should be artistic or follow formula or be like Chekhov or the last metropolitan fad, or anything. The virtue of the story is its reality and its meaning for any one person: that is its pungency.

At any time that you have seen outlets appearing with the record of this kind of personal, family, labour experience, you will have seen hundreds and hundreds of new, original stories, of intense interest to the people they are written for – the small-town people, the trades-unionists, the unemployed, the elderly sick, anyone, anyone who is unrecorded. It is not necessary that these stories should be masterpieces. The idea of masterpiece and of great writer is good enough for professionals; the essential for us is integrity and what is genuine. Just look at the collections that appeared in the '30s: not all are memorable stories (some are), but all record the realities of the days when America was suffering and looking for a way out and thinking about its fate; and – look at those same today – they are a vivid and irreplaceable memento. That is what is best about the short story: it is real life for everyone; and everyone can tell one.

The story has a magic necessary to our happiness. In the West no one knew of the thousand and one nights, Oriental stories in Arabic, until they were translated by the Abbé Antoine Galland in France. They were a wild success. Fashionable young men collected round the Abbé's home calling for him; and, when he appeared,

cried, 'Tell us another story, Abbé, tell us another story.'
(That happens in New York at night, too, when, as I have
seen, friends gather and tell their remarkable, endless
folklore.) And the belief that life is a dream and we the
dreamers only dreams, which comes to us at strange,
romantic, and tragic moments, what is it but a desire for
the great legend, the powerful story rooted in all things
which will explain life to us and, understanding which,
the meaning of things can be threaded through all that
happens? Then there will no longer be a dream, but life in
the clear.

And now, the other day, being lonely, I was looking for
a group to join. There were clubs for stamp collectors,
coin collectors (I don't mean bankers), hikers, old folk,
and even a writers' club; but the last appeared to have
been organised by an enterprising agent for amateurs.
There was a UNO society (what do they do?), and others
too. In the end I found a small local friendship society and
joined. Though very near London, part of the web of
streets, it could have been in a distant country town, a
plain group that looked at old films, sometimes put up
foreign visitors, and had a modest bar, mostly beer and
sandwiches. No one seemed active but the treasurer, that
tall, dark, lithe angleworm sort of man, like a country
schoolteacher, who organises intellectual life in small
places. Christmas was upon us; they proposed, having no
money (and not really wanting any), to have home
entertainment – the films, the lottery, the gift stall, and
then . . . everyone was to tell a story.

What a scare! This is what comes of joining clubs.
What was I to tell them? Christmases I have known
(New York, Lausanne, Sydney)? A pungent Grimm, like
the 'Singing Bone' (a Cain and Abel story)? Or that idea
of the sensitive Franco-American writer, Julien Green,

that everyone is affected if not formed for life by a folk tale, a legend of childhood. I had already asked people about this. An economist was shaken, as a boy, by 'The Saltmakers' (why the sea is salt). A king invited saltmakers; the ship sank but the saltmakers went on grinding salt. I was enthralled by the legend of Roland and Oliver. I don't know how many times I read the legend of Roncevalles; and in my inner life there was always a Roland seeking an Oliver.

However, it all turned out differently. The treasurer got up from the little kitchen table they had placed out in front and said he himself would begin, not by telling a story but by reciting a poem he had learned at school; and which had affected him then and all his life. ('I was not good at school, though my parents did their best for me; and I did not remember much but I remember this.') It was 'Abou ben Adhem.' After him a woman read a long, carefully written story about an incident in an inn: it happened to her. It was a Pat and Mike story; and, after her, her husband, a Welsh schoolteacher, told at length a story which truly happened in his neighborhood in Wales. It was hard to believe it – I looked round anxiously. I knew it. I had heard it in New York. It was, though, a gaptoothed, woolly wildman, the ancestor of the story gone back to nature, and with a respectable end. How did that worthless little story get over into Wild Wales? Then another storyteller rushed forward – there was no stopping them. They jumped up, raised their fingers, said 'I want to . . . ' The girl from the inn, the Welsh schoolteacher, all wanted to talk again. They had to be held back.

And in the meantime I had thought of a splendid story – something that had happened to a friend of mine in Inner Mongolia about forty years ago. But would they believe it? – that he had inherited the armor of Genghis Khan? In the meantime, more and more and nearly everyone, those stuffy and snug people came to life, became mouths out of which bubbled stories, poor and ordinary or before unheard-of. And, as for me, they did not know I was a writer at all. 'Didn't you write a letter to the *Chronicle*?' (prized local weekly) said the treasurer, troubled by some memory. But because I was a newcomer they were too polite to ask me.

But there it was, the ocean of story, starting out in drops, drops of hill-dew, or sweat on the mountain's brow, running down, joining trickles from the rocks, just like Smetana's *Vltava,* broadening and sounding deep and moving in its fullness toward the ocean of story. The same thing could have happened anywhere; and anywhere it does. The short story can't wither and, living, can't be tied to a plan. It is only when the short story is written to a rigid plan, or done as an imitation, that it dies. It dies where it is pinned down, but not elsewhere. It is the million drops of water that are the looking-glasses of all our lives. 'The people have no history,' says Jean-Henri Fabre, 'throttled by the present, they can't dream of keeping the past in mind. But the forgotten bundles of family papers, would be instructive archives, most of all, comforting and in good odor, speaking to us of our forebears, their patient struggles against sour destiny, their tenacious efforts to build, grain by grain, what we are today. For individual interest, no history has such value. But things are so that the hearth is deserted and once the nestling gone, the nest is forgotten.'

In the USA most of all, I think, the short story has come to have just this value, these thousand and thousand grains of sand of individual lives have been partly recorded. Start a magazine anywhere there and you will find pouring in hundreds of tales, both authentic and borrowed, imaginative and plain. How can anyone store up this vast natural treasury? It is inexhaustible. There is so much that it can be wasted commercially (as it is) and men of talent can exhaust themselves through commercialisation, but there is always a free and fresh supply. All that is needed are a great number of places for the stories to be printed and told (they need not be printed). Some may and will die; but man's story never.

1 The Early Years – Australia

The Old School

The brick school in its yellow playground lay south west from and below Lydham Hill. One morning the wind-break on the knoll half sank to the horizon like a constellation wheeling; the house lay close to the breast of clay, shawled in pines. It turned out that there were trees in the school ground too – a Moreton Bay fig, a pepper tree with outstretched arms and in the lower part, near the headmaster's house, some flower beds for the infants.

The rumour about the school among the very small children who had never been there, was that children were beaten there and prisoned, 'caned and kept in, even the babies'. Mistrial and injustice were common at home, but there never was any particular conclusion, while in this new yellow earth, there were strange administrators, and things had a beginning and an end, the end at four o'clock, the conclusion liberty, sometimes delayed 'kept in half an hour'.

Cause and effect were much clearer than at home,

effect often unlooked for, doomful and needing analysis. Cause and effect mostly concerned the boys. A boy who jumps over the fence in the evening and shouts while playing stolen football, who picks a pansy from the infants' garden, who takes a pear from the Jollys' fruit stall, will soon be seen at the headmaster's table waiting for six cuts. There are even trusties, worthy little boys who do not seem to earn much respect, who are willing to take him there. And it is known pretty soon that the boy who stays away a whole week, a truant (that is a terrible word) in the hot silent gully, hidden by trees, paddling in the shallow creek, will go to the reformatory. The shadow of the reformatory was steep and dark. The informants – there are always a number of small sages about – know all about it. It had barred windows, food was bad, beatings the usual thing and you only came out of there to go to prison. In any case, in there they wore blucher boots. Blucher boots were stiff work-boots with heavy soles, cheap and long wearing. It was accepted that children who came to school in blucher boots would leave school early and do rough work. They might even work on the road alongside their fathers, who, too, wore blucher boots. The very word was socially significant: 'he's wearing blucher boots!' The nice girls looked down and away in shame, the dirty girls grinned. Nevertheless there was Tom Biggar, a fleshy chestnut and rose boy often good at drawing. Mr Roberts put upon the varnished table a blucher boot to draw and beside it some potatoes. There were protests from the girls and the nice boys. They also did not want to draw potatoes. Tom's were very good though. Mr Roberts said he might be an artist. Tom laughed, 'I'm going to work on the road with father, when I can.' He did not mind the prospect at all: he would earn money like his father.

All the outside information, these certitudes, were spread by the informants, natural moralists, two or three to a class and as far as I knew, all little girls. There were girls and boys in each class, but in their own society, that is in the playground, they did not mix. There was one moral little boy, though: he was called after one of the greatest English poets and had a good memory. Once the whole school was assembled in the long room to hear of a most serious crime. 'Who did it? It is a mistake to think you must be loyal to your classmates, when such a thing has been done.' The headmaster marched up and down and called 'Speak out'. Many moral questions were debated by the girls in large circular evasions but this was an obsolete law never debated. (The informants knew that someone had scandalously coupled the names of male and female teachers in stolen chalk on the boys' outhouse.)

In all the school assembled, only one child had the moral courage to tattle, Dryden Smith himself, an under-sized clerkly boy of ten; 'It was Snowy Thorne.'

This delation froze the school in lessons and caused the playgrounds to move with wagging heads and hands, as a fern-slope under wind; whatever the verdict, Dryden was left alone, contaminated: such a lesson in public morality lasts through life. Even the informants dared not become informers.

At the end of the year, Dryden won a prize *From Log Cabin to White House* given by Mr Roberts, a man who protected children, and Dryden recited before the parents and the minister 'Horatius at the Bridge', standing up trembling but brave. I can still see his pale serious round face as it rose, twice, once for the denunciation, once for the poem. And I saw him once more, at Christmas, at the old Anthony Hordern's with his little face just above the counter, where they sold men's ties. We saw each other but made no sign. He was at work. I was at school. I too had won a prize, 'Feats on the Fjord', which struck me as second best and I recited 'There was a sound of revelry by night'. I could see, as I proceeded, that the parents were stupefied with boredom and good manners.

The informants, our moralists, had clean dresses, pink, blue or sprigged, patent leather shoes and white socks, and curls natural or rag. They did clean school work too, even when we got to pen and ink. Goodness alone knows how, with their pink cheeks and shiny curls and neatly dressed brisk little mothers, they got all this news about jails, reformatories, judges and sentences, lashings, canings, bread and water.

When wrongs took place in school or grounds, the informants instantly knotted together, a town moot: they discussed, debated and delivered an opinion. What the teachers said was brought forward but only as hearsay. I never had an opinion to give; in one way I did not understand and then I was always puzzled. I thought then that cruelty and unjustice were natural and inevitable during all of a poor creature's life.

Now Snowy Thorne, the accredited bad boy of the school, a ten-year-old orphan with straw hair, tear-stained face, a good Norfolk suit given him by his aunts and blucher boots – if the little girls picked him out for gossip and innuendo it was because the teachers had picked him out first. The headmaster, a grey haired small-headed socialist, a mild moderate mediocre fellow, thought he had been slighted in being sent out to this distant suburban school, a revenge for his opinions. He hated Snowy Thorne. Some iniquity discovered, Mr Fairway would call together the three upper classes (fifth was top class then), pack them into the long room which

was built in a court house style, and make Snowy Thorne
walk up and down, up and down, all the length of the
room, by the three blackboards, up and down from the
desk where he got his canings to the door to the yard
through which he could escape (but Mr Roberts stood
there), in his neat but yellowing Norfolk suit and his dull
black boots. What annoyed Mr Fairway was that Snowy
Thorne would not admit all of his crimes, until after
being baited and exhibited and worn down he cried and
was caned; and even then no one was sure. But who else
threw ink into the new fish pond that Mr Fairway had
just put in at his own expense to cheer up the boys'
playground? Who else wrote certain symbols on the
wall, for example, a rooster and a strange eye with long
lashes? Whose pale poll was seen at evening star time
alone in the playground and whistling to itself? Where
had the toffee apples gone from the IXL shop? It could
only have been the butter ladies' boy (his aunts sold
butter). I do not know what became of Snowy Thorne.
Poor Mr Fairway! The school was given more class-
rooms, a better grade; and a new assistant head, smart,
conceited and lively and, worst of all, with a B.A. degree,
came to push the aging man about.

When we first came to school, we sang a pretty song
about the old bell,

> I was hung in my place when the village was young,
> And the houses were scattered and few,
> In the old dingy belfry for ages I've swung.
> But my song is the same as when new.

Though I knew it was about another place, it also seemed
to me to be about Bexley, where the houses were scattered
and few; but by the time Mr Bobsley B.A. came, closer
settlement had begun, many old paddocks were closed to
us.

The first teacher I knew was a confident pretty neat woman, married, with two young children at home. She told us about them almost every day: luckily for her in these children she had met her ideals. She had large blue eyes and crinkled hair; and her children were fair, too. The school children called her 'very strict', not a slur. This was another moral issue often debated – who was the better teacher, the strict or the slack?

'If I hear a single sound you won't go home to lunch, you'll stay in all day and I'll make rabbit pie out of you and eat you,' she said. This threat caused some of the infants to sob out of hunger in prospect; other sobbed out of fear. We were very young. Each shiny morning she looked up and down the ranks as they marched in and standing at her desk would cry, 'Millie fall out, Jack Dodger, Will Hill, Polly – fall out' and by the time the class stood at its desks there would be on the floor a ragged line of the guilty, surveyed by the others with interest and guilt. It was not always possible to understand why they were guilty. It was easy to note some, torn jacket, hair 'like a birch broom in a fit', and Maidie Dickon of course, for truancy, though she hid in no sunny gully. We sang the first song, 'Good morning to you, glorious sun', sat down and the moment came, the review of the sinners, more exciting to the teacher than to them. Some after a homily would be sent back to their seats, two or three were left to tramp up and down. Then a general explanation of the law. If parents could not afford boots they must send a note explaining; but if children had boots and came without, then – and so forth. Children had the duty of asking their parents for boots and shoes; if the soles were worn out, they themselves must take them to the boot-mender's. I myself stood there once in broken boots, but was saved. As I stood there with flushed cheeks and resentful, the class sang its second song, with the chorus, 'Shoo, shoo, go out black cat'. At this moment the headmaster appeared twinkling (he was younger and happier then). He pretended to be a black cat and ran out: the delinquents were sent back to their seats. When the class set to work, Maidie Dickon would be called to the desk and her case gone into. She had been away eight days, say, and only returned in response to the teacher's note. She must now go home and bring a note of excuse from her mother. The dark haired little girl went out silent, passive. As she clumped to the door, one of the informants, the censors (who felt themselves enabled to speak in class) remarked that Maidie was wearing boys' boots, blucher boots. So she was. Presently another who had been sent to the head with a message, returned to say that Maidie was sitting in a corner of the shed, doing nothing. So she was, she could even be seen from our doorway, quite still, head drooping. A willing messenger was sent to tell her to go home. The next day she did not come; but at mid-morning on the following day someone saw a motionless bundle there, with her two bare legs in the boots, crouched in the infants' shed: she had no note.

For a few days after, she sat in her desk in front, clumsily doing lessons with a book and pencil from the school cupboard. In those days, new books and pencils from the cupboard were given out sparingly: you had to bring your own. The censors were indignant (though well provided with books and pencil cases). There was a considerable outcry, 'It isn't fair' they exclaimed. Usually a new book was given as a sort of prize, for very good work. Maidie would begin a new exercise book and then stay away for so long that the book would belong to someone else by the time she returned. She came without any property at all, no pencil box, sponge box, slate pencil, pencil, school bag, lunch, handkerchief, forlornly destitute.

The censors (the informants) were astonishing newsgatherers. How could they know? – but they did – that Mr Dickon was a roadworker who had been on strike (for them a criminal thing), that Mrs Dickon was a washerwoman, never home in the daytime. When she got a query from the teacher, Mrs Dickon always answered at once, on odd pieces of paper, bills or newspaper, which were exhibited and read out to the class by the clean gold haired teacher. These notes would say 'Maidie had to help me,' and once she said 'I have a new baby and Maidie had to stay at home to help.' Maidie knew a brief popularity then: the informants loved new babies.

Monday mornings were bank mornings. Children with prudent parents brought each a shilling or a sixpence and went to the headmaster who wrote down in each bank book the sum brought. He complained about it – how did we know that? – and we could not understand his complaint at such a privilege: a moaner, evidently. I also banked one shilling a week and one Monday the shilling was missing. Neighbours and busybodies (informants should I say) helped me look for it, said it was stolen. Knowing how confused I was, how I always lost things at home, I thought I had lost it myself. We turned out the little lunch case, poked at its seams and everyone studied the floorboards. 'Who stole it?' very soon became 'Maidie Dickon stole a shilling.' 'How do you know?' 'She must have, she's poor.' Even the teacher was shaken. Maidie Dickon remained as before, silent, forlorn. I felt guilty. I felt sure it was I. Justice without evidence took its course. The following Monday when I opened my case a shilling piece lay on top. 'Maidie Dickon must have put it back' they cried. As for me, I believed that I had overlooked it, that it had fallen out of a seam, a pocket. That notion of Maidie Dickon climbing up all those stairs (I was at the back in a banked classroom), opening cases, taking out, putting in and all with such cunning and stealth, she who never moved, was always late, did not fit. Even now, she never spoke, never volunteered word or action. There she is though, the little girl in white, with her bowed heavy shoulders and black eyes, in my mind; and with her, the horror of money.

She was sitting there one morning hunched more than usual because of the dress. Someone was reading the lesson, 'A man in a land where lions are found was once out late in the day far from home' (a phrase I have never forgotten), but the little girls' interest was glued to a topic right at home and they interrupted the fascinating lion story (I remember that the man hid in a hole under the cliff and the lion leaped right over him into the gulf), to remark to the teacher that Maidie was wearing a new dress made out of a sheet. 'No, it's a flour bag, her mother hasn't got any sheets.' This was a serious argument without malice. 'Mrs Taylor, she shouldn't come to school in a dress made out of a sheet' – craning, inspecting, deciding. They had been simmering with this news, waiting for the moment to let it out. Before school, she had pulled away from their inquisitive puzzled fingers and eyes, little sparrows pecking at the odd-feathered one, her large opaque black eyes on them and then away – with what feeling? Even in the lines that morning, they, the good, had been disorderly, fluttering. And now, when the bright haired woman settled them all, they told her she had been obeyed. Maidie had only stayed away the last time because she had no dress to wear. Now she had a dress, 'It's made out of a sheet.' 'Flour bags?' 'No, it's a sheet.' The teacher, curious, went right up to Maidie's desk and studied the dress.

It was soft old thick cotton, made in fashion, with a deep yoke, long sleeves into wristbands, several inch wide pleats into a waistband, tucks and a wide hem to let down. It was white and remained white, though certain marks (which had made them say flour bags) had faded with washing.

Maidie never had any lunch. During the lunch recess she sat by herself at the far end of the wooden seats which ran round under the high brick walls. The rest of the girls in groups in the noonday shade of the buildings occasionally glanced her way, during a lull in their busy colloquies, condemning her for her misery, some, perhaps, curious about her life. If a newcomer, a wandering casual, not yet incorporated socially or perhaps even kind-hearted, approached her, the playground leaders at once dispatched a messenger, 'You musn't talk to her: she hasn't any lunch,' and some other parts of the indictment might be added, if the wanderer hesitated.

Some hungry children ate their lunches in snatches under the desks during school hours and had none left when noonday came. Some of these grasshoppers cast eyes on their friends' lunches and even begged; but they got little if anything. They too had the sin of lunchlessness, though it was understood they were more weak than sinning. Was it one of those who in the morning poached another's lunch? In the middle of the morning Dorothy (a sweet little girl who was not an informant) found her lunch gone. 'The thief – the thief' a word they liked to shrill and who could it be? Yes, Maidie it might be – but for some reason the informants had grown a little careful since the episode of the shilling. They must have had doubts, too. But what a din!

She listened at her desk, motionless: she sat in the shed

or playground. At last, the lunchless one, Maidie wept, but no one pitied her. They sang the midday song, 'Home to dinner, home to dinner, hear the bell, hear the bell, bacon and potatoes . . .' etc. Dorothy lived too far away to go home and the teacher gave her money for the IXL shop.

It is a hard cruel knot that has gathered in the shade at the top of the yard, looking over their shoulders fiercely at the girl in the white dress, a bundle of submission in the sun sometimes shaking her black basin-crop which she scratches ('she has nits') and glancing mildly round her: perhaps she is shortsighted. 'Thieves oughtn't to be allowed in school,' and they bring into their talk the reformatory, these pink and blue girls, whispering secrets, boasting and harsh; and yet all are afraid. The reformatory for Maidie, there with coarse dishes, coarse clothes, sleeping on sacking or planks, there children are flogged, though it serves them right, there is the cat o' nine tails, there they are put into cells alone, there are iron bars on the windows and if they escape the police catch them. The little girls in pink and blue know the names of the jails – Long Bay, Parramatta, Bathurst. Where do the charming little balls of fluff, their mothers' happiness, gather this awful lore? Mrs Taylor, the teacher, comes round the corner of the infants' building where Maidie sits in the midday sun, close to the side gate leading into the headmaster's dark snug cottage. Mrs Taylor speaks,

'Are you hungry, Maidie?'

'Yes.'

'Have you any lunch?'

'No.'

'Don't you ever bring any lunch?'

'No.'

'Come and have lunch with me.'

She takes her by the hand. They go round the corner towards the infants' building where the teacher has her packet lunch, done up in a white damask serviette, on her desk.

The teacher does not acquire merit by this action. How set back the informants are now! 'She oughtn't to do it!' Yes, morality has got a black eye. The teacher has fallen from grace. 'She shouldn't give her lunch when she never brings any.' What Mrs Taylor does will henceforth be debated with less than latitude: she has sided with the luckless, rebuffed the righteous. I was there. I was never able to make up my mind about things; and so it is still there, clear to me, the ever burning question of good and bad which (to be fair to the informants) so greatly occupied their minds. I always thought it strange that adults do not notice how profoundly little children are engrossed and stirred by moral debate. They are all the time sharpening their awareness of the lines and frontiers.

The Milk Run

Lydham Hill was the name of the knoll and of the cottage, too; it was painted on the stone pillars where the iron carriage gates closed the now unused drive. The cottage stood on the crest of a high ridge overlooking Botany Bay, some eight miles distant and was built foresquare, east-west, so that they could look from the verandah straight between the headlands, Cape Banks and Cape Solander, to the Pacific.

They could see from the attic windows the obelisk standing where Captain Cook first landed with his botanists, Banks and Solander, and they could see on stormy days the little launch they called *The Peanut* tossing between the heads as it went towards Kurnell. The cottage was built of rough-hewn sandstone blocks cut in the quarry down the hill and hauled up in the old days. The trees round the house, Norfolk Island and other pines, pittosporum, camphor laurel, were seventy and more years old and the pines had seeded in the old neglected orchard where the seedlings grew higher every year, faster than the children. The knoll itself was iron-stone capped and penetrated by heavy, thick and almost pure clay, gamboge yellow, stained red where the iron-stone stuck out its nodules.

It was almost country still; few houses, large pastures, unpaved streets of sand or clay, foul and grassy gutters. The short street Lydham Avenue, which went over the hump before the house, westward, was a hazard, almost impassable in wet weather. Cartwheels, horseshoes, boots, umbrella ferrules were sucked in by the clay. In the hot sun the clay soon turned to dough and then to pottery. A messenger boy, the young postman, the women and children of Lydham Hill, had to cross the clay to get to the tram or the shops and might lose a handkerchief, a parasol, a shoe, a parcel; and after poking at it gingerly, afraid to fall in the muck, would abandon it and struggle to the clay bank and look back just as if the thing had been carried out to sea. The postman's prints, first of a sandshoe which he lost as he crossed to Lydham and then of his naked foot, and a copy of the *St George Call,* which he had dropped while trying to get his shoe back, remained week after week. The footprints and tracks remained and even at the next big rain they did not disappear, but only formed little foot-shaped puddles and long canals.

The Council occasionally sent men with a cart and shovels to scrape off the surface; and with it, they gleaned the lost articles and went away with the cart, leaving behind an identical clay surface, but with the banks higher now, until the people in Lydham Hill had to cut steps in the bank, yellow clay steps.

It was warm, October, summer just beginning. October is the month of the roof-raising equinoctial gales, which shouting, bring down trees and capsize sheds. It was a Saturday. The day and night before there had been gales; rain in the morning – in the evening, a sunset the colour of the saffron tearose at the gate. Matthew, going for milk on Friday had lost a sandshoe. 'Clumsy ape,' said his father, goodnaturedly, flipping his cheek with the nails of his left hand and at the same time explaining that he and Matthew were lefthanded; and he went on to explain how very difficult this made things for his neighbours, a lady say, at public dinners; and that Matthew later on, would find it awkward, too. Matthew was seven. Then his father, going barefoot, had squelched happily out into the mud and got the shoe back. It needed soaking and cleaning. Said his father, 'From now on you go to Dappeto barefooted; it's good for the feet anyway.' Dappeto was his grandfather's place, where he got the milk.

All the week, in the evenings, his father with his elder brother Jimmy-James, had been lopping the lower boughs off the Norfolk pines down the horse-paddock side. They called it the horse-paddock because it was rented to a brown horse for one pound a week, a lonely horse that could be seen streets away on their slope and which people thought was their horse; but they were not allowed to speak to it.

With the cut branches the three of them built a gunyah, an aboriginal shelter, placing the tall boughs against a goodsized trunk, lacing them together with small branches. It made an odorous half-tent, green, dark, with a floor of old brown pine-needles, nine inches to a foot thick, so that even now it was dry and warm, on the slope.

Matthew had dragged some of the other boughs to the bottom of the white paddock, a pony's paddock, so called because it had a white railing. In it they kept two fullgrown emus named Dinawan (a native word for emu) and Dibiyu, (a native word for the whistling duck because this emu whistled). Dinawan and Dibiyu had come to them newly hatched chicks, striped and about the size of fowls. Beyond this fence at the bottom Matt had built this gunyah to share with his friend Lyall Lowrie, also seven years old, a boy who lived in one of the new brick cottages downhill. There was building all around them, fascinating for the boys.

Matt and Lyall were sitting in the gunyah close together, talking in low interested voices. It was quite warm, though the sun was striking higher at the trees as it westered. Matt, though he did not say so, was hiding from the house. The boys had torn away the rough pine-needles and were poking in the soft blackish felted earth. They had found some small red ants.

'That's the beginning of an ants' street,' said Matthew.

'I know, one street on top of the other,' said Lyall.

'Like a city of the future,' said Matthew.

A whistling began. Matthew peered through the pine-branches. A woman's voice came down the hill. Matthew said,

'I have to go for the milk. Do you want to come?'

'Where is it? The dairy?'

'It's my grandmother's place: about a mile.'

But Lyall had to go home. He climbed a branch, reached out for the fencetop, dropped down, shouted, 'I'll see you tomorrow.'

'If I don't have to work,' said Matthew.

Matthew toiled up the orchard path, made of pebbles stuck in clay. At the south end of the house was a lattice, with one panel sagging from the gale. His father was repairing it. A tall strong fair man, burnt red by the sun, he stood in the opening leading to the brick yard, a courtyard almost entirely enclosed by domestic buildings in sandstone, a shelter from the hilltop wind.

'Milk-oh!' said his father.

'I made a gunyah,' said Matthew.

'Good-oh. And now skedaddle.'

Matthew was a fair sturdy boy who closely resembled his father. His sunbleached hair was whiter; he had a thick down over his temples joining his pale eyebrows, and it ran over the sides of his cheeks where his beard would be.

As soon as he came in sight of his father, his eyes became fixed on the man's face, he smiled with an unconscious faint rapture and, his head turning, his glances followed his father, a restless, energetic man, never still.

'Do you love your Dad?' said his father, smiling with coquettish cunning at the child.

The boy burst out laughing, 'Yes, Dad!'

His worship of his father was a family joke, a public joke and something that irritated his mother. They talked about him when they thought he was not listening. He was always listening idly, his head turned away, while he played with ants, bees, wasps; and mooned, as they said. The ants, bees, wasps did not sting him; they would hang resting on his hand. His idling, playing was not a ruse. In his dreamy pastimes, he liked to be a part of what he heard, the snatches and inconsequence of their talk, part of the wasps, the rush of wind, an entire life, vague but delicious. He could sit in the sun watching the ant-trails for hours; he never hurt the ants. His father told him they were ant-engineers, ant-architects, ant-soldiers, ant-nurses, ant-scouts; but he scarcely thought of it. 'Perhaps another Darwin,' said his father; and he said the same when it turned out that Matthew was slow in school. Darwin was slow in school. But at other times, Matthew galloped about shouting; no one knew what he shouted.

His father was pretending to block the way. Matthew could get very angry. His father was curious about it and teased him. With a rough push, the boy got past and went to the kitchen. The milkcan stood on the table, a workman's billycan of grey flecked enamel with a tin top that served as a cup. He set off. His feet were bare. They were solid well-formed feet, with the skin grown thick and horny on the soles and blackened underneath, dark grey with dirt you could not get out, yellow-splashed at the sides, with deep cracks on the soles right down to the red flesh. He was used to having sore feet and dug deep into the soft mud, soothed.

He went down the grass slope outside the iron gates, where they were now laying the foundations to build. The men had gone and he picked up a few bright nails from between the floor joists for his father. The men liked him and let him take nails anyway.

At Wollongong Road he scanned the dairy farm opposite. The he crossed the road and walked along by the two-rail fence. The farm buildings of whitewashed planks lay slightly below the swell of the meadow, towards Stoney Creek gully. Matt trotted down the deeply rutted tussocky footway. He had not gone far, before the boy he feared came out from the brick wall of the old house where he had been waiting, with a mad scowl, his features jumping as if on red and black wires, his teeth showing. He rushed to the fence and swung his greenhide thong on to Matthew's shoulder and face. He did not say a word but with a fierce grin of hatred jerked and swung.

'Don't,' said Matthew. He hurried along, the milkcan swinging wildly on its wire handle. His enemy followed him to the next panel and the next, but did not get through the fence on to the footway. The greenhide bat, about fifteen inches long and three or four inches wide, slapped down on Matthew's left side. He started to cry and ran along the ruts, the milkcan insensately hopping up and down and doing somersaults. But the boy, having caused terror, ceased after a few more panels and walked diagonally towards the milking sheds, turning round to make a face. The cows were coming up from the gullyside and gathering at the door of the shed. The milkman's son was a thin muscular boy of about ten, with dark hair and regular features; but when Matthew saw him, he was always snarling, scowling, grinning in fury.

Matthew reached the next block, all small redroofed houses; but it was some time before he saw the ochre-coloured picket fence of Dappeto. Until a fortnight before, it had been his sister Emily, a clumsy girl of eleven, always in the wars, as they said, who had gone for the milk to Dappeto, every evening after school. Then one day, almost home, she fell in the clay and sent the can flying. She came home dirty, her long fair hair wet and dark-streaked over her red cheeks, with no milk for the baby and the story, 'a boy beat me'. 'What boy?' 'I don't know.' Though Matthew knew the boy, their unbelief made him think it was a lie, too.

Now, though they did not believe her and he was smaller, it had become his job to go for the milk. Even his mother had made no protest.

Here was his grandfather's house, Dappeto. Inside the fence grew all kinds of trees, camphor laurel, pittosporum, swamp box, eucalypts, wattles. He went down the lane to the side where was a big gate for the buggy. He dug his toes into the asphalt softened by the day's sun. There was the old camphor laurel with the broad low arms good for climbing and hiding, there the giant Araucaria Bidwilli, with shining dark green stabbing leaves. There was the man Tom Grove, called The Man, in the cow paddock at the salt-lick. Matthew went in under the archway where were the feed bins and up into the second kitchen. No one was there. Up a step into the kitchen. Mary the maid sat at the window knitting.

'I saw you coming. How's your mother?'

'All right.'

'What dirty feet! Where are your shoes?'

'I lost one.'

He went up another step, on to the verandah, turned right; there was the double pantry: preserves beyond in a dark room; here on the shelf three large shallow pans of milk for skimming. Mary came and poured milk into his can.

The parrot sitting on his perch on the verandah, put down his head engagingly, said 'Cocky want a bit of bread and sugar?' Mary dipped a crust in milk and sugar and gave it to the boy.

'Give it to Joe.'

'No, no,' he said, flushing. The parrot had a cunning eye and heavy beak.

'Emus have bigger beaks,' said Mary. She was a country woman from Hay ('Hay, Hell and Booligal,' he knew) and saw no sense in keeping emus.

'Emus don't bite,' said Matt.

Mary, in her long flowing skirt, stepped along the verandah and handed the parrot his crust. He was a handsome Mexican said to be forty years old, as old as Mary herself.

'Go and see your grandmother; I'll get some butter for your mother.'

Up another slate step into the house, where right beside the door there was a little room called the housekeeper's room, where his grandmother liked to sit.

'Is that you, Mattie?' called a voice very like the parrot's voice.

A large solid neat old woman, with white hair strained back into a little bun, in a black dress with white trimmings, a housekeeper's dress, sat in an armchair stuck between the table and the wall. She could look out through two windows in the angle, one towards Wollongong Road, one towards the greenhouses. She smiled fondly but did not stop revolving her thumbs in her clasped bloated hands.

'Look at the dirty feet! Doesn't your mother give you shoes to wear?'

'I have sandshoes.'

'Where are they?'

'It's healthy to go without shoes.'

'Come and kiss Old Mum. How's your brother?'

'Jamstealer is all right. He's playing football this afternoon.'

The grandmother said suddenly, 'Jamstealer is not a nice name to call your brother.'

'It doesn't mean jamstealer: it's a name. Daddy calls him that.'

'It's not a nice name for your father to call his son.' Matthew frowned. The old woman rose and took his hand.

'Come and I'll get you some flowers for your mother. How is she?'

'Mother's lying down.'

She plucked flowers from the beds along the cracked asphalt drive. Her flat monk's shoes slid off the grassy verge.

'I nearly fell down on my bum,' she said, began to laugh, opening her mouth wide in her creased floury face. She kept her eyes on the little boy, 'What would your father say to that?' Matthew was shocked but said nothing. 'Milking we had a stool called a bumstool,' she said. She had come from a dairying family on the South Coast. He eyed her straight. They came back to the kitchen.

'Tell your mother to come and see her mother one of these days.'
Mary handed him the butter in a bag and the flowers and the milk.

'Scratch Cocky,' said the parrot. He lowered his head and ruffled the feathers, showing grey skin.

'Beat the gong,' begged Matthew.
Mary picked up the chamois-headed stick which hung on the gong beside the back door. Joey shifted his feet in a slow respectable dance. Mary hit the gong twice: Joey screeched,

'Stephen! Walter! Edward! Anthony! John! Arthur! Matthew! Robert! Frederick! Albert! William! Leah! Rachel! Pitti!'
It was a country woman's screech.

No air-thin boys and girls came gambolling from the paddocks and orchard, from the gardens and bowling-green, hungry for dinner; though in years long gone they had come racing, in flesh and blood. Those were his uncles and aunts and Pitti was his mother, the youngest, 'Pretty.'

Matthew went back up the asphalt drive, the home-made butter in one hand, the flowers and the quart milkcan jostling in the other. When he came back to the dairy on Wollongong Road, he hesitated. He could cross towards Forest Road, heading round a triangle of land just being fenced in and invisible to the dairy boy. But he was a little afraid of the new route. He crossed and came along the other side of the Wollongong Road, along a tall apricot-coloured fence of new hairy boards. At the farther point of that triangular plot, too, was an interesting wooden post, very old and grey and eaten inside by termites. It had been smouldering for weeks, set alight by the sun, not extinguished by the rain. The sun was on the horizon. Shafts of red touched him across the dairy. He reached the end of the new fence and Lydham Hill could be seen with its great head of trees. He stumbled on a big tussock and fell. Though he kept hold of the things, the milk spilled. He got up quickly and righted the can, but there was very little milk left. He tried with the lid to catch some milk from the ground, but it had soaked away into the sand, leaving a light stain. Just a few of the grass blades held a dew of milk. When he shook them, the dew fell. He did not know what to do. He was too tired to go back to Dappeto. At home, they might beat him, worse, shout and deplore. As he still poked stupidly about looking for milk, he saw a gold coin, a sovereign, under the tussock. He knew it, for his father brought home his pay on Saturdays, spread the coins on the table, gold sovereigns and half sovereigns, silver and let them finger it. He was proud of it, what he earned.

Matthew picked up the gold coin and hurried home up the yellow clay, past the saffron tearose, the 'Chinaman's Finger Tree', a tree with yellow bell flowers, so called because they put the flowers on their fingers and rushed at each other, shrieking, 'I'm a Chinaman.'

He had his statement ready, 'I fell over the grass and spilled the milk.'

His mother was in the kitchen in her grey silk dressing-gown, with the silver and gold dragons on it, at the bottom gold water-waves and a gold tower. She had a baby's white shawl round her head, a sign of neuralgia.

'I was tired,' he complained.

'Barely a cupful,' she said contemptuously. 'Open the condensed milk, Eva. What's that?'

'Butter and some flowers and Old Mum says to go and see her.'

'I'll go and see Mother tomorrow. I wish I could leave this darn windy barn. And the emus walked in this evening and ate your father's cat's-eye waistcoat buttons that were lying on the kitchen windowsill.'

'I found this,' said Matthew, 'it's a sovereign.'
Until he had shown it, he had not been quite sure about it; was it really there?

The two women came close. 'Yes, so it is,' said his mother; 'some poor brute of a workman lost his wages and is getting a tongue-banging this minute, I know.'

'Can I keep it, Mother?'

'I don't suppose so. We'll ask your father.'
But his father said, 'It's no use crying over spilt milk,' and he said Matthew could keep the sovereign. 'You can start a savings account at school on Monday.'

Matthew turned up his fair flushed face radiant and looked at his father's face: it seemed to him all pure love. He exclaimed, 'Tommy Small whaled me; with a greenhide bat.'
They drew back, inspecting him curiously.

'Where?'

He pulled up his sleeve and there, to his surprise, there really was a broad bruise. He now expected his father to break into shouts of indignation. His mother stood in doubt; his father also stood away with a strange expression, a queasy, almost greedy expression, yet shy and frightened, too. Matthew felt that they would do nothing about it.

'It's a dirty dairy,' said his father.

'Must I go for the milk tomorrow?'

'Of course, gee-up, milk-oh!'

His mother said, 'You must be a man, my son.'

They did not believe him. They thought he was copying Emily. He did not go further. Muteness crowded his mouth: his throat closed. He saw they had abandoned him, and expected nothing. On Sunday he went with his mother for the milk. 'It isn't half a mile,' she said. After that he never saw Tommy Small again. This too was something he did not comprehend; he began to feel that perhaps he was a liar, like Emily. But then the gold coin was inexplicable; and what astonished him most, in secret, was that it was he who had found it. He knew he was not clever or lucky. A thought grew inside him, evolving out of doubt and fluff, 'Perhaps later I will have just one big piece of luck;' and the gold coin remained shining in the soft animal darkness of his mind.

When the new houses were finished and he could no longer go there for nails for his father, people came to live and presently a new dairy sent round a cart. He would rush out when the milkman came, glorying in the spurting foaming quarts that they took in, in two big jugs they had bought. He stood on the brick landing outside the kitchen and watched, his tongue at his teeth. 'Two quarts, please,' his mother always said, standing in her long pink dressing-gown, her black hair fluffed out. Oh, the milk! The flowing milk.

A Little Demon

The Masons are one of those large inwoven families, sprung from a prolific and managing father and mother, good in business and able to provide for all. The children of this old pair, now old themselves, all married young; but they have small business ability and few children, perhaps one to a couple, no more. They all work, but after work they pass their time in the timeless land of the family, happy, active, with the same notions, friends and foes. Some of their friends were friends in youth, others were drawn in forty years ago and have remained part of the story every since, just as if they were brothers or sisters. But they can take in new friends too; and, after a time, the figures of the new friends are drawn on the pattern, in the right colours and attitudes, with little differences embroidered and attributes given, as a man with a falcon, a woman with a bouquet in old weaves. And after this, the falcon or the bouquet or the reaping-hook, this figure too, is part of the family legend.

In this easy-going dreamy way, life is passed in houses

and on properties the family have slowly acquired, based on the investment and energy of the original Mason couple. The conversation is about family affairs, old anecdotes which take the place of fairy-tales in other childhoods, witticisms invented long ago, by the dead or living, and family personalities, all briefly stylised.

The family, because it is essentially and from beginning to end a family, is radical or liberal in its political opinions; they well understand the need for a republic, free speech, free purpose. And just as in politics, caricatures emerge. Each character has a part long assigned to him, which he can never change; even when his hair changes from dark to pale, his character from bad to good, his fortune from poor to rich or the other way about, even if he changes his wife or his profession, he remains, 'Charlie the gate crasher' let us say.

But there is one thing diminishes a Mason and is quite incomprehensible to the family, frowned upon, and bitterly spoken of – it is to leave the city, county and country anciently picked upon by the founding father. He is an artist – he must go to South Africa on a tour! That is no excuse! He is an airman, a pilot and must fly to Europe every week: a very thin, unreliable and giftless thinking he must have, a shabby temperament: the Masons shrug.

Anyone admitted to the family, who have this invisible but ever valid passport, receives all their news, lore, fable. He hears of many people, all ticketed long before he meets them. He even gets to know them quite well, their route from birth to age, though they may live and die without coming face to face. So with Old Edie and her five bachelor sons, whose lives she soured and ruined, a powerful bitter self-centred woman who suckled her own youngest brother – an action described with uneasy laughter and a felt shudder, and one could be in Thebes and afraid of the oracle. Edie was a bad cook and a good contralto. Was she like that? But appeal against legend? There was Fat Harry and his joke about the five-barred gate and the five dollars on Saturday and where did you leave your uncle. Everyone laughed at this old joke and so did I; but I never understood the joke. One of the family figures was Stevie, the little demon. My friend Jeanie, one of the kindest women in the world, lively and witty, friendly and girlish, exclaimed,

'Wait till you see him – just see him! No one would want to see him. No one likes that kind of child.'

Stevie was Jeanie's grand-nephew, only child of brother Rolf's only daughter, Mariana.

'Mariana's adorable, she is adorable and she just can't understand where she got such a little demon. Oh, well, Carrie, you know Carrie' (no, I don't), 'Mariana's mother, how adorable she is, what an angel! She wouldn't say anything about a fly! Well, even she admits that Stevie is a perfect little devil. You know that cat Fluffy' (yes, I know Fluffy), 'well, Fluffy I never did care for. I think there is something wrong with Fluffy; someone put her in the garbage can and put the lid on. And I will say one thing for Stevie, he actually rescued it and brought it home. They asked him, "Where did you get that cat?" He said, "In the garbage" and of course they didn't believe it. They thought he had stolen it. But after that, he never touched it. Just hates it now. Well, that poor Fluffy – what a life she leads! You know Mariana's loving heart – with Rags and Duff and Boiled-Beef, those dogs; and Duff, that is Rags's mother, even bigger than Rags, but they're still puppies to her. Mariana of course is simply wild about Duff, but she adores Rags; she simply won't go anywhere without Rags. She says she will never let her have puppies and I quite agree, to spoil a beautiful big doll like that, what a shame! Oh, poor Mariana, the way she carried on when Duff had puppies, even though one of them was Rags, well, I thought she'd never get over it and it was after she had Stevie, too. But she was furious, really furious and wouldn't talk to her mother Carrie for six weeks, when she found out that Duff was going to have puppies. To spoil that darling Duff, she said. And now the fact is she prefers Rags to Duff.

'Well, you see this cat Fluffy upset the dogs and Stevie took her part, just for a day or two; and then he saw which way the wind was blowing and lost interest. Well, where Stevie comes in – I think Mariana resents Stevie, too. But why not? I would. A little boy, I think, with no feeling for animals and no notion that Rags and Duff have feelings like us – like us? – more than us. We become hardened I think, but dogs never. They become more sensitive to us as they love us more. Yes, I suppose, it is cupboard love, I say so to myself, they just love you for the mince and bones; but why do children love us? Well, poor Mariana, she has this lovely great big dog and this naughty little boy and I really think she prefers Rags, no wonder. Why is he so naughty? She can't love him. You'd say a devil had got into the child; an imp is no word for him. What that child will do! And nothing brilliant either, nothing witty like those sayings they put in magazine columns – I suppose they are polished up a bit; but still amusing, suitable for that age of childhood. But if Stevie does anything, it's mean, glim, scary, just ugly; he has an ugly temper. Does everything he can to be disagreeable, to annoy, to tease. You'd think he knew. I believe he does. He knows how it hurts and annoys, even adults; but not animals, not dogs. He has no feeling for

dogs and that is why I know that he has no real understanding, just a kind of intuition for the bad, not even like
animals, but something connected with a low grade of
intelligence. He says vile things, pert and cruel. I really
hate him, though he's Mariana's child. We all hate him,
his grandparents, too. You know Carrie, how sweet she is
– she tries to defend him: he's young, she says. But how
long does a child stay as young as that? Anyhow, understanding the feelings of animals is a thing a child is
supposed to know first; and then to understand its mother
long before it can speak, just by looking in her face and a
sort of intuition. Well, but not this beastly little rat. Oh, I
hate him! We all hate him. Dirty, he smells, -ah-ha – he's
dirtier than a little dog and rolls in his blankets all dirty
and picks his nose and puts his finger in his ear for the
wax and eats it and scratches his hair and no dog is like
that.

'Mariana, she's so sweet and fair, is that the word? So
sweet and fair and she can't stand this nasty smelly little
brat. How can a child, think, a child, be like that, rotten as
a pear? It is something missing; he must be defective; oh,
we all feel he is a defective. But that's the strange thing,
the worst of all, you'd say he does it just to spite them. In
school he's quite normal, he's more, he's bright. After
tearing the house to pieces, he goes to school and not a
boo out of him. They were terrified about letting him go
to school, because of his character, temperament, whatever it is; and then they knew he was backward, a cretin,
and they didn't want to expose him. But at last they had
to send him, just to give Mariana a little rest from him and
the father had to take him. He took the morning off and
took him.

'Well, his father, Glenn, understands him more, but he
understands in another way how bad he is. Mariana was

always so sweet, though a bit disin – indifferent would you say? She could have done anything, but she has no interest. Don't you think that's the secret, having interest?

'Well, she told Glenn he must tell the teacher about the kind of boy Stevie was, to be fair to her; and to keep her eyes peeled and to tell the teacher if he played up in school to send a note home and they'd beat him.

'For about six weeks they heard nothing. They began to worry, for they thought the teacher was afraid to complain; knowing what most parents are. So Mariana got up the courage to go to the school and told the teacher she must tell her what Stevie had been doing; for she was so worried; and if he'd been doing anything, to leave it to her and Glenn. She said, "We'll make the little monkey pay for it."

'Do you know what happened? The teacher was quite surprised. She said, "Why, he's very good in school. He never makes a noise and he's almost at the top now."

'You can imagine how they felt when they heard that. They could hardly bear it. Mariana was simply furious to think of that hypocritical little monkey making such trouble for her at home and then putting on a smooth face and sitting still in school, a regular little Uriah Heep, she said.

'Can you understand a boy that age being so deceitful, playing a double game? It's not normal, I told her; and I really think and his grandfather thinks too, there's something radically wrong. They thought right away of taking him and sending him to a school for feebleminded or retarded children; but the teacher didn't want him to leave.

'Well frankly, Mariana didn't believe the whole story; she thought it was an act he put on and she waited. But he kept it up at school – not at home, oh, no! That's another strange thing about the boy. He knows when he's fooling people and he'll act so sweetly and behave so nicely, if he thinks some stranger doesn't know his record. He'll fool them completely.

'That's incredible, isn't it? It shows something wrong. I know that boy's twisted in some way, a mental hunchback, probably quite dangerous too; for the way he can scheme and not in an obvious way, but like that – fooling his parents, playing a double game, and no feeling for anyone at home, not even for Rags and Duff; and you know, a boy and a dog – it's abnormal. It quite frightens me.

'Oh, I hope they don't bring him here this summer. I am nice to him; but he knows at once, like an animal, that I can't stand hair or hide of him. His instinct isn't natural, it's like a dog's, but a dog is kind and humble and just slinks off – while he, he knows it too, but he won't answer, he turns his back and walks off, out of the room. A child – and at his age! No good will come of him. If they don't put him away in a feebleminded home he'll be a curse to society. I really do think that would be best, preventive arrest, best for society.

'But what gets you most is not his wits, poor boy he can't help that, though it's a tragedy for Mariana, but his slyness, the way he sees through you – a born crook. Nothing good will come. He's too quick and not in a smart way.

'Well, in a letter this morning, Mariana says they'll bring him; they have to; there's nowhere they dare leave him. You'll see him and you'll know at once, because you're quick at human beings, you will see. I'm just dying for you to see this dirty little warped thing. Oh, I can't wait for it. I hate the little wretch, but I can't wait to hear what you'll say.

'What he does, I can't begin to tell – bites, scratches, pinches. They shut him up in the toilet, so that he'll do his business and they say, "Why don't you do like Rags?" Rags does her business every morning and so she does, a cleaner dog never was. He stays in there out of obstinacy and does nothing. Mariana tells everyone how he is, hoping to shame the little devil, but she can't shame the devil out of Stevie, no she can't shame the devil out of the little pinhead.

'When he does come out, he knows he's bad and he just slinks away, not listening to the scolding; and she is so ashamed of a boy like that. He goes out and sulks all day and it's his fault, not hers. She tells me she's in despair. If I didn't have Rags, she says, I don't know what I'd do, I'd run away. She often told me, "I'd give him away. I never wanted anyone like that." I said, "Oh, no, no, no one would take him." And I heard her tell him, "No one would take you, you little devil or I'd give you away."

(I thought to ask what Stevie looked like.)

'A stick – so thin and pale and dirty, you can't bear to look at him, undernourished, although they feed him enough. Mariana's always at him, nags him, in fact. No. He just slinks off in his usual way and then he steals food! Think of that! Oh, the end is, we'll see him in jail and not so far off and not too soon either. We wouldn't even care. It's so clear.'

One Saturday morning in the summer we heard that Mariana, Glenn and their son Stevie had arrived at the grandparents' home, just down the dirt road. I passed the day in anticipation. The country life is calm and there is time for pleasurable anticipation. But Stevie did not come that day. My friend, Jeanie, his great-aunt, telephoned Mariana, saying that I was hopping with excitement to see the awful little boy, I had heard so much about the little demon. And she brought me the message, 'She won't be so anxious to see him, when she sees him.'

The next day about eleven, I saw the grandfather, Rolf, a tall, wiry goodlooking man, in his best clothes, leading by the hand a small slender boy in a new white suit. My heart began to beat hard, for though they were far off, I knew it must be Stevie. I am interested in and sympathise with turbulent children; but I am afraid, too, that they will lash out at me with their sharp tongues; and I came down the orchard path slowly and quietly.

I was exceedingly surprised to see a handsome sallow boy with thick wavy dark hair and a dissipated tormented face, yet innocently curious in expression. He was tall for his age: he was a little more than five years old.

He looked straight into my eyes, offered his little sallow hand and said goodday in a sweet voice. All went well, though his strained face did not relax. His grandfather went round the corner of the house, leading him by the hand. Soon I heard Alfred, the artist, Jeanie's brother, like Jeanie, married with no children, laughing nervously in his studio. I looked in the studio window and saw Alfred hitting Stevie on the head with a roll of paper. I went in. Alfred laughing still, said,

'You see, Stevie, really is a naughty boy. He snatched the paper out of my hand when I shook it at him.'

Later, I went down into the town with Mariana, a beautiful woman of the ephebe type, with her smallboned dark young husband and Alfred, such a happy, good-natured, kind man, small, plump with nutcracker features. In front with the couple sat Rags, a splendid fawn Great Dane who constantly licked Mariana and laid her head on her knee. Mariana sat in the car while Glenn and Alfred did the shopping. She was lively, sharp, impatient, full of elegant twitches. She kept kissing Rags on the head, nose and shoulder. 'Oh I love you, love you,' she said in the tone of a manly declaration, 'I wish I had more like you.'

'You love her more than Stevie,' said I boldly; (I had known the family for years). She said at once,

'Yes, I only wish Stevie were a bit like Rags. I hate Stevie. I'd like him a bit if he could be like Rags.'

This was on the way home. No one started or stirred: Alfred laughed and said, a family standby, 'Why don't you give Stevie away?'

She said between her teeth,

'I would. I'd have a motherly instinct if I could; but I can't with Stevie. I'm sorry he was born. I have a motherly instinct with Rags, so that just shows. It's Stevie's fault, the little damn devil. He's taking a child's place and he's no child. That's what I hate about the little damn imp. Glenn can't take him either.'

The fascinated husband did not object. I said,

'Stevie seems bright.'

'He'd seem anything just to spite us; don't make any mistake about Stevie. He isn't bright, he's stupid, a foul little brat; but he seems bright just to get back at us. He's the greatest simulator you ever saw. I never met up with such a dirty little hypocrite. But I'll pay him out yet. He won't get any mother love out of me: that's how I pay him out, the little devil.' And half-laughing, she dragged the meek dog to her and kissed it passionately.

'I love you, Rags and no one who isn't as good and sweet as you.'

In the afternoon the grandfather took Stevie to the town. The grandfather was a jokester and always had names for people in the town, or the family; he invented them and they stuck. He was considered very smart, the smarter perhaps because he had come from far away, from 'Liverpool, England'; and yet he made such a go of it, became rich. People in the family, people in politics or business, he called Coonskin, Goon, Goop, Aky-kaky. He was fond of Stevie and took him everywhere. So the boy heard him naming, nicknaming, joking. This summer day coming back up from the town, where his father had given him money to put in the juke-box, Stevie saw a milkman, one of the old native families, coming from the hill; and he said, 'Hello, Maky-kaky, Crappy Maky;' and the grandfather laughed. Stevie turned and said, 'What are you laughing at, you old pisspot?' Grandfather did not laugh.

2   *Apprentice Writer*

A Night in the Indian Ocean

The night was rayless and sultry and phosphorescent jellyfish heaved in the round black waves. Two sailors came and closed the cannon ports. The rush of the sulky ocean could be heard through them. The ship was beginning to heave a little, like a sleeper taking deeper breaths. The clock on the staircase leading up to B Deck was stopped at 11.30. Bells kept ringing and, when they rang, lighted numbers appeared on the electric indicator-board between the stateroom corridors on B Deck. When the lighted number 17 showed, the girl got up from the nightwatchman's table under the staircase and went into the corridor on the port side.

The bunk in the single-berth cabin was under a small porthole. A shaded lamp stood on a bedside table. Under the bunk, at its foot, and against the other wall were hatboxes and heavy cases. On the bed, the covers thrown down to the foot, lay a pretty young woman with fair hair. She was made up with eye shadow, lipstick and rouge, but carefully so, to bring out the exceptional translucency of her skin. She was dressed in a transparent white nightdress, trimmed with small lace and ribbons. She was well formed, tall, with flaccid breasts, slender arms and legs. With a spoiled expression, she said, 'Damn her!' and had her fingers on the bell again, when the girl, Stella, came in.

'Are you awake again? Can't you sleep?'

'You know damn well I can't sleep,' said Babs. 'Oh, forgive me. I can't sleep. If André only would come he'd bring me some gin. He smuggled it in last night. Then I can sleep. Put up with me, please nurse.' Her voice dragged, strained. 'Oh, I know you're not a nurse. Oh, why don't you stay here and rub my feet? Who's out there? Only that old man? What does he talk about?'

'He's going to retire to Margate after only two more voyages; and he says I cannot get the dole till I have worked six months,' said Stella laughing.

'There, that gives me relief. You have a lovely touch. You could be a real nurse. Only don't do it. It's hell. I've had nurses and made life hell for them. Poor kid. I suppose you're tired. What time is it? Look at my watch.'

'It's 12.10 by your watch, but ship's time is still 11.30. They don't start the clocks again for ten minutes yet.'

'Rub my feet! Where's André?'

'He's just gone down to sleep. They had a dance tonight. Everyone's tired. André had to play the guitar in the orchestra too.'

'Oh, I can't understand him going down without coming to say goodnight. I believe the captain told him to stay away, damn him. That captain's a pu- milksop. He's afraid of me because I've got money. He came here alone and I shouted him out of the cabin. Then he came back with the doctor and Mrs Montorgel to stick up for him. Yellow coward. That didn't stop me. I didn't shut up. I shouted: Fools, damn imbeciles. Then they all backed out. The doctor is rotten soft, too. Probably disgraced on shore; got caught doing an abortion and changed his name and went to sea. All ships' doctors are idiots who can't make a living ashore, did you know that? I know all about ships. I travel six months every year to avoid taxes. I know the doctors. Who but failures would live in a mean little cabin all his life and listen to the women who vomit and the women whose bowels won't work and the drunks like me? And most captains are cheap snobs. They lick for money.' Her voice softened, she smiled, 'But not all captains and not all doctors. I have known some nice ones.'

Stella, rubbing her feet, asked, 'Do you feel sleepier now?'

'I feel better,' said the rich girl. 'You have a lovely touch. You could make something out of it. But you haven't the muscles for a masseuse. It's a pity, they make plenty of money if they know what's what. Did you ever try mesmerism?'

'No. At least, only once on my little brother – but I think he was sleepy anyway.'

'Oh, of course you did it. You have a certain thing. I must get you to practise on me. It will be good for you too. I'll get used to you and you can put me to sleep. I could introduce you to people. I know people. I could sleep now but I'm so thirsty. Give me some water.' Suddenly she was demanding, 'Hurry, I'm perishing! Oh, this terrible thirst in my throat. It's like dying in the desert, or something.'

She drank a whole glass of water at one draught. 'Give me some perfume now; it sends me to sleep. There on the table, *Little Blue Flower*. I'll tell you something. If you're ever in Paris, go to the Champs Elysées, Guerlain, and get this *Little Blue Flower.* All other scents are vulgar beside this one. Men, especially refined men, go wild over this one. It is so feminine.' She said curiously, 'Are you interested in men?'

Stella said shyly, 'A little.'

'Do you know any interesting men?'

'I know one or two. I have a friend in France. I'll see him when I go over.'

Babs looked her over smartly, 'If you get a chance, marry him. Take my tip. Don't wait and don't you live with him without marrying him. It doesn't pay. I know men.' She repeated bitterly, 'I know them.' She thought for a while and continued, 'By the way, what was the dance like tonight? Did you hear anyone say?'

'No.'

'You don't know anything,' said Babs crossly. 'Oh, André could have told me. Leave me now. I'll sleep.'

Jares, a tall ugly dark man in a worn dark blue uniform, without a cap, came peering down the top steps of the staircase from B Deck. 'Hiss!' he said. He peeped through the banisters at the girl reading at a table under him. There was a burst of silly laughter in two voices, male and female, from a corridor on C Deck and Jares retreated upstairs into the shadow. From the smoking room corridor Captain Blount appeared in evening dress with Mrs Seymour, with smart hairdo, golden nails, a lowcut black dress, and diamond bracelets. Both were tipsy. Jares reappeared faintly in the shadow above, with an interested leer. Halfway across the stage Captain Blount showed a bottle of whisky he was carrying, put a finger to his lips. They tiptoed towards the staterooms. A bell rang staccato during the passage of this couple. They pantomimed 'Hush!' to each other and vanished with ballet steps. The bell rang again. Jares, above, went towards his own staterooms with an impatient gesture. Another bell began to ring continuously on C Deck and simultaneously the number 24 flashed on the board. Mr Parker, the nightwatchman on C Deck, walked in from the port corridor carrying a small tray with two cups of coffee and a plate of sandwiches. He limped on large flat feet. He was of middle size with a broad sanguine face, loosening and fattening with age. He wore the same sort of uniform as Jares. Stella looked up.

'Do you have coffee when you're alone here at night, Mr Parker?'

'Sometimes the kitchen man slips me a cup when I take the captain's coffee, up,' said Parker. He put down the tray in front of the 'young lady' with a friendly flourish, and was about to sit down, when 24 rang again.

'It's 24,' said Parker. He went into the stateroom corridor and a soft conversation was heard. When he came back, Parker sat down heavily, drank his coffee and asked, ''Ow's your young lady this evening?'

'I rubbed her feet for about two hours and she went to sleep.'

Parker rinsed his mouth with coffee and swallowed it. 'It's a shame to see 'er in that shape. She's a pretty young woman. You know she tried to kill 'erself before they got you? You know what brings 'em to it?' He nodded and mimed the pouring of a liquid from a bottle. 'You know what I mean.' The bells rang again. He twisted round to look at the board. 'H'm. Them bar stewards work plenty in first class. Just listen to them bells. It's 'is.' He pointed upwards to where Jares lurked somewhere. 'Last night I crep' up and there 'e was asleep on a chair. "What're y' doin'?" I said. "The 'ole switchboard's goin' off like a packet of fireworks, I get a 'eadache listenin' to it the 'ole night long." "Answer it yourself," 'e says, "'Ere's the water bottle for number six, get it filled," I says to 'im. "Oh, stick it somewhere," 'e says to me, "'E's a rude man. I 'ate that in a man. "It's ringin' on your deck all night," I says. "Oh, you go to," well I won't repeat it, "and lemme sleep," 'e says. Well, because I couldn't stand the ringin', I went and filled the bottle. "Where in blazes 'ave you been?" says the mister; "and bring me some soap and look lively." I got a bit and give it to 'im up there. "Take it to number six," I says. "Oh, stick it somewhere," 'e says; but 'e snatches it from me. I don't like 'im. You'd not believe the 'alf of what 'e does; and there's somethin' real vicious about 'im. 'E makes trouble for me, 'e does and knowin', too.'

'Is that what he's like?' asked Stella.

' 'E's a nasty kind of feller. You can't trust 'im. Listen, are you 'ungry? Should you like a bit more coffee? It's weary down 'ere all night, wearyin'. I'm an old man now. I drop off in a minute. I'll get you a bit more coffee. Then I'll sit 'ere and be so kind as to give me a nudge when you 'ear the watch comin', will you? Give me a tip off when you 'ear the rounds.'

Looking up, Stella saw Jares leaning on the balustrade above the old man, a grin on his devilish face. As soon as Parker was out of sight, Jares said 'Hiss!', came down a few steps to the first landing and dangled a two-string pearl necklace, the sort they sell in the bazaars in Colombo for a couple of shillings.

'Give me a kiss,' he said with a laugh, 'give me a kiss and you'll get this.' He dangled the necklace, crooked his elbow, drew it back, laughed. 'Pearls, real pearls,' he said with a laugh. She said nothing.

Parker returned and Jares melted into his upstairs dark.

'Jares was just here,' she said in a low voice, pointing; 'He pretended he has a pearl necklace.'

The old man became very anxious and in a low voice warned her about Jares again; 'That feller's no good. And 'e's after my neck; 'e said 'e was after my neck.'

'Why?'

'Because I wake 'im up to answer 'is bells.'

'Thank you for getting the coffee.'

'It gives me somethin' to do. It's not time to take the captain's yet.'

The old man put his head on his arm and instantly fell asleep. The nurse read her book, got up to take a few steps, yawned and sat down. She heard the watch, wakened the old man. Presently they came, four serious men in uniform marching together, eyes right to the table, eyes towards the staterooms, the cannon ports, round and down the other way, seeming handsome and strong in their perfect earnestness. Mr Parker sat down and before he began to doze, he said, 'Don't let that feller Jares come down 'ere. One night 'e tied a string on the stairs to break my neck.'

A bell rang and 17 flashed on the board. The sick woman was trying to get out of bed. 'Help me to the W.C.' She was so weak that she could not stand up, could not straighten her legs. Like a beach doll half filled with air she hung over the girl, and helping herself with her weak thin arms she was dragged to the W.C.

'Shut the door and wait outside,' she said severely.

When she was in bed again, she lay looking at the girl and then said, 'Sit here and talk to me.'

'All right; but I must go and tell the nightwatchman to keep watch.'

'Is it the watch?' he said lifting his blurred face.

'I must go to Miss Prescott.'

'I'll walk about then.'

When Stella returned the young woman was still lying

on her back with the covers down, looking pensive.

'How old do you think I am?'

'I don't know. Twenty-two?'

'I'm thirty-one. I can't get any older-looking. I blame my looks for the way I live. Don't tell Mrs Montorgel. She treats me like a child. It's better. I had a child. No, don't believe that. Yes, I had a child. My sister has it. It doesn't want me for a mother.' She paused. Then she said fretfully, 'They say there are six multimillionaires on board. Well, let me tell you, this is the dullest ship I ever was on and I've been on *some*. Six millionaires and everyone afraid to walk, talk or drink because they're not in their class. Millionaires are the goddamnedest dullest crowd in the world anyhow. On the last trip we had cocktail parties from breakfast on. As soon as you came out, there was a cocktail party going on in the corridor. We had dozens of them on deck and plenty of gay young men. Are there any decent men about this evening?'

'There was a rather good looking man with a lady; she called him Captain Blount.'

Babs said impatiently, 'He must have got on at Colombo. I don't know him. He's an Indian officer going home on leave. He must be a good sport. What was he doing?'

'He had a bottle of whisky and he was going with a lady in evening dress towards the staterooms – the other corridor.'

'Did he come out again? Did it look like his wife?'

'Oh, it wasn't his wife; you could tell.'

Babs stirred, turned her back to her attendant. 'Oh, it's rotten, rotten being here. There must be some fun on board. He sounds a nice man. I'm so weak I can't talk, otherwise that cowardly doctor couldn't keep me here.'

She turned round on her pillow and leaned towards

Stella fingering her nightdress. 'Get nightdresses like this, they're the best. They're cheap. You can have a dozen. Get a nice one, not too much lace, pretty small lace, small. Men like it. Transparent is best! It's so graceful and men like it. I must have things about me that men like. If I didn't feel at any minute of the day or night that men would like what I have on, I'd go mad. Don't you ever feel you want to scream at the dullness of everything? Oh, you're so good, so goody-good; don't you want to break out and have a good time?'

'I have a good time.'

The rich girl fell back on to her pillow. 'I suppose you do; not my way. My way's a rotten way. I can't help it. See that photograph? That's a picture of my mother. Do you like it?'

She watched Stella cunningly, while Stella got up and looked at the photograph. Stella looked at it for a few minutes, casting glances every few moments at Babs; then she said, 'She's very pretty and young.'

Babs boasted, 'She was fifty when that was taken and you'd take her for thirty-five at most.'

Stella said nothing. The woman in the photograph was smiling, bending forward slightly in a winning way. She was wearing a big hat and carrying a large handbag, ready to go out. This woman was standing by a doorway. On the other side of the doorway was a bedside table with a bottle on it and in the bed a young girl, very young, soft, appealing, smiling shyly. She was wearing a nightdress with a soft frilled neck. One arm in a long sleeve was on the bedcover; in the other hand was a glass, half full.

Babs saw her looking at the photograph, which was on the wall where it could be seen from the pillow.

'How old do you think I was?'

'Twelve?'

'Eighteen,' she said with intense bitterness. Then more quietly, 'A friend of my mother's took it. They were going out. When they went out she sent me to sleep with gin.' Again bitterly, 'I keep it to remember how my mother was, what she did to me. It's hard to remember when a woman has that face. She didn't care. She did it to make me like herself. Oh, she isn't dead. I say so; but she isn't. She's stronger than I am. And she ruined me. That man who took the photograph, her friend – he was mad about me. They made it seem amusing. I thought it was the real way to live.'

The girl sat and looked at her and her nakedness, which seemed shameful to her. She pulled up the sheet. The rich girl impatiently pushed it down again; 'I'm burning and perishing with thirst. Anyway André might come in. He likes me like that,' she said with a sudden gaiety. 'He pretends he doesn't. But I know.' Then she said seriously, 'André is very decent to me. He's a really decent man, though he's only a steward. He's much better than those men up there, that Captain Blount you told me about. I know that type only too well. Well, talk to me. You know I tried to throw myself overboard and that's why they moved me into this cabin with the little porthole? Oh, you don't know what it is. You probably don't drink.'

'No.'

'Listen, tell me about third class, if that's all you know. They say there's a terrible crowd down there this trip. Mrs Montorgel knows someone there. She says her friends have a little club of their own up near the hospital and they don't mix with the others. Mrs Montorgel's like a mother to me; the only one of this rotten, dirty three-halfpence worth of small town snobs that doesn't despise me because I drink. I was carried on board drunk. Did you know that? It takes some sort of courage, some stamina. They get tipsy over one cocktail, the fools, the – When I was fifteen I never went to bed without a bottle of gin at my bedside. Is that a way for a young girl to be brought up? I began to grow up and the men went mad over me from the time I was eleven or twelve. She began to give me drink. I thought I was becoming one of them. I became one of them . . . Tell me about the third class.'

'At the last port of call, I heard, they put ashore three women from first class, because men were visiting their cabins.'

'Really? How interesting! That bitch Mrs Montorgel tells me nothing. What else?'

'Well, there's an English girl down there in a red petticoat and bare feet, married to an Italian fisherman going home to Sicily. She does tricks on deck with cards and glasses of water. There's a missionary girl from the South Seas who's going home for the first time in fifteen years. She wanted to marry the minister in her parish. While she was away the minister divorced his wife and married a girl out of the choir. This missionary didn't want to go home, but now she has a tropical disease and must live in England again.'

'I know, I know. He lived with this missionary when she was young and in the choir; and then he said he'd stick to his wife and she went away. And then he married someone else. The usual thing.'

Surprised, Stella said 'I don't know if that's it.'

'Of course. Why do you suppose she went to the South Seas? You don't know. I lived with a man for two and a half years. I loved him; he was mad about me. Then I had a baby. He left me. My married sister's looking after it. He hates it now. I took to drink for that reason. No. I always drank. That's why he hated me. My mother did it. She drank all her life. Look at her! With those looks she could get drunk every night and no one suspected it. She gave me too much to spend. I'm rich, very rich. That's why I travel. In that trunk are forty pairs of shoes of all kinds, just tossed in. They tossed them in in the hotel: they hated me, they didn't pack for me. I'll never wear one of them. I'll buy more when I get to London. Open the trunk and look in. Go on!'

Stella opened it, and looked. It was nearly full of all kinds of shoes.

'I'm rich,' she said fiercely, 'and I can't even get a pony of whisky. I have to depend on the favour of a steward, damn his eyes. André's a darling, though. Never mind that mess, that's powder I spilled. André can swab it up in the morning. Let Mrs Montorgel do it: she's such a mother to me,' she said with hatred. 'You come to me before that boat docks at Port Said. I'll give you a telegram to send. Mrs Montorgel has made arrangements for me to be met by an ambulance at Tilbury. I'm having a friend take me off at Southampton. I'll give you the money and the message, and don't tell anyone, not even André. Will you?'

'Yes.'

'I knew you would. Listen. Go away now. Don't believe all that rot I told you. It's rot. My mother's dead: she died a long time ago. And I didn't have a child either. Go and bring that nightwatchman here at once.'

When Stella came back with the old man, the cabin smelled of fresh perfume. Babs was still naked in her transparent dress. Parker came timidly to the doorway with his eyes cast down. She laughed, 'Come in, Mr Parker. You're not afraid of me, are you? I'm not used to men being afraid of me. I've got to have company. The days are twenty-five hours long at present and it's filthy weather and the fan in this cabin doesn't work. Go away, Miss! Listen Parker, look at me, men like to look at me. And can't you wake up André? If he's sleepy, tell him to come and sleep here on a mattress beside me.'

Parker said, 'It's impossible, Madam. 'E 'as to sleep in the gloryhole with the others.'

She begged, 'Oh, couldn't you do it without telling anyone? Be a sport, Parker.'

'I'm the nightwatchman, Madam,' said Parker, seriously.

'And what about Captain Blount going into a lady's cabin with a bottle of whisky, eh?' she twitted him.

'I don't know nothin' about it, Madam.'

'No, you don't. You only know about me. Like them all. And my only friend is a steward who isn't allowed to come near me, because he's kind to me. And a couple of women out of third class. I know that the doctor put up a notice about me and begged for volunteers out of third class to look after me. Because no one in first class would give up their fun to come near me. I hear their cocktail parties start at eleven in the morning on B Deck. Oh, Parker, I wish I could get up there. I could have fun. If only they would let that Captain Blount come to see me, we could have fun. He sounds all right; he'd bring me a bottle. He's the right sort. You don't understand. None of you understands. You don't know what it is to live. Oh, Parker, I'm so sick, I'm so miserable; and no one to know how miserable I am. Parker, Parker, send me André.'

Parker, who had been trying not to see the young lady's legs, and who had pity on her, said, 'You'll catch cold, Madam. The young lady can cover you up.'

Babs had pity on him, too, 'Go away, Parker, and put your head on the table. Stella will wake you up when the watch comes. Perhaps I'll sleep too. What time is it?'

'It's nearly two now, Madam.'

'Two o'clock is the zero hour when people die; when you wake up if you've managed to get a few hours' sleep; and when babies are born. I'll sleep after two. Send the girl in, Parker.'

'Yes, Madam.'

When she came in, Babs said, 'Well, what happened? Did you see Captain Blount?'

Startled, Stella said, 'Yes. He asked me to go up on deck.'

'And did you?'

'No. I said I had to look after you.'

'You are a fool. I should have gone. You must be bored. That Captain Blount sounds just the type. Is he out there now?'

'No, he's gone to bed.'

'To whose bed? I don't mean that. Well, next time you see him, tell him to come and cheer me up.'

'They won't let him.'

'Oh, how awful. Oh, what a terrible ship. What weaklings men are! And you'll find the weakest at sea. Go now, go I said.'

Stella went out the door.

'Miss! What is your name? Stella! When you see André in the morning, before you go off, tell him to come to me. Will you?'

'Yes, I will.'

'He'll pack for me. You'll send the telegram and I'll cheat them all.'

La Toussaint
(All Saints' Day, November 1)

The half-naked trees lightly blowing on a watery sky introduce November; and the flowerstalls along the boulevards, bright with chrysanthemums, have written on their slates: 'La Toussaint': it is All Saints' Day, which is in France an important religious fête, and the day of the commemoration of all dead. The soberly dressed Parisian crowds roll out towards Père Lachaise, Montparnasse, Montmartre and the other burialgrounds of the city, carrying flowers; the pavements are strewn with the wares of the plant merchants, occasionally church bells ring, the cafés are crowded. The cemeteries are swarming with visitors, but the boulevards are also busy and most people have come out to celebrate a rare holiday in the true French style – a little family walk, a glass of coffee in a café with a glass of grenadine for the child, a visit to grandpère, and return home for supper.

In the cemeteries the family chapels are open, the vases are filled, the priedieu freshly linened: the stranger who goes out of curiosity or sympathy with the movement of the crowd, finds himself not in the presence of mortality but in a ground stirring with activity, the home of the living dead: there is even no feeling of immortality, but instead, of a prolonged life, as if the funereal earth underfoot were breathing, moving slightly; and one might hear, with the ear to the ground, a slight crepitation, like the movement in an anthill. There is the family burialground held in perpetuity: on the headstone a great number of names, some dating from the early eighteenth century: the number of living in that family must seem small in comparison with the dead, a frail pendant to a pyramid of skeletons – and with whom rests the future? The skeletons. This cult of the dead, in which the French resemble the Chinese, and the frequent use of family chapels, makes the cemetery a true necropolis and no mere patch of clay where a body lies. Only in the Jewish section, which has few chapels and little ornamentation, do the dead sleep in eternity, and is there the sweet decayed tranquillity which we associate with graves in fine weather.

The cemetery is cold and wet underfoot, a rare wind blows the yellowed trees and the crowd of mourners splashes through the mud and the piles of rubbish, bits of flowers, papers and broken pots. Sometimes there is a large family group, whose women arrange the flowers while the men stand by with heads uncovered: sometimes it is two young women in black, one arranging the grave, embarrassed while the bereaved one prays long, leaning over the iron railing: or there is a gay young married couple with one child, cheerfully chattering and carrying two gigantic chrysanthemums, for the grave of some old relative some time dead, a benefactor: there is an old woman with golden hair and rouged cheeks, looking ill, unhappy and discomposed, as look old women without a husband or a fortune, splashing along in suede shoes carrying a pot of chrysanthemums: there is an old woman with her hair in a handkerchief and an apron over her working dress walking in slippers – she searches up the whole alley of graves, but turns from each one discontent, and disappears for a moment with her handful of flowers picked up on a heap, behind some other grave.

Everywhere is the small Parisian family of three persons, bending and rising, arranging, retreating a few steps to see the effect, bending again and talking quietly: in some places they hold back the rose boughs and ivy sprays which cover the names of the persons long dead – the eldest son, aged fourteen, deciphers the names and attributes of his greatgrandparents, while the little girl of five plays with the small clipped hedge and rosebushes round the railing. Sometimes the grave is entirely covered and banked with flowers and that is one which had been lately opened: two of these were buried only yesterday. The richest floral tributes are on the graves of young men who 'died in the flower of their age on the field of honour'; or accidentally, on the threshold of a brilliant career; nothing is more cruel to a family than the death of the young male who shows intellectual promise: 'To . . . aged 23, doctor of laws, doctor of philosophy, cruelly ravished in the flower of his youth'.

The monuments to distinguished men are rarely decorated and some of the chapels of very famous families, famous even overseas in our country, are unopened. That is the true death: their lives were so full that their death was sensible: none feels that they live. The poor it is who chiefly cherish their dead: and here is the poorest, a poverty stricken couple arriving with a bouquet of elegant flowers which must have cost them two months' savings, they, poor, meagre, dried and crushed, the blooms like fat dowagers shaking their palsied heads and displaying their pendulous charms.

After the visit to the family grave the visitors wander round the cemetery admiring the flowers, the rich or peculiar monuments, reading inscriptions, supposing histories: small rites are being observed – the father of a child dead some years ago is digging the moss from the inscription: the woman who has arranged her flowers in nine and nine and nine, having some left over, thoughtfully places them on the sunken and withered bed of a neglected grave whose headstone is defaced: three women walk behind their friend, a young woman dressed in the deepest mourning, who nevertheless walks proudly alone, as if conscious that the day is hers and its celebration magnifies her sorrow.

One walks miles on this day, in a cemetery: and fatigue, more than the old superstition, fills the benches at the gates: the superstition is this, that on leaving a cemetery, you must sit down for a time at the gate, so that the ghosts who are following you, will become discouraged and return to their own dwelling-places; if you walk straight out, they have the power to follow you. Outside, the crowd is beginning to turn: the florists have done a trade which must pay all overdrafts: but it is blowing rain – the people hasten to bus, tram and underground to reach home, fire and coffeepot, or else to the cafés, for the most economical family permits itself a discussion over an apéritif on a day of fête.

'O, If I Could But Shiver!'

The day Lludd started work at Brice's, the rubber-stamp maker's, a dingy little hole down under the railway bridge, he ducked stuttering Andy, the senior apprentice, in the river. At night he related that he had seen Andy capering in a dunce's cap with his shirt-tails lifted, his way lighted by three dancing donkeys bearing lanterns, whispering in each other's ears and hee-hawing, followed by three geese and led forth by a suckling pig standing on its tail. Andy had a long face like a shoe, staring, beaded with fat sweat, and he wiped his brow constantly on his arms, so that its impression came off and his arms were presently covered with staring long faces. Andy stepped ever closer to the river, walked in, next trod in up to his knees and at last was drowned with only his old felt hat floating down the current, while the church bell gave out warning tones like the first grumblings of a storm. At this point in the story, Andy's father appeared with Andy pale as a junket, and Lludd, after staring for a second, burst into a lively laugh and shouted:

'Look at the senior apprentice! He knows his trade; he shivers like a half-set jelly, like a wet shirt on a clothes-line, and I can't shiver at all. Oh, what a trade is that that men learn, that the innocent can't do at all and that old buffers do to perfection, shivering and palsying until the grave stills them for ever. What a man I should be, what a rubber-stamp maker, if I could but shiver!'

That night the church bell jangled for a quarter of an hour in the middle of the night, and when the sexton went to investigate he was pitched head first down the stairs by a bogey and broke his leg; pigeons and fowls were loosed into bedrooms, goats and dogs strayed about the streets, the barnyards were stirred up, ghosts walked, bugles blew, lanterns flickered, door-bells rang with no one on the step, milk-bottles left on steps were filled with urine, letters were flung through letter-boxes threatening terrorism and extinction by the 'Horny Hand', and other freaks and wonders took place which were blamed (and rightly) on Lludd and his juvenile band of townsboys. In the morning flocks of citizens passed by the public-house of Lludd's father threatening to boycott the house if Lludd did not leave town. Lludd very gladly agreed to. His father took him aside and said:

'Lludd, do you want to end up in prison? Have you made up your mind to a trade or a profession yet? I will do what I can for you, for no boy ever started off worse in life.'

'Father,' said Lludd after a moment's thought, 'do you know what it is? I can't do one thing, I can't shiver; that's what's at the root of all this. I'd like to learn to shiver, first of all.'

'Get out of my house, you jackanapes,' cried his father; 'don't let me see you again: you have no brains and no feelings.'

'Well, I'll go since you talk that way,' said Lludd. The old father watched him out the gate, called out 'Wait!' and Lludd waited. After a long time the father came out of the house with a bundle and a purse in his hand and said:

'Lludd, you're my son and you've been spoiled by a foolish mother: I blame her for your weakness, but perhaps there's something of me in your wildness, too: I ran wild myself once – but I know it leads to trouble. Still I can't let you go empty and naked into the world, at the next turn of the street to fall into God knows what company and monkey tricks, with your habits. Here's twenty-five florins I've saved, and here's a bundle with a shirt and a sandwich in it. But you get all this on one condition, that is that you swear me a solemn oath never to tell your name, or your birthplace, or your father's name and condition, to a living soul. You'll keep an oath you swear to your father whose face you'll never see again.'

'I never lie,' said Lludd, 'I'll promise.'

In fact, only those who can shiver can lie.

'You can break your promise if you come back wealthy, honourable, famous or otherwise respected,' said the father, lingering a bit when the moment of parting came.

'I understand,' said Lludd, and turned away.

Lludd went cheerfully down the road, waving good-bye to dozens of people who had had fun with him. He went down the road and over the top of a rise and never thought to be seen in that town again. He cried out aloud:

'Now, I'm launched; a rover I am, a man I'll be; I'll make my way, I'll teach them a thing or two, I'll cut a figure in the world'; and he loped along the highway singing aloud to himself, 'O, if I could but shiver! O, if I could but shiver!'

At sunset a man came by and heard this song. 'Is that a folk-song, son?' he asked.

'A folk-song? No, it's no song. I've set out on foot to learn to shiver, because I can't. In fact, they've kicked me out of house and home simply because of that.'

'Impossible,' said the man; 'what, you've never shivered? I'll teach you to shiver in double-quick time.'

'Then, I'll give you ten shillings,' said the boy; 'there's no harm in your trying, but I warn you, no one has taught me yet.'

'Here is the spot,' said the man presently.

On a rise near the top of a hill near a thick, low copse, seven corpses hung on a great tree, the remains of seven murderers and robbers, so it was said, caught in a band when robbing a deserted castle.

'I will learn here?' said Lludd, uncertainly.

'I'll take my affydavy on it,' said the man.

'All right.'

The evening promised to be lowering and cold, the sun had gone down, swans and bitterns squawked over the sky and a wind had come up.

'Stay and see if I shiver,' said Lludd, 'perhaps I won't know when I do it.'

'You'll know,' grinned the man, 'after you've danced at the wedding of the Seven Ditch Crows with the ropemaker's daughters, for dance they will this night; but not I. You say you're out to learn; well, you'll learn this night from stiffs to fly and your skin will learn to creep. But for me, a bed in the inn and a steak: the steak is good if the inn is queer, and if the woman's garrulous, she keeps good beer. I'll come and collect the ten bob in the morning.'

'Good-night, sleep well,' said Lludd.

The man went off laughing to himself, and Lludd went

up to the Seven Ditch Crows and sat under the dead men's feet for company, for he was most companionable. He lighted a fire, but at midnight the wind grew so cold that he did not know how to keep himself warm. The wind swung the bodies backwards and forwards and the ropes creaked, and Lludd said:

'They are rubbing against each other to get warm, but listen how they complain of the cold: here I am freezing by the fire; how much colder must they be up there!'

Then he climbed the tree and cut them down one by one. He blew up the fire and placed the dead men round it. As they could not sit up by themselves, he propped them up with bits of brush. They sat there and never moved even when the fire caught their clothing.

'Take care, look out there, brother,' he kept crying, and he hopped about putting out the flames which caught their clothes and the brushwood, but when the flames burned the clothes right off one he got angry and shouted:

'Look after yourselves better, or I'll hang you all up again.'

The dead men remained silent while their few rags burned up – miserable sights they were, naked, dirty, scarred from their struggles, charred where they were burned, and the ropes trailing from their necks. But Lludd was tired; he had been walking all day; so he lost patience and hung them all up on the tree again, although they were very heavy.

Next morning the man came back and found Lludd ready to start.

'Now,' said he, 'you shivered, I bet.'

'How should I learn it with nothing but dead men around? Those fellows over there never opened their mouths and they were so stupid that they let their clothes burn – as for shivering, not likely! *They* don't know how.'

The man looked at Lludd nonplussed and went away saying:

'Never in my life have I met such a queer customer'; he was uneasy, he hastened his step and was soon out of sight.

Lludd walked a little way and perceived a small settlement beneath him, a country hotel, with a garden and one or two cottages about, and beyond, coming up through thick old trees, the smoke of a chimney.

'A nice place,' said Lludd, 'and if I didn't have to learn something in life, I'd stay here. But something's hidden from me; there's something wrong that I can't shiver.' And without thinking any more of the dead men he went on his way singing his tune, with the words, O, if I could but shiver!

A carter walking his horse along the road caught him up and asked:

'Hey, where are you from?'

'That is a secret.'

'A fine secret: who is your father?'

'No one must know.'

'Who wants to? What's your name?'

'I'm not allowed to tell.'

'It's not far you've come from; your shoes are clean.'

'I wiped them this morning on dead men's rags and all yesterday's dust is gone.'

'Where are you going to?'

'Wherever they teach men to shiver.'

'What's that?'

'I'm out on my travels to learn to shiver; then I'll make my fortune.'

'What do you see on my cart?' said the carter.

'J. Snooks, General Merchant,' said Lludd.

'Well, J. Snooks, General Merchant, supplies every-thing to the neighbourhood,' said the carter, laughing, 'and even shivering I'll guarantee to supply. You'll shiver this night.'

Very soon they came into the dining-room of the inn, where the carter began calling:

'Mrs Coppers, here's a customer for you; he's off on his travels and wants to learn to shiver.'

The landlord put his head round the door and exclaimed:

'Yes? Then there's work for him in this part of the country.'

Lludd stared at the landlord's face, which was exces-sively red and grown with very thick eyebrows, whiskers and beard, while his nose was too large. But with this grotesque and clumsy face went dark, quick moving and observant eyes.

Near, in the middle of the small forest Lludd had seen, they said, was a great castle, perhaps the largest in the land, but deserted for fifty years past by the ducal family that owned it because it was haunted and could only be freed from ghosts, and its hidden treasure revealed, by a youth in his first bloom who would stay in the castle three nights in succession.

'Many have tried and none have dared stay even the second night,' said the landlady sadly. 'Seven men who tried lately were found hanged on a tree, on the hill beyond, in the morning. Don't try. What does it matter if you can't shiver? I don't see it can harm you; you're not so sensitive as other people.'

'You think so?' said Lludd, 'then that's it perhaps; and I must learn to shiver, at all costs.'

Then they told him the castle could not find a buyer; and the noble duke who owned it was obliged to live in a gamekeeper's cottage with his three daughters, and try to marry them and keep a son in a cavalry regiment and two nephews in the navy on the miserable means left him. How he did it no one knew; but he had sold half his giant estate to a suburban development company for bungalows.

No one dared approach the castle, they told Lludd. Lights appeared at the windows at nights, fearful howls, hollow sounds of gongs and desolate cries were heard by those who went within a thousand yards of the walls at night. A cold wind blew continually from it, and the trees growing older and older, untrimmed, grown with moss and mistletoe, thick with rooks' nests, were fearsome even by day.

'There is one curious condition,' said the landlord: 'he who goes into the castle may take three lifeless objects with him.'

'Then,' said Lludd, looking carelessly out the window and seeing objects in the backyard, 'I'll take a fire, a wire and a piece of wax.'

That night, set in the great hall of the castle by the duke himself, whose eyes resembled the landlord's, Lludd picked all the locks he could with his penknife and his wire, melted the wax at his fire and took impressions of the other locks with the wax. On the second and third nights, despite some wretched bogeys and katzenjammer contraptions arranged in dark halls and doorways, and the effective use of tom-toms, bugles, sirens and other little wheezes, which the duke had fixed up to frighten off the scarey, Lludd discovered a very complete counterfeiting plant and a store of prohibited drugs in the castle. He now understood quite well how the duke kept, on his dwindling rents, three daughters to marry, a son in a cavalry regiment and two nephews in the navy. Then, because he was unable to shiver, Lludd was employed by the duke to distribute the counterfeit money round the country in the most handsome manner. Before a year was out he had a letter from his father telling him that he might tell his name since he had succeeded so well; but Lludd didn't care to. Lludd saw that the duke paid him off in good coin at the end of a year, when he thought the business in counterfeit coins had reached saturation point, and went his way, after having fallen in love with and seduced in turn the duke's three daughters and his middle-aged maiden sister. The duke, very properly enraged at his conduct, had Lludd arrested while discoursing with a dozen workmen in the ditch on the public highway adjoining his forests, because Lludd was heard to say (while exhibiting a bad coin to the workmen):

'See how rotten the king's head is! And you'll see that he's turned upside-down on that date . . .'

So Lludd was locked up for three years in a country gaol. He fretted and fumed, and his only thought was how to get out of gaol before the year was up. One day he went to the warder with his best manners and said:

'The men have nothing to do in the yard; why don't you let them dig little gardens round the cells?'

The warder, a kind man, agreed to that and gave the men small spades. Then Lludd began digging in his cell under the bed and made a tunnel. Each morning he covered up the hole, and before daylight put the excavated dirt outside the cells to make a garden. When he had made a hole so deep that a man could go into it and he needed a truck to take out the dirt, he collected matchboxes from all the men in gaol and made from the matchboxes a long train of little cars with which, patiently and laboriously all through the nights, they took the dirt out of the cell. Presently, after a couple of months, the tunnel went under the wall and came up into the bog which surrounded the gaol. And one night Lludd and a mate escaped and were never caught or recognised. For of course Lludd had not told his name. In this way Lludd was turned against the law.

Now, he was a long way from the place where he had concealed the money given him by the duke, but he began to journey towards it along the highways and byways. He lived miserably, poor amongst the poor, but nothing daunted him, simply because he could not shiver. He assisted at murders and druggings; he slept, without turning a hair, in a country inn with a trapdoor in the bar-room floor where drunken men were robbed and thrown head first, down into a deep well. In the stews, he slept one night with a Javanese girl of great beauty, whom he found dead the next morning from plague, puffed up, black and stinking. From her room he ran out naked into the streets, avoiding arrest by shouting 'I've got the plague, the bubonic plague.' He passed the night under a cart with a dead man and tried to warm him back to life by pressing his warm body against him, and he awoke in the morning with the dead man's jaw biting his cheek. He came once to a large town in the north and could find no hole to sleep in until he came to a decaying court hidden in a maze of rotten tenements, so bad and old that they seemed to tremble as you trod. He found them not deserted, but inhabited by more human creatures and more families than could fit into ten times as many mansions in the west-end. The one back window on the foul, green, rotting staircase, covered with rags, cobwebs and filthy emanations of households, was almost black with dirt. The pans had overflowed, and the mingled excreta and spittle of all the families in the house, most of whom were consumptive and otherwise ill, ran down the passage and the stairs, and in the centre of the court children played horses and made immature love round an open cesspool. In the basement a family of skeletons lived. The mother lay in a sort of slime in which rags could dimly be seen; she had just given birth to another skeleton with staring eyes. Little bags of bones which, worse luck, couldn't even be sold to the rag and bone man, clawed at him and begged in a gutter dialect. They were covered with sores and their hair was matted; they looked like animals, but they spoke Lludd's native tongue. Lludd looked at these creatures strangely, and he cried with true feeling:

'O, if I could but shiver,' for he realised that there was something wrong with him that he couldn't shiver at that. Thus he tried to tear out of his breast, in his boyish ignorance, the secret of immense success. He left this town, having had no luck in it, and struck out again along the high road, but when he came to the place where he had hidden his cash, he found the secret discovered and the money gone. Merrily he set out again, whistling and occasionally pondering on the strangeness of the world and its madness, beyond all that tales of ghosts and fairy-tales had taught him.

One day he saw a strange thing, like a large, tattered bird hanging to the telegraph wires. When he came closer he saw what it was, a man with burned clothing, blackened, contorted. Just then, some workmen came past and with hands wrapped in newspapers they got him down, the poor scarecrow. It was Peter Brownet, a down-and-out yokel who joined the army and who was accused of stealing the company cash-box because some money had been found on him. He committed suicide by climbing the telegraph wire and electrocuting himself. When Lludd looked at the death-dealing coins which still remained in the poor recruit's pocket, he saw that same bad shilling with the bad king's head which had caused his own imprisonment. But Lludd couldn't shiver although his middle was wrung with anguish. And he said:

'The open road, the free life, the tramp's life is too full of miseries; you see too much. I want to be cooped up, I want to wear blinkers, I'm going back to town,' and back he went.

In town Lludd met his brother Page, a theatrical manager. Theatrical people are very superstitious you know. The stage-manager somehow gets mixed into their religious beliefs – they think there's one aloft who's interested in their blowings and puffings and what they gross. Well, Page took Lludd to Madam Maritana, a wonderful parti-coloured ogress. Lludd walked up a littered lane between garbage tins next door to a theatre, where badly-mixed cats prowled, dogs sniffed trousers and old men poked in the rubbish. Up a wooden staircase black with age lived Madam Maritana behind a cretonne curtain. She wore two Paisley shawls and old Turkish slippers, had a moustache, gold-filled teeth and a port-wine breath.

'Do you wish to learn the secrets of the unknown,' enquired Madam Maritana after drawing the orange curtains; 'do you know what fate lies before you in the courses of the stars?'

'No,' said Lludd, 'I came to learn to shiver; I thought my brother Page explained.'

'To shiver,' exclaimed the lady, in a baritone voice, 'ho, ho, you are the young man who cannot shiver? You'll learn.'

'In this way?' asked Lludd a few moments later, when the lady, after gently massaging his hand and the back of his neck, approached her mouth to his own red and pouting lips. Maritana advanced the smallish foot in the Turkish slipper to Lludd's foot, murmured:

'Many learn this way.'

'Not me,' said Lludd.

The seer then rose, changed her dressing-gown in the corner, sprayed herself with Black Zebra perfume, brought into the room a large parrot and a crystal ball, and proclaimed:

'Lludd, prepare to see futurity!'

She put the ball in front of him and begged him to keep his eyes fixed on it. She pressed a button, not unobserved of Lludd, and clouds assembled in the ball and began to fade away. The old one, leaning over his neck, grunted:

'Boy, what do you see now?'

'Nothing,' said Lludd.

'I see, I the seer.'

'You should.'

'I see that you will take a long journey, come into pots of money, marry a beautiful innocent girl who has known much misfortune.'

'Good, but when do I shiver?' said Lludd, who was single-minded.

'Now,' said the lady, 'your father's spirit stands before you, and with his index pointed at you says, "Son, I have a message for you; I can see you unseen and hear you unheard. Be here at Madam Maritana's place at three to-morrow afternoon and you will meet your fate and fortune." '

Well, Lludd fell into Madam Maritana's net too, but he made money out of it; he was no sucker like Page. He became the Fakir Prahna, the most celebrated society fakir of our day. He made lots of money. The women were all swarming at his feet; he performed for everyone of distinction, all the rich noddies, the old girls taking beauty treatment with their pekineses, the timid Theosophical widows living on the alimony of husbands in India, the actors, the Monte Carlo hounds – the world of spirits, if you please, is just wild about them. His bank account swelled like a puff-ball, and Edna Freedom, the beautiful, wild and middle-aged wife of a leading rich Socialist minister, threw away home, reputation and husband to live with him.

Lludd had no bad habits and he got on. In this way he met his wife. She lived on an estate in the country with four brothers who were anxious to marry her off because she was almost forty and sentimental. She was severe in dress, cultivated in conversation, religious in practice and had a giant library. Madam Maritana saw how the land lay, introduced Lludd to her as secretary and librarian. The lady, named Esther, fell madly in love with Lludd and invented difficulties in the way of marriage to induce him to run away with her to Gretna Green. But Lludd waited, for her honour's sake, he said, for the marriage contract, which was not long in coming. The next year she had a child by him and he immediately became the perfect family man and she the perfect virago. The little brat had hardly learned to squawl like a human and not like a kitten before Lludd was festooned with the chains of domesticity. She was wifely too, the rich old bride; she put his slippers by the fire, had the finest dinners cooked for him, gave him a nightcap at ten at night, when he was used to sitting up larking, reading, dancing, listening to music till two o'clock in the morning. She even gave him an allowance for 'private pleasures', went to the tailor's and chose his suits with him. She never left him alone for a moment, winter and summer, night in, night out. But there were no nights out, except when she went to the theatre and displayed the family diamonds. Then the young women used to look after Lludd regretfully and jeeringly as the smart young Alec who married the family diamonds and had been converted into a safe-deposit.

But pretty soon, Lludd met one who delivered him – in a way. He went down to an antique bookshop to get something rare and curious for Esther's birthday. Alone in the shop was a young, serious girl, in colouring all red, white and ebony, with hair beautifully curled up from her neck and the perfect, young, delicate, elegant beauty which looks divine with a long neck. She was retiring in manner because a maiden, and troubled by the sensation her beauty caused everywhere. She had a hesitating lower middle-class accent. What a beauty she was! Lludd dared not look at her straight but stole a thousand side-glances at her. After a few minutes' stiffness and silence, she moved gracefully about showing him the books he asked for. He found an erotic book which would please Esther, and as he stood looking through the illustrations she moved off and stood at some distance like an alabaster lamp in the dim of the shop. His heart was soft wax and moved round her image. He walked along the streets with wide and gleaming eyes thinking of the beauty, and he felt desire too, but that tender, painful desire which always overcomes one at the sight of a peculiarly beautiful and intricate design, as one of Cellini, or at the sight of very fine stone Venus. The next day Lludd awoke from dreams of the girl with a burning love. He went back, bought Esther many books and made love to the girl. He told her all his ill-fortune, how he had been tricked into marrying Esther – a long and plausible history – how unhappy he was and the restrictions he suffered in. The letters he wrote her! He blushed himself when he re-read them, stealing them from a wooden box she kept them in.

They ran away. He went with very little money, no clothes and a railway ticket, and she had a little bundle. He took a canoe moored in the river which ran through the estate and came into the great river and so to the city where she met him. At the landing-stage they set the boat adrift; nothing more than that.

After waiting two years, Esther divorced Lludd; but alas, by that time he had already taken and forgotten three or four girls. He particularly liked the bluff, artistic, ignorant art-school type of girl, a mixture of Burne-Jones and Marie Laurencin in face, odd greens and handwork in dress, who believes in Wiener Werkstätte work and art in a garret, on papa's meagre allowance; who is raving mad with love and spouts muzzy eloquence, deep-voiced from a deep bosom. He liked, too, the revolutionary girls who believed in themselves and the flame of revolution and were equally mad with love and ambition. He vowed never to marry again – but he did. He married a girl with a china shop who had two thousand pounds of her own. She immediately gave him twins and they ate up the money (one thousand pounds as it proved) in no time at all. First of all, of course, they furnished a luxurious studio with Nepal furniture, Madras cloths and Chinese rugs, and after that they lived in the cheapest sort of hotel in one room with only their valises and the babies' crib. This second wife, Wanda, left Lludd in a year or two and went to live with her people, opening a second china shop. In the meantime, Esther sued Lludd for alimony, made false representations of his financial position and wanted him in gaol. He was now penniless, somewhat shopworn and couldn't recuperate his fortunes so easily; and he had an accident. In a fight with one of the art-school boys about one of the art-school girls he got his nose broken. It was reset at the public hospital by a harassed young doctor who was sandy and very plain, and it no longer had its fine outline.

Well, to make a long story short, just when Lludd was getting on foot nicely with a little business in ladies' gloves, financed by a madam who wanted to give up her house, and who would have married him, Esther had Lludd thrown into gaol for the alimony. There he stayed six months until Wanda, the second wife, got her people to pay it off. But by that time, of course, more was due and in six months Lludd was in gaol again. Lludd wrote to Esther from gaol a most pitiable letter, and Wanda went to see her showing her the twins and her belly in which was a third. But the four brothers threw them out bodily on the country road and Wanda came back sick, suffering, and full of reviling, to her parents.

Lludd came out of gaol and went to see Esther's brothers. The youngest, who had a little heart, took him aside to say:

'Esther doesn't want the money, she has more than she'll ever want: she wants to keep you away from the other wife – don't you know a jealous woman's a tigress?' and he advised Lludd to skip the country. So he started to leave all his troubles behind and begin in somebody's colonies. But Wanda got wind of it and had him arrested at the boat for wife desertion. For they had both heard of the amorous madam and were mad with jealousy. You have to beware of these great passions, they flow equally in all directions.

At last Lludd heard the charges were lifted and he was a free man. He walked out of gaol with greying hair at thirty and hid himself from them all under yet another name, and with a moustache. He didn't answer telephones and moved from place to place. Soon again he had got someone to advance him the money for a refreshment shop business. He made a temporary husband for many a lonely girl. They were all grateful to him for his kindness and helped him when he was in trouble.

Then he got a delicate little note in the handwriting of Adora Lester, the beautiful girl from the antique bookshop. She told Lludd she had her job again and that her father would get him a job in the city if he got himself divorced and married her, since he had come to understand that all along Lludd had been the victim of misfortune. She mentioned a time, seven o'clock in the evening, when the shop closed and it was darkish. Lludd got himself presentable and went up with a little button-hole of carnations for her; but there, on the spot, was Esther, looking plump, well-dressed, and dark about the eyes. She had begun to make up, and as she got older resembled Madam Maritana more and more. By the hand she held a boy of seven or eight, Lludd's son, as he supposed, a sickly, dark, timid child, dressed in a lace collar and silk socks. When Lludd came up, he smiled and gave her the bouquet, and she said:

'I suppose you brought me a bouquet because you knew by thought-transference I would be here, you old mind-reader,' and with that she raised her arm, which she had held behind her back, and brought down across Lludd's face a great green-hide thong. Lludd let out a yell, but Esther laid it on, and presently people came running, although it was quiet there, near a museum, and heads popped out of windows. Men held her off, and presently, with his face and neck horribly marked, and the boy howling, Lludd made off. But Esther shook herself free and ran after him. Lludd was almost blinded and stumbled as he ran. He presently fell. In a moment she was there, pushing off the policeman, and saying:

'It's my lowdown runaway husband; I'll teach him to leave me for a pack of bitches.' She sang this out in her rich contralto, which had something fearsome and inspiring in it. When Lludd attempted to get up, Esther let down a couple of stripes and yelled:

'Your madams won't like you now.'

They pulled her off, and she began to cry, saying:

'Lludd, if you'll come back, I'll forget everything; I worship you, I'll clean your boots.'

'I won't come back,' said Lludd, and fainted.

When he came to himself he was in a great, dark room, cool, sweet with the scent of flowers. He didn't recognise it at all. He felt a soft, kind hand on his and thought:

'It is Adora; at last she has brought me home.'

He felt around and switched on the bedside lamp. There, grinning horribly with love, like a man-eating ogre, with the green-hide bat across the chair, sat Esther.

'Lludd,' she said in her deep, coarse voice, and she opened her dressing-gown preparatory to coming into bed. She had got much older; she was wrinkled and wasted, but he saw the fires of passion still burned, from her intense and almost beautiful look and her welling eyes. She vaulted into bed, the savage, and at that, yes, at that, Lludd felt himself convulsed in a long network of cold sensations, as if a delicate knife gently lacerated and penetrated his skin and muscles; from head to foot shuttled the blades in all his limbs.

'Why are you shivering?' said Esther anxiously; 'why, you have learned to shiver!'

'Who is this coming?' said Lludd's mother a few days later, when a splendid automobile drew up before the public-house. Looking out of the window they perceived a dark, fat, rich woman in furs and a delicate pale man with a silk hat.

'It is Lludd,' cried the father; 'he comes back riding in his own car: what a boy!'

'My brother was born under a lucky star; there he

wallows in the Pearmain Million,' said Page at the theatre.

And Lludd, by shivering, shivering, day and night, made his money and keeps his place.

About the House

Mrs Fairchild, Dorothy called Girlie, invited Alison Darling to have tea with her in town. The two women met in the ladies' tearoom at the Civil Service Stores where Mrs Fairchild and her sisters had always had accounts. Mrs Fairchild sat down and threw back the new satin-lined furcoat she had borrowed and took off her gloves. After she had ordered tea and cakes, she looked hard at the young woman.

'I didn't know you were so young. How old are you?'

'Twenty.'

'I am forty-eight and so is my husband,' said Mrs Fairchild. 'We have been married twenty-one years; we were married before you were born. My eldest girl is your age. We have brought up a large family and my husband is a devoted father. I do not intend to leave home or have my home broken up. In the next five or six years my children will be growing up, marrying, Apsley is a large house and we expect some of them to make their homes with us. What can you hope for?'

'I love Alan and Alan loves me,' said the girl. Mrs Fairchild was looking at a wellgrown young woman comely in a plain way with brown hair under a schoolgirl's hat and the dark blue silk dress and severely tailored coat of a senior schoolgirl. She had new flat-heeled shoes, a plain bag, wore no gloves and had neither manicure nor makeup.

'Alan does not approve of gloves or makeup,' the woman said smiling slightly and looking at the girl's hands.

'No, I know and so I don't wear them,' said Alison. The wife repressed a smile.

'Has this been going on long?' she asked quietly.

'For four years, since I was sixteen,' said the girl. 'We were out in the country – with others, with a group; we had just struck camp. We had come along a road full of animals, a dead kangaroo, a dead wombat, a dead sheep, all run over by cars, a mob of emus dancing about inside a fence and a bluetongue lizard and a goanna and a snake. Alan tried to catch the snake but it slipped into the bushes. I was glad. He was annoyed because he loves snakes. It was just getting dark. We suddenly fell in love, both at the same time.'

'I am sorry for you. You are still only a girl and he and I are almost fifty. You have wasted four years of your life when you might have been looking for a young man who could marry you. Don't you want children? You cannot have children born like this, beyond the pale, such children are marked for life and what would their mother be, you, a disgraced woman. They used to say a scarlet woman when I was a girl, but I suppose they don't any more.'

The girl blushed with anger.

'I suppose you don't care,' said Mrs Fairchild.

'There's no talk of children,' said the girl in a low voice, but in anger. 'We love each other and I am not going to try to stop. He needs me.'

'It's incredulous!'* burst out Girlie, looking at the girl, who sat straighter. The wife wavered; she felt there was something wrong. 'It's incredulous – don't you feel any shame?'

The girl was looking at her with silent scorn. Her makeup betraying her, looking witchlike, Girlie rolling her brilliant, dark eyes, glared at Alison, 'You're a university girl, aren't you? A graduate?'

'Yes.'

'And is that what they taught you at the university, to have sneak affairs with older men, break up homes, to take their food and shelter away from children and women who can't help themselves?'

The girl's face grew grave and silent with contempt.

'You don't answer. You know there's no excuse for what you're doing.'

'There's nothing to excuse. I love Alan. I haven't done any wrong. He needs me. He told me he was looking for love, that he was lonely and he needed me.'

'And that's enough for you?'

'Yes; that's all.'

'You've had a good education,' said the older woman, somewhat relieved and taking a motherly tone. 'Alan is old enough to be your father and I am old enough to be your mother. I know girls get crushes on their teachers and older men. It's because you need to settle down and

* Mrs Fairchild's use of 'incredulous' where she means 'incredible' is strange, since she speaks correctly otherwise. 'Incredulous' appears in both versions. I can only assume an [unusual] error on the author's part.

you idealise the first man you meet. I don't suppose you have much experience of men,' she said contemptuously.

The girl flushed, 'No, I met Alan when I was sixteen and I never thought of anyone else.'

'Then he ought to be ashamed of himself,' said the woman but could not help a hypocritical tone; she heard it herself.

'Oh, no, I am grateful to him. He saved me. I was very lonely and had nowhere to turn,' said Alison, sincerely.

'But can't you think of the consequences of this? What do you want from him?'

'I don't want anything.'

'Then for nothing do you think it is right to hang round a man meeting him in sneak interviews and talking about love and kissing, when you don't mean to do anything and you don't want anything?'

'If I ever can, I'll marry him and I'm willing to wait.'

'I have never heard anything like it,' said the woman with stage indignation, but baffled. 'I do not intend to break up the home and I shall insist upon Alan's breaking it off with you; and it is for your sake too. Haven't you a mother and father, haven't you someone I can talk to to get you to see how wrong and how hopeless it is?'

'I live at home,' the girl said, 'but my father and mother were always very unhappy; and they should have divorced long ago. I believe in divorce because I know what an unhappy marriage is.'

'You will feel differently when you find a man of your own and have your own children,' said the older woman drily but not unkindly.

'I will never feel differently.'

'Well, you are quite right. If I could have got a divorce after my first child, I would have,' said the wife suddenly with desperate truth, 'but I couldn't. I didn't know what to do and they had got rid of me at home, they didn't want me back. I am sure a good many women stay married because they have nowhere to go. Women usually only get married because they have nowhere to go.'

The girl said nothing.

'But it is too late now,' said Mrs Fairchild. 'You have nothing to hope for. I couldn't leave if I wanted to. And I have to see my children grown up and out of it. If I can prevent it the girls won't marry; anything is better; any mess is better. But I suppose they will be fools like all of us. Now Miss Darling, I have to go and catch my train. I do not want you to see Alan any more; it is not fair to me or to him. Not that I care much about him, he has got you, me and himself into this tangle with his sentimental talk. I know it. I've heard it. He caught me with it and you're not the first young girl that he's got sympathy from. I want you to leave him alone. Don't write letters. Get over it. Get one of your professors, go out into the street and get a man. There are plenty and you are young and fresh ... Well, have I your word?'

'No,' said the girl.

'What? Hasn't anything I've said meant anything to you?'

'No.'

'I've met a girl like you before, Selborne, Alan's niece. He was always mad about her, and now she has gone to Queensland without even saying goodbye to him. You are just a substitute. You're a niece to him, not a sweetheart.'

'I know about it,' said Alison.

'But you're wasting your life.'

'Oh, no; it isn't wasted now; it was before.'

'There's no more for me to say here,' said the wife.

They stood outside the store on the pavement in the late home-going crowds.

'You may think you're very clever and can carry this off, but I shall not permit it. I have other lives besides our three to think of and as for yours, I don't care anything about it.'

And then with a gracious nod which she called a bow and a wave of the hand, the wife said, 'Goodbye.'

'Goodbye.'

Mrs Fairchild sat in the train huddled in her furcoat which Alan had not seen for he did not approve of furcoats. She felt like 'an old hen' as she said. She considered the girl a waste of time. 'What does she understand,' she thought, 'it's to Alan I must speak. At least he's my age and has been through what I've been through. And I know he'll never give me the children; what else has he to show?' She looked at herself in the train window and powdered her face before she got out at the big suburban railway station. But when she came through the gate, her daughter Emma hurried to her saying, 'Are you all right, Mother? You look so tired.'

'And I am so tired. Take this coat upstairs where the man who loves animals more than people can't see it and make me some tea. I had tea but I was talking and drank it without noticing. And when you're upstairs get me a tablet. My head's bursting. I don't feel as if I'm going to sleep all night. And I have got to talk with your father before then. Matthew, go and tell your father that I want to see him in his room. I have something to say.'

Matthew, a tall bigfooted quiet boy of thirteen obediently ran off. In a few minutes, Alan Fairchild in the worn dungarees and sandshoes he wore round the house, his thick fair hair on end, stood at the door of the kitchen, filling the doorway and looking at her flushed and with indignant bloodshot eyes.

'Girlie, I forbid you to send orders to me by the children. If you want to see me, you can ask me properly. Is that tea, Emmie? Bring me some into the dining room. Your mother can come and have tea with me there.'

'I'll never drink with you,' she cried indignantly. 'It'd be too easy to throw it in your face. You always so candid, frank, so honest, so open – and you are a sneak.'

'Don't dare use that word to me.'

'Yes, I will and others too. I know what you have been doing and saying.'

'What does that mean? Explain yourself. I detest innuendoes.'

'I have been to town, in that furcoat I borrowed from Jean, I went to the Civil Service Stores to have tea with a young woman. I asked her to meet me and she at least had the politeness to meet me. You know,' she said tossing her head and with a cunning smile and her voice and manner were extremely artificial, 'I believe you know her too; her name is Alison.'

He looked shocked and then thunderous, 'How dare you interfere with my affairs?'

She tossed her head and laughed the laugh he hated and said, 'If you don't want all your children to know the details, then go. I order you to go and wait for me in your bedroom. I will be up presently.'

He heaved a deep breath, a deep sigh, he was a tall strong man and seemed broken. After a few steps he returned and said in a broken, natural voice, 'You took a letter from the clock, then?'

'Yes, the day before yesterday; and I am keeping it.'

'I'll be up in my room,' he ended.

Sitting there with a fierce thin dark face, a determined expression, Girlie sipped and swallowed her tea, had another cup and a slice of bread and butter, and then went upstairs to her husband's room and shut the door firmly.

The children who knew nothing unusual in the quarrelling, for all they had ever seen was the noisy antagonism of the pair, went about their games and household jobs; and all they actually heard of it was when Girlie came out and their father standing at the door said loudly, 'I will not allow you to blacken my name,' to which their mother replied, 'I am going to do what suits me best. You have given me my freedom.'

'I am not going to allow you to put me in the wrong.'

To this her answer was her high trilling laugh, a girl's laugh that she had preserved. Then stopping at the head of the stairs, she said loudly for all to hear,

'If you drive me out of the house, you'll regret it. We will see what becomes of your fine name.'

But after that, other talks took place, long murmurings and arguments of a quieter sort. In the end Girlie called all her children into the diningroom, one blustery October afternoon, and looking very strange, very bright with her large hazel eyes blazing, her hair pulled tightly back, her face pale and her lips purple, she said,

'I want you all here to know what is happening. Your father has fallen in love with a young woman the same age as your cousin Selly. Your mother cannot remain here while your father carries on with another woman and especially makes a fool of himself with a girl young enough to be his daughter. He goes or I go. As he does not choose to go he says that this' (she threw her hand up and tossed her head towards the ceiling), 'is his home and so it is not my home. I don't want you children to choose between us. I want you to go on with your schoolwork and sports, whatever you are doing. But I want Boysie (Ralph) and Emmie to help me find a flat, or room not far from you so that I can be near you and you can visit me every day. I am being thrown out of my home and taken away from my children, after the years of torture I have put in for your sakes. I want only two things, that you will come to me and that soon some of you will help me. For I have no money, your father has no money either. He is so much a coward that he will not allow me to put his name in the papers and get his rights and so I must make do with what I can get. He has told me that I must not go to law and get some help and my rights, because of you children. Very well, I take it for what it is worth and it is for you I am doing it. All I ask is that you will not allow that other woman to come into this house while I am your mother.' She said a few more words. Matthew stared at her all the time astonished; he was unable to take it in. He had spent the past stormy weeks thinking of his school, football, friends – he had shut the trouble out of his mind. He had only a vague idea of what she meant by another woman; a houseworker? They had had one once. But the little one, Philip, the kindhearted one burst into tears and going round to his mother's side put his arms round her and said, 'Don't go, Mother, don't go.'

The older ones, though surprised, were so used to their kind of family life that they only began considering ways and means. What the elders had decided was settled: now what was to be done? Hence though Boysie said 'I'll come with you, Mother,' and Emmie asked if she should go to the stationer's and look for the notice of a flat, and whether it should be in the next street or whether next door would be all right, and while the younger girl kept saying, 'Oh, that wouldn't do, you can get a better flat in Double Bay where Auntie used to live; or why don't you go and live with Aunt Sophie and then we could come and stay?', they stood there in reasonable excitement and discussion. Their mother was not much unsettled by the children's practical views; and the idea of freedom, of having a flat to herself, where she need not work so cruelly and hopelessly hard amidst an uproar and without letup and where she might spend the rest of her days resting, pottering or playing cards perhaps with a friendly neighbour, whist or bridge, had begun to have a small attraction for her. So she suddenly said with a laugh, 'And let's find a place out of these dreadful winds for one thing.'

They ate their meal rather quietly and when they got up from table Matthew went up to her and said, 'Mother could Boysie and Phil have your room, because it is a big room and Phil could sleep on the verandah and then I could have the room to myself and not with Phil.'

'You must ask your father; it's his house now. But please wait till I go. I haven't found a place to live yet.'

Crestfallen, but thoughtful, Matthew went away and presently they found him moving his things out of the tiny leanto he had always shared with Philip and into a corner of the larger room adjoining where Geoff and Boysie slept. Though there was a fight about it, he kept his things there and in the evening said to his mother, 'Geoff doesn't mind if I sleep in his room. Boysie can have your room to himself if he likes.'

No sooner had she moved than Boysie announced that he was engaged and that he had a room and would soon be married; and would bring his bride home to Apsley soon after.

(And so on. Don't know.)

Uncle Morgan at the Nats

'You may notice the noise I am making,' said Uncle Morgan, champing with his jaws. 'You know what I have told you: masticate, denticate, chump, chew, and swallow. Now all together, masticate, denticate, chump, chew, AND swallow.'

The five children chumped, chewed, and swallowed in rhythm with pleasure. There was a loud noise like a hippopotamus eating sugarcane.

'That loud noise,' said Uncle, 'is a healthy noise and if you were in some countries, they would take it as a compliment, that you were pleased with the food; and you would be obliged to smack your lips, smack your bellies, and belch; and in fact,' he said, becoming excited, 'explode with greed and satisfaction in all directions, ears, eyes, nose, mouth, belly, and lower down. We will now smack our lips, roll our eyes, shake our ears, heave with our lungs, and belch if we can. Those who can't belch must try. It relieves the stomach of gases which accumulate and which if not relieved will go down lower, ro-oll around the large and the small intestines and rumble in the rumble-seat.'

The children broke out into cries, chuckles, and guffaws. Aunt Mildred rolled her black eyes in revolt. Her beautiful, black-fringed eyes rolled in her thin, yellow face, she shut her purplish red lips and with a look of disgust went out to the kitchen.

The orgy degenerated into horseplay, which Uncle Morgan took in hand. 'Enough,' he commanded, 'Gilbert the Filbert!'

'Morgan the Gorgon,' answered Gilbert cheekily but with his charming little grin. Morgan relaxed and sent a sparkling blue glance to the boy.

'Now when I was young I had digestive troubles,' pursued Uncle Morgan, with an agreeable air. 'I was a vegetarian, I wrongly believed that it was meat that upset me. Never say I don't change my mind. When facts present themselves to me, I change my mind. If I like the taste. In this case it was a meat-stew brought to a Nats' picnic by a lovely, serious young woman, who admired your Uncle Morgan. I did not know it then; I was too serious.'

'It was my friend Nellie,' said Morgan's younger sister, Beatrix, 'you were keeping company.'

Morgan passed this over, 'Morgan has never been known to ignore a fact. Aunt Mildred he MAY ignore when she is in one of her whimsies and whim-men have whimsies; Aunt Beatrix he MAY ignore when she forgets to collect the porridge plates – ' Beatrix got up hastily '– and when her hair is sticking up –'

'Now, Morgan,' began Beatrix with chatty ire, 'you have twisted your own hair into horns, into yellow horns.' This was a habit of Uncle Morgan's.

The children looked at the horns but did not laugh; but

Aunt Beatrix giggled and her timid, little, brown-haired, three-year-old daughter, Renee, broke down and giggled too. It was pretty to see how her round face changed, broke, mottled, dimpled, shifted, as she bent her head down, bashfully.

'Now, Grandmother,' said Morgan, gravely addressing the three-year-old.

Her eyes shone, she flushed.

'Now, Grandmother,' he said ominously, 'will you do everything your Uncle Morgan tells you? Do you love your Uncle Morgan?'

'Yes,' she piped.

'Then,' he said looking gravely at her, 'put your hand in the fire for your Uncle Morgan. Will you, Grandmother?'

This was before Uncle Morgan took down the chimney and dug out the fireplace, to avoid fire risks; and at that moment, half the breakfast fire was still blazing away in the grate, behind Aunt Mildred's armchair. Renee (Grandmother) looked from her uncle to her mother; she paled.

'Grandmother?' he said sternly.

'Will you, Gilbert the Filbert?' he enquired.

'No,' said Gilbert.

'But Grandmother *will*!' said Uncle Morgan gravely. 'Grandmother, get down from your chair!' She slipped off her chair and leaned over the seat, her face already working; but she did not dare to cry yet.

'Morgan, don't be so stupid,' said Beatrix.

'I mean it,' he said instantly, 'Trixie, I am training the child to obey, I know what I am doing. Leave it to me.'

She waited.

'Grandmother, go to the grate.'

She tottered away from the chair, looked at her

mother; she was crying now, but not loudly.

'Go to the grate and stand in front of the fire.'

She did so.

Her mother looked at her and said gently, 'Don't cry, my lamb. It's only fun.'

'Grandmother,' said Uncle Morgan, 'this is one of the most serious moments of your life. You are now learning something that will affect your whole life.'

'Morgan,' burst out Beatrix, 'how can you tease the baby?'

'Grandmother is not a baby,' said Morgan. 'Grandmother! Put your hand in the fire.'

She was sobbing loudly now, but she bent forward slowly and held out her pudgy hand with one fat finger advanced.

A thunderbolt tore into the room from the kitchen, the curtains blew about. Aunt Mildred, blazing black fury, was there.

'Morgan,' she shouted, 'how dare you tease the children!'

Uncle Morgan lifted the milk jug off the table and with a sweet laugh, parting his lips and showing many of his white teeth, he made as if to hurl the jug at Mildred.

'Let's see if I can land it right on her nose,' said he.

Aunt Mildred rushed forward and Aunt Beatrix rose to her feet. There was confusion. Morgan sat there, sanguine, grinning. 'Down, women!' said he, putting down the milk jug.

'You see,' he remarked in a pathetic, gentle tone to the children, 'when a child is getting social training, when its character is being formed, the women interfere and ruin its character. Now my character fortunately was not ruined, because my mother was a stern old Methody woman, good, loving but firm –'

'She was our mother too, Morgan,' said Beatrix, 'and she made me promise to obey those rules she believed in and which have kept me straight and true ever since.'

Aunt Mildred was now retiring to the kitchen and Beatrix said, 'Come here, lamb, to its mother.' But Morgan instantly changing his tune, commanded. 'Grandmother, back to the fire! You have not done what I told you.'

'Oh, Morgan,' said Beatrix.

'And you, Beatrix, don't butt in,' he said rudely, 'ideas come before sentiment. Granny,' he began in an ingratiating drone, 'do what your little Uncle asks, Granny, your little Uncle is asking you. Granny, do what oo is told! Granny be a dood girl. Granny, put your hand in the fire for Uncle Morg!'

Trembling and weeping the child put her hand out, felt the heat that surrounds the flame, blindly weeping, unquestioning, while Uncle Morgan ducking his head and grinning whispered to left and right, 'She'll do it,' gleefully, 'Granny will do it!'

'Renee!' shrieked her mother and fell on the baby, pulling the poor thing from the fire.

'She touched the fire, she touched the fire,' the children shouted, jubilating, dismayed.

'Granny did not al-to-gether touch the fire, Granny let her Uncle down, Granny did not obey her Uncle,' said Morgan, in a repulsive weeping tone.

Aunt Mildred was marching up and down the cemented kitchen floor with her arms folded, her eyes black. She stared through the window like a witch and if the crooked, smooth, silver arms of the fig trees had been broomsticks, she would have flown off on them.

Aunt Beatrix, weeping with her child, rushed into the kitchen to Aunt Mildred. 'Mildred! My poor fatherless baby!'

'You're a pack of fools, all of you,' said Mildred.

She went into the boys' room next to the kitchen and started throwing the mattresses about in a rage. Beatrix sat down on the rickety kitchen chair and began combing Granny's soft, curly brown hair. She soon smiled, her eyes rounded and shone and she whispered, 'Uncle Morgan didn't mean you to do it, love, Uncle Morg was having fun, Uncle Morg loves you, darling.'

Aunt Mildred could be heard hissing. She turned the mattress with such a thump that the iron bedstead of Sid, her eldest, slid halfway across the cement floor bringing to light Sid's heterogeneous collections and also a board he had cut loose in the wall to make a secret cupboard. Aunt Mildred surveyed this with contempt, pushed the bed back and muttered, 'What a pack!'

In the breakfast room, Uncle Morgan was saying cheerfully, 'But all this interrupted what I was going to tell you about the Nats' Dinner.'

The Nats were the Naturalists. The night before they had had their annual dinner and Uncle Morgan had not been re-elected Chairman. They had instead made a rule, the week before, saying that no chairman should serve more than two terms consecutively; and Uncle Morgan had already served three. He felt injured. At the same time, he held the Nats in contempt for having to pass a new law to get rid of him.

'At the Nats' Dinner, Ratty Atty,' by which he referred to Mr Atkinson, a lively naturalist, tall, thin, dark, whom he regarded as a rival (though of no account), 'was in the chair and sat at the head of the table, so that your Uncle Morgan –'

'– Morgan the Organ,' contributed Gilbert the Filbert.

Uncle Morgan smiled in the corner of his mouth, not

wishing to acknowledge this hit, but proud of it, '– had to sit at the side of the banquet table; and since I am left-handed,' he said, illustrating with knife and fork, 'I was inconvenienced; and my right-hand and left-hand neighbours were also inconvenienced. When I eat, I cut with my left hand and my elbow sticks into my neighbour's elbow or his side or shoulder, or his eye, it depends on his size,' said Uncle Morgan with a spiteful twinkle, for he was tall, large, and strong, 'and the eating rhythm of the table is disturbed, whereas when I am Chairman, if my arm moves to left or right, no one is disturbed.

'Last night I was sitting by a lady, it is true she was only an old schoolteacher with a bun, but a very fine woman, a woman of intellect, who admires your Uncle Morgan –' he continued with a marvellous genial expression of malice, for Aunts Mildred and Beatrix were not women of intellect, but read the bestsellers and the women's magazines; and Aunt Mildred called intellectual talk 'snobbish talk by gasmen', while Aunt Beatrix did not listen at all, only waiting to 'chip in', as she herself said.

'– and because my right arm was only holding the fork and her sharp elbow was coming my way; in fact, she was continually nudging me in the elbow! – because my elbow stuck out to wrestle with a tough bit of gristle and I made the fork twang and the plate whistle, and her elbow would be poked out as she went for a juicy tendon, for it was prime wether mutton about fifteen years old, though not so old as Miss Wetherby and perhaps that is why he bought wether, or I don't know whether. And on my other side, was Miss Rosemary Atkinson, Ratty Atty's daughter, beautiful as a rose, so that when the old lady with the bun jabbed my elbow and I jabbed hers, my chop skittered across my plate on to Sweet Rosemary's plate and I had to fly after it with my fork and we both said at the same time, 'Not much chop!' and laughed. But it was difficult for your Uncle Morgan to laugh because at that identical moment I had in the side of my cheek, my right cheek, on her side that is, a large ball of half-chewed tendon and gristle, with a little bit of bone in the middle. I didn't want to swallow the bone, and I didn't want to spit it out, so I had embedded it in a ball of refuse, much as the dung beetle builds up his precious hoard from droppings, and I could smile but I could hardly speak. I carried that ball about in my mouth for an hour after dinner and it was only when I was walking in the back of the house, in the conservatory with Lady Wassail and she asked me, 'What is the name of that little plant with the heartshaped leaves, Mr Jackstraw?' that I could turn round, while pretending to look, and could rid myself of the downy greyish ball. For by now, it had been completely chewed up and also had bits of salad and strawberry in it. For a whole hour I had been rolling that ball between my plate and my tongue and cheek.'

'What plant was it, Uncle?' said Gilbert.

'Of course she knew, she just asked to please me, to get my attention. It was *Orosera rotundifolia*, a sundew,' said Morgan carelessly.

'Another thing, when I am President and hence Chairman of the Nats and sit at the head of the table, no one can hear my plate clicking. Your poor Uncle Morg –'

'Morg the Dorg,' said Gilbert who had been only waiting for this.

'– Morgan,' said Uncle Morgan firmly, 'no matter what certain smarties who think themselves very witty may say,' (Gilbert the Filbert grinned conceitedly), 'was a very poor boy and is an autodidact, that is to say, he gained his education at night school and in the Library of Life and also of Knife.'

This was greeted with the usual appreciation and he proceeded, 'And Morgan Jackstraw did not have the chance you children have; hence he had to have his teeth out by the roots, when they could have been stopped from going, but they went.'

He smiled at the titter and continued, 'And I who am a natural speaker and have great natural charm, especially with the ladies; and with any men and boys,' he turned an eye on the boys, 'who believe in reason, logic, the true, the beautiful, was obliged to learn to speak through impedimenta, the impediment of my ivories. They click. You children know that however poor the fare at home, for a man like me, who has eaten in the company of lords and magnates,' (he said, ridiculing himself), 'I prefer to eat at home, because I can click at ease.' He clicked not only at ease but demonstratively and went through a series of denture acrobatics, wobbling, tossing, clicking, and pretending to shoot his plates out on the table. 'Plates to the plate,' said he. The children greeted this with a roar of laughter, while Aunt Mildred, rushing through the room, groaned and tossed her head. He replaced his dentures with a lick of his agile tongue.

'Lady Wassail then asked me the name of another plant, which incidentally was a *Hardenbergia Sydniensis*. I believe, children, that she feels for your Uncle Morg. She told me something I could quite agree with,' he said artfully, 'that she did not enjoy this banquet anything like the last two, for she loves to see me shining at the head of the table. "The head is my natural element," I said to her modestly. At which she tittered. For your Uncle Morg,' he said mournfully, looking round the table and especially at Renee, 'may not be appreciated by Lilliputians at home; but many is the beautiful woman who has wanted to run her long slender fingers through his golden hair.

Your Aunt Mildred may pretend to be in tantrums, but time was when she used to sit and dream over your Uncle Morgan's golden hair.'

At this grotesque idea, the children burst into laughter. Uncle Morgan shook his head sadly, '*Tempus he fugit*,' he said. 'You kids have no idea how I was as a boy. You girls have no idea. Trixie there has an idea; but you don't know now, with my beard getting rough, my plate clicking, my catarrh, my digestive troubles, my appendix, my photophobia, my antrum, my torticollis, the pain in the small of my back, all of which I fight bravely, what I was like as a boy, a young god; only that there aren't gods; but man is a god. Ah, kids, you missed me as a boy. When I went to work, a boy there named Nunneally, I was thirteen, he was seventeen, used to stroke my arms and say "Like satin, Morg, like white satin, like a duchess!" '

Beatrix giggled and then seeing her brother's astonished eye on her, she said apologetically, 'Yes, Morg, you were a handsome boy and with such a dreamy look as if you were too good for this world.'

'And so I was,' he assented, 'I was too good for the world, I didn't know there were evil men; I thought, if I was good, people would be good to me. But you see, kids, what happens? The Nats,' he said lugubriously, 'the Nats do not see me as I am. Can I blame them? They are naturalists but also men, and men have failings. Well, let me tell you, these dinners are an ordeal for a sensitive man, but next year Ratty Atty will have to vacate the seat and you will see the Padrone Morgan, the Patroon, at the head of the banquet table.'

'Morgan,' cried Beatrix breathlessly, 'do you know what I dreamed last night? I dreamed I was at the dentist's and he put out his tongue –'

'When I am going to have trouble, I dream of a yellow-bellied sea eagle; he comes to warn me,' said Morgan.

'Mowed down by a bird of ill-omen,' said Beatrix rushing to get in, 'and the funny thing is that though I knew it was Nell, I kept calling her Mrs File –'

'The sausages are burning, Trix,' called Aunt Mildred sourly.

'Yes, Millie dear,' said Trixie eagerly, 'and I woke up and it came to me out of a blue sky –'

'– in the middle of the night,' contributed Gilbert.

'The sausages are burned to a cinder,' said Aunt Mildred glaring.

'Trixie's cooking is a pillar of cloud by day and a pillar of fire by night,' said Uncle Morgan.

'And the dentist scratched my stocking and the funny thing is there is a run in my stocking.'

'Those are my stockings,' said Aunt Mildred.

'Mill's stockings are on Trix's last legs,' said Uncle Morgan.

Trixie brought in the sausages. It was Sunday. The children did not have to get ready for school.

'I adore Sunday,' said Trixie, and sang.

The kitchen became full of her sprightly chatter, the clash of dishes, and her gay soprano. Uncle Morgan had retired to the cane lounge where he lay at full length, 'expatiating', as he said.

3   *Pre-war Europe*

The Azhdanov Tailors

Jan Kalojan organised some eight thousand Yiddish-speaking tailors in Poland. Before that, they had belonged to the Bund, an old-fashioned organisation. Kalojan had learned Yiddish to do so because many of the tailors were Jewish and were not friendly with the Poles. The Jewish workers were tailors, carpenters, and factory workers. Some were very religious and wore the gaberdine; but the factory workers, who for the most part had to cut their beards and hair, were regarded with some contempt by the truly religious ones and called 'half-Jews'. It happened that Jan Kalojan himself, son of a rich mine owner and of a Viennese society girl, was really a half-Jew.

He told Otto Bauer, the Socialist leader, that he would organise the Jewish workers. Bauer said to him, 'No, you will never do that: you have bitten off more than you can chew, you will lose your teeth in it.' Jan was a very young man then, short, strong, blue-eyed, redheaded, and he had not lost any teeth, but that was the expression used.

Otto Bauer said, 'If you get together four thousand workers I will come and speak to them' – for fewer than that he would not stir, for he was a great man. 'How will you do it, Kalojan?' 'In many ways. When I was organising the printers, I wrote a story about printers and they printed it. I will now write a marionette play. I go about Europe juggling concepts and I will write a play in which concepts are dolls. There will be labour-value, surplus-value, the exploitation of labour; and there must be a little love. That is how they sell books. Then I must learn to smile – I blow up, I shout; that's not right. A smile conquers everything and everyone. A sense of reality is perhaps not as good as a sweet smile such as my sister Mrs Rock has. They would not let Jewish orphans into the orphanage and I became angry; but she said, "Let me go and talk to them." She went, she talked to them, she smiled at them and they allowed some Jewish orphans into the home.'

Jan Kalojan organised eight thousand Jewish workers.

One day he went to speak at Azhdanov, a place near Cracow. This small town was run by religious leaders who owned a paint-works producing ochre paint, a factory making hessian sacks, some tailoring and tobacco workshops, and all the businesses in town. They ran the churches and were town councillors.

Kalojan had a new tailored suit, gloves, a flower in his buttonhole, and a heavy stick. He took a first-class ticket; so that when he got out at the Azhdanov station, the three or four workmen who had come to meet him were standing at the other end of the platform. The first thing he saw was a big, elderly woman with a figure like round pots of all sizes, put together with a wig, a shawl, and the black clothing of repectable old women. She was at least forty and she seemed aged to the young man. With

astonishment and a little scorn, he saw her rush up to him
and throw herself on her knees before him. She pulled at
his trousers and coat and at her own shawl and began to
sigh and call out, 'Aie-aie-aie!' Tears ran down her face.
'Oh, please don't ruin me,' she cried out, 'don't take away
my life, don't ruin us and bring the killers, have mercy on
us, think what you are doing – have pity! You must have a
heart; you can't be as bad as that; think what you are
doing to us all, poor men, women, and children – don't
bring this scandal into our beautiful town. We are happy
here – just go home and think it over! You're a young
man. Go back by the next train without taking another
step and you will be glad later on! Think of the wicked-
ness of bringing the black terror here, where everyone is
so happy! Will you bring this disgrace on my daughter?
Oh, go away before the worst happens –'

Kalojan put his stick under his arm and began to move
sideways out of her grasp. He thought she might be mad;
he thought she might be cunning; he did not know what
it was. He was angry and thought to himself, 'If they
want to try to influence me, why don't they send a
beautiful young girl, not a fat old woman who ought to
hide in shame.' But he hardly thought anything; he had
no time for her. At that moment, the workmen who were
waiting for him, came up to him and said, 'This woman is
the rabbi's wife and they have told everyone that you are
coming here to organise a pogrom.'

They went out of the station and warned him that it
was going to be difficult. Kalojan had begun to organise
the Jewish workers in Azhdanov. To begin with, that is
some time before, he had gone to a little café where they
sat and read newspapers. He spoke first to one, then to
another, then to two or three; and the workers gradually
fell away from the synagogue. This whole thing had been

begun before his time, because of the work in the factories.

As they walked from the station, the workers, one of whom was named Henryk Portnoy, told him that there had been bills posted on the churches, the synagogue, and the walls of houses saying, 'A certain Kalojan –' or 'One Kalojan – is coming on such and such a day from Cracow to cause a pogrom,' and much more of this; and it continued, 'All are warned to stay away from him,' and much more. Kalojan, who was at that time about twenty-three, a fearless and bold talker, took no notice of what he heard, but sent the workmen away to tell the others he had come; and to hurry them up to the meeting-place where they would all be together and in force. Portnoy and the others were unwilling at first. 'The town is ready to burst into flames. The priests, the rabbi, and their friends have incited the people to violence and done things with their own hands.' The books from the workers' library had been taken out, torn into little pieces, and burned; the workers' centre was damaged; any people who stood about and looked on were dispersed.

But Kalojan now went on toward the centre of town near the synagogue where the Jewish workers' centre also was, because he did not mean the town councillors and the priests to keep this town, entirely a working-class town, in servitude. Holding his stick in his hand he went on, determined.

As he walked, he noticed two or three little children who ran around him: they were poor with their shirts out at the back; that is, very small and some had bare feet. They ran around him and pulled him. Then older children came, nine or ten who ran around him and followed him; but he took no notice and went on walking, though they tugged at his stick. He put it under his arm and buttoned up his coat. Then still older ones came and he took no notice of these either; and then youths and young men and men in their thirties fell in, from the doorways, or yards, or side-streets, and by then he knew it was an organised demonstration against him; but he kept marching on, thinking, This means nothing to me; I can manage this; and in fact, he felt no particular fear.

But the crowd grew and grew; they opened up before him so that he could keep on walking, but they squeezed him on both sides and pushed him at the back so that he could not move his arms and could scarcely breathe. Soon he felt them sticking needles into him, sacking needles which were used to sew up the hessian sacks in one of the factories; he felt cold and heard the cloth being torn; he heard shears snipping. They hurt him and tore at his new suit of good material. He kept marching, though now he knew it was serious and he wondered if they meant him to arrive there naked. He was carried onward and soon had to pass the synagogue, where now the crowd was very thick, an excited crowd, shouting and threatening; and now he could no longer move but was being crushed slowly in on all sides. He was a short man, but sturdy.

He now saw some of his friends, high up on a wall and some on a scaffolding. The Jewish workers were also carpenters and builders in this town. Suddenly two of them dived into the crowd of people headfirst with their arms spread, as if they were going for a swim, but they could not get to him. At the same moment, a Town Councillor came out with friends all round him, on the steps of the synagogue where he could be seen; and loudly, with his arms out, he cursed the intruder from Cracow, and shouted at the crowd of people who were mostly Jewish, telling them Kalojan had come to start a pogrom. Some people tried to start fighting, but the crowd was too thick.

Next, several policemen pushed their way in and arrested the man from Cracow for causing a disturbance. The police knew very little and the Town Councillor was a religious leader, a factory owner, and a very rich man. He was obeyed, even though Jan Kalojan protested, saying that he had a right to visit Azhdanov and a right to speak to his friends and that he himself knew people in Cracow more influential than this Town Councillor. He said he had bothered no one but had himself been attacked. He was taken to gaol still protesting, and now he looked disreputable, with scratched face and torn clothes; but he insisted upon writing out telegrams to the Chief of Police in Cracow, to Victor Adler and Otto Bauer in Vienna, and to the lawyers who looked after his family estates. His father having died, he was now, though so young, chief of the Kalojan family council; and the family owned mines, warehouses, country and town property, and was even well-connected at the court in Vienna.

Kalojan was not sure of help, but he thought he might impress them. The police became anxious and agreed to let him go to the station if he would go by small back alleys. Jan said, 'They will all think like you, they will think of back alleys; so you must take me by the main streets.'

Then they wanted to put him in a carriage; but he refused. He said, 'I am going to walk, I want everyone to see how you treat a man who comes to organise the workers.' The police were anxious for their own skins, but he forced them to walk along with him to the station.

Near the station, the back streets and the main street converged and the organised crowd which, just as he had foreseen, was expecting him along the back lanes, saw him passing along at a distance and rushed forward yelling. But he got on to the platform, and though they had some time to wait for the train, the police protected him. Meantime, he could hear the threats and insults shouted outside, 'The workers' friend is an *elegantchik,* but doubtless his shirt has not been washed for weeks!' This was their idea of a deadly insult, suggested by their own lives. 'Now that things are a little hot, he is taking a first-class ticket back home.' This was true, of course. Kalojan was not angry or bitter, he was reasonable; he knew how all this had been arranged and why these things were said. Besides, he was upset about his suit. A charming young girl sat in the ticket office. He asked her if she could do something about it. She borrowed a needle from one of the demonstrators outside the station, found some thread and sewed up the worst tears in his costume. 'See what the tailors' workers have done to my suit,' he said to her.

When Kalojan returned to Cracow, he found an excited crowd of workers at the station and in front of them was his sister, Mrs Rock, very pale, almost white, looking terribly anxious. She rushed up to him and kissed him to make sure he was there, safe and sound, for he looked very strange; and in fact the news had got around that he had been killed. A great deal was already known about the demonstration.

But this was not all. Kalojan was arrested in Cracow at the insistence of the same Azhdanov people and held in gaol for trying to make trouble against the Jews. He was brought to trial. He pleaded not guilty and related all the circumstances, so that it was clear what had happened; but the rulers of the small town of Azhdanov had got stupid people together and suborned witnesses, among

them a servant girl, a religious fanatic who cried in court
and testified that he had called out, 'At them, hunt them,
kill them, kill the Jews'; and others who testified that he
had said, 'Loot the Jewish rich men'; and others again
who said they had heard him shout, 'Burn the Jewish
workers' centre!' The proof was that the workers' centre
had been looted and the books had been burned. There
were many such witnesses.

At last the judge, who was a man of Kalojan's own
society and knew him and Mrs Rock quite well, had him
taken to a private room. The judge came to him and said,
'Look, sir, you plead one way and twenty-five witnesses
have come from Azhdanov to testify to the contrary. It is
not a question of justice here but of preponderant testimony. If you can take other measures, you had better do
so.' Kalojan realised he would not get a judgment and
that he had better follow this advice. The case was
postponed for a day or so. Kalojan was allowed to go to
local people, authorities, and friends. He found out that
some of the witnesses had various concessions, a tobacco
concession and so on; so Kalojan arranged through his
friends for the witnesses to be threatened: 'Your concession will be withdrawn if you do not take back your
testimony and complaint.'

The thing was settled in this way; and Kalojan was told
he could get damages for his ruined suit. He said, 'I have
other suits, but the workers in Azhdanov have not got
other books.' The Councillors, priests, and witnesses
were obliged to restitute the burned volumes. It was
amusing to see them sending to Cracow for the socialist
classics; and the workers watched at the station to see that
the parcels of books came and were not somehow lost on
the way.

Portnoy, one of the four at the station, went to the United States some time later and became a tailor in a town in upper New York State.

Some years after the beginning of the Nazi terror, he heard from another immigrant tailor that Kalojan himself had fled from the Nazis and was living in New York City.

It took Portnoy some time to find out where Kalojan was living, because in the long years between, Kalojan, now a man of sixty, had lived all over the world. At last he got his address, and at the end of a year, during which he saved, he went down to New York by train and came to a side street off upper Broadway, where he found a big courtyard and an apartment house in it. On the fourth floor he found the number he had been given and rang. After a long time, the door was opened and there stood a strange old man with thick orange-coloured hair and a face that was entirely cherry-red. His eyeballs were red too and in them pupils of such a startling blue that they seemed to rush out at the visitor and stand before him like two floating globes on two golden threads of light. There was a strong smell of gas in the place. 'Come in,' said the strange old man, 'the gas will go away soon; I opened all the windows when I heard the doorbell.'

He was dressed in a frayed cream-coloured suit with a silk shirt of French style, in thin red, blue, and black stripes, and he had onyx cuff links.

Portnoy was embarrassed. He could not understand how the man could have such a complexion and he did not know who he was; but he soon found out that he was Jan Kalojan and had received Portnoy's letter. This old man was nothing like the young man he had known, except that he looked Polish, and that young man too had

had startling blue eyes and orange-coloured hair.

'I did not recognise you,' said Portnoy. 'How is your sister, Mrs Rock?'

'It's a curious thing that you came just now,' said Kalojan. 'I fell asleep in the kitchen and I was just going to put a goose to roast, but I forgot and left the gas on in the oven and I had not even lighted it. You see, I live alone.'

They sat down by an open window, while Kalojan brought his visitor something to drink: 'Are you American now? Do you like Scotch? Or sherry or Campari? And I have slivovitz.'

He bustled about, an experienced host.

'My sister, Mrs Rock, died some years ago. She was picking up coals for orphan children. It was a bitter winter day and as you know, she had got the rich people to found an orphan asylum, but there was not much coal, so she used to go picking up coals along the railway, where they fell off the railway trucks. It wasn't necessary for her to do that, she could have bought the coal; but through worrying about the orphans she had come to behave like an old pauper woman. That day she caught cold and in four days she died. Half an hour ago I was thinking about her and about all the others who have died. I just received news that my sister who married a Polish Jew in Lodz, my brother, and others in my family were sent off and murdered in the Nazi murder trains. My brother had a little daughter whom he loved and who died in childhood; he never recovered from it, but for the rest of his life, which is ended now, he was gloomy and apathetic. I am not like that; but I was thinking of them just half an hour ago, and that is how I forgot about the goose and left the gas jets on. I'm glad you came. I do not intend to die.'

'It has taken me more than a year to save up the train fare,' said Portnoy.

'You can call me a tailor, I suppose, but I do mending and cleaning mostly, in a workshop that looks right on the railroad. The cinders come in on the clothes; you understand, it's an unsuitable location. But now I know you are here, I have something to live for and I promise you that every year I'll come down to see you; and there is a friend of mine who knew you in Azhdanov who will come down, too, perhaps at Easter.'

Private Matters

After an early lunch, we set off for Gheel where Jack's nephew lodged. We took a taxi; Jack had a car but did not drive. Maria, his promised bride, usually drove, but she had gone to Berlin for her brother's funeral. Jack had a chauffeur but he did not want the chauffeur to know where he was going. Jack had a nephew Claud, now twenty-five years old, who had been staying with a peasant family in Gheel; but he had tried to kill his hosts and had been taken to the asylum. Jack had had to authorise the strait-jacket. But Claud had escaped, taken a bicycle, set out for the Dutch frontier, been recaptured.

The taxi streaked through the flatlands of Antwerp province in the lovely afternoon, through high fields and leafy avenues until, nearly an hour out, we came to the poor village of Gheel. We had had to ask the way several times, but all local people knew where the village lay; there were eighteen thousand people there and four thousand of them were insane, for the most part not of that region.

Jack was silent throughout the trip and we said little. Jack Brame was the youngest of five in a poor Scots family, the only boy, the only rich one. He looked after his mother, a poor widow, and his four poor sisters, some married. His favourite, Rose, a widow now, had a small newsagent's shop in the East End of London. Her only son, Claud, a brilliant boy, ready for the University at sixteen and Jack ready to send him, went off his head and was called incurable. Rose said he was too sensitive; the doctors said something else. When Claud tried to kill her, Rose begged Jack to buy them a farm in the country where she could look after him. It was her fault; she had not understood him. But since Jack had a business in Belgium, she agreed to try the village system in Gheel.

Jack left us at the asylum, a big glum building on the outskirts, and we walked on into the village. There were a few cafés where the signs said, *Bière à pression, plats chauds à toute heure, banquets, noces* and we sat down. Some cyclists and pigeon-fanciers were sitting about, a family party getting noisy, a couple of quiet seedy men at an empty table drinking nothing. The Belgian army was at autumn manoeuvres somewhere near; motor cyclists were tearing through the streets. The bar owner spoke to the two quiet men, who got up and went away. A cropheaded young man with a brown pouch slung on his shoulder stood near the village pump and played with the trickle of water, smiling to himself and childishly at passers-by. Round the small railed green in the middle of the square men hung their heels. One or two were haranguing their withdrawn neighbours or the cooling afternoon air. Some of the men looked gloomy, some satirical.

A very tall middle-aged man walking uncouthly, passed and re-passed the café, his head hunched into his shoulders, brooding, startling. Another tall man with a pleasant round face came with a little book. In silence, he opened it to show a collection of green beech and oak leaves with designs on them. He was very poor. He murmured, 'I go into the forest and get the leaves; then I punch designs in them and sell them.'

He took out of a breast pocket his punch, a teaspoon handle.

'Do you do it all with that?'

'Yes, that's all.'

His manner was gentle, pallid, humble, yet complete; and it was as if on second thoughts, he offered a leaf; on a delicate background of veins, the green flesh remaining represented a pair of lovers in hats, town clothes, gloves, embracing.

There were other scenes, a man on a horse, a village with steeple, made in the green flesh of the leaves upon the network of veins, which suggested forest boughs. I kept that marvellous little work of art many, many years; it turned brown, fell to a sort of ash.

A Belgian family at the next table looked at the leaves, passing them round, giggling and uncomfortable. 'What could we do with them?' With resignation he picked up his leaves and moved off.

In the central square another visitor, a well-dressed courteous man, speaking French and English, saluted us and walked up and down with us. He was pleased when we said we came from Brussels.

'And I live here.'

'Are you a doctor?'

'No, just a resident.'

He told us the shopkeepers all around were 'very nice' to the insane. 'They know what to do. Did you come to live here?'

'No – we are visiting Gheel – it's famous.' He seemed to withdraw.

'Are you man and wife?'

'Yes.'

'But you did come to live here?'

'No. A friend is visiting his nephew here.'

'His nephew lives here?'

'Yes.'

'He has something wrong with him,' he said with gloomy conviction.

'Yes.'

'I know; they all have something wrong, here. They are all out of their minds.'

He asked questions trying to place us – London, Paris, Brussels, the stock exchange, the commodity markets. He satisfied himself and then said eagerly, 'Then you would know the name of Lowenstein, the Dutch millionaire who made the markets in –'

'Yes. There was an accident; he jumped from a plane in mid-Channel and his body was found near Cape Grisnez.'

The man brightened, 'Yes, he left everything to his mother and to Baron Smith. I am Baron Smith.' He watched and then went on, 'He left me 17,000,000 guilders and that is why I am here. If I could get away I could get my hands on 17,000,000 guilders. If you help me –' His air was half serious, half hazing, and he began a sort of act; but was seized by some excess and poured out fantasies, exaggerations, romances; and all these were normal abnormalities as if he had read the books about madness; and I think he had. It was as if he were telling us, 'I have such and such a disorder and you must recognise it.' He looked keenly at us after each of his statements about Baron Smith; and at one moment,

'My wife is keeping me here. She put me in Gheel as soon as I got queer. She has all my money. She could have kept me with her.'

This was said in a heart-rending voice.

He caught himself up, changed tone, 'You see those soldiers going through? There is going to be war. I could get away then.'

(At that time all the businessmen in Belgium and Holland had rough plans for hasty escape in case of invasion).

He talked straight politics for a few minutes, what should be done about shifting funds; and then said with his previous stagey air, 'As it is, the Germans have already poisoned all the wells, their spies have done it. Even everything we eat. It is a new method of war preparation. We are all poisoned already.' He continued, 'Do you mind if I walk with you?' He seemed relieved and quite gay now that he had shown himself.

'I am rotten here,' he said, touching his forehead.

'You must not say that.'

'Yes, yes, I assure you,' he said earnestly.

'You will get better and go back to your wife.'

He was silent. Then, 'You have really come to live here. You are poisoned, too.'

'No, no.'

'You don't notice anything wrong with me, do you?'

'No.'

'Brussels is a beautiful city,' he said with longing. 'My wife said I was mad; to get my money.' He looked cunning, 'But there *is* something wrong, you must see it.' Tears came into his eyes. 'She told me I was sick, sick in my mind. It is miserable here. Look around you – a peasant village, it is terrible to live here and I can't get away.'

'Would you like a drink, friend?'

'No, no.'

We insisted and went to a café with an open terrasse, vines twining round trellises. He was pleased, but stood timidly while we sat down, and had to be invited again. This shyness went oddly with his face and clothing.

'I only take water.' He removed his hat and showed us a pustule the size of a pea, on his forehead, and when he saw this was understood, he began more stories. First, that before his marriage he had led a merry life; and then, that the trouble came from his grandfather, a gay dog, a cavalry officer, a devil of a man, who did not give a snap of the fingers for his children.

When we thought it time to go for Jack, he got up hurriedly, offering to leave us and swept a glass off the table with his sleeve. The pretty waitress came forward, smiling at him and picked up the pieces; 'It is nothing, it doesn't matter.'

'I can't help it,' he said helplessly, looking about with wet eyes. 'I suppose you are going now,' he said forlornly.

'Yes, we must.'

'Perhaps I've bored you with my talk?'

'Oh, no.'

'I liked to talk to you about Brussels and London and the markets. I don't meet many people who know anything about it. These are peasants; they work in the fields and have cabins. I am a rich man; I had houses, servants. My wife doesn't want me. If only I could get to Brussels to see her –'

He began the whole story again, packing it hurriedly into the last few moments; then, on the instant, recovered himself and began to walk with us to the high street leading out of Gheel and to the gloomy high building.

'Is he there?' he said nodding at the building.

'Yes.'

'Is he a young man?'

'Yes.'

'He must be bad if he is there. He won't get out.'

Then he said, 'They'll put me there some day, but I am all right so far.'

'Don't you think you will get better?'

'No, I won't,' he said sadly, with understanding. 'No, I'll never get better. My wife was right. She was a nice woman. But the minute I get bad, she sends me away, she puts me here. Can you imagine a wife doing that?'

He went with us a few steps more along the road to wipe out any bad impression and stood waving his hat, smiling friendly in the late sun. Then he turned back, hunched his shoulders and tramped towards the railed green.

When we left in the taxi Jack was dispirited. Claud would never be cured. We said, 'Take him away; this place will make him madder.'

Out of his corner came his low unhappy voice, 'I have paid the board for three months, so he has to stay until Christmas. They want me to take him away. He is dangerous. He is in a strait-jacket now.'

'Jack, this is only a mediaeval way of doing it, farming out the poor sick mad; it's not for him.'

'Well,' he sat up; 'I've paid his board until Christmas so he must stay until then.'

And now for the first time, another private matter emerged. Rose, his sister, was in Gheel and had refused to return with Jack; she wanted to spend a few more days and nights seeing her boy. If she could talk to him, she could calm him. She joined the doctors in begging Jack to take the boy away. She never ceased urging Jack to buy them a farm in the country where she could live with her son. She did not believe the doctors. 'People are not kind to him; he's a brilliant mind; he needs understanding.'

On the way back to Brussels, Jack began to think of other things, he leaned forward to urge the taxi on. He had to get home, get his overnight bag, get to Berlin. He had to attend the funeral of Arthur, Maria's brother.

He had to get things straight about Arthur's will.

Maria had taken Mitzi her maid with her and also Arthur's will; but her mother was already in Berlin spending hours with a lawyer, for she had another will; and then Elena, Arthur's 'woman', had a letter in which he left her 100,000 Swiss francs and he had also given her a house. Maria, 'Mimi', was outraged. What men do! Even a brother, a beloved brother. And there was her mother too, trying for an unfair share.

Jack cheered up. His wife was an heiress and her father, now eighty-nine, was dying. He already managed his wife's affairs and Mimi's affairs; he would have a look at Elena. Poor woman, a sort of widow – and there would be men around her, sniffing; she needed help.

'Will you be home the day after the funeral Jack?'

'Don't know,' he said in the low husky murmur he used for private matters. 'Got to bring Mimi home, stroke her mother down, see this woman' (his voice sank out of hearing). 'Wouldn't be nice to leave Mimi, she's very sensitive, very cut up. Then got to see what cards the mother holds.' He laughed with a gay boyish look.

We all laughed, the first laugh of the day. We went to the station, kissed goodbye. Off he went.

We went back and had dinner with Bosch, Jack's Antwerp manager. Bosch was no Boche, but a Walloon (French/Belgian), who planned to become Minister for Food when the revolution came.

When the revolution came (for a brief period), so he was.

Lost American

One time when Benjamin F. Cullen, Pete's friend, went over to the American Express to get the letters with his quarterly allowance from his Philadelphia family, he invited Pete and me to meet him in the *Café de Rohan*, in the Place du Louvre, after work – our work, he did none. Pete was delighted, 'I've always wanted you to meet Ben.' I had heard of him.

Beside one of the plate glass windows on the terrasse of the *Café Deux Magots* looking out into the colonnade, a man stooped over a table dipping his pale moustaches in a Pernod. He rose, shook hands in a distant manner and when he had ordered our drinks, retired into himself. Pete gossiped with his usual gaiety, but Mr Cullen seemed disgusted about something, and from his demeanour it was easy to imagine that that something was me.

'You ran a printing press in Heidelberg, Mr Cullen?' I asked, recollecting this out of all the rumours and anecdotes. He dipped his moustaches in his Pernod. I saw by his face he was deaf and there was a scar, so I said louder,

'I should like to see some of the books you printed privately in Heidelberg, Mr Cullen.'

Cullen mumbled and gave me a cross look. I saw an oval, self-indulgent face, a soft bad skin, yellowish teeth blackening at the roots, under a walrus brush. In his almost inaudible voice, he began to ask Pete about the stock exchange. Cullen lived on dividends. I said no more. About a quarter of an hour later, when Cullen was on his second Pernod, a voice floating in the air said, 'You must call me Ben.'

I looked round but Cullen was absorbed in his drink and Pete seemed to have heard nothing. An illusion. Later, I said to Pete, 'I don't think Ben likes me.'

'Why,' exclaimed Pete, 'he thinks you a very fine person; he told me so.'

We shifted our quarters to the Left Bank soon after and began to see Ben every day after work, where he sat, as he had sat for the last twelve years, on the terrasse of the *Deux Magots*. There he had his breakfast of coffee, pastry and absinthe. Sometimes we saw him there before work and sometimes we saw him there after work, when he was having his afternoon allowance of three absinthes. He despised all other Paris cafés, would never go to Montparnasse, not far away, or to the Latin Quarter, another short walk. He never went along the Boulevard St Germain farther than the Cluny Museum and saw the Right Bank once in three months, to get his cheques. He lived for a couple of years in each of several mediaeval lanes within a few hundred yards of the *Deux Magots* (called matily the Duke's Maggots). He discovered and ate in various working class restaurants within a few minutes' walk. He would nose out the place, help to make it famous; and when the proprietor began improving it, putting in paintings, new tablecloths, attracting the American tourist, Ben moved out and sought another chef of unpublished genius.

We had our apéritif one afternoon, at the *Deux Magots,* although this was not yet our habit. 'How do you do, Mr Cullen,' I said shyly to the stooped head.

'Sit down.' He said, 'Call me Ben.'

He was drunk, but eye, hand, voice were steady; he was simply a shade more lively than the time before.

'Do you know the tale of Petronius, the young girl and the Term?' he asked. It was by accident that I heard his faded voice; a breeze had scurried round the corner in our direction.

'No, Mr Cullen.'

'Ben.'

He told it, giggling slyly and only for himself, into his drink; and then suddenly lifted his head, looked kindly at me.

'Do you know Corsica?'

'No, Ben.'

'Ille terrarum mihi praeter omnis
Angulus ridet.'

'I don't understand Latin, you know.'

He translated, 'That is best of all places on earth to me. Horace. There is a tale about Lucullus. He kept giant eels in a fish pond at Naples and fed them on slaves to make them fat and delicious. You should read –' Cullen kept on and on, stringing tale to tale, while I bent to hear. Lucullus was mixed with Virgil, Horace and the couplet, contests of the Esquimos, which got mixed with the story of an illegitimate son he had in Finland, with Samoyed eyes, and with a certain strange cloud in the sky in Texas which had preceded a fierce funnelling wind he had lived through, while it ripped the paint from his car: and a young Italian beauty with whom he had swum naked in the Blue Grotto at Capri.

There were others on the terrasse saying the things Americans say in Paris, talking about the stock exchange, the daily *Herald-Tribune* crossword puzzle, places to eat; I sat isolated in a cavern in Ben's peculiar planet listening to Prospero's whisper; aching because I had not yet got used to his threadbare voice. Even when I did, in the end, I often did not catch more than the drift. He always signed his receipts Benjamin Fitzgerald Cullen and people frequently called him that. He thought well of himself, carried his six-foot odd with dignity, standing up straight; he was well-shaped and not clean, he looked the decayed aristocrat. He was nearly forty, years older than we were. He let everyone call him Ben from their first meeting, except rarely when he was sober and in one of his pets; he called all women at once by their first names when he felt friendly and by their surnames when absent and he wanted to backbite them; but this did not include scandalous gossip about their sex behaviour, for he saw nothing scandalous in that respect. If they were mean or narrow, that was different. Women by him reputed to love him, wrote to him from Helsingfors, Heidelberg, Berlin, Milan. The very first moment, Ben, with the avid experienced instinct of the raconteur, had seen in me that precious thing, a good listener; and he gave me a very warm welcome whenever I turned up at the *Deux Magots,* warned me against drinking anything so strong as Pernod, told me his stories if he were in company, and if alone, spent a cheerful hour, backbiting all his absent friends. He avoided only the pompous, was delighted with people who showed pettiness, vanity, sham. After about four Pernods at one sitting, when his eyes were fishy, he would gently begin to tweak those present about their character deficiencies. Very far on in the night he would become mildly quarrelsome, but always in that unedged voice.

After several months Ben said, 'I want you to meet Jeanne,' and that evening we had dinner with the couple in the *Restaurant Pré-aux-Clercs*.

'Is Ben married?'

'He doesn't know.'

'He doesn't know?'

'He was married once, in Charleston. It's quite a story, ask him sometime.'

But I never asked Ben anything. Jeanne told me about herself. She was a farm girl of good physique and complexion, plain, about ten years younger than Ben; she had sense and between Ben and herself was the under-standing of a long-married couple. Ben would never say anything about Jeanne but 'Jeanne's a good girl.' She had come to Paris to get a job typing and got one. When she despaired of getting a husband, a friend took her to a marriage broker who arranged marriages, 'under-standings' of all sorts between men and women. Jeanne's friend Anne-Marie was very pretty, very young and when she came to Paris, the marriage broker had introduced her to a middle-aged count, who had kept her for three years and then 'done the right thing' – given her a dowry and married her to a young businessman, who, of course, knew all the circumstances. Jeanne had confidence in this broker. She had answered a few advertisements in maga-zines and met a few young men, but had been dissatisfied with their appearance; she was afraid to go to an unknown agency, because a bad person would try to send her into prostitution or would take her money and do nothing, or demand too large a percentage or fee. Anne-

Marie's broker in fact introduced Jeanne to a young worker who wanted to settle down and have children; but Jeanne hesitated; and at this moment, the spirit of adventure which had prompted her before caused her to answer Benjamin Fitzgerald Cullen's advertisement in the Paris *Herald-Tribune* –

'American man resident in Paris would exchange lessons with French girl. Benjamin Fitzgerald Cullen'
and a box number. The name interested her and gave her confidence. That was five years ago. Jeanne's brother and his family, respectable working class people, had moved to the Buttes Chaumont and now wanted Ben to 'regu-late the situation' and marry Jeanne. They had written to America, discovered that Ben was respectable, of good family and had an interest in the family estate. He had treated Jeanne kindly and she was thirty. It was time to have a family.

Soon after I heard this, Ben showed me a photograph of a dark plump girl, standing by a desk in a tall room with French windows.

'That's my wife Madeleine. I married her when she was sixteen. She's eighteen in that picture. The funny thing is the day after I took that photograph, she ran away with another fellow. You see that desk? She left a note on that desk telling me she couldn't stand me any more.' He said this with interested calm.

'You didn't go after her?'

'Why?'

'And then you came to France?'

'Heidelberg. I studied chemistry.' (Ben was very good for kitchen hints).

Ben put the photograph in his breast pocket. 'I gave her the house and came away to Heidelberg, then to Bordeaux, where I went into the wine business; I gave that up. I thought I might publish in Paris, but when I got here, I didn't go into it. I published a few rare books and erotica in Heidelberg.'

'Did you divorce her, Ben?'

'I wouldn't divorce a woman,' said Ben with a touch of hauteur.

'Did she divorce you?'

He laughed his rather foolish laugh, 'I don't know. Now, they say so.' His mother, a handsome matriarch of family and property, wrote to him regularly. He would give the letters to Pete or another, saying, 'See if there's money in them; don't tell me any of the news; they only call me names.'

Few Americans can or will give any coherent idea of their country to others when abroad. Ben Cullen was not like that. He tirelessly described the states and towns he knew – Baltimore, Philadelphia, Charleston, Boston, Washington, Long Island, Connecticut, Texas and Arizona, with the humour of a Twain, the observation of a Marco Polo; and bright little stories of his own boyhood. He was not a fairy, he hastened to say, but when he was at Harvard, the boy who shared his room was. He grinned foolishly and remarked, 'We got on very well, so why not?'

Finally, a friend arrived from Philadelphia who told Ben that he had seen his ex-wife with her husband. They were living in fine style in Ben's ex-house and were socially popular, while Ben's own name was under a cloud.

'Did she divorce me then?'

'Eight years ago, didn't you know?'

'When you go back get me some proof will you? If it's so, I'll marry Jeanne; she's a good girl.'

Just before the marriage, we visited Jeanne's family, the

Barrats, in the *rue des Buttes*. It was an old and poor apartment house. The Barrats owned it. The apartment was wretched, with long windows looking out on a grey street, but it was high up, over Paris. All the famous monuments of the Paris streets were visible from there. While they were getting dinner ready, a pretty, gentle young girl came to the door and got a bowl of soup from Jeanne's mother. They explained that it was Rosalie, the little girl who rented a room from them in the attic. She was a prostitute and she had caught a cold walking in the streets. 'That's no life,' said the old slipshod mother, a widow now, who lived with them. She shook her head like a grandmother, 'You've got to be sorry for her.'

In one room Ben had piled his books on 'the curiosities of love'; publications of his earlier days. While they were still getting dinner ready, he stacked them on the old stained wash-stand, burrowed in, found 'The Perfumed Garden', recited from it, both in the original and in French and again translated some sections into English.

At dinner were Jeanne's married sister and the brother-in-law, who had brought a pheasant for dinner; it was closed season but they had run over it accidentally in their car. Their children were there and Jeanne's other brother, a gay widower, a tight little black fox of a lawyer's clerk, who had acquired this house and the one next door, when they had fallen in on a bankrupt estate. He clipped his seven-year-old son on the ear, joked a lot, played up to Benjamin Cullen, showed off to the foreign visitors. It was a grand celebration in the *rue des Buttes*. Soon Jeanne was to be Madame Cullen, a country girl who had married a rich and well born foreigner, and all without any kind of looks or dowry; and they said the name properly, Cu-lenn.

The dinner was good, but the pheasant was too fresh;

after, they had preserved cherries, coffee and liqueurs. Throughout dinner and the conversation after, it was amusing, pathetic, to see Benjamin Cullen playing head of the family, dignified, not talkative, polite, with a ready and crushing opinion on politics, which they did not contradict. It was easy to see that they all thought him effete, yet respected him for what he meant to them. Jeanne was genuinely happy; and it looked as though he was beginning to have affection for Jeanne, as well as respect.

Jeanne became Madame Cullen shortly after and Ben was seen no more at the Duke's Maggots. It was not decent for a man to sit all day in a café while his wife worked in a radio factory for nine hundred francs a month. Jeanne studied English hard to get a better job. Ben began to nose round the American offices in Paris and for the first time in Europe mentioned his family name, his connections. During the whole of this time, he was cranky, opinionated and altogether bad company; he began to have moral judgments on other people, and he told no more Marco Polo stories. Everyone complained about the change in Ben, but no one blamed Jeanne; 'Jeanne's a good girl.'

Finally, Ben sold some of his small property in the States and bought the Barrat family a small stone cottage, a *pavillon* with a tiny bit of ground, in the suburbs.

We did not see him for years after that. He had become ambitious, touchy; he wanted to become a political reporter. About seven years later, though, we did run into him, taking a Pernod with Jeanne at the *Deux Magots*. They had come into town to buy some stuff for the house and looked happily married, Jeanne buxom, frank as ever. They had a son Benjamin; the whole family still lived with them and all wanted to see us, they said. So we arranged a day and after an hour or so in an ambling suburban train, we came to the station and, after walking half a mile, came to a country street, bordered with mud and daisies and to the house, a white-faced peeling cottage with four square windows, a door in the centre. It was now nearly mid winter. The house was ice-cold and heated only by one stove in the hall downstairs. There were four bedrooms, all in stale disorder, a bare dining room with pictures cut from newspapers and magazines, a heavy sideboard. They opened the sideboard and took out a number of apéritifs which they offered; and showed us round the house, the grounds. In the garden were rabbit hutches, hares, newly hatched chickens, kittens, roosters, hens. The kittens kept on climbing up the fruit trees and miauling. The mother cat prowled round the chicken coop. Benjamin, a little boy, and his grandmother, more dishevelled than ever, took turns at the spit on which was a fat rooster, in the outdoor fireplace.

'That's Benjamin's rooster,' said Benjamin Cullen in French; 'we killed it for our party.'

The dark eyed pretty little boy looked proud and smiled.

'His name was Cock-eye,' volunteered little Benjamin. He had no timidity; he was pert.

'He's good and fat,' said the grandmother; 'Benjamin fed him every day himself.'

Little Benjamin smiled with cunning.

Cullen took us down into the cellar, where he had several barrels of small wine bought specially from little vineyards in the south, vineyards he had known in the old days. We tasted the wines, saw the ones he had selected for lunch and dinner.

Lunch went well. Everyone kept shouting 'Marie' at the top of his voice, to bring out the sixteen-year-old husky maid, who ran willingly but was never fast enough and who answered them frankly, without any feeling of servanthood. She was only half respectful to Ben, who sat in a grand manner, at the head of the table and commanded his small army. Next to him sat little Ben. Big Ben talked to him tenderly, commanded him with an old-maidish squeak in which impotence and affection showed. The little boy, cavorted, whined, Jeanne and the grandmother smiled.

Presently, the *pièce de resistance,* the fat cock, was brought from the spit, smoking. Ben carved it and as a special favour, and by general vote, the baked head with its baked crest and eye, was put on little Ben's plate: 'There's Cock-eye,' said the grandmother.

The little boy looked at the plate, looked round the table, in a confused unhappy way.

'It's Cock-eye,' said big Ben, mildly.

Everyone began eating the bird, which was fairly good, although too well done and tough; everyone said how good it was. Suddenly little Ben gave a howl and pushed back his plate.

'Eat, my son,' said Jeanne.

'No,' howled Ben turning away his head.

'It's Cock-eye, darling,' said the grandmother.

'I won't eat Cock-eye,' said the boy and began to weep, aside. With a curious expression, half embarrassment and half amusement big Ben pushed the plate towards his son, 'Eat, son, it's Cock-eye, you know Cock-eye. He was your rooster, you used to feed him every day.'

With rising flush, and eyes glittering with excitement and fun the rest of the boy's family urged him,

'Don't you like the head, darling? It's only Cock-eye's head, he's dead, he's cooked. Why you know old Cock-eye, you're not afraid of him. It's the baked eye. It's the eye he doesn't like. It's the comb and the eye: cut them off. Don't you like the head, son? Take it away from him. Come on then, son, eat it up; you said you wanted us to cook him. Shall I cut off the comb and the eye, Ben?'

The little boy howled and ran from the table into the house. The servant ran out, 'What's the matter? Doesn't he want to eat Cock-eye? Well, what do you make of that?'

'He's sensitive,' said the uncle, Jeanne's foxy brother. Ben looked fierce, shouted, 'Ben, come here this minute.'

'Let him go,' said Jeanne, 'he's nervous, you won't force him to eat now.'

The dinner went on, everyone was pleased, amused. They went on shouting for Marie and began joking, saying they must sooner or later buy a bell. The brother began telling off-colour stories and flattering Benjamin. Jeanne's grandmother pulled out of the worm-eaten sideboard a special liqueur that she had made up.

'Don't you ever think of going back to see the USA?' Pete asked.

'What for?' asked Ben nettled; 'Jeanne's faithful, French women are faithful. A husband is everything.'

We left Paris for London, London for New York, and in a few years war broke out. The war was nearly over when we got a letter from Benjamin, from Switzerland. He said that he had married a Swiss nurse and was coming to the States in a Red Cross boat and wanted to put up with us. We had a room. We waited. He wrote a letter from his home town, Philadelphia, laughing about the American girls, 'They don't even say hello, just Hi! They don't seem to know they're just here for sex, what else are they here for –'

He came to the house with his bag and knapsack, grinning and raffish, his teeth longer and looser, his mustachios dripping deeper into the wine glass.

Jeanne? The silly girl had refused to work for Vichy – she was wandering about somewhere. His son? In the country, he thought, with the grandmother. Then Jeanne was divorced? 'I never divorce women.' The Germans? 'They're all right, you can get along with them. As long,' he tittered, 'as they gave me my Pernod. I wrote political articles and they got me my Pernod.' Pete made enquiries, for Benjamin had never been strong in politics. Benjamin tittered, 'A little Jew, a Jewish doctor, in hiding – I found him, he wrote them for me, I gave him something.' Shining with conceit and satire, mocking American opinion, he stretched his long handsome legs, gulped down his wine, drank more.

In the mornings he was up before anyone else. When we came out to have coffee, he was already sitting in the chair that had become his chair, overlooking Sixteenth Street, in a dressing-gown, and slippers, stretched at ease, with a flagon of wine beside him. He did not take any other breakfast. The first morning, he just said, 'I'll finish this wine.' Then he grinned in his old silly way, 'They told me in Paris if I keep on this way I'll die in two years. They told me in Switzerland too. The nurse took me there.'

'Where is the nurse now?'

The same vain grin, 'She's there. She got me the place on the Red Cross ship.'

'What's wrong with you?'

'Cirrhosis,' he said, self-satisfied.

He went to the movies, in an old place off Fourteenth Street, now closed. They were showing Charlie Chaplin's 'The Great Dictator', with his comical take-off of Hitler. Benjamin whispered, 'Do they allow that? Do they allow that here?'

'Of course. Why not? Do you think they like Hitler here?'

'But I didn't know such liberties were taken. Won't they close the theatre?'

'Didn't you ever hear, in Paris, that other countries don't like Hitler?'

'Some news came to us through Finland; but I didn't know it was like this. I didn't know the USA was like this.'

'You thought the USA loved Hitler?'

'They think so,' he said plaintively: 'they think the USA meant to go in on their side; it was the mistaken alliance with England.'

It took him a few hours to get back his happiness.

Then he said a friend of his was coming to see him. He had his old cynical grin when he said it. When the friend came, a young dark easy-speaking man with a slight accent, it was lunch time; I was alone, and I had laid the table for Ben and me. The young man had a lot to say in an eager, confident way about meeting people upon business. I did not offer him a drink, though Ben was drinking, and I did not ask him to lunch; 'Your lunch is ready, Ben,' I said. 'And Herman will stay to lunch,' said Ben. I brought in the two plates.

'Aren't you eating?' said Ben.

'I'll have mine in the kitchen.'

Ben had a curious expression, mixed emotions.

When his friend left, Ben said, 'He will come back tomorrow. We have business to discuss.'

I said, 'You must go Ben. You cannot stay here. You must go tomorrow and meet your friend elsewhere.'

I packed his bag for him and in it I put the set of silver teaspoons he had given me when he arrived. I told him so. He said nothing and again the strange expression, a sort of gleam, an acknowledgement.

'Goodbye, Ben.'

'Goodbye. Thank you for your hospitality.'

'Yes.'

The moral which we drew was that sensualists should never mix in politics, though it was for absinthe that he did it.

4 ===================================== *New York*

Life is Difficult

Emma was a small child, born when her mother was forty-seven. Next to her was Frederic, a young man at the university, intending to be a doctor like their father; and there were seven other children, the eldest over thirty, married and with children older than Emma. Several of the boys had gone to the USA, so that Emma and her young sister Anna were left with the old couple and surrounded by a close-knit set of relations, complacent stay-at-homes. Their home was in Riga and they were lively as all seaport people and critical of the world which came to their doorstep. They were a German family; but they also spoke some Russian, and the children learned French and English. They were Jewish, liberal, free-thinking and did not speak Hebrew or Yiddish. Anna grew tall, handsome with rich pale hair; she was lively and romantic; she grew taller than Emma. Emma remained squat; she was sharp and ready. She had dark hair, large brown eyes in Tartar eyeholes and a thick white skin which could fold and unfold in excitement.

Emma's manner was old for her years. It was hard on her to hear always about Anna's looks. The Kobols were one of those satisfied intellectual families where everyone goes into ecstasies over talent and looks; talent in men and beauty in women. 'Such a beauty, *eine solche Schönheit, a kracavitzé*,* such shoulders, you can kiss your fingers, an angel,' they would gabble in their polyglot at the coffee-table; and they early began reckoning up the eligible young men, budding lawyers or doctors, who were there for Anna.

At twenty-two Anna married secretly. Her husband was a poor schoolteacher. The Kobols were a family of doctors, lawyers, professors. They were humiliated. Anna went away with her husband; and just where she went, became a secret. She had gone to France. The Kobols were one of those German families who say, 'The French – pooh! the French – La Grande Nation, pooh – they do not keep their houses clean and make all sorts of sauces to hide poor food.'

Emma now lived all alone with the old parents. She was studying medicine and was laughed at for it. There were few women doctors then. Old-maidish and disap-pointed, she heard them say; and would wipe her large beautiful eyes in the hall and at the stairhead. She hid her feelings and sat in the midst of her relatives, aunts, brothers and sisters, a small full-bodied wiry woman, who had learned to be witty in a family that relished gossip – sprightly, full of scoff and innuendo and all the time fighting for a foothold. Her late birth, her plainness and smallness turned her into a sort of orphan. People were always making meaningful remarks about late-born children. That was the reason for Anna's flightiness,

* Polish for 'beauty'.

'such a beauty marrying a school-porter' – for by that time the legend had got down to that; and then jokes about his pale face, holes in the seat of his trousers; there was Emma too, not the marrying sort, stuck in her books.

She surprised them by sailing for New York to her brothers there, quite taking away the breath with which they would have accused her of selfishness and of leaving two old people alone in a house of three storeys. They were perturbed; she had been a handy servant and nurse.

At home in Riga now, they pictured her as character-less, lightheaded as Anna without the excuse, running off because she had not found a man, ready to take anyone, even a cowboy. Yes, how they laughed at that. They said she had a mole on her upper lip, which was rather too long, she had a putty nose, was fond of her food and that she licked the ladle in the kitchen when she made their soup. They said she had gone off for her own pleasure, leaving two old people to die on their hands. The old people died on their hands two years later and were regretted by none. The eldest of all, however, Richard a lawyer, felt himself head of the family and wrote her a letter.

They were surprised to learn that Emma had married a young lecturer named Foix, a French-Canadian, introduced to her by her brothers, a man a year younger than herself.

The family was disconcerted only for a moment; 'she didn't lose much time lassooing a weak-kneed French-man; she probably learnt it on the plains.' He was talented, ambitious, a university lecturer in medicine. The photograph showed her in the modest wedding-dress provided by her brothers, her hair puffed out in a crown; and beside her a short powerful man with stormy black hair and wide open blue eyes staring truculently at the camera. 'She'll have trouble with him,' they said. When they heard that Augustus Foix was a year younger, they were delighted. 'Well, no good comes of cradle-snatching; she had better have some children quick.'

They were poor. Emma went to work teaching the piano and languages and tried to study for her medical degree. But they soon had a child, a sickly withered girl who could not live long. Emma, so strict, so clean and housewifely, neglected everything for the poor baby. It had large eyes, a worn little face, just as she did. 'Oh, how pretty she is and so intelligent,' she told her husband. She also soon had a vivacious dark-eyed little boy, healthy and loving, fond of adult society and argument; and she loved him too, but not in the same way.

Her husband abandoned her and having little money, sent little and later nothing at all. Emma moved to a slum street not far from the middle-class block on the East Side, near Coontjes Slip, where her brothers and her cousin Belle, also from Riga, had houses. One brother was a doctor, one a lawyer; and they had introduced Belle to a lawyer, middle-aged, successful, infirm, who married her without love, for company. He promised her the house, a grand piano, furnishings and money. Luckily, in Emma's district, there were plenty of parents, Italian, Jewish, Spanish, anxious for their girls to learn the piano and French. At visiting hours, Emma went to see her daughter Eva, in the Home for Incurables. Eva died there. When she returned from the funeral, Emma had not a cent, but one of her relatives said, 'It will be easier for you now, Emma with only one child.' Having not a cent, she gave lessons the same afternoon. She could not say anything about the child's funeral to her pupils, because one must not wound young hearts; and there were the parents.

When she was out giving lessons and her son Freddie returned from school, he went to his uncles' houses for bread and jam. 'Emma's child', they called him with a certain disesteem for both, something a child knows at once. There were no children's books in those houses; so he read books of medicine, encyclopedias, dictionaries and lawbooks. He was of a very gay nature and natural goodness; he flourished and everyone said he would become a doctor or a lawyer and look after his mother.

However, there was no money and Freddie went to work at fourteen; and after a while became a journalist. Every man in Emma's family had had a university degree. She knew no other way for a boy to succeed in life; and now she became very restless, worrying at night about their future. She was forty, her hair was almost white and she began to say she was old. 'I am old and bitter and I will die soon.' Perhaps she thought it would make Freddie serious.

Journalists made money, became famous in New York, met fine people; but Freddie did not. After work he spent his time in back rooms, libraries and in political meetings. The only people he liked and knew were socialists. One of them, a French-Canadian named McEwen, with the Scots passion for protecting orphans, took a great liking to Freddie as well as to three other gifted lads from the slums and began to help them in their careers. But as he himself had graduated from the university of hard knocks, he wanted them to succeed in the same alma mater. He found positions for them in business and made Freddie his secretary and manager of a farm he had in upstate New York.

Emma's divorce had been paid for by her brothers. Hers was the first divorce in the family and considered disgraceful, a failure you might expect of Emma. She told

everyone she was a widow. She told McEwen she was a
widow, Freddie an orphan with none to help; and she
hoped that McEwen, who had made a lot of money in
engineering, would make Freddie his heir. Freddie, a
truthful man, was obliged to back her up.

Emma coughed at night thinking about her troubles
and running through episodes in the life of her dead
daughter, as other people go over their love-affairs when
they are lonely; but she could not speak about Eva to
people, she could not say Eva had died of an incurable
disease, neglected and in the most miserable poverty. She
sometimes said that she had had a daughter, 'much
brighter than the boy and a beauty, such a beauty, a *solche
Schönheit,* what a pity, a daughter loves her mother better
than a boy; I would have had a friend, a boy runs out of
the house all the time, day and night.'

Fate sent her a friend, her niece Elena, her sister Jenny's
youngest, a beautiful simpleton, who, laughing, told her
aunt that she had led a dissipated life with officers in the
garrison, since the age of eleven. Now they had sent her
to America to start a new life and get married. Emma
counselled her, 'We will say nothing about your mother
and father – it does not look nice to leave parents; people
wonder why. We will say you are an orphan and we will
not say your real age; you look very young, we will take
off five years; we will say you expect some money when
your uncles die in Riga. We must say nothing about the
officers in the garrison. And you must not say too much
about Riga – people don't like foreigners here, though
God knows they are all foreigners; but of course, the
nicest people are not. You must get a job; I cannot keep
you. Freddie works, but the boy's foolish and spends his
money on books. The way he goes on, he meets only
trash with no money. I don't want him to marry for

money – eckh! – but rich girls are nice too.'

Elena immediately got a job in a laundry and all the young men and some of the married men between home and the laundry gazed at the gentle longcheeked smiling Venus. A tailor's son in a little shop in the same street, said to her, 'Marry me: I am dying of tuberculosis, I have not long to live, let me have some happiness, I adore you.' His parents came to the house and begged Emma to agree; he was their only child. Elena could refuse no one. She married him and lived with him in one of his parents' rooms, where there was only a double bed, a table and two chairs. Soon the young tailor could work no more but stayed at home all day coughing. Elena went on working in the laundry. In eleven months she was a widow, just as the young man had promised; and she went back to living with her aunt Emma, though the tailor's family begged her to stay with them. 'You will remind us of him.' She cried sometimes, and she might even cry in the street; but pleasant things happened in the street and she soon felt sunny again. When she got off the bus, the new young bus-conductor said, 'Do you get this bus every day?'

'Yes,' she said softly with a shy uplifted smile.

'I'll be looking for you tomorrow.'

She could refuse no one and began a life of quiet dissipation which she concealed in no way from her aunt. 'I saw a feller on the bus and he asked me to walk out with him,' she would say in her modest way, and with a slight smile.

Her aunt hid the scandal and explained it all away to the neighbours. She scolded Elena, but she said to her in a soft voice, 'You must look about you, not pick up garbage collectors. You must get married and settle down. Such a beauty – and to go out with a waiter in a German restaurant! It's unheard of! You must be happy, my darling. I am old and bitter; I will die soon.' Elena laughed at these scoldings long and sweetly. She laughed at everything; and she was very kind to her aunt.

Meanwhile, Freddie was never to be seen. If not in the country at weekends with Mr McEwen for whom he did some work still, he was going to classes, meetings in halls and in the houses of friends. Though he had no degree, he conducted a course in economics. 'Pfui! Nothing but nonsense from you,' said his mother, 'how can you teach when you have no degree? I don't believe it.'

Freddie showed her a printed course which he had written for a friend of his, a university professor. 'Students who learn this course, get their degrees,' he said laughing.

'Then you must take it and get your degree,' she persisted harshly. He laughed and was gone. 'Always laughing! Never serious. What is he doing, what is he doing? It's all wasted.'

Freddie and Mr McEwen were socialists. Emma herself was a socialist; but she knew that people do not care for socialists; you do not get on. He came in late and she brought in his breakfast with a black face. 'Two o'clock in the morning, who knows what you were up to?'

'We had a session after the meeting in the baker's shop at the back.'

'At the baker's! Stuff and nonsense.'

'Goldenweiser was there.'

Her face quickened, 'Tell me is he from the Ukraine – they say so. Very brilliant they say. Tell me, Freddie.'

'Yes.'

'No, no, tell me Freddie, is he from the Ukraine?'

'Yes.'

'Freddie! Answer!'

'For the third time, yes, Mamma.'

'For the third time – who hears, who knows what he says and if it's so? Let me tell you something – I am old, my dear. You can be what you are but don't let it interfere with your life. Now if Goldenweiser knows you –' Freddie laughed and was gone.

Freddie and Mr McEwen were pacifists. When the war came, Mr McEwen arranged for Freddie to get to Mexico to avoid the draft. Emma was very glad; but Emma had to explain to every woman in the house that her son had not been called yet and that Mr McEwen had got him work in another State. They were surprised that Freddie did not send her money. To make it look natural, she cloaked her rancour, 'Oh, we must not ask too much; youth must have its day; young is young and old is old.'

But when they said he was thoughtless and unnatural, she agreed and sighed, 'A daughter is different. Daughters love their mothers.' When the police came looking for Freddie Foix, she said it was a mistake, she knew no such person. After that, she changed her address, taking Elena with her.

It was not the first time the police had called. Elena had at one time taken up with a petty thief, who had entered their rooms, coming over the roofs after midnight and hiding there for three days. Mrs Foix had had to explain to neighbours that he was her nephew who was not well. Freddie got tired of exile, returned, went to a quiet gaol and afterwards began to live with a girl who had been one of Emma's piano pupils, a very pretty diffident girl who always seemed dejected, and who was unhappy at home. Her parents and family, named Grandison, a lively lot, ran a delicatessen which did not flourish, partly because they ate their own goods. But the war was finished; it was boom time; they went in for building an apartment house on credit. They were ambitious immigrants from Russia; the father was a mason. Emma now had to explain that her son was living away from home and that he was engaged to a rich and beautiful girl. Freddie and the girl were married, first at City Hall and then at a synagogue wedding. Emma did not want to say her relatives were Jews and she did not want to say she was a free-thinker; so she did not give her neighbours any details and this caused unpleasantness. Once or twice she burst out with, 'Oh, it was such a grand wedding –' and subsided into a mumble and then no more. Yet Emma was very happy; it looked as if her luck had changed. The wedding, the feast, everything had been marvellous; her new relatives were big spenders; they did not mind big debts in the least; it was part of their large natures. Yet Freddie and his wife Dorothy continued to live in the same small room and both went to work.

Meanwhile Freddie, who had simply been a socialist, had become enthusiastic about the Russian revolution and so had his wife Dorothy. Her parents were overjoyed at the October Overturn. 'Is it true? Is it true? Ivan the Thief is gone?' ('Ivan the Thief' was the old regime.)

Emma herself was glad Ivan the Thief had gone; she was like the thousands who on the morning of the first news had rushed out into the streets in a tumult of disbelief and happiness.

'Your time is past: you should have children now. The revolution is for them, if they want it,' she said to the young couple.

Emma from her slum, where she taught the piano, now went for two weeks each summer to the large hotel the Grandisons, her new relatives, ran in the Catskill Mountains, a hotel visited by many big spenders. The Grandisons had succeeded in business because of the energy of Ruth Grandison, the mother of all, and to go to *Mountain View* a big Kosher hotel was the regular thing with many Jewish middleclass families. With contentment and joy the poor piano teacher sat rocking all day between meals, on one of the verandahs of *Mountain View.* There were two beautiful Grandison daughters and her moneyless son had married one because of his talent. She rocked and talked, said who she was; and who should be closer than two mothers-in-law? She was envied; though she wore her best, they saw she was poor; but they imagined the Grandisons helped her. And how lucky her son was (a fine man, of course), to have married such a beautiful girl! What did he do? What synagogue did they go to? Who was the Rabbi? Where did they live? Where did she come from?

Ah-ha, she was very cunning. She did not give them a thread to follow; she kept her secrets; her heart was a labyrinth. 'They talk, but I say nothing: they don't know what I am,' she said to her son and daughter-in-law. Her daughter-in-law, an unhappy person, despised her; but in her joy, Emma could not see it. To her mind it was natural for a beautiful woman with a rich mother to be cold; though she sometimes said to herself the word 'unfriendly'; but sometimes, too, in her joy at being there, and at her son's marriage, she would say quickly and eagerly, to Dorothy, the wife, 'Sometimes a daughter-in-law loves her mother-in-law better than her own mother. Yes, I've heard it said and I've seen it. How do you account for that?' Dorothy would turn away.

Emma worried that they had not a child; and often spoke of it. After a few years they had a child, a girl. Emma's happiness was now complete; she had nothing to wish for; except of course that Freddie would settle down, give up his meetings, attend to his career.

Dorothy rarely saw her husband: she went to her mother in the country for the child's health. He had his work, his lectures in town; he was writing a book. Emma begged him, 'Settle down, you have responsibilities now. That kind of thing is for schoolboys. Books are all very well, if you have money. Without money, it's bohemian. It's unheard-of, a married man with a child. When your uncle Jules died they found university medals in his desk: he said nothing about it, he worked as a pharmacist for his family. How terrible it is. What they said of you when you were a child! Oh, Mrs Foix, the principal said, that boy is a marvel, a prodigy, he's somebody, a personality, it's a pleasure to talk to him. It was in 28th Street. A man came, a reverend, with such a lovely child – what Nature can create! A boy like a wax doll, with cheeks like apples. If it had been a girl! What did he say? "Mrs Foix, your little girl is prettier than mine. Oh, is that a little boy? I thought a girl." Yes, I kept you straight. If you spilled something, I rapped your knuckles. And now! What's the use? It's a world full of trouble. It was a great crime – yes, I blame myself. I didn't want it. Why did I bring a boy into such a world? And now you want to change it! Very good – but you're a father now. It's different for a boy. Well, well – who knows? What a mystery!' Emma begged him to give up meetings and go to night courses and get a degree. She begged Dorothy to have another child. Instead of this, they separated and Emma had no more summer invitations: she sweltered in town.

Emma had to explain all this as best she could to the neighbours, the people in shops and the people she sat with in the park. She had other difficulties. During the war she had to be careful not to speak any German and then when the October Revolution came, she had to forget her Russian and say not a word about her family in the Baltic Provinces, though she worried about them. Then there was her sympathy with the new Russians. She did not of course believe the absurd gruesome tales her neighbours believed. She had to listen, shake her head and say 'Mm-mm'. She took to behaving as if she were a little off her head. It was safer. The ladies in the park went to church. She was now living with her son in a district near the university where the people were mostly Protestants; and she never liked to offend. She concealed her free-thinking and that she was of Russian, German, Jewish origin. She admired the women, in fact; she called them 'real Americans, real American ladies'; and she listened to all they had to say about the after-life and God in the most cordial way. She had an accent, she knew and she used occasional French phrases, *'Ça c'est bon, il n'y a pas de quoi',* so that they thought her French. When she went home, if she were alone, she could vent her irritation aloud, 'Such good people! God is on everyone's side, *cela va sans dire,* but someone loses. What roguery, what trash! God decides. Is he interested in our gutter squabbles? And the sparrows too! Why not say right out he decides the baseball game?'

At that time Elena was no comfort: she talked too much, she laughed with the doorman. All that Emma could tell the neighbours was that it was hard to find a good man with a steady job nowadays. 'My niece is so trustful; she does not understand men.'

Freddie now came to the house alone; Dorothy never came. Once in a long while, Emma put on her best dress and went by herself to see the little girl, a black-eyed beauty called Flora. Her daughter-in-law received her in the same gentle cold manner, listened as if deaf to her requests, did not have a cake for her. Still, there was the splendid child. She spent the hour or two she was there expressing her ravishment at the child's beauty, 'and a daughter, oh, how lucky! A daughter is better than a son,' and urging her daughter-in-law to take certain steps. 'He is not bad, he is unsettled, that is all.' Dorothy said, 'I certainly will never call him back. He left me; I can't overlook that.'

Emma returned to the house, her head whirling. Things should have been simple, but they were not simple. She explained it all to the women in the house as best she could. She had boasted all the time, in her ease and joy, about the rich and wellknown Grandisons and their beautiful daughters, had told every word of the whole story over and over again. But the inquisitive women did not understand why Dorothy did not visit her, why they did not have a car, why they did not take her to live with them in their fine apartment.

She thought of reasons for everything and when Freddie came to the house, she advised him to mention casually to the doorman, for instance, that his wife was travelling in France with rich relatives. The war was over. 'That will explain everything. Why should they know our business? Least said, soonest mended.'

From bad to worse. One day Freddie brought a girl to see her, a girl about twenty-four, pleasant enough but quite plain, even pale and tired to look at. Emma called her my dear and pretended to be confused. She put a black scarf over her head like an old Russian woman, put out her hand like a claw asking for stamps and money, ran about with bent shoulders and when Freddie was out of the room, came close to the girl and said gently and reasonably, 'Think of the child, my dear; you will under-stand when you have your own.' The girl said nothing and Emma ran quickly into her room and began mud-dling up her clothes in the trunk and drawers. Then she came back and said to Freddie, 'I am going to Europe to see my brothers, Richard must be a hundred years old and I must see them before I die. They won't remember me. Who knows if they want to see such an old monkeyface. Yes, we are descended from monkeys. I look in the glass, pfui! a baboon!'

Freddie put up the money and she went there and back all alone, having strange adventures arising from her assumed old age, her fear of poverty, the old age of her family and all the new conditions in Europe since her girlhood. Freddie met her in Berlin and brought her back.

Worse still, Freddie took to live with him the new girl. In the park she talked about her lovely daughter-in-law and grandchild and the rich family they belonged to, with a hotel in the Catskills and another in Miami, and about her summers in the mountains, all that part of the dream that had come true.

She now had no friends but those in the park and on the esplanade. She told them about her young sister, Anna, who had died of love, unable to marry the officer she wanted; and about her two beautiful nieces who had been clever students at the university and who had gone abroad, without explaining that the two nieces had long ago been sent to Siberia as revolutionists. When asked about her church, she said she was Episcopalian or Protestant or whatever seemed right at the moment, so as not to get into trouble and lose a friend. One of her park friends was Catholic and she went to church with her, though not to confession.

When the ladies saw Freddie walking in the street with his new girl, named Harriet, Emma explained that Freddie was going to sponsor Harriet for a job, that she had been helping out in the house, being of a very great kindness of heart. When Harriet became pregnant, she explained that the girl was unfortunate, had been deserted by a man and that she and Elena thought it right to give the girl a home till something could be done. 'Why, you would look after a sick dog,' she said. When the time came, she explained they would place the child in an orphanage and the girl could go to work again.

She explained that her beautiful daughter-in-law was ill at present and needed care, and her grand-daughter was living with the other grandmother who had plenty of money and saw that she had a nurse, a governess and servants, to take care of her; but that it was far off in the country and she, Emma, could not go. 'It's a pity, a great pity,' she would say and wipe her eyes. She would describe the wonderful little girl.

But it was all too much brainwork for her. She became exhausted and annoyed with the ladies that they expected so much of her. She began to complain. She told her troubles, but not in so many words, not to betray herself and so many others, in the long and inexplicable struggle with fate. She told the ladies she was hungry, ragged, penniless, ill-treated, bruised and beaten, that she had been threatened with a broom-handle and had fallen to the floor and left to lie there. She could see that the ladies were horrified by this and did not draw closer to her: they drew away. She knew why, too; no one likes trouble. She would still come home and babble about the ladies in the park and on the esplanade, what splendid homes they had, so many rooms 'four rooms and a kitchen,' and how beautiful their daughters were, 'such rosy cheeks, such shoulders.' 'When did you see their shoulders?' Freddie would enquire laughing, for he knew that was a modest family word for breasts. 'Oh, stupid, dumbbell – what it is to live with a dumbbell! I know what I know,' she would exclaim angrily. 'Ah, what is a son? He's an angel, a cherub when he's a child, and then later, a good-for-nothing.' But then she would light up eagerly and say, 'Do you know a woman there, I must say, very nice, a real American, but she was ten years in Germany and she asked me the words for potatoes. Did you ever hear the like? *Kartoffel,* I said. A head made of wood; a lost case, my dear. But ladies they are.'

One day she asked to see her cousin Belle, the one who owned the house on the East Side. Belle she had always considered very lucky. She had married a man who did not care for sex; indeed it was thought she was still a virgin, though she was now sixty-eight. Her husband had given her a beautiful house, a grand piano, a maid; and she had never had to have children. She looked younger than her years, she was a real Kobol lively, witty, comfortably lodged; and now that she was a widow – what a life! She did entirely as she pleased, just sat at home, played the piano and ate cakes, cream cakes if she wanted them. 'Ah, what a life,' said Emma. Besides, this Belle was very kind and sensible. Belle came, the doctor came and after that Emma went to a hospital.

Everyone came to see her, her daughter-in-law with the beautiful little grand-daughter, Freddie with his new girl and baby, her cousin Belle who spoke to her in Russian, someone else who spoke to her in German. Her room-mate was inquisitive, but the old woman said only, 'That is my daughter-in-law Dorothy, isn't she a beauty? She belongs to a very rich and wellknown family and I go there in the summer.'

'And who is the young man you call Freddie, who calls you Mamma, with a wife and child?' 'Oh, that is a nice boy, a dear friend, he lived with me once and got to calling me Mamma, isn't that funny? Mamma, Mamma, just like a baby. And that is a friend of mine, a nice girl who lived with me once when she was sick. "You were very kind to me, my dear," she said. Why not? One must be kind. Otherwise we're no better than dogs.'

On the morning of the third day, Emma was awakened by the birds. It was spring and they began their cries about four in the morning.

'It is my daughter's birthday,' she said to her room-mate. She looked very strange when the daylight came and her room-mate called the young nurse. The young nurse hurried in and spilled a glass of water on the doorsill. 'To speak French,' said Emma, 'you must speak like the birds, chirrup. Do you hear?' Her room-mate thought she was wandering and said to the nurse, 'She is a clever woman, she knows French and Latin and other languages.' The nurse cleaned up the floor and when she returned the room-mate said, 'I think she is going; I have seen them go.'

The young nurse came to the bed. Emma, now an old wrinkled woman with thin white hair in a plait, murmured to her, *'A quoi bon? A quoi bon?'* 'She wants fresh water,' said the nurse. 'It was all no use, my dear,' said Emma and died.

At her funeral Dorothy sat in one part, Freddie in another and the new girl in another, so as not to offend. Some of Emma's relatives came because they were sorry for her; some stayed away because she did not have a religious funeral.

'Poor aunt,' said Elena, crying, 'I understood her.' 'What are you going to do with the extra room now?' said someone, as they were walking away from the crematorium. 'I suppose Elena will get the fur coat,' said another. 'Well, if your mother left you a little money, you deserve it,' said another, grudgingly. 'And to think,' said Belle to Freddie, 'that she died before her twin sister, after all.' 'What twin sister?' 'Why, your mother was a twin; Anna was her twin.' 'Anna! The girl who ran away with an officer and died young?' 'Anna ran away with a poor schoolteacher. Your family couldn't swallow that; he hadn't a degree. She married him and they went to France to live. Emma always wrote to her; she was very fond of her. Yes – I think when Anna first saw him in amateur theatricals he was dressed as an officer.' 'But why didn't she say she was a twin?' 'Ah, yes – well, it was embarrassing in company to say that they were twins; everyone would look and say, "But Anna is so beautiful!" Emma looked older, so she thought it was better to say she was older. And you know the Kobols, what magpies for clatter! So she changed the story – and then she went to America anyway.' 'Poor Mamma. I suppose I had better write to my father; I don't want to, but I ought to.' 'Your father. But the professor is dead!' 'If he is, he's a very lively corpse. He's living in Detroit with his third wife.' 'Ah, I see. She always said – Well, poor Emma. Life is difficult.'

A Harmless Affair

Everything went right in this love affair from the beginning. It began just after Lydia had thought, 'It's spring and an empty spring; it's years since I felt really in love, I must be getting stupid – never looking outside my eyes, never longing for anything else.' The next day she went to a party and there met a lot of distinguished people, people who had all arrived at their destinations. Lydia hated this sort of party – to be with people who were famous made her feel that life had stopped and there was nothing more to live for, whereas she wanted to keep on living, and for that reason preferred people who had not arrived, at the top, or anywhere else, but who still nourished impossible ambitions and desires. There had been some unpleasantness about the invitation, on that account. The woman invited her: she wrote and accepted the invitation and she had not known the woman was famous: she only found it out after. And then the woman had not invited Lydia's husband. Lydia was known as 'Miss Parsons' in the laboratory and so she often used the

name outside. This woman was a doctor, a simple ordinary woman, and after accepting the invitation, Lydia had
discovered that she was not only Dr Brown, but also
Mary Cohoet, a great social light and humanitarian, and
one who was so far above the battle that she believed in
meeting people from all strata of society – radicals,
conservatives, revolutionary artists, writers in society
papers and so on. Lydia had been invited because she had
done some work in bacteriology and was still a young
woman, and had travelled – she had some social graces in
fact, although her parents were very poor.

Lydia put on a French dress and shoes and arrived late:
the studio room in the duplex apartment was nearly full,
people were drinking sherry and cocktails, and yet there
was a flat, round-shouldered air in the room, which
revealed, at a glance, that the guest of honour had not yet
arrived. He was a man who had lived in China a long
time and was going to make a plea for aid for the Chinese
people.

Lydia felt very much at her ease, for a wonder, that day.
It was an early spring day: thin sunlight slanted through
the great studio windows and made the scattered people
look untidy. Lydia saw she was the best-dressed woman
there – not the richest dressed, but the woman with the
best cut frock. The hostess was even a little surprised at
her appearance, evidently, and began to introduce her to
the people there. Lydia tried to remember the names, but
only seized one here and there. There was a line-up of
young men more or less ill dressed standing in the sun, an
accidental line-up – they had been standing in a group
and the circle had opened out into a parade line when the
distinguished hostess appeared. Dr Brown named them.

'Dr Lyall, my cousin, Dr West, Roy Finch, Captain
Paul Charters, Herr von Wirtz . . .' and so on. After one

or two more introductions they had reached the other end of the room. Lydia received a cocktail and was left to herself. Seeing no-one there she knew and everyone awkward, she turned back to the group, which again opened into a parade line when she approached and going straight to a tall young man with a black thicket of hair, said, 'Did Dr Brown say Paul Charters, or Paul Charteris?' He laughed, 'Well, she says Charters, but *I* call it Charteris.'

'Then you're the journalist and soldier,' Lydia said confidently. He laughed, 'Yes. I'm the journalist and soldier.'

The other men had discreetly moved away by this.

'We have all your books at home,' said Lydia. She bubbled with uncommon good spirits.

'All,' she went on: 'so if you ever find one's missing, come and get it at our place. My husband's a great admirer of yours.' Charteris was in a good temper: for some reason, she beamed at Charteris, she felt idiotic and yet delighted. Dr Brown tore them away from each other to introduce the guest of honour, Mr Henri Lafargue. Lydia began to chat with Lafargue in an inspired fashion: she became terrified, for fear that this singular animation would leave her in the middle of a sentence and Lafargue would find her stupid. But no, Dr Brown tore Lafargue away from her, with something of a frown; she had no right to hog the guest of honour, she knew, but she was in a very strange exhilarated state and did not wish to come back to earth.

Later in the evening, Dr Brown came back, 'I did not know you were married. How stupid you must think me not to have invited your husband too. Please forgive me.' Lydia was puzzled, then remembered she had mentioned her husband to Paul Charteris.

She was different that evening from any time in her life. She liked a lot of the people immensely: she invited at least half a dozen of them to come to their apartment and meet her husband. She came away by herself and walked a long way by herself in the dark, missing several subway entrances on purpose. There was plenty of time to go home and take up the cordial connubial relations she enjoyed with her husband.

About a week later, Charteris telephoned at ten o'clock in the morning, asking if she had really meant her invitation and if he could come and see them. Suddenly the same confident exhilarated mood took her and she answered, 'Yes, of course, whenever you like,' but in a voice and mood quite unlike herself.

'Can I choose my own date?' asked Charteris.

'Of course.'

'Any time?'

'Any time.'

'Thanks,' said Charteris and rang off.

She told her husband that the famous Paul Charteris was really coming to see them. But he did not telephone again and she almost forgot him. Then a month later, he telephoned again, 'Hello Lydia,' he said coolly: 'can I come and see you today?'

'Yes, of course.'

'At three o'clock?'

'Yes.'

'Thanks,' said Charteris, and rang off.

Lydia scarcely gave a second's thought to his coming, although generally she fussed round the house, tidied herself up for hours before even the most uninteresting visitor arrived.

Charteris came at four o'clock. 'I'm sorry,' he said. 'I was with Anna Brown, getting things ready for

Lafargue's lecture. How are you Lydia?'

Lydia felt herself trembling with joy. 'This is my husband, Tom Dunne,' she said. It was with a vague disappointment that she saw the two men take an immediate liking to each other.

Charteris' coat was greasy and old, his hair uncombed and his skin was bad: she could see he was not living well and that he was over-tired. Just as they sat down, and her husband had begun some question about Charteris' work in China, the telephone rang and Tom said, 'I know that's for me, that's my broker,' with the good natured parade of influence he sometimes made, and he dashed to the telephone and began chaffing the broker, calling him by his first name and putting on a wonderful variety show for the benefit of Charteris and herself. She sat down in his vacated chair and said to Charteris, 'You have been over-working, haven't you?' Charteris looked straight at her, and said,

'Oh Lydia, I never had any of the luck in life,' he hung his head and then suddenly looked again and smiled softly.

'How do you mean, Paul?' She felt towards him as towards Tom in their quieter marital moments.

'I have no luck,' he said looking at her with meaning. What meaning? She could not quite believe that he meant what he seemed to mean, that is, that she was already married. Tom had suddenly ceased his jokes and cutting-up at the telephone and was finishing his conversation in brief businesslike words.

'I didn't know you were married,' said Charteris. 'Anna Brown didn't know either.' He said it very coolly, with wide open eyes on her face and he seemed cunning to her, for it was impossible to tell whether this followed from his first words, or not.

'No,' said Lydia.

Paul smiled into her face with a look of humble affection, and yet there was a cunning in his coolness, that made her speechless. However, she was thinking very fast, weighing her chances with him, his chances with her, the outcome of love between them.

All this happened in the first five minutes. Their conversation had been carried on in a low, but natural tone, and Tom had hurried back from the telephone, as if intrigued, all the same. Thereafter Tom, of course, led the conversation on to China. Lydia had always admired Tom's brilliance and scholarship and was very surprised to see that not only was Paul equal to him in brilliance and scholarship, but seemed cooler, surer of himself, and moreover had exactly the same kind of thinking as Tom. Tom talked, talked, Paul answered him, argued with him, opulently showered him with his own ideas, and every few minutes would turn on her a golden smile, the kind of smile, Lydia had always thought up to now, that was only exchanged between lovers. And she felt herself giving him, too, those rare golden smiles: she felt very happy, at ease, as if floating on an inland brook, in midsummer in full sunlight. She had never felt at ease with a man like that in her life before, except with Tom, but in a different, more maternal way, with Tom. She had no maternal feeling towards this stranger, but no sinful nor vulgar adulterous feeling either. Only a feeling as if the love of the ages of gold existed between them and would never be disturbed.

Presently, because she could take no part in their conversation, which had become 'a feast of the intellect', she retired to her own workroom and went on with a monograph in bacteriology she was doing. This did not please Tom very much: he always liked her to be there, to listen to his brilliance, and to love and admire him; so he called her, 'Lydia! Make us some coffee.' She came out at once, as she was used to doing, and as she passed the door, Paul smiled at her and said, 'Well, if you come like that when people call you'll never get your work done. *I* wouldn't do it.'

Everything about him was natural and sweetly audacious. When she gave him the coffee, he smiled at her as if he were absolutely sure of her love. 'What a strange thing,' she thought: 'I must be seeing things! I'm just mad, that's all. He's being pleasant.' But she saw he smiled at her husband coolly, carelessly, with the faint air of an adversary, and would turn from one of those rather crisp looks, to give her one of those smiles that was slowly dissolving her out of herself, out of her wifehood, back into her childhood, into the romantic and rapturous child she had been. She felt that Paul knew instinctively the kind of child, girl and woman she had been up till now – the kind of family life she had had, all about her, her secret thoughts were the most open things in nature to him. She was obsessed by him, but it was a kind of dream: and when the door closed on him, she rushed into Tom's arms with a quiet rapture. Standing there, thinking of Tom's goodness and their happiness, she found herself looking at the hall mirror.

'Tom,' she said slowly, 'who does Charteris remind you of?' Tom looked into the mirror too, 'Of someone,' he said thoughtfully.

'Of someone we know very well?' said Lydia, puzzled.

'Yes: someone we see often,' Tom continued.

'Tom,' Lydia continued in a low voice, 'look at me.'

'Yes,' her husband answered, after a scrutiny: 'you are right. He is so like you that you might be twins.'

She looked closer at the glass, 'All the time, I had an

odd feeling that I had known him for many years. But it was only myself!' She laughed: and noticed on Tom's face a baffled expression.

It happened that soon after that Tom and Charteris began to work together on a textbook, and all their meetings were at some office in town. Lydia encouraged this and even refused to go with Tom: 'Why? I just sit there while you two gas.'

And again shortly after this, Tom got an appointment in another state, for two years. They returned to (. . .) at the end of that time, on a Sunday evening and went straight to Broadway to see a movie in the 'stinkoes' along Forty-Second Street. At the corner of Broadway, Lydia saw Paul, looking very pale and untidy, and with a young woman.

'Why, there's . . .' she began.

But Paul hastily turned right about and crossed to the Times building. Lydia said 'Tom, there's Paul, there's Paul . . .' and dragged him with her. At the bus stop Paul, with a tired and almost frightened expression was standing, with a badly dressed and tired, but pretty girl who had also a timid expression.

'Hello Lydia,' he said so awkwardly, that she knew he had seen them and turned away purposely. She looked at the young woman with a friendly smile.

'This is Rosetta – Rosetta Myria,' he said.

The girl seemed glad that they were friendly.

'Let's go and have a drink,' proposed Lydia. She felt masterful, confident. She wondered why Paul had wanted to avoid them, but did not care. They went to one place after another and found them nearly all crowded. At last they found a 'tavern' that had booths and almost no-one there. They sat down and looked at the gallant frescoes, ordered wiener schnitzels and beer and Paul, very ill-at-ease, conscious of his dirty collar, untidy hair and greasy coat (the same as two years before) began cracking bad jokes. Rosetta and he had been to France since they had met, and in fact, this evening had only just got off the boat with only ten cents between them and had not even tipped the stewards. This made Tom feel very jolly and he urged them to eat and drink and lent them some money. Paul easily accepted the money, Rosetta looked relieved. Lydia invited them to come and see them and they accepted for the next Saturday. Paul put on a bold air as soon as he had eaten and told some broad jokes. He was always a frank fellow and tonight he seemed to want to appear as rollicking as they had known him before. What had happened to make him so blue?

Lydia looked at him curiously. 'This is the man I nearly lost my head over.' He certainly looked very like her, when she was looking tired and blue: his reactions were just the same, except that he was a man. When she felt 'scraggy' she tried to avoid people and then she tried to be bold, laugh it off, be vulgar. She looked at him feature by feature – he seemed miserable and ordinary, and yet very comprehensible and she was ready to defend him against the world, as one is a member of one's family. She was careful not to offend the girl Rosetta, by showing the affection she had for him. Paul sought her eye and her smile once or twice pitiably, without confidence.

She did not wait for the Saturday night and had no feeling against Rosetta. 'I don't want him,' she thought, 'and I'm glad he got someone to console him for his unhappy married life of the other year.' When Paul came, she spent the whole time talking to Rosetta. Rosetta was an agitator, conscientiously going from factory to factory where she was not blacklisted, organising the girls. Once or twice, she looked at Paul: Paul was not so talkative, he was letting Tom talk and, rather discouraged and tired was sitting back, stretched out in the comfortable armchair, with his eyes fixed strangely and quietly on Rosetta. 'He loves her,' thought Lydia. They gave her their address: she was to come and see them. 'He was never really mine,' thought Lydia.

A fortnight later, he rang up and asked if he could come at once to see them. When he came, an hour later, Lydia craning in the darkness of the passage, at the woman behind him, saw his wife. 'I am so glad you came, Mrs Charteris.'

The woman, plain, unhappy and tempestuous, looked round the flat. 'It's very small,' she said, 'and you can see the bedroom so plain.'

'It is,' said Lydia: 'we can't do a thing here.'

'It's hard to find,' complained the woman: 'I don't know how anyone finds you.'

'Oh,' said Lydia, 'we leave the lamp in the window, and then Paul was here before.'

'Yes,' the woman gave them all a bitter look: 'he was here before of course.'

Some other people came – among them, a friend of Paul's, a journalist equally brave and famous, and with him his wife, one of the most beautiful women alive, delicate, slant-eyed, porcelain-faced. Mrs Charteris and she discussed the Spanish and Chinese wars and Lydia, who knew nothing of them, worked on an embroidered bedspread she had begun years before. She had begun it superstitiously, 'She would not marry Tom till it was finished' – but she had married Tom long before. The three men talked: when she looked up she saw Paul, stretched out as before in the very same chair, looking as bitter as old age at his wife. When they went, they all heard them begin to argue bitterly immediately outside the window and down the lane.

Their new place was in the centre of the city, near

Paul's place of work. Paul dropped in several times with a manuscript he wanted Tom's advice on, and once or twice he ate there before going home to his wife. They were very poor and lived a long way out of town: he did not get home till eight in the evening. Once Paul spoke of Rosetta 'Yes, I left her and went back to my wife: it's my own fault I suppose.' Rosetta? Lydia was sure she loved him. That evening, she noticed how seedy Paul was, how a little beer paunch was developing on him, and crows' feet round his eyes, although he was not much older than herself. The hard, discouraging and dissipated life was drying him.

He began to drop in. Once she spoke of some young poet she knew and lent him the book of poems: 'This one is splendid,' she said: 'it's his finest.' He took it unwillingly, but politely. Afterwards she repeated the poem to herself: a glorious but stirring and sensual poem. She felt ashamed and yet thought, 'He will understand I meant nothing by that.'

He came in one afternoon about two o'clock to return the book. It happened that Tom was off from work early that day and he was in the apartment. She answered the door and there stood Paul, tall, wind-flushed, with his curly dark hair and a certain timidity, 'I came to return to you your books.'

'Come in, Tom is here.'

'No, no.'

'Yes, he would love to see you.'

She forgot everything that had intervened: it was as if they stood there, meeting awkwardly in a doorway in the first flush of a love affair. He entered. A journalist was there who hated Paul Charteris, a political opponent: he instantly went out, crushing on his hat, scarcely muttering 'Hullo'.

Charteris looked surprised, gained his full manhood in a moment, but merely said, 'I don't think he likes me!'

He was amiable and full of ideas after all. He went promising to come soon. He came the next day, at four o'clock. No-one was there, but Lydia. She was nervous. She sat on the edge of the couch, with her whole body hidden behind an armchair, her arms and chin resting on it and began to talk. She could not stop herself talking. He listened, looked at her, in an alien way, never answered a word. She went on feverishly talking, in a high squeaky voice, as it seemed, that she detested. Suddenly, 'What is the use?' she thought and fell silent, and frowned. It was too bad of him not to answer at all. At the frown he jerked and began to talk – about himself, his brothers, his idea of writing a novel of his youth. When Tom came they were both relieved. Paul came the next day. She gave him liquor, which he liked very much. They talked about parties – she had given one which had fallen flat. 'Why?' he asked: 'give them rough liquor and beds to make love on, and no party falls flat.' He laughed tipsily. She was hurt. When Tom came home early, she was glad, and sat down in the deep armchair doing her bedspread. When he went Tom had some stories to tell. He had been talking to friends of Paul's. Paul was a heartbreaker, a Don Juan and so on: he had a new flame every five months and everyone was disgusted with him. Lydia excused him to herself, but she observed that Tom was capable of pinpricks. (And Tom had once said 'If another should love you, I'd be proud to know this lover: I would never stoop to jealousy.') A day rarely passed without Tom getting in a gentle hint about Paul's lovemaking, some little joke 'the ladykiller'. It ended by Lydia forgiving Paul entirely in her heart: 'So he is, and I love him for what he is.' She didn't know when she began speaking thus of the tender feeling she had for the erring Paul.

Paul began to drop in every day. When he went one day, she would say, 'Come tomorrow if you can, Paul: Tom will be home about five.' Paul would always come at the time mentioned and have wine or cocktails. He liked drink and Lydia always had it for him now. Tom was always there and there would be a long session of political discussion. Lydia would say nothing – just do her work and look at them both. Winter was approaching and the evenings drew in soon: in the semi-darkness Paul sat, with his legs stretched out, resting back, with a fatigued look in the deep armchair. Sometimes answering Tom and sometimes letting his inspiration flow. When he answered him, it was always pungently, with a personal philosophy. Paul had studied a long time abroad, and was an original. Lydia watched them and in these few evenings, the tender and familiar feeling she had for Paul, changed: she fell in love with him. When the lamp was lighted, he shaded his fine almond shaped eyes and listened still. At first he came two or three times a week, then every day. When they were out of liquor, she left them talking and ran out to get it. The cloak hooks stood in view of the chair he always sat in. Neither of the men made a move to go out and get the things. As she got into her things, she could look in and see Paul stretched out there: whenever he saw her he would turn and give her that melting smile of his and she would smile back from the depths of her heart, a smile that was the fulfilment of romantic love almost, something dreamed about in poetic youth. And so when she came back. Tom saw little or nothing of this, which was the only interchange they made all day, except when she asked him a question 'A little more port? Another glass of beer?' He never refused. One day, when she was going out, Tom asked her to go up the street and get some carbon paper too. Paul, at this, gave her a quaint tender smile, one of those he was a past master in. She was as happy as a schoolgirl to whom a professor has smiled in the street. Her heart beat fast and cheerfully going along the lane. She got into the street in a high state of mind. In the shop waiting for the boy to wrap up the carbon paper, a dark storm rushed on her, and for a few seconds, everything in the room whirled round in a glorious delirium: the dark wind rushed on, but left, where had only been a joyful excitement, the surge of adult passion. This was not like her earlier crushes with their blind rages and aches: she had been living happily with a man for a long time and she knew what happy passion was, and this that was left with her now was the night-darkened heavenly garden of love. She desired, with every sense, Paul of the tender smile and understanding heart: and joy rushed over her too, 'I thought I would never feel it again, and God be praised I am madly in love: what splendid joy.' She went back soberly, but like someone to whom glorious tidings have been announced in the street. 'I have won the lottery, yes, really,' she thought. She hastened out of her coat and hat, did not look at any of them when she came in, but began pulling corks and so on.

When she came in to give him his drink, Paul was saying, 'Yes, I'm going to China again and I'm never coming back this time: what have I to stay here for?'

No-one tried to dissuade him: that was his business, and everyone felt it was his fate. He was not happy here: the reconciliation with his wife was a torment for both: stories were being whispered about his affairs and people were turning against him for no good reason, chiefly because of his wife's unhappiness. But it was a long way off. Lydia saw him as always to the door and asked him to come again tomorrow, 'Tom will be home at five.' 'All right,' he said, in his sweet manner.

When he came the next day, she had been through hours of desire – the first time she had ever waited for him to come, or deeply desired it. He sat there this time, in the lamplight of the early fallen day very silent, hardly saying a word, and she kept looking at him, quietly, little glances that no-one could notice.

'How is it possible,' she thought 'that I am so madly in love with this man I've seen so often, and who is after all, like me, if rather handsomer and sweeter?' She began to look at him, 'Is it the mouth? Is it the eyes?' She found that each item gave her a pang and that in fact, it was each item that she had not, and then had, fallen in love with. She went out silently, unnoticed by the others and looked at herself in the mirror in the bathroom – pulling her eyes up and down, trying to get the sweet expression Paul got so easily. Her smile did not seem much like his: but in her happiness thinking about him, she caught herself looking rather like him when he smiled. This made it nearly all pure joy. She came back and stole fresh glances at him – she began to notice the parts of his body. He seemed so potent, full of manly strength that she felt like fainting: she seemed to get a little delirious although she had not drunk very much, and began to think that he was all honey, all roses, and so on. She found that she had moments of absence, when she heard nothing of what was going on, but only heard beautiful words about him, 'His limbs gather passion as the bees honey and I am the hive . . .' Her feeling this evening was so powerful that she could not believe he did not feel it, that Tom did not feel it, it seemed to have thickened and made fluid the air. He said very little, shading his eyes with his hands and looking through them, while Tom went on about Ethiopia.

When she saw him to the door that evening in the usual polite and indifferent fashion, she thought suddenly 'Oh, if I could only walk in the street with him a few minutes.' The moment of greatest joy had passed and she was already beginning to feel the pains and aches of desires, but very much more powerful than before because of her marriage, and almost uncontrollable, as convulsions or childbirth are a giant revolutionary spasm. She thought at once, 'I must not see him again.' She had to control her thought and face during the evening with Tom and have his caresses from which she had never once turned away, but all the time she was realising with more plainness the gulf of passion and drama on which she stood. 'Another moment,' she acknowledged 'and I would have walked out into the street with him, without a hat or coat, without a penny or in my slippers: and it wouldn't have mattered how long the street was – even if it was as long as the country – that's how I felt. If he had asked me, would I have had the heart to refuse? I would follow him barefoot: I would not have the heart to refuse him.' She never had the smallest idea of leaving Tom nor of hurting him, and she loved Tom deeply and wholesomely. She then realised that she was in danger, and thought 'I must never see him again.' She began to think how she could manage this without arousing Tom's suspicions or Paul's. She could be absent, once or twice – but not more than that. 'What am I to do?' The conflict had begun: it was not a conflict between one man and another, for her relations to each of them had never changed from the beginning, she loved one because of their marriage and the chances of their coming together, but in Paul was some secret command from her own destiny, he was destiny, and they both knew it. In his wilful wayward and inconsiderate way, if he cared to ask her to do something (he would plead, with an appearance of weakness), she would do it without a second's thought: it was foretold from the earth's youth that she would meet him. She was his equal, she knew her own powers, she knew she was like him, she did not grovel before him, she knew his nature without any blindness and the things she thought of obeying him in were – following him in his many wanderings more than anything else, for as to the result of desire, she knew that he was made this way – he adored love for its own sake and if she mentioned her love to him he would love her, for the sake of love. So there was no unhappy crushed desire in her feeling, only this singular feeling of destiny which came upon her with a sure ferocity. It was the strangest and most perfect of loves. 'O, Gods,' she kept thinking 'I have known it: this is it, perfect, spotless, boundless love: how lucky I am.' To her he seemed the most imperfect of mortals, with a godlike power over her. And naturally, when she realised this, she knew she could never see him again. She feared him.

The next morning he telephoned to say that he had an immediate assignment to go to China and that once there he would never return: he would die there. These were his strange words. 'I have nothing to live for here nor there,' he said.

He could only come twice before he went, because he had so much to do. He came for one or two hurried visits then and the whole time was taken up by the journalist who was politically his opponent and who almost lived with Tom and Lydia, in the hope of gibing at Paul before he went out. They had no last moments with him at all. He went on a Monday night.

Lydia felt little that night: 'He has gone – well, fate's relieved me of him.'

The next morning she was so deeply in love with him

that she could do nothing. Tom went to work and instead of starting her work herself, she pulled down the blinds and thought about her lost love, about his face, limbs and sexual beauty, his charming smile and tenderness: it was as if a smouldering fire had been poured into her flesh and she had no bones or sinews. She could do nothing, eaten up with tenderness and cruel desire. About twelve she roused herself and put on her hat to go and buy some envelopes, thinking 'Why does this happen when he's gone?' when the doorbell rang and she opened it to see Paul standing there. She took two steps forward and murmured in a low voice 'I thought you had gone.'

'It's put off till Saturday,' he said.

He came in and talked in a low, inconsequential way, almost in a low fever, of various things, but had not been there more than ten minutes when the talkative journalist, who was his political enemy, rang up and said he would be over.

'Shall I put him off?' asked Lydia, her hand over the receiver.

'He doesn't like me,' said Paul.

But she could think of no reason for putting him off: he only wanted to come over for a cup of coffee and a chat. She said, 'Paul Charteris is here.'

'Well, I won't come then' said the journalist nastily. 'You don't want me if that red is there.'

'Don't be silly, Edgar.'

'No, I won't come,' said the journalist in a pet.

'All right.'

The journalist suddenly relented: he couldn't pass up his gossip. 'Well, if you want me?'

There was no way to put him off decently. He arrived and began a sharp discussion with Paul and after that, in came Tom again, not working in the afternoon. It was really odd that, at whatever time Paul came, they could never have a minute alone. And yet she had nothing to talk to him about: she hadn't the faintest idea what she would talk to him about if she had no interruptions. She had got so used to Tom taking up every conversation and engaging everyone's attentions, that she had got out of the way of rousing herself. Perhaps Paul thought she did not care for him.

Paul came every day that week, although he was very busy – and always at different times, just when he was free, but every day that week the gossipy and touchy Edgar was there too, and every day that week also Tom was home incredibly early from work – in fact, one day he did not go at all. He liked Paul and he wanted to see him as often as he could before he went away for ever.

'It's unlikely I'll ever get to China to see you,' he told Paul.

'Oh, I'll die there this year,' said Paul, rather bitterly.

'You won't.'

'Why not? Yes, I will.'

Lydia said nothing, sitting there wondering about him. Why was he going? Why did he want to die? Why did he come so often? She knew he was going and so she quietly gave herself up to contemplation of him: she would never see him again. No-one noticed anything. When he came to see them for the last time, Edgar was still there. Paul said nothing the whole evening but let Edgar rail against him and his cause and the Chinese: Paul sat with his face covered with his hand and drank everything he was given. Lydia drank a lot too: whenever she gave Paul a drink, she drank too. Tom was not much of a drinker and Edgar preferred to talk and was slow getting through his drinks. She felt herself presently very drunk, but very cool too. Paul stayed as long as he could but presently had to go home to have his last meal with his wife. Everyone offered him gifts – a pair of fur-lined gloves, socks, marching boots, a fountain pen and the like, but he turned them all down but the boots and gloves.

Edgar relented at the last moment and offered the gloves. He had always said that that rat would never go off to China and now he saw him going he felt ashamed but he still said, 'He'll only sit in Hong Kong or Canton in a cosy café and send home despatches, he'll never fight.' Paul said nothing to all this. It was very strange. Lydia knew why Edgar was so biting – he was jealous that they had become so friendly with Paul: he wanted to be their bosom friend alone, himself. That was why he had been there every day that week – to be sure that she and Tom didn't get sessions alone with Paul and to find out what Paul had to say that interested them so.

Presently Paul got up to go, got his hat, and everyone said 'Goodbye and good luck.' Paul was to meet Tom on the next day to get the measurement of the boots and the gloves, but this was the last time he would call. Lydia was very jolly, took him to the door, then decided to go out to the lane with him. Paul was silent, surprised that she went to the lane with him. He was surprised that she had drunk so much. At the lane she stopped, 'Well, goodbye, Paul.'

'Goodbye,' he said indifferently. She held out her hand and he took it, when suddenly she grasped his hand in both hers and pressed it hotly. He lifted his face with an expression of great surprise and smiled in delight: he searched her face and waited for what she would say.

'I'll go with you.'

'Will you?'

'I haven't got the money yet.'

'Can you get it?'

'I don't know. No.'

'No,' he said shaking his head.

'Well, goodbye, anyhow.'

'Goodbye,' he said smiling. He went off and she ran up the stairs.

It had only taken a minute and a murmur and no-one would notice her absence. Tom was rattling away, but Edgar laughed and said, 'Here comes Lydia all excited.' Jealousy makes him say that, that's all, she thought: he's so glad Paul has gone. Heaven above, she thought, I actually said I'd go with him: I nearly walked out into the street after him. I must be careful she thought: I could never never let Tom down, never. But I forget everything in the world beside the imperative Paul. She got their dinner ready and no-one remarked anything. Paul had gone, but she was not sorry, she was inflated, ecstatic. Paul knew she loved him now. What a cool customer, she thought smiling to herself. She would have been ashamed to let any other man know she loved him, but not Paul. To Paul love was an autonomous thing with its own rule, the creator of life; he admired it for its own sake. A man able to get women from other men by sleight of hand, without struggle.

But Paul did not keep his appointment with Tom the next day. Instead he came early and to lunch. For lunch they had a visitor, a young boy who hero-worshipped Paul and who would not take their hints that they wanted to see Paul alone at the last minute. He wanted to see the famous Captain Charteris himself, especially as he was leaving for China. He stayed through lunch and after lunch: and only after a painful silence on everyone's part did he take the hint and go. It was then late, within five minutes Charteris himself was leaving. The men put on their hats to go and buy the boots and then Lydia noticed that Tom came into the passage looking rather pale (and) startled.

'He wonders if I am going to kiss Paul goodbye,' she understood by this. She was too rollicking with Paul and it was not a farewell at all. Tom stood at the door staring at them both, still with that startled look. She tried to think of something to ask him to do so that he would leave them for a moment, but she could think of nothing rational. 'Goodbye, Paul.'

'I'll try to come back for a moment later,' said Paul gently.

She was so surprised that she answered stiffly 'Oh?'

Paul was discomforted, 'I don't know if I'll have time.'

'No, no,' she said: 'no, no, you'll be busy . . .'

She was worried by the staring pale face of Tom, minutely observing the two of them.

'And so goodbye.'

'Goodbye.'

Paul hesitated again, worried, 'And you do my work for me.'

'I can't do that.'

'Try, Lydie.'

'Until you come back.'

'Oh, I don't think I'll come back.'

He was gone. She was so astonished by everything that she could not collect her wits. What did it mean? She saw in an instant that she had never really understood him, how clever he was.

It was a long time till Tom came back, and she thought, 'He will come back from China of course, and by then we must be out of the way: I must never see him again.' For the conflict had arisen now between the two men. The angelic, patient and deserving Tom who had been faithful to her for ten years was there, and also the underserving but imperative Paul. Who would win? She envisaged all the consequences of going with Paul. She and Paul were too close to have any great surprises for each other – there might simply be the amusement of being with your twin for a while: after a while, Paul would have another flame – and she would get angry with him, she was sure – his dilatoriness, his flames, even his beer parties and his little paunch, which had disappeared at present, but would come back when he returned to ordinary life. Also she could sense that Paul had given up most of his ambition and hope in life: while she had not, she was still mad with it and she hoped always would be. She would make Paul laugh and Paul would seem dull to her. 'It would never work,' she thought 'and I would hurt Tom forever and for no good reason.' But she knew that if Paul said in his yearning and understanding way, 'Come to me,' she would find it hard, perhaps impossible to resist him. 'That's the end,' she said: 'if he comes back twice as large as life, I will never see him again.'

She was so resolved, that she did not miss Paul, and never thought of writing to him, although she knew other people were – Anna Brown and all the friends he had worked with in causes. Why? She and Paul understood each other: that was all there was to their friendship. It would always be so. She regretted that she had not known Paul's love, that would have been she was sure the revelation of love: and she bitterly regretted not having in her body a child of this dear and intimate man: that was what she really wanted of him, a child of him, a child like him, a child to be her perfect joy for ever, of which he would be the distant father. She wanted to love him but not live with him. She felt that she had already been married to him and lived with him for years. But with

Tom, life was a constant excitement and pleasure: she felt she had only lived with Tom a few weeks, even after all this time.

Three months later, they had a telephone call late at night, telling them that Paul had been killed in action. She said nothing, a feverish activity began in her soul, she began to lament like a woman in a Greek play, in long rhythmic phrases: her heart began to slowly weave Paul's funeral dance and in her ears rang long phrases of lament. When the light was turned out, she lay in bed with Tom seeing night for the first time.

'How dark it is when the lamp is turned out,' she said. Tom listened and after a moment asked 'What do you mean by that?'

'I never noticed before.'

At that moment the church bell began to strike the hour.

'Listen to them ringing,' she said: 'Why do they ring for the hours that are gone: all the ages that are dead and they still ring the hours: it's so little – such a little sound in the night. Even the dead hour just past doesn't hear it: the people dead the past hour don't hear it and what do we care? We live tomorrow – not an hour or two, but endless days of life.'

'Lydie?' he asked in a small voice, curiously.

'Oh, Tom, let's leave here. What is there here? I don't like it.'

'Why do you say that?'

'I don't know. My heart isn't in it here.'

He was silent. She realised what he might take this to mean and hastened to talk a lot about their circumstances. Meanwhile she was realising what it had all meant that she had said, and that Tom perhaps guessed too – she turned away from his affectionate hands. A light from another window fell on the pillow: it was a fine pale yellow light. Among the words in her ears, she heard ones she recognised, 'Oh, Jonathan, Oh my brother Jonathan – very pleasant was thy life unto me, . . .' The words went on repeating themselves. Suddenly a great sob shook her and she began to cry uncontrollably.

'Lydie, Lydie,' said the good Tom, 'Lydie what is it?'

'I never knew anyone who died before. I'm so silly, it's just new to me,' she said.

But she spent three days in uncontrollable sorrow, in tides of regrets that came and went: Tom could not help knowing that it was more than shock and be came angry on the third evening. On the third night he made love to her and she who had never refused him in her life didn't dare refuse him now.

Tom began to talk to everyone cheerfully about Paul saying 'Yes, I knew him, he was a great friend of mine,' and 'The last time I saw Paul he hardly listened to what I was saying: I guess his mind was on some girl: he was a great lover of the ladies,' and 'Oh, yes, I knew Paul intimately, I collaborated with him, but Lydie knew him even better than I did.' After a little while, this seemed very comic to Lydia, and whenever they began to talk about Paul's death and Tom said this, 'Yes, we were very close to him just before his death but Lydie knew him better than me, didn't you Lydie?' she would say 'Yes,' and begin to laugh. Everyone always looked astonished, but Tom's little gag continued to strike her as very funny. Meanwhile for quite a long time, perhaps two years or three, she knew that if the choice had been between lying in his Chinese grave with Paul or living her happy, unclouded and fertile life with Tom, she would have taken a long time to choose and what would have been the choice?

Paul had said 'Do my work for me,' but no-one can do another's work for him and who cares to? We only want to do our own work. She thought, though, 'I will work till I do a very fine piece of work – that will be in memory of Paul although no-one will know it (and it's better that they don't, they'd laugh at both of us, the three of us) – and then I won't mind what happens.'

And whenever she went out into company, she dressed very carefully, tried her hair various ways, wondered if tonight, or next week, she would meet the other Paul that the contemporary world probably held.

I Live in You

Peter, a lover, is dead now. He was a middlesized boyish
fair man about forty then, appealing, not jaunty, in an
English tweed jacket, suede shoes, a scarf and in the
coldest New York weather, a short loose coat just below
the knees. No one else then wore such a coat; he had got
it in the army surplus store. He worked in Madison
Avenue. After work, he roamed New York, visiting
unexpectedly. He gave invitations when he had loose
change; at other times, he was a guest. He had a good job
and good money, but he had several ex-wives to help out.

He had with him a bag of wishes, dreams, happenings,
like the Man in Grey and he poured out its contents on
the café table or standing in the doorway, or at ease in the
apartment, trying out the lewd, coarse, smutty, strange,
unheard-of, romantic, trying to fit you, poetry of artists,
customs of the race-divided southland, craft erotica, as of
laundrymen and undertakers, the love-hunger of living
and dead.

It was curious that he did not hold his audiences.

Perhaps that is why he blew about from one set to the other; for he did not have any set; he liked all sorts of people; he was a stray, a sample, from a swatch of metropolitan man. Or he did not hold them because he did not hold his women, loving as he was; and he admitted he did not hold them. Or perhaps the minstrel must wander: and he was a minnesinger. He told the horrors of war, (as Goya says 'Great deeds against the dead') how American soldiers in Alaska mutilated their victims just as the Welsh women did in *Henry IV* and hung their trophies on their tents to dry in the sun, a biltong or pemmican to take home to show their girls: and their camp could be nosed miles away, like reindeer, in the cold waste. He told about girls in closets, hearing the conspiracies of other girls, all naked; 'That is for you' he would say to an artist, 'you can use that story, I give it to you.' He would say to a writer, 'You will understand this, it happened to me in the rue d'Alésia in Paris,' and it would be a famous prostitute with a fullblown rose between her breasts.

Peter had how many love affairs! – If every wish and dream, contact and word of mouth, sentiment of desire and glance of admiration is a love affair: and to him all these were. There were the affairs with several women who had been or might become his wife; desires for girls who had kissed him at parties, who had married other men. This was love to him; it is love if you think so.

One day he said,

'When I was just married three months, I used to meet Janet my wife, in the public library. I stood near the pass-out gate with my stick, gloves and hat waiting for Janet, who worked there. I hate waiting and she was often late. I would look at the feet of people coming in for their books, if they went slow or fast. This time, I saw a woman whose feet attracted me. They were not beautiful but sexual. I looked up and saw the woman. I don't remember much; she was not beautiful, but her eyes looked straight at me and *knew* me. She had a faint smile and looked right into my eyes as if she knew all about me, had my number. Only her eyes and her feet – and I was will-less, almost trembling and did not notice my wife coming down the stairs only five or six feet away. I dropped my hat, gloves and cane, my strength was gone. The woman passed on, my wife came up and never knew; she thought I had been careless and dropped my hat and gloves.

'I worried about it for fourteen or fifteen days and was afraid to go to the library, but it was what I had to do. I was frightened. I had only been married three or four months. I was not spoiled then and I loved my wife. I still love her, though we are divorced. We remarried and redivorced. She divorced me in the end for my infidelity. I love women. She could not do otherwise. I agree with her.

'I began to look vaguely in crowds for this woman. I would watch feet. We had an apartment downstairs, feet would go past the grating, I would think to myself, "I know what kind of person that is." I would sit there, waiting for her. Some time later, I actually saw her again, on the corner of 42nd Street and 5th Avenue. I think I was just walking along towards the office when I passed her. I saw her, the feet sexual as before, the eyes. She looked at me, knew me, faintly smiled and passed on. She paused about eight yards away looking back. I looked at her, a pain went through me and I at once thought, "If I go after her, I will be helpless, this is a turning-point. If I go on to the office, I will be all right." I forced myself to go on to the office; it was a great effort of will and I kept regretting what I was doing. Perhaps the best way is to face these things, go towards the person, not away;

combat them and overcome them. But you can't combat those people. They have the Indian sign on you. They look at you and know. Just the same it must be the best of all experiences, to be completely possessed; and the worst? You could not win. They could not love you. What they want is possession. I still think and worry about it. But at the same time, I thought about Janet and bitterly, hopelessly regretted her; that was before I even lost her.

'I like to go up to people, to accept; I don't like to say no. You may be doing wrong to someone.

'Last week,' said Peter, 'I was going out to Connecticut and someone had left a ticket for me at the booking office. There was a queue and when my turn came, I asked for my ticket and said my name, Merryden. A woman behind me tapped me on the arm and said, "I live in you." That's the name of a town. She was an ordinary looking girl, nice and gentle.

'I was in Paris with Janet. I was about twenty-six and Janet was two years younger. We hadn't much money, just enough to get around a bit and go home to New York. One day, sitting on a café terrasse, on the left bank, I heard a woman going agh-agh, hoarse breathing. I looked round cautiously and saw an old woman. After a while, I saw her beckoning and I went. She told me she was all alone in Paris and wanted me and my wife for company for the afternoon; did I drive? Yes, but I had no car and no licence. She said she had plenty of money and showed me her alligator-skin bag full of money; and told me to engage a car or cab. I did that. She didn't want to go to the Bois. "Just go where you will feel happy and talk to me," she said. We drove around all the afternoon, from bar to bar and I had only beer for I saw it was going to take time.

'You get tired of beers. I wanted her to go home and rest. We drove to a big famous hotel, where she lived. She begged us to stay to dinner, because she felt sad. We went to her room, she sent for dinner, we had it with her and then she said she could not be left alone, she wanted us for the night. After some argument, she engaged a room in the hotel and we spent the night sitting up with her, in turn. This went on for three weeks; and during that time we were not alone together, for we took it in turns at night. We kept our room in the little hotel on the left bank, because it was always "just for today, just once more" and the expenses, which she paid, were also on a day-to-day basis.

'We sent for a nurse; but she quarrelled with her. She said she must have her friends, her only friends.

'After three weeks, a woman rang up asking for Mrs Gollardy, though I have forgotten her exact name, and when she heard of her condition, she was annoyed. "Why didn't she let me know?" This woman was Mrs Gollardy's friend and was not only a trained nurse herself, but kept an agency in Paris for Americans who needed nurses, sitters, such. Mrs Gollardy was the wife of a famous American artist, now dead. They had lived in Paris many years, knew everybody: she spoke French fairly well, was at home there.

'Hearing this, we left. She always had her purse under her bed gaping and in it always thousands of francs. She kept saying I reminded her of her son. When we left, she gave us two presents nicely wrapped, one for Janet and one for me. Janet's was a pink cotton nightdress, very unattractive, mine was an expensive alligator-skin wallet, empty. All this time the big open alligator-skin bag had been under our noses, under the bed, full of money. We went on with our holiday and went home.

'Some years later, Mrs Gollardy telephoned me in New York and asked me to cocktails. I came to the café with my wife Binnie and the woman without looking at Binnie, or asking about her, asked me if I would go to Greece with her as her chauffeur. I said no. About a year after that, her son rang up. He said he was her son, and that his mother had died in Greece, all alone; and in one of her last letters, she asked him to telephone me to thank me for my kindness. That was her last wish. That was all though.'

'Last Monday,' said Peter, at another time, 'my wife Mary left me. I was best man at her wedding and she loved me, not the bridegroom and she came to me and we married. I don't know why I didn't marry her first. Now I am waiting for her to come back to me. But she says she has left me; she won't come back, she says. I meant to leave the apartment and I should have given notice; but I didn't. I keep telephoning Mary to come back and I will wait. I am going to wait. If she doesn't, I will just sit there with my cases half packed and I won't do anything about it. I love her and her alone.'

He was away for a while on a business trip and next time we saw him he said, 'I was in California staying with a friend who is an undertaker. I know a lot of undertakers in California. There is business there. Undertakers are drinkers and very erotic. I went to their banquet and they told a lot of stories.'

Here he told some of the stories, wild, repugnant, agonising; and he continued, 'This man I stayed with told me about a love-affair. The undertakers, you see, have a trochar, an instrument they use, about the length and appearance of a steel for sharpening knives. It has blades so thin and fine you can't even touch them with the finger, they cut right in. It is hollow and in it is a tube and something to work the tube. It is used for withdrawing blood, juices and things like that. A young couple about twenty-two had gassed themselves; she was twenty-one, I think; and they had committed suicide in a love-pact. The bodies were removed to separate sections, male and female. My friend had to prepare the female body. He undressed her, thought, a nice looking girl, nice figure and with a certain feeling of admiration, he inserted the trochar. After a minute or two, I'm not sure how long, the girl stirred, sat up suddenly, looked at him; he could see she was aware. She screamed. There was only one thing to do; her injuries could not be repaired. He knocked her out, finished her, murdered her and went on with his work. That was all he could do.'

We took Peter to see a friend of ours, an unlucky woman, very handsome but with white hair and too fat, so that she kept losing lovers, and was always looking for new men. There were some Manhattan people there, all wellknown, good company and we had a good dinner with an exceptional mixed salad, lettuce, artichoke hearts, palm hearts, avocados, tomatoes, I think. There was plenty to drink, Peter liked to drink and was at ease, full of romantic anecdotes. When we left one of the women came with us, a full not yet heavy blonde, who was working as a typist in a publishing office, but not for long she said; she wanted to be an editor. She had an apartment not far away up a long flight of stairs I had never noticed, next to a hotel in University Place. 'Can I come up with you?' said Peter, who had been talking bawdy. The girl laughed a little, 'No,' said she. She went up the stairs and Peter climbed up after her. The next day the whitehaired woman telephoned to ask Peter's telephone number. 'He's to my taste,' said she; 'and I can see what he is.' But Peter had some reason for not going. 'She was complaining about her lovers: I don't like that.'

He then told more about California. 'I was at a party where I met the Stonebecks and other famous people like that, but not all rich. It was in the hills. Not many had cars and the man I was with drove the Stonebecks home. We also brought back two guests, a young woman and an oldish woman, in a strictly Greenwich Village get-up, a kind of monkey jacket and a long dress tied round her with a cord, lowheeled shoes and white or grey hair cut in a long bob, also very Village. She had a plump face, big eyes, signs of age, but she had confidence and fun. She was the last guest in our car and Marty my friend wanted a drink, so I dropped him at his house saying I'd take her home. We were speeding up towards her home along a road rimmed with trees or cut through a plantation. It was full moon and I was very drunk, but exactly on the hairline, the backbone of the ridge, so very alert that I saw the grains of stones on the road, the outlines of leaves, and the shadows cast by the full moon, almost green it shone so full. I thought, It's a blue moon. I was aware of smells, noises. It happened that my driving was too perfect, a touch and it turned, a touch and it stopped, or went on. I touched it, it stopped a small distance from the woman's home and I thought I would light a cigarette. I don't know why I did it. For some reason I turned the key and the car stopped, I just had a general feeling of exhilaration, command, on top of the world. I tapped the cigarette on my hand, lighted it, the light of the cigarette and the slant of the moonlight fell on the woman's nose, slender and young and her large sweet eyes. In a second, I had thrown away the cigarette, embraced her and was conscious only of a young girl. We got out of the car, nothing said, and went into the trees and there I took her and again, nothing said. Her breasts, too, and all about her seemed a young girl. Afterwards, when she was walking towards her house, where her husband was waiting for her, only about seventy or eighty yards away, I went down to the car. An instinct told me not to look round, but after a few steps, I did and I saw, climbing the hill, an old woman, back, buttocks, bent head of an old woman with the boyish cut unsuitable for her grey hair.'

Peter went on with his adventures and lonely life. He did not care for politics, though he made the curious ingenious observations of the unengaged. He liked food and drink, would play tricks to get them; at the same time, was always out to oblige friends; and sometimes, his pride would be hurt, and his friends had to wait for him to come back; he always came back, full of kindness, with never a reproach. Or if he made a reproach it was quite incomprehensible; and if he reproached you, you might have to pay for a drinking bout before the smear was wiped off you. But no one reproached him. He had spoken about knives in his middle. When he went into hospital for the knives, Mary his wife died; and when he got home, they had sent her luggage to him. For months, he lived on in the apartment with the cases and bundles set around as the men had left them. He opened one, saw a nightdress, shut the case and never unlocked another. He kept them there that way until he died. He did not live to old age.

My Friend, Lafe Tilly

Lafe Tilly wore his hatbrim down, and his coat collar up; there were round spectacles over his hollow eyes. A little of the yellow face could be seen. He stood by the lamp, looking down. He did not take off his gloves.

'I was at a funeral last week. There was the widow and another woman, the man's brother and I myself, his only mourners. Once he had hundreds of friends, thousands perhaps. Hundreds of women loved him.'

Lafe Tilly smiled.

'He was cremated; and before that they had to embalm him and make him a new face. His was gone.'

'Gone?'

'Eva and I knew them years ago, years before any of us were married. I was a stunt pilot then: I lived in Brooklyn like everyone in our crowd; and Joe Cornaco stood out in the crowd, very political, a big talkative man, dark, thin faced, greedy for women, spending a lot on dress, always clean shaved. He treated all the women badly. We believed in sex equality and did not think any woman had the right to complain. I married Eva, the first to marry; and soon after that Joe married Donna, a woman in our set who had been with us for years.

'She was a few months older than Joe and he talked about it. He made her a partner in his real estate business. She became his office-manager. She worked hard, stayed back every night to clean up business; she looked after the staff and did his work when he was out with girls. He was out nearly every evening.

'She had been working since she was fifteen. She had never been to college. Joe had a younger brother Victor who was sent to college and became a lawyer. Donna turned out to have a good business head, better than Joe had; and she put her savings into his business, about five thousand dollars.

'Although Joe was never sentimental, always calling a spade a spade, he got into trouble several times with women. A young woman who was always dressed in black, a thin thing, committed suicide. She tried several times; no one believed her and in the end she managed it in the bath.'

He smiled most curiously. It was like a waxen face reflected in moving water, not a smiling man.

'It was after that that Donna asked him to marry her, for his own sake. He knew she was in love with him and he liked that, the quiet, loyal, patient woman to whom he complained and who understood him. They had a talk; he put his views to her: she agreed with everything he said.

'He said, "You are getting the best of the bargain, since you will be both my wife and my partner; and you are getting the man you love, whereas I do not love you." "Yes," she said. "Therefore," Joe said, "we had better have an agreement to safeguard me. You agree to look after my business and my home; you study at night to get a degree so that you will be my equal. No children. I am to have my entire liberty, as I have now, as an unmarried man." Donna agreed to everything. Between them they drew up the marriage contract and they made his brother, Victor, a lawyer by then, go over the clauses. Victor told Donna that it had no validity being contrary to public policy. She said, "If I keep to it and he keeps to it, it will be binding. We both know what we are doing." "But if he divorces you?" "He will not divorce me. He will have no reason to." "But what about you, Donna?" "I love Joe and I never expected to marry him. I know I'm not good looking. I consider I'm lucky." "Why get married?" people said to them both. But they were satisfied. A friend called Cowan and I signed the contract as witnesses. Cowan died years ago.'

He looked straight ahead, continued, 'Now Donna took into her office young girls who attracted Joe and she made friends of any other women he wanted. It was strange how they all trusted her. When, at home, he went into the backroom with a girl, she sat chatting with the others, or read a book, or did the housework till the couple came out. If they stayed there for long, she went to bed. She always said that jealousy had been left out of her nature. She didn't know how it was. All women are jealous, aren't they?' said Lafe Tilly smiling.

'Joe's brother Victor was tall, dark, fleshy, with red damp lips. He was very fond of women, too; but he went after them differently, explaining his troubles, abusing Joe, using the word love. When Joe was away for the weekend with some girl, Victor would be at the house, eating and drinking with Donna. If ever Donna complained, it was to Victor. Victor had always been jealous of Joe and he would go round spreading gossip; Donna told me this. Joe had illegitimate children, all being supported by the mothers. Donna had no children. Victor sometimes stayed the night at Donna's apartment. It was a long way to his mother's home in Queen's. "I want children," he said to Donna; "when my mother dies, I will marry. I am sorry you have no children; you would make a good mother." But Donna did not sleep with him and never had a sweetheart. She was respected and had a following among Joe's male friends.'

After a pause, Lafe said harshly, 'She was a bawd for Joe, she played on the trust the girls had in her. She was good to them as long as he wanted them and afterwards she might dry their tears for them. It depended on how they stood with Joe.'

Lafe Tilly laughed suddenly; and then became serious and reasonable as before.

'I used to see Joe on the street. He was always the same, smart, spending money on himself; and they were making money between them, a lot of money. He nicked himself once when shaving and the nick didn't heal. He went about with bits of sticking plaster on his cheek. The scratch grew and he would go about without dressing it saying the air would heal it. Later he had an operation and he kept going to the hospital for skin graftings. He went about as jaunty as ever. People began to avoid him. I did. But he didn't understand it. I know Donna tried to persuade him to stay at home; and when he insisted on going to work, she wanted him to go in the car and come straight home afterwards. They had some rows over it. He thought she was trying to keep him away from girls. He said, Remember you signed a contract with me; keep your word. The worse his looks, the more frantic he was about girls and he thought everyone was standing in his way.'

Tilly glimmered a smile.

'Naturally, I guessed. I told him to go home and stay home. He got very angry and I didn't see him again.

'About four months ago, I had a note at the office from Donna, which said, "Joe says please come to see him and bring Eva with you. Come Thursday afternoon." Underneath this was written, "I have written what Joe asked me to, but do not bring your wife. If you want to see him you had better come now."

'It was a new address, away out, a wooden house, on an earth bank in a long dusty street of such houses, all three-storey, with steps in front, downhill off a four-lane highway. There was a funeral home a few doors down.'

Lafe showed the sharp point of his tongue as he drew in his breath.

'I found the number which was one that Joe had always thought a lucky number. The windows were shut, with drapes on all the windows; it looked well cared for. The door was opened by a good looking young girl, serious, fair type, in a house dress. She showed me into the front room and went away. There was complete silence for a while, then Donna came in. She had changed very little. She had healthy looks; her cheeks were fat and red, her black hair was braided over her broad head and she had on some sort of aesthetic smock, brown, with hand embroidery and unusual buttons. She collected buttons. It was the same sort of squaw outfit she had always worn and which she liked better than shop clothes. It was part of their revolt against machine-made things. She had fine eyes, but solid as stones, denser than dogs' eyes. Otherwise, she is short, thickset and has a slow flat voice.

'When I started to get up, she said, "Sit down, Lafe."

'She spoke in low tones, like the girl, and said Joe was

asleep. He needed all the sleep he could get; he would be
in a bad temper if not rested. She said she'd get me a
drink. I said, "Not yet, wait for Joe." She said, "You'll
need it." She went out and came back with a full bottle of
Scotch whisky, which she opened and put in front of me
on the table, with one glass. She didn't want any. She
asked me if I wanted some water and went away for it; but
did not return.

'No one came. I thought I heard a whisper once; apart
from that, the house was quiet. I poured myself a drink
and had it. After a long time, the young girl came in with
a jug of water and some ice. She seemed to be a servant, so
I didn't offer her any; and Donna stayed away. I just sat
there and drank by myself. It was hot and still. Sometimes
I thought I heard a soft noise somewhere in the house or a
car on the dirt road; that was all. There was nothing to
do, so I just sat there on the sofa and got quite
comfortable.

'The curtains were partly drawn. The sun fell on blue
patches of carpet and various yellows. The place was kept
very clean. On the wall were crude paintings, the sort we
used to collect when naive art was the fad. Besides these
and the furniture, there were two mirrors, a long one
between two windows and a big square one standing on
the floor, very large, with a lacy acanthus-leaf frame, the
frame about eight inches deep and with rusty gilding. It
was out of place. There was a woman's hand-glass on the
mantelpiece, some bookshelves with old intellectual best-
sellers, nothing for me to read. I could see the door of the
room across the hall; that was all.

'I had drunk at least half the bottle when I heard
footsteps and something being dragged. There was a slow
shuffle coming nearer. A door opened, there was a
whisper and in answer to it, I heard a strange voice, a

cawing. People were coming along the hall together. Then three people stood in the doorway. There were women behind and in front, in a dressing-gown, and slippers, wearing an eyeshade was a man. He had an immense lipless mouth, the cheeks were blown out and he wore an eyeshade. There was a paisley scarf round his neck up to the chin. They must have just fixed the scarf round his neck, because he was impatiently pulling if off as he shuffled into the room. He took no notice of me, but he approached the glass on the floor, which was at an angle so that he could see himself walking. He signalled, and they put the hand-glass into his hand. He dropped the scarf on the floor and took off the eyshade. Then he began taking a careful look at himself, turning his face this way and that. He made a sound of irritation and gestured. The girl switched on the top light. The man continued to observe himself in detail. While this was going on, the girl went away and returned with a tray of coffee and other things, which she placed on the table near me. Donna stood there calmly, looking from one to the other. Presently, she said, "Lafe Tilly is here, Joe."

'The man made an irritable sound which they seemed to understand.

'The wife said in her flat commanding voice, "He's at the table by the window, if you'll look, Joe. He's been waiting."

'The man turned. I started to get up. I was drunk perhaps. I looked at him and fell back again into the soft old couch. Joe seemed to laugh. He touched his cheek, shook his head, uttered sounds and looked at me, nodding his head slowly. Donna said, "Joe says he thinks he has improved this week. It is the hot weather which does him good." The man said something. The wife said, with calm shining eyes, "Joe thinks you can understand him and that I am insulting him by interpreting. Tell him you can't, Lafe."

'I said, "Are you feeling better, Joe?"

'At further sounds from him, the girl left the room; but the wife said, "Joe, I must stay if you are going to talk to Lafe. Lafe doesn't understand a word you say." She continued to me, "Lisbeth has gone to make more coffee. Joe's is cold. Joe always drank very hot coffee, you remember; but now he never gets it. It takes so long to drink. Well, it is not our fault, Joe." There seemed to be mirth underlying her stubborn words. She continued, "Joe is not allowed to drink whisky. It would choke him. He would choke to death."

'Joe made conversation. He drew me out about politics, contradicting everything I said. He talked a lot about his health, with which he was fairly satisfied. He had improved considerably, he said, since his teeth had come out. It was a good idea of his doctor's; and it should have been done years before. He ate better and felt better. If the teeth had been taken out years before he would not have had the skin trouble. He had always had excellent teeth, always sound and white; so he had not thought of it. "Joe always had a bad skin," said the wife.

'She interpreted everything he said, being constantly interrupted by Joe. She laughed once, saying, "Joe says I am treating him like a child; he just has a speech impediment for a short time, but his speech is coming back."

'Lisbeth came with fresh coffee and poured a cup for Joe. He took a drop on his tongue from time to time and complained. Donna said. "It is no use getting mad at us, Joe. You drink so slowly that it can't help getting cold. You take a whole hour to drink a single cup of coffee."

'Joe was sitting at the table facing the long mirror between the windows. He held out his hand and Lisbeth brought him the hand-glass. He continued to study his appearance with care, while he drank.

' "Ah-ah-ah," said Joe.

' "Joe wants to know why you supplied such bad paper for those new books. The ink shows through."

'I said, "We were told not to waste paper; but to use paper that the men could tear out and use in the latrines."

'Evidently Joe was laughing.

' "Ah-ah-ah."

'Joe says "Are you still with Tacker and Taylor?"

' "Yes."

'Joe says, "Is Ben Taylor still a melancholic?"

' "Just the same."

'Joe says, "He never did appeal to women. He couldn't get them."

'Joe was trying to shout with rage. In an undertone, Lisbeth said to Donna, "Let him talk."

'He wrangled with the women, equally furious if they translated or if they neglected his remarks; and at times, he rolled a drop of cold coffee round his tongue. He made enquiries after people and asked why Eva had not come.

' "She used to be one of my girls in the old days. She had a crush on me. She always had her blue eyes fixed on me." Joe laughed.

' "Donna had the crazy idea of moving out here where no one can reach me and where I can't get into town. She made a promise to me. You know that. She is not keeping that promise. I'm a prisoner here. These women keep me in jail. Afraid of competition, they're not getting any younger."

'He kept insulting Donna and Lisbeth. Donna translated the insults without emotion.

' "I'll soon be back in circulation and I'll make up for lost time. You won't cheat me!"

'He showed temper, shouted, caught sight of himself

and once more began his careful inspection.

'Presently, they helped him to get out of his chair. He wanted to lie down; he was tired.

' "Rest is everything. Sleep rests the skin. I look much better in the morning when I get up," he said to me.

'Donna went out to the front gate with me and I said, "How long will it be?"

' "The doctor said it might be two months; he's starving."

' "He doesn't seem to suffer much."

' "He's drugged all the time. He's full of aspirin. And they did some slight operation. Joe's last message to you was to bring Eva. Don't bring her and don't tell anyone. I can't have people."

' "Who's the girl?"

' "A girl he wanted me to engage about eighteen months ago. I don't know whether she fell for him or she was sorry for him. I don't know if they had an affair. What does it matter now? It's six months since that. But he wouldn't understand it if I sent her away. It's all he's got. It was always the greatest thing in his life, his way with women. He would never have gone in for politics; he didn't care for the business. This was the greatest thing. It's not his fault, is it? It's a fault of nature."

' "And he doesn't know it's over?"

'She laughed shortly. "It's hard to believe; but he has just bought two tickets for himself and Lisbeth to go to Lourdes. It's only a lupus he has, he says. It's nerves. He'll be cured there. He read about a thing like that in Zola. The girl in the book washed her face in the fountain and the lupus at once began to heal."

' "And you, Donna?"

' "I'll keep on looking after the business. We've done very well. There'll be big changes round here. Victor helps me. We got the land and houses cheap years ago. I'll be all right."

'A couple of days ago,' said Lafe Tilly, 'I got the funeral notice at the office. Eva knows nothing about it, so don't mention it to her.'

'No.'

'She used to admire Joe in the old days; he dazzled her. Eva never understood men. She's naive. Joe took her sister and left her; that is why she married me. Eva and her sister were always rivals. I thought of marrying her sister, too.'

After a pause, he continued quietly, 'Lisbeth was at the funeral. Joe's brother Victor was there, assisting Donna. I think Donna expected to marry him. I went back with them to the gate. Donna said, "You'll come in, won't you, Victor?" But he jammed on his hat, said he had an appointment and hurried up the street, his big legs going fast.

'Donna did not seem to notice anything. She told Lisbeth to wait at the gate and asked me to go in. I went. She gave me a valise and a box tied with string and asked me to carry them to the girl at the gate. Donna stood on the porch and called out to the girl, "You must go away now. You can't stay here." The girl took the bag and box, said goodbye and turned away.

' "Come in, Lafe and have a drink," said Donna. "In a minute," I said. I said to the girl, "Where are you going? Home?"

' "No, they threw me out. I'll find a place."

' "Can I get you a taxi?"

' "No. I have no money. I'll find a place."

'I went in just to see what Donna would say. "You don't mind letting the girl go like that?"

' "What has she to do with me?"

' "But you lived together for eight months."

' "I don't know her name or her address; she is nothing to me. She took my husband from me. I don't care what happens to her."

' "But Donna she has nowhere to go."

' "He never cared for her. She threw herself at him. The women are shameless these days. You can't blame Joe. I was not like the others. He married me."

' "Would you like to see Eva?"

' "No. No women any more. I don't have to now."

' "Donna, why did you go through with it?"

' "You know I signed a contract with him. You were there: you witnessed it."

' "And you stood it for that reason?"

' "Joe and I had a contract. We agreed on everything. We understood each other."

'I passed Donna today,' Lafe said. 'She looked just the same, leathery skin, with a slight moustache, a dark felt hat, a black belted dress, her satchel. Her eyes were on the sidewalk and her brown lips muttered occasionally. I was going to meet a blonde, so I avoided her.'

He glanced sideways. 'Donna's a virgin. Imagine it.' He grinned.

'Why do you tell these stories, Lafe?'

He said nothing.

'Because you feel the pain?'

'Yes, people live in pain.'

'Would you like a drink?'

'No. Goodbye. Don't tell Eva.'

'No.'

An Iced Cake with Cherries

Mrs Anderson was very busy one Friday evening. She went to bed early, scurried about in the night and had a good deal to say to herself. When she was having breakfast she put her finger on a spot of coffee and remarked:

'Wet. Those who travel understand a lot. For example, I was told, a certain man told me, that 'wet' in Dutch means 'law'; Wetstraat means Law Street. Naturally, a man with a gift for languages. You're either born with it or you're not. However, you can talk for an hour and not say anything.'

She continued disgustedly: 'I prefer those who speak plain.'

'Then you must speak plain and not in crossword puzzles,' said her son Gilbert, laughing.

She spat fire. 'Plain! Yes, it's very suitable for a plain old woman. I speak plainly – others do not.'

Gilbert and his wife Nellie laughed. Said Mrs Anderson:

217

'Very well, laugh. I know what I'm talking about.'

'I know you do, but we don't,' said Gilbert.

'You can judge a man by the way he treats old people. If a man has respect for old people, then he is a fine man. A man who never gives a thought to anyone but himself is either a miser or he's greedy. He never puts his hand in his pocket! A miser! An egotist! That's disgraceful for a young man, unmarried.'

'What is the trouble, Mamma?' said Gilbert.

'Never mind, never mind.' She sat grieving. When asked to have more coffee she said: 'Never mind, not for me, not for the old.' But later she took some.

When Gilbert went shopping he asked: 'Is there anything you would like, Mamma?'

'Oh, don't trouble yourself, you're very kind,' she said charmingly, making her little bow. Before he had made a step she went up close and remarked sagely:

'Old is old. We must not complain. There's nothing can be done about it. Arsenic cure in Romania perhaps. Bogomolotz they said; but who knows? They advertise. I digest nothing. For example, sardines are greasy and hard to digest. Even the best – say, Portuguese or French. They're dear, also they're just as indigestible. Then they smell out the icebox. What a pity! Who can eat a whole box, too? So much money thrown in the street, you might say. Of course, there is the taste, very good. I read in a medical magazine that doctors are beginning to discuss whether it is more than a question of calories and vitamins; there is taste, too. Why is taste given to us? There must be a reason. Nothing exists without a reason. Well, there you see, perhaps a nice-tasting sardine makes a nourishing sandwich.'

'Well, I'll get some sardines, then.'

'Sardeenkee, Gilbert, sardeenkee, do you know that is what the Russians say?'

'And what else, Mamma?'

'Oh, but Russian is such a pure language, no one, no foreigner could learn it. No, it's no use. It is too pure.'

'Mamma!'

'Sardines, I am sorry to say, are a very good taste, but what is there to them? A bite and they're gone! It's not practical, my dear. The young cannot understand and it is better so. An old woman is better off taking oatmeal. Only it happens in my case that I cannot digest oatmeal. Besides, what is it but an excuse for taking milk and sugar? I would do better to take milk and sugar in my tea; and then the tea remains hot longer. At the same time, I prefer lemon tea – it's more delicate. They say eggs have come down; did you hear that? Of course, eggs are bad for the liver. I knew a woman, a lovely woman with twenty-seven rooms, she ran a boarding house and she never ate an egg. Oh, my dear, she had bright eyes, like stars! "What is the reason for your remarkable health, Mrs Saxon," I asked. We used to meet in the afternoons, in the park. "I have a very poor liver," she told me; "and my son too. We never touch eggs." You can learn from everyone.'

'Well, I'll get eggs,' said Gilbert.

Standing there, in the same bright, touching and philosophical manner, Mrs Anderson discussed the way to make omelettes (above all, a special pan, oiled but never washed, though she never touched oil), meatballs (a combination of veal and beef, finely chopped), string beans (bad for the liver); and she also mentioned several surgical cases she had heard of. There was a man, a native-born citizen, who had his stomach removed and the large intestine joined to the oesophagus, and after walking bent double for eighteen months he had been able to become a waiter in the Palace Hotel. Gilbert observed that he knew a literary man who remained a literary man after the same operation. Mrs Anderson became worried. She said in a gloomy manner:

'And there are some who live entirely on salads; but in my opinion salads are full of water and lead to dropsy.'

'Anything else, Mamma?' said Gilbert, opening the door.

Mrs Anderson clung to the doorpost and peeped around it, looking frail and irresolute. It was hard for her to mention anything outright; it was a breach of diplomacy. She said shamefacedly:

'Who knows if brown bread is better than white?'

'Well, I shall get some brown bread.'

'Brown bread – naturally, some people live on nothing but that. As for the Russians, what beautiful teeth! Oh, like pearls! Every tooth in their heads sound until they're a hundred, perhaps more. But as for their cooking, it's that of barbarians. And the Romanians broil bits of raw meat hard over an open fire. No, give me barley soup or some white fish, even a pancake – I can manage that sometimes.'

Gilbert said; 'Well, I'd better write this down.' He made a note. He knew something more was required and waited. There was a silence. Mrs Anderson crept to the doorsill and coming very close, took hold of his arm and said:

'Supposing anyone comes in the afternoon – suddenly, unannounced! There's tea – what's that? In China, even when you're doing business, people put a cup of tea before you: it's mere custom. Coloured water! There should be more. Say, a chocolate cake!'

Having thus expressed her wish, Mrs Anderson drew back and looked quite cross.

'Why, is anyone coming this afternoon?' he asked, knowing that someone must be.

She turned her back and looked sulkily around.

'Who knows? Who knows? Strangers knock at the door. They say: "How are you?" Must I turn them away? They say: "Don't you remember me?" We met twenty years ago, perhaps. Or ten years. I have a head like a cat. And who remembers a child? But men are boys. A chocolate cake is never wrong.'

Gilbert said; 'Ah-ha! So it's cavaliers now, gigolos at teatime! Valentines!'

Mrs Anderson turned pink; but she smiled roguishly. 'What an idiot!' She pretended to be waspish: 'Naturally, here I sit all alone, no one visits, no one knows me. Incognito! Life draws to evening and I must sit like a mouse in a hole.'

Gilbert laughed outright: 'Don't try your tricks on me, Mamma! Tell me the name of the man.'

She half turned: 'Go on, go! I must put the dishes together. A person lives with you three years and never brings you as much as –' (she showed the tip of her little finger) 'that of a cake. No thought, no heart. Another person, who scarcely knows you at all, calls upon you and brings you an iced cake with cherries on top. I call that good manners. Manners are born, not taught: they come from the heart. To be kind to the old is a sign of good character. We have nothing to offer; so if they love us, we are grateful!'

Gilbert cried out; 'Theodore! My cousin Theodore is coming.'

'Theo! Pooh! You know nothing – a grown-up child.' Suddenly she cackled angrily: 'Theo! He spent three years in my house and never thought of bringing home so much as a sausage, not a solitary piece of chicken, not an egg.'

'But he paid us rent,' said Gilbert. He became enthusiastic. Theodore, his cousin from Germany, had knocked at the door when Gilbert was fifteen and Theodore about twenty-six: 'I'm your cousin Theodore from Hamburg.'

Gilbert reminded his mother of this. She now said:

'Yes, it could have been a highway robber; I come back and there I find a man in my house.'

'But it was Theodore.'

'It could have been Al Capone – a gangster! At five you had more sense than at fifteen.'

Theodore had studied medicine, qualified, become a sailor, joined the merchant marine for three years, skipped ship on the New York docks. He had nothing but the address of an aunt he had never seen, Aunt Mollie Anderson. Mrs Anderson said now, looking angrily at Gilbert:

'You would believe any story. Your work in Wall Street. Where did it get you? You should get a degree.'

Gilbert chuckled: 'They don't give you degrees in Wall Street.'

Theo had found a job as a labourer and lodged with them for three years, paying rent; a quiet steady man who read books and went to bed at ten o'clock.

'And then he got married suddenly to an *Italienische*, without telling me and without inviting me,' said Mrs Anderson.

They had a few words about Theodore, Mrs Anderson getting sourer and sourer.

Gilbert said: 'Well I want to see old Theodore. I like him. He's sedate but he's honest.'

'Honest! What do you know? Your tongue wags but you say nothing. It's George who's coming.'

'How do you know?'

'He appeared.'

'When?'

'Mm-mm! Such good manners!'

'When, Mamma?'

'He paid me a visit about a week ago. I don't know. He had to hurry away – he had business.'

Gilbert went to do the shopping. When he returned he talked about the family. He also wanted to see his cousin George. George and Theodore were the sons of a dead brother of Mrs Anderson, a man full of promise, a man of genius, she said, who died early in life. He was too modest, said Mrs Anderson. It was only after his death that they found in his desk his gold medals for law and philosophy. He was not one to boast. Mrs Anderson's family was medal-bespangled.

'Mother always calls him Emil, the Genius, the Soul of Honour,' said Gilbert to his wife, at the table.

'They talk most who know least,' said Mrs Anderson.

Gilbert continued: 'And then we have Heinrich the Angel, and Herr Doktor, the Professor, my father; but you will never hear Mother mention Moritz der Zwerg, yet Maurice the Dwarf was the brightest of all. He turned Catholic, took his wife's name and taught philosophy in France. The name of Maurice the Dwarf is never mentioned by us. He was as small as Mamma; he barely scraped five feet. And there was Aunt Thekla who wrote romances for servant-girls.'

'Pfui! Trash!' said Mrs Anderson, 'but a so rich woman, never mind.'

After lunch, the table was laid with an embroidered cloth, the tea-things were set out; the chocolate cake put in the centre. George, when he had 'appeared' the week before, had brought an iced cake with cherries on top, which the two of them had eaten. Now it was right to reciprocate, mere good manners.

'It is a nice cake,' said the old woman, 'yes, very nice,

chocolate is good. Of course, there are no cherries, but never mind; it is nice as it is. Imagine, so poor! He had no coat, only a shirt with no tie.'

'And he had been in Holland,' said Gilbert.

'Holland! What nonsense!' she cried angrily.

'Not in Wetstraat?'

'Tt, tt! Never mind. Who knows? People don't talk. I ask no questions.'

They lived on the ground floor, right on the lobby. Beyond their front door, which was up two steps, was a considerable space, with two lifts, one near them and one near the front door, the doorman's desk, palms in tubs and in the middle a staircase. Immediately to the left of the building was a park built on a cliff-face and descending into Harlem.

George arrived in a jacket, a tieless shirt, cotton trousers, and sandshoes, a middle-sized man with a harassed boy-face. He carried a big unframed painting. He rushed past Gilbert, who opened the door, hurried along the L-shaped passage, looking into the rooms, found a bedroom to the left, ran in, opened a cupboard door and placed the painting inside. Meanwhile they stood in the passage with welcoming smiles, dodging as he ran past them. He came out of the bedroom saying:

'It's a painting someone gave me to sell. It'll be safe here. I've just been put out of my room and the weather's so tricky I can't take it with me. Tonight I'll have to sleep in the park.'

Mrs Anderson grasped his hands, reached up to kiss his cheek, hastily begging for details.

'Are you so poor, Georgie, you can't pay your rent?'

Gilbert said in a jolly tone that it was all right, we need not worry, the painting could stay there 'until the cows come home'. Where did he intend to sell it? George had had an offer; he expected to get $10,000 for it. But he must lie low for a couple of days. The police were after him on account of his rent. Then, unluckily, the room in which he had spent only a week, had before that been rented to a sneak-thief. The police had mistaken him for the thief. He had had to make a getaway over the roofs.

'Over the roof, George!' said Mrs Anderson with anxiety. She looked him over; no bruise, no broken limb. 'But couldn't you explain who you were? You have papers!'

'Get beat up first, explain afterwards,' said George, walking to the table, which he could see through the glass doors. George sat at one end of the table, his legs stretched out, talking in an undertone to his aunt, who hung over him, her little white head and her big black eyes nodding at him. He was tired and hungry; he seemed exhausted. But he ate and drank with excellent manners and only glanced once or twice at the chocolate cake before he was asked to have some. Then he took four slices, as they were pressed on him. He was polite to everyone, yet in an absence, like a sick person. He suddenly said:

'You don't know what trouble I'm in, Aunt.'

He had not eaten properly for a long time, had nowhere to sleep, no clothes. He could come back here and spend the night on a divan in the livingroom; and he would be no bother. Then he seemed anxious to leave. She lifted her hands high, pressed back the loose hair, straightened his collar.

They stood at the door. George left them in a curious way. He opened the lift door, next to them, and went up in the lift. Perhaps he had a friend in the building. They shut the door.

A little while later the doorbell rang and there stood a policeman to ask if a Mr Joe Miller was there. Did they know him, a young man with dark hair selling men's shirts? At that moment another policeman entered the building and seeing his mate in conversation, approached. Behind him a young man's quick slight figure, carrying a valise, slipped down from the stairway and hurried into the street, turning towards the park.

'He is somewhere in the building,' said the policeman.

Gilbert, full of friendly, lively denials, left the policeman with the doorman at the desk. He closed the door.

Back in the diningroom Mrs Anderson was weeping. Oh, the troubles of poor young men with nowhere to go! At the same time it was evident that she was very nervous. George had seemed so worried. He had brought nothing, so unlike a boy with his manners. Something else worried her – what was it? Gilbert said:

'I think there's something fishy about George with the good manners; I think he's a phony, Mamma.'

'Your tongue's wagging like a clapper in a bell and doesn't know what tune it's playing,' she cried, darting up and seizing the tea-things to carry out. 'Such a remark! A poor man with nowhere to sleep and he's fishy. I gave Theodore a place to sleep for three years; and you, Gilbert – all of your life.'

'Don't be angry, Mamma.'

'And who was that at the door?' she asked hysterically.

'Who, at the door? Such a nuisance. Nothing but magazines and vacuum-cleaners. We're on the ground floor, never in my life – anyone could walk in. Who ever heard of such a thing? You're old enough to know better.'

'It was the police at the door,' said Gilbert.

At this Mrs Anderson froze, grasping the dishes tighter; then set in motion, like a machine, she ran out to the kitchen.

'The police! What nonsense! They call on everyone these days. What a state things are in!'

'The police,' repeated Gilbert, who had had time to get upset. 'They are looking for a young man selling shirts.'

Mrs Anderson was silent.

George came back at a quarter to twelve at night. He looked worn and tear-stained but he said confidently that he had been at a business conference and that now he would remain with them for a few days; he had the promise of a room soon.

They all slept badly on account of the police; and then there were quiet noises in the house. It was Mrs Anderson 'creeping about like a mouse', as she said; and there was a soft light in the hall. George was on the divan in the livingroom.

Mrs Anderson was sitting in her best dressing-gown, her hair in two tiny plaits, by the bedside of the young man. He was lying on his back with his large dark eyes open and looking upwards. From time to time he turned his face to her, with an expression of trust and intimacy.

Her hand was lying on the eiderdown pleating it and she said:

'You were right to come to me, darling. Here they are all selfish – in America they have hard hearts. They laugh and enjoy themselves. And it's no use talking to those here about your mother. Least said soonest mended. I realise she could not look after you, a widow. Leave it to me. I'll write to her. But hush! Not a word to them. Here you might as well be in a robbers' den. He and she, he and she; that's all. A bird fell in the courtyard, they took it in and fed it, but it died. They threw it out with the rubbish, a living creature that had died. They will do the same to me. They will throw you out if they know. Not a word, you hear!'

The young man, turning his thin face to her said very low:

'Aunt Mollie, I knew I could come to you. The trouble is nowadays people simply don't believe anything and don't want to help. And then, about mother . . .'

'Sh! Walls have ears. They ask questions in this house. No one is safe. You are safe with me. I am penniless. I haven't a bankroll sewn in my drawers, as you might think.' Here she laughed. 'But if anything comes my way, if I can save or get from them – never mind, I'll give it to you for her, poor Rosa. I know you, you would never beg. You stay here, darling, and never mind what is said. I'll give you some money – a little bit, no more than chicken-feed, for what have I? Selfish is the world, my poor boy. Stay with me. I'm alone, you see. And there's room: it's as big as a palace.'

She leaned over and kissed him. He put both hands on her ears and drew her head down:

'Dear Aunt! I was right to come to you.'

She whispered: 'Sleep now! Stay here and don't go out till evening. There was a giant on the esplanade, a policeman, a giant, when I went out. Giants to frighten people! I'll say you're ill, have a fever.'

The next day he was querulous and feverish. He said:

'Don't answer the doorbell. I have a terrible headache, I'm feverish. I'm worried. I can't trust my business partner.'

After dark, he went out and returned with a valise. He brought it into the diningroom and opened it on the table. He said to Gilbert:

'A friend of mine got a lot of shirts, very cheap, a bargain, from the warehouse, no middleman: do you want any? I can let you have them at $2.50, but it's for a quick sale. Look at the material.'

Mrs Anderson laughed with pride and joy, drooped when Gilbert refused. She ran to show him a shirt, so well made, such a good design, modern. He had paid $5 for the last one and you could sift peas through it.

Gilbert calmly shut the valise, picked it up and put it into one of the large unused cupboards in the old kitchen.

She was shocked: 'Such a shame not to help, and the boy shows enterprise; he is trying to get money to open a men's store, all the latest for men, on Broadway.'

The young man went out on business very early the next day, and when he was gone Gilbert told her about the shirts:

'They're hot, Mamma!'

She believed him; she was terrified. But when Gilbert came back from work on Monday, in the afternoon, the two were in the kitchen, the gratified old aunt and the yarn-spinning youth, cutting into an iced cake with cherries on top, which he had provided.

UNO 1945

The Howards left before the conference ended and set out to drive to their new home in Beverly Hills. They had spent all this time and money on the UNO conference to write reports for the New York *Labor Daily* and the Washington *Liberator,* at a time when Emily's Hollywood agents were waiting for two scripts; and her New York agents for the manuscript of a new book in her moneymaking series, *Mr and Mrs Middletown,* humorous books of family life. The couple quarrelled before starting, about the opinions in Emily's article for the *Labor Daily;* but she posted it unchanged. As soon as the car started, the tiff began again.

'This is not for money, Stephen, and I'll say what I like; it's the truth.'

'Oh, damn the truth and damn not for money. You'll offend the left and you've wasted a week rewriting your article when your agents are screaming. But it's OK, your soul is white and the children won't eat next week.'

'Your goddamn article was a palimpsest by the time

you'd finished achieving a wise, dry, prescient tone. You had to telephone it to Washington,' said Emily, but she began to laugh: 'In Europe contributors to radical sheets go about with the soles off their shoes and gnaw a dry crust in freezing attic rooms: and we live on the plunder of the land, best hotels, three-room suite, long-distance calls, swell car to run us home to our latest residence: that's American radicalism I suppose. They can't pay us so we pay them.'

'Well, it's worth it to see my name flown at the masthead,' said Stephen nastily.

'That's a petty selfish view. If we waste all this money, it's what we owe the country for our unnatural natural luck.'

They quarrelled again and the last part of the journey was passed in silence. When they got home, Emily went round the house fast, talking in a lively way with the servants, the children, the neighbours' children who were in. She looked through the children's clothing and the laundry, checked the contents of pantry, icebox, deep-freeze and bar, ordered dinner and took her large bundle of letters up to her room; a little room at the stairhead, and overlooking the side and back gardens. Manoel, the manservant, brought up a pot of black coffee; and she locked the door behind him. Her room was furnished mainly with steel files containing copies of her volumi-nous writings of all sorts, her diary, her correspondence, the material for many novels and stories, copies of all her lectures and articles, bundles of clippings, household bills and the children's school reports; as well as the exercise books in which she carefully went over their lessons with them. Besides this, there were wire baskets, a few refer-ence books, a table, a chair and an excellent typewriter. She drank the coffee, took a pill from a little locked drawer in the table and began to read her letters, with shouts and great guffaws and sighs. She began typing replies at once.

Downstairs, in a large front room well furnished as study and library, in his own room, Stephen sat discontentedly going through the notes his research worker had sent him. He had a partners' desk, a pale blue-grey carpet. The panelled sliding door communicated with a charming living-room decorated with chintzes, French paintings and flowers arranged in Japanese style. Stephen found it hard to settle down to work, for Emily's agents, the studios and her publishers kept telephoning Emily; and every conversation in which, in her jolly, loving, languishing manner, full of good sense, outrageous hope and bonhomie, she promised and put off, threw him into a frenzy. Last year she had, without effort, made $80,000 in Hollywood. But she consumed hours, weeks in all, writing to friends and otherwise wasting time. A river of money was flowing through the telephone: she had only to direct it into their pockets. The thought poisoned him and stung him. Their expenses were large. The Portuguese couple who managed for them cost considerably over $400 a month; his own research worker had cost more than $5,000 in the course of five years.

Yet upstairs Emily flirted with the idea of writing a great novel. She sketched out one idea after another, and in each of them she wanted to tell some truth that would offend some section of the community. Some of the truths would offend everyone and get them on the black list. Also, she prepared lectures and courses for workers' and students' education. She wrote impassioned letters about her troubles to her friends, gave advice to young writers, worked harder on articles for 'those snoots' on the *Labor Daily* than on a script for Twentieth Century Fox.

Emily came downstairs, very cheery, bustling the children to wash their hands, fix their neckties, come in to dinner.

'What have you been doing?' he said sourly.

'Writing a letter to Phyl Robinson.'

'The house is full of unpaid bills and Hollywood and Bookman Bros are telephoning and telegraphing every hour. You've got a market shrieking for your work. Why don't you do it?'

He said this before the children and Manoel the butler who was serving. This was not unusual. They always talked with the greatest freedom before intimates.

'My writing's crap,' she shouted, 'I don't want to do it. I'm not proud they pay me gold for crap. That Mr and Mrs stuff is just custard pie I throw in the face of the Mamma public, stupid, cruel and food crazy. I find myself putting in recipes – ugh! – because I know they guzzle it. They prefer a deepfreeze to a human being; it's cold, tailored and shiny. I don't believe in a word I write. Do you know what that means, Stephen? It's a terrible thing to say. You believe in what you write! Why should I work my fingers stiff to pay off the mortgage on this goddamn shanty with electric lights on the stair-treads so that the guests don't roll down when they're full – let 'em roll – and with dried sweetpea on the airspray in the linen closet –'

'That dried sweetpea makes me gag,' he sang out irately. 'All right! Let's get out of the crappy place, though we've only just got in, and find something cheap and nasty with no towel-rails. Let's go to one of my family's modest little tax-saving apartments or a cabin in Arkansas. Let my family see I'm a failure. Let's get rid of

Manoel, who's my only friend and get a char smelling of boiled rag and with hair in her nose. I'll do the buttling. Why not get a job as a butler? I'd make a good sleek sneak sipping the South African sherry in the outhouse. Let's wear our shirts for a week and save on the laundry.'

'You're eating my heart with your aristocratic tastes,' she roared, beginning to cry, too. 'Moth and rust are nothing to what a refahned young genteel gentleman from Princeton can do to an Arkansas peasant girl, when a spot on the carpet to him is like pickles to a stomach-ulcer. Oh, Jee-hosaphat, what was the matter with me, marrying a scion? You've ruined my life, darn it. I want to be a writer. I don't want to write cornmeal mush for fullbellied Bible belters. Did I leave my little Arkansas share-cropper's shanty for that? I was going to be a great writer, Miss America, the prairie flower. Now I'm writ-ing Hh-umour and Pp-athos for the commuters and hayseeds.'

She helped the children with their homework. Both parents went up to sing to Giles in his cot, a song invented by Stephen,

Oh G, oh I, oh L, oh E, oh S!
Sle-ep, sle-ep, sle-ep, sleep!
Oh, Gilesy, Gilesy, Gilesy, sleep!

Stephen ran a bath, while Emily went downstairs; and after writing out the menu for the next day and saying, 'I will make the crêpes suzette,' she went to the butler's pantry where she mixed herself a strong highball. Just as she was carrying it into the living-room, Stephen came down in fresh clothes. He scolded her for taking a drink and for the expense of some new handmade shirts which had just come in for the three boys; Lennie, aged twelve, Alun, eight, and Giles four. Emily defended herself: what was he just saying about a char with hair on her eyeballs?

She was in a good humour. 'I've got an idea that will work for my script; it's so cheap I blushed for shame.'

Stephen picked up the evening paper and glanced over the headlines. They began once more to tear at the great wound which had opened in their love, mutual admiration and understanding and great need for each other. This was an equally fundamental thing, a disagreement about Amercian exceptionalism; the belief widely held in the USA that what happened in Europe and the rest of the world belonged to other streams of history, never influencing that Mississippi which bears the USA. The flood of American energy could and perhaps would swallow those others: the watershed of European destiny was far back in time and drying up. To this belief, Stephen liked to adhere. Emily accused him of servility to a system which had made his grandparents and parents millionaires; and Stephen would not have been so tenacious, if the Government, and all the political parties right down to the extreme left, had not agreed that America's reason for invading Europe, joining the conflict, was to spread America's healthy and benevolent business democracy everywhere: the western answer to communism. Stephen had everyone at his back, but a few. Emily found this 'a pill too big for a horse to swallow,' to quote Michael Gold; and she declared that this local doctrine, held even by the communists, was wrong.

'They know their theory better than you and me,' said Stephen querulously: 'at any rate better than me; and I don't know what to answer. I can only follow blindly; but I intend to follow. I went into Marxism for personal salvation, I know; a despicable reason; but I have to stick to it or where am I?'

'I'm not going to follow anyone into a quagmire. And I don't want to be saved.'

'You're an individualist: individualists become renegades.'

She sprang up from her chair, 'Don't you dare call me a renegade! I'll scratch your eyes out. I won't stand that.'

They quarrelled so bitterly and such unforgivable things were said that she packed a valise, got a seat on a plane going east the next morning and telephoned the studio that she'd post the scripts from New York. 'And I'll be able to work there,' she shouted, 'not worried to death by a limpet throttling me. Maybe I'll give up the whole crazy game, get myself a hall bedroom and really write.'

Before it was time to leave for the airport next day, Stephen took the car out. Emily telephoned for a taxi. But Stephen returned with a jewelcase, in the velvet lining of which lay a deep amethyst necklace from Russia. Emily loved stones in yellow, green and purple.

She was dressing and sat before her looking-glass in a linen slip with a square-cut neck embroidered in small scallops; and a bronze silk dressing gown, fallen round her hips: her hair was disordered, pushed back and in spikes. Arranged on her rosy solid bosom, set in the low bodice of white embroidery, the gems look superb. Seeing her comical, robust fairness in the glass and Stephen beside her in pale blue, pliant, placating, absorbed, she began to laugh with tears in her eyes.

'Oh, Stephen, it's so beautiful and it's such a filthy insult, to think you can buy a writer's soul with money.'

Stephen said, 'Don't let Browder and such bagatelles separate us, Emily. What can I do without you? I know you can live without me.'

She sat thrown back in the dressing chair, looking at the necklace and her grotesque fair face. 'By golly, I look like a Polish peasant dressing as a countess,' she said laughing, her blue eyes bright and flushed, lucent, wet. 'I look like any kind of peasant, I'm so goddam earthy, no wonder I fell for a silk-stocking. I like to hear you talking to waiters in icy tones, "This *Graves* is not cool enough, wait-ah!"'

'I do not say waitah.'

'The prince and the pauper.' She began to take off the necklace, tugging impatiently at the catch. 'Help me with it, Stephen,' she continued in a hearty husky tone, 'it's lovely, I love it, but get thee behind me, Satan. I guess you don't know me after all. Hasn't any woman ever told you it's a damned insult to try to buy a woman's affections with Russian crown jewels and a fur coat? Is – our – whole – future,' she continued, breaking into sobs, 'to-be-built – on my selling out my belief in the future of the world for some gewgaws of Czarist Russia? It's a symbol, all right. I guess that's the kind of women you've known though.'

'Oh, Lord!'

'Of course, your mother and your sister are like that; they believe in Cincinnatus labouring the earth with a golden ploughshare. And what is the harvest? The corn is gold. The country's rich and right. Why dear Anna, your mother, would think it the hoith of foine morals intoirely to give up dirty radicalism and wear a clean fortune round your neck. I don't say sister Florence. Florence is not all lucre. She'd pawn it at once for a hundred cases of Bourbon –'

'I got this from Florence. I've got to pay her for it, somehow.'

'Take it back. It's for her sort,' said Emily decisively pushing it along the table. 'I like it; but after you saying you'd divorce me if I didn't believe in the American way of life –'

'I did not!' he shouted.

'American exceptionalism! What else is it? And you'd leave me for not believing in Hollywood, the art of the masses; do you think you can buy me back with a stick of candy? I don't think you could have done that to me, even as a child. The only thing you could buy me with then was affection. I loved people. They didn't love back.'

'I didn't mean to hurt your feelings; I don't seem to do anything right. So I've lost you!'

'Will you give up your belief that revolutionary Marxism is right; and consent to be led by the nose by the quiet man from nowhere, all for an amethyst necklace?' said Emily loudly and scornfully; and throwing the box with the thing in it on to the carpet, where she kicked it away. 'Pooh-ah! What triviality! Is that what you think of me, Emily White? You can buy me with a string of beads? When I whore, I'll whore for plenty, for the whole works. They'll have to come to me with the whole world wrapped up in their arms! And with the Bible too and the whole of revolutionary history, man's struggle, too, and say: Debs says you can, and you can prove it by the Haymarket Martyrs, the crimes of Cripple Creek; lynched labour organisers led to it and Sacco and Vanzetti died for it. Manoel! Is the car ready? Put my bags into it. Drive me to the airport. Stephen, I've left everything arranged; the children's diets, their dentists' appointments, when to change their clothes; everything; I've paid all the bills, I was up all night. Now, this is final. You can divorce me if you like.'

'Forgive me, Emily,' said Stephen.

'I don't forgive you. I'm goddam mad and I'm going to stay mad.'

But Stephen ordered Manoel out of the car, got in

himself; and while he was driving Emily to the airport, he talked her round. In tears, quite overwhelmed with shame, Emily was brought back to the house. They spent the day together talking over many things quietly and sincerely; kisses and endearments were exchanged in the vegetable garden, down by the river, behind the trees that screened the barbecue, by the children's swing, in the dark of the garage and while they were spraying the vines with DDT against the Japanese beetle. Not far off, Manoel and Maria, in their rest hours, could be heard talking and laughing; once they screeched with laughter. Two or three times Emily ran to the children, who were being kept together by the English nurse named Thistleton. Emily hugged them all, kissed the eldest, their nephew Lennie, in the dark curls that fell over his pale narrow forehead. 'Oh, my darlings,' she said to them once, 'if you only knew what a mother you have! You'd do better with a snake, a gila monster, than an earthworm like me. Oh, Miss Thistledown, I'm a poor weak woman without character.' She hugged the nurse, 'Let me kiss you,' she said, pressing her wet round cheeks, rough and warm as fruit, to the middle-aged woman's thin face, 'you English are all so strong, you're just and strong. My God,' she said, turning away, and aloud, 'if my fighting forefathers heard that blather! I'm fat with the buttering and the licking afterwards.'

At dinner, Emily, a good chef, made the crêpes suzette as planned. She was wearing rings, a hair jewel and bracelets. She was flushed and her tongue wagged frenziedly. 'Oh, if only we were Jewish,' she cried; 'we'd stick together. What a beautiful family life the Jews have, so closewoven; and they make more of blood than we do. It's beautiful that tree of life with all its branches, under the mantle of all its leaves. Oh, how lucky you are,

Lennie, to have had a Jewish father. If only I had Jewish blood I'd make you happy. I'd have the art of keeping the fire in the hearth forever. I used to go down to the Jewish quarter as a child and just stare in, glare in hungrily through their windows on Friday nights, when they had their candles in the windows! Oh, how tender it was, how touching and true! The family is the heart of man; how can you tear it open?'

Stephen listened, smiling, grinning: 'Lennie's father, my brother-in-law, was a nasty little man! Any family life is poison. I'm sure Miss Thistleton and Manoel think they're having a season in hell. Read what Plato said about the family!'

'Plato was a homosexual!' declared Emily. 'Stephen, listen to what I say! Family love is the only true selfless love; it's natural communism. That is the origin of our feeling for communism: to each according to his needs, from each according to his capacity; and everything is arranged naturally, without codes and without policing. Manoel, why don't you bring in the coffee? This coffee is not like we get at your sister Florence's. But of course, there's only one liquid that means anything to her –'

'Stop it!'

But she did not stop and held them at table while she discussed Stephen's family and their money habits, for a long time. Lennie's grand-uncle had dieted himself to death, being a miser: having apportioned his estate among his children to escape death duties and family hatred, he found them all sitting like buzzards around his semi-starved person to tear the pemmican from his bones. Stephen's mother, Stephen's sisters – the rich girl the family wanted Stephen to marry –

Miss Thistleton, embarrassed, half rose from her chair. 'Stay where you are!' roared Emily, 'I haven't finished speaking. You're the children's guardian. If I leave, you'll be their mother! You may as well know what's in them!' Last, with an imperial gesture she dismissed them, the children to their homework or beds; and when they had sung the Giles song, she said to Stephen, 'Let's go to the movies; I have a need to sit in the dark with you.'

They went downtown. At night, they went to bed but did not sleep. In the film, the word *fascist* was used and Stephen exulted, 'There you are! Hollywood is not all poison. Reaction is on the way out, when the radical writers in the studios can put over their ideas like that.'

'Oh, poohpooh,' said Emily; 'people don't even know what it means. It went by in a second! Who heard it but politicomaniacs like us?'

And with this one word, the bitter wound opened again.

'I shall be ill if you don't let me sleep,' said Stephen. 'Last night, too –'

'Sleep! When our futures and our souls, I mean that word, it's all we have that's worth fighting for – we've got to think this thing through. We can't sleep anyway.'

'I could if you'd let me. I've got you; my children are with me; I have no other wants. I don't want to have ideas. Ideas are civil war. Let us drown our ideas, Emmie: let's live in a friendly fug. I'm sick of it.'

'In the first place, what are we fighting about, Stephen? Let's get that clear. We're mixed up. We like New York, but you want us to stay here and make a fortune in the movies, so that dear Anna and Florence the Fuzzy and Uncle Shongo –'

'I have no Uncle Shongo!' he squealed.

'Uncle Mungo and Uncle Cha will see you are not a failure; you, too, can make money. I don't mind being a failure because my people remain in the mud of time; but

you do. I'm from hoi-polloi and you're from hoity toity
–'

'Stop it! Was there ever such a fool! I married a clown!'

'Anyway, for some reason, we've got to believe in MGM and the mistakes of the left.'

'Goddamn it, they are not mistakes. Who are you and I
–'

'For myself, the writers like what I write when I like what I write; but the agents don't and you don't and even – but leave certain names out of this shameful story. If I write the way I like, it'll be poverty for us; not this monogrammed sheet, but mended shoes and tattered pants and not enough vitamins; and that's not fair to the kids.'

'We're not philanthropists. It's theory and practice for everyone in the world, except the unquestioning and thankless rich – lucky dogs! You don't want our kids to grow up like Clem Blake's, eating out of cans with many a fly twixt the can and the lip.'

'Golly!' she laughed: 'I guess they'll grow up, too.'

'If they don't die of botulism.'

'I thought that was from botflies.'

'What are botflies?'

'It shows I'm a farmer's daughter. Well, they'll grow up, too.' She sighed. 'Oh, well, what the hell! Maybe the oral hygiene and the handmade shirts are just hanky-panky. Maybe that's no way to raise heroes of labour.'

'I don't want to live with heroes of labour,' he said pettishly. 'I've seen lots of them. Starvation and struggle are no good for the soul; nor the stomach. What are we fighting for? Not to make people like the workers are now. Good grief! I had "a love the worker" phase; but I wasn't sincere. I walked along working class streets and saw their stores and their baby-carriages and hated 'em. I wouldn't raise anyone to be like them. Why are the French so revolutionary? Because of their good cooking and good arts of life. And what the devil – you can make money, so make it! If we starved, it would be a whim, the whim of the rich. Why should we starve? You've only got to do two days' work and we'll be in $30,000. It's a whim and a selfish one to throw that kind of money back in the studio's face and talk about art and poverty and your soul. And if you're a red, you ought to show you're one just *because* you can come out on top; so they can't say it's grousing. You ought to be a shining – red – light. The rest is just moral filth, mental laziness and infantile behaviour. You want to be back in Arkansas, the school-girl who read through Shakespeare once every year, and dreamed about making a noise as a great writer. Fooey! You know I hated Princeton. Well, one of the reasons was, I spent my time trying to live up to the noble secular trees and noble secular presidents. I starved myself trying to live on what I thought a poor scholar would live on; and fancied my parents admired me for spending so little. Rich imbeciles like me think there's something mystic, some intellectual clarity and purification of the soul in sobriety, austerity and poverty. I got over that. Now anyone can keep me, my family, you –' he said bitterly, 'or Lennie or my son.'

'Lennie is your son,' she said: 'we'll get him.'

'My lazy vampirism feeds on my nearest and dearest: I gnaw their white breasts.'

'Oh, Stephen,' she wailed, 'oh, don't say that. I love you. Don't say those things. If I have a vulgar streak which enables me to make more money than you, aren't I, in those moments, like your moneymaking grandfathers that you despise? And I feel I'm tanned like a tanned rhino hide: I'm secretly afraid you'll leave me and get some decent woman who never sold out. Despise me; but don't despise yourself, Stephen. What else am I working and selling out for? You're my whole life, my rayzon d'ayter. If we haven't got each other, we've got nothing. Our life is so hideous. With each other, we can work it out, we can hope. Otherwise, what has it all been for? You gave up millions, I gave up my hopes, dreams and ideals; and our hearts are being squeezed dry.'

'You've made me better than I was,' said Stephen. 'First out of Princeton, I used to hang around with those wistful carping critics of the critics groups. I was young and stupid and I think I still am. I hated those arty people, Emily – all – with the bitterest hate of envy; and then I took up Marxism because I thought it gave me a key they didn't have; it raised me above them. I got out of the grovelling mass in the valley and felt the fresh air blowing on me; but it was all selfish –'

'It was NOT,' roared Emily, 'don't be crazy!'

'Yes, it was. They seemed to get women without even trying.'

'Jee-hosaphat! Did you want to get women?' She began to laugh, rolling about on the bed and looking at him with her red and yellow face, surrounded by loose fair hair. Her face was made for laughter – a pudgy comic face with deep lines only when she laughed, the deep lines of the comic mask. 'Oh, Stephen! And you so beautiful! Why on earth you picked a puttynose, a pieface like me –'

'A what?'

'I look as if some slapstick artist just threw a custard-pie in my puss –'

'Don't insult the woman I love!'

'And those freckles remind me of the oatmeal in a haggis –'

'You're the most beautiful woman I ever had in my life, that's all. It's the beauty of the mind –'

'Oh, if we could wear the mind inside out! I don't get it. You're fascinating, Stephen.'

'Well, the only women who go for me are those who wriggle down to the platform after meetings and ask me to explain. You know what that fellow in the bistro in Paris said to his son that day? "Don't fret son, study the cats. The females always go for the ragged, bleary-eyed, whiskery, dirty old tom with cobwebs on his eyebrows."'

'But is it true?'

'I envied them all,' said Stephen sourly, 'and you provide the final revenge against them. You're so wonderfully, truly, profoundly potent and you're nothing like them. They were so genteel; they wouldn't be caught in an enthusiasm: the sad little band of *nil admirari*. I had my intellectual revenge when I studied a few scraps of Marxism too. I learned they stood for nothing. They, if they learned a bit, they dropped out halfway. They married a bit of money, a schoolteacher with cheques appeal, took a house in a restricted suburb; no Jews, Irish or Italians, they're all too enthusiastic. They began to owe money and have plenty of nothing; they get sleek and terribly bright and wise – and so terribly empty. There's nothing to prevent them jumping off Brooklyn Bridge right now. Because only an idea and a belief can prevent you doing that.'

'Oh, well, who the hell cares for them? You got out.'

'Yes, but they've no doubts. I employed a poor scholar, a tailor's son, to teach me Marxism: the old noble getting out an insurance policy against the revolution! You're real. I knew right off you were a genuine person, a wise and rich woman, strong and meaningful.'

'How did you know that?'

'That awful dress you wore!'

'Stephen!' she cried, blushing; 'and you always said you loved it.'

'So I did and I do. I made you keep it forever. I love it. The vines and the grapes and the flowers –'

'Stephen! I did think it was lovely and warm,' she added thoughtfully. 'I loved it too. I still don't think it's awful. Of course, dear Florence wouldn't have –'

'Don't spoil it. And the story you told me of your growing up and the things that happened to you! The man in the house that fell down when you were in it: Jimmy – the man who rented out condemned buildings and introduced you to Donne – well, I never met such people. And then the rotten men – whom I understood, with all my failure, better than you. It all showed me the depth of life and love and passion and ability that could be. And lacking just one thing, the ability to be warped.'

Emily said nothing.

'I felt so cut off from the rest of mankind and you bridged that for me. I felt I was still up in that hospital in the snow slopes and pines, where I was cut off for three years. But I know I'm down on earth again when I'm with you. And I live for you,' he said obstinately, 'and only for you. Would I live for myself? You don't like me to say that; but I must. I want to call it out, to shout it out. I thirst for what you give me. My life drives me into sterility; I can't give and nothing bears for me. But you did.'

Emily turned about restlessly, 'You mustn't say that. I told you not to. It makes me feel ill. Suppose I died? Anyone can die.'

'Don't say that please.'

'All right. But you mustn't found your life on one person. It's dreadful. You throw yourself on another person's back and bear them down. They bow right down to earth with weeping and sobbing for you and them. You kill them. The feeling's unspeakable. I'll die.'

Stephen laughed, 'Well, that's me, though. Too bad. You must live for something. I think I'm lucky. A lot of those men I knew had nothing to live for and now they're slipping along a moral skid row. They're looking sideways furtively at the milestones. I guess the only thing that stops them putting their heads in the gas oven is that all they've got is an infra-red grill. I know what I'm living for: for you. For anything you live for. I don't care what it is.'

'That's fabulous. I won't have it,' said Emily angrily.

'Perhaps I could be different in another society. I wonder. But I think a bad man, a real bastard but a strong villain, would be better for you than me. At least, he wouldn't pretend to be an intellectual or moral hero and take up your time and waste your affections.'

'Oh, I don't know what to do,' said Emily frantically. 'I'll give you a beating. It's more than I can stand. I'm going mad. You're killing me.' She threw herself from side to side as if avoiding bees. 'I'm burning. Don't, don't, don't!' She threw herself at him, 'Stop it, do you hear! It makes me feel desperate. I'll burst.'

She jumped out of bed, opened a small drawer in the dressing-table; and he at once snapped, 'What are you doing? Taking some of those damn pills?'

'I've got to calm down. How can I work tomorrow? And I've got a lecture in the evening.'

'What lecture?'

'Adult education.'

'That's it, that's it! Your whole life is filled with giving, doing. I'm nothing but a barnacle on the wheel of progress.'

She jumped back into bed and kissed him furiously, all over face, neck, hair, chest, arms. Then, she lay back and began to reason. 'This life doesn't suit you, Stevie. It's a gambling racecourse crazy life for touts and bums, not for you. You're a scholar and should live in peace. This double or nothing, boom or bust scares you and nauseates you. Your attitude towards money, so different from mine, is disturbed in this mad Hollywood carnival. You respect money. You shouldn't. Fancy respecting the filthy reeking stuff. I don't respect it. To me it's not part of a highly organised respectable society, the just reward of pioneering valour: nor a medal pinned on the virtuous starched bosom. To me there's just as much virtue in Skid Row, or as little. Moneymaking is gangdom, grab or someone else will. Of course, you're right too. It's the high established church of our great land. Lincoln said, "As a nation of freemen we must live through all time, or die by suicide." Suicide! Oh, God! A great nation cutting its throat! Could it really happen? As long as the razor is of gold and the noose of amethyst –'

'A country can't die,' said Stephen indignantly. 'We can, the poor lice on its hide, but thank God the country can't die. If I thought it could, I'd die of empty horror. Do you know the story that has haunted me since I was a boy? The man without a country.'

'But that's bamboozle.'

'I think I can even understand the cranks and crooks who are put out of Russia and write lies for bread. They want to be noticed; they're Russians too. It's the infant screaming for its mother.'

'Don't waste your sympathy,' she said drily.

'I suppose it's envy, too,' he conceded. 'They're best-sellers; though it's a nasty mean way to make a fortune, running down your country. I know you don't believe I am as good as that. I couldn't write a book that would sell, in any terms. So I ought to be out earning a living and giving you the chance you want.'

'I wish I could,' said Emily, thoughtfully and gently. Then she began to fire up, 'I'd like to write a book about the revolutionary movement, the way I see it and what's wrong with it. Here we have the greatest organisation for socialism in the western world. Look at the size of the labour union movement! A state within the state. When it says, Go, we go: when it says, Stop, we stop. Organised millions of conscious workers: what would the early socialists have said to that? The millenium! Though, it's not. But isn't it a great big poster saying, It can be done! Or is it already too late? Are there too many labour opportunists, too many finks and goons? Or are we what's wrong with it, the goddamn middle-class opportunists? I'd like to write this book. I'm dumb enough to think it would be good. But who would print it? We would all of us end up in the railroad wreck and not a single finger lifted to take the engine off our neck.'

'You could do it,' said Stephen without force; 'but you'd get nowhere. I ought to build fires under your ambition. It only shows the kind of punk I am. But I'm representative. You could have me for one of the characters; a clay lay figure covered with the fine patina of soft living, a radical arguing man, busy with top secrets and who's who in Washington, softshoeing in the antechambers of the lobbies of Congress, a radical dandy, dispensing the amenities of another caste, paying his way into the labour movement, following a boyish dream; take the underdog along with you to the White House; heel, sir, heel: misinterpreting everything to suit the silk-lined dream and with laughable ineffectiveness exhorting a stone-deaf working class out of the blind alley of porkchop opportunism to lead them down the blind alley of rigid righteousness. For what have we to offer them? Something we don't believe in ourselves; socialist austerity and puritanism for the better building of steel mills.'

'I wouldn't see it that way,' said Emily slowly. 'This would be a cruel book. I wouldn't spend much time on theoretical errors or an analysis of our peculiar applications of theory; but I'd try to put a finger on essential human weaknesses; the ignorance and self-indulgence that has led us into bohemia. On that score, there's plenty to say. Ought we all to live well, have our children in private schools, training them for the *gude braid claith*? I ought to say how everything becomes its opposite not only outside the besieged fortress but in: how we misinterpret the mission of America, the position in the unions, ourselves; and what our lives are, that are going so far astray. We would sneer at Utopian communities; but we are trying to live in Utopia.'

'It might be an epitaph of American socialism: I'd like to see it,' sang out Stephen.

'No, no! It would be for the real rebels, the real labour movement, against all vampires who take all that's best in the world, even the name of the most sacred causes and use them for promotion; shepherds killing and eating the lambs. That's it. Socialism can't die! Don't we believe that? But it can die – suffocated, here! By us! That's horrible.'

'It's horrible; especially when we're in it up to our necks,' said Stephen restlessly: 'if I had to be born in these days, why not a Russian, where it's all settled?'

'Why not a Jugoslav, a Frenchman, anyone but us? Yes. The world's going to be implacable towards us, Stephen. Let's face it. There's going to be a lot of stuff in between; but that time, the day before yesterday, was IT, *die Ende,*

Schluss, Fini. I keep seeing the weirdest thing dancing before my eyes – like a dagger, like a cup of poison: choose fair maid, but both are death; ha-ha! Gromyko round the big table, eyes straight ahead, shoulders back, jaws grim, pad-pad, round and round, silent, but brain radiating what we all felt only too damn well: "If there's a war you can't win!" Oh, God! And we have to be on the WRONG side in the bad time coming! To be in America, to like America, to want to be an American and to be wrong, to be martyred by Americans – because, by golly, how the Americans love to make martyrs! They make them so wholesale, they never notice. Every few years some innocents have to be offered up on our altar, the giant footstool before the infinite altar of the brassfaced Philistine god. I know my people; I'm from deep America. What did Lincoln say in that address before the young men's Lyceum in Springfield, 1838: "– till dead men were seen literally dangling from the boughs of trees upon every roadside and in numbers almost sufficient to rival the native Spanish moss of the country as a drapery of the forest." I read that often as a child and I trembled. Later I thought, things have improved since then. But now I know they haven't. Can you see us as martyrs, Stephen? I'm not made for that. I don't believe in it.'

'Neither do I,' said Stephen, 'but it happens. Every day someone's name is called and he is conscripted into the army of blood.'

'I don't like to be a martyr, I won't be a martyr. I don't want to be on the wrong side. I wasn't born for that. How short life is! And what about the children? Oh, my, my! For them, one can't be on the wrong side: and yet we have to choose. What's the right side? I mean morally, and in terms of our natural lives? Oh, Lord! We can be torn to pieces. I won't give up the kids; and your mother and Florence will drag them from us like lightning. And they'd have every right if we became outcasts, outlaws with the community riding us on a rail and throwing stones through our windows. The court could be enquiring into our bank accounts and laundry baskets; and Grandma and Florence would be seen white as snow, for guzzling is not considered wrong in this country –'

'Oh, for pity's sake!'

'All right, Stephen,' she said, furious: 'you know you want to keep the children!'

'Yes, I need them: I love them and I need the boys' money.'

'You can't touch it,' she said.

'I could charge them for keep and education and foreign travel – we can travel maybe: and I can influence them, I hope. Imagine two little boys in my household are multimillionaires; and I'm a poor man. Life hoaxed me.'

'If they were settled, our hands would be free,' said Emily without joy. She sighed, 'It's the damnedest thing! But I won't let them go. And besides, with us they'll escape the tumbrils.'

'What tumbrils?' he said testily.

She sighed, 'Oh, well, if we weren't socialists, I suppose *agenbite of inwit* would make heroes of us anyway. We'd have to start out and join Daniel's little glorious band marching to extinction. Ugh! But that would finish us with your family. Now we can contend, with dear Anna and all our dear lucre-men, that communism was a youthful jag, "our Spanish Civil War phase", as the renegade hath it; and they can see it as an enthusiasm we're too decent to abandon. But, start in now and it would be crystal clear that we're middle-aged delinquents, not mad but bad. Yet we can't abandon and join those other bastards whose names are writ in shapes of crap.'

Stephen lay rigid and was silent. She became silent, too. They went to sleep.

Emily rose early, ordered the food for the day, and, taking a tray of black coffee up to her little room, she began on one of her scripts, a story with humour and pathos about a freckleface in the big city. She worked hard through the day, drove down to the village to buy some bottled French sauces and herbs from a specialist, visited a workman's coffee stall, the owner of which was a political friend, and hurried back to make over her UNO article into lecture notes for the evening.

In the evening she drove to downtown Los Angeles and in a small hall addressed forty to fifty people, among them Mexicans and Negroes, giving her impressions of the San Francisco Conference. Emily spoke in public as she spoke in private. On the platform, she was earnest and incisive and also rollicking and fatly funny. At the end she said, 'A man I knew in the Middle West had someone in City Hall tip him off about condemned houses; he rented them out privately as flophouses for whores and bums. He showed me a few of his houses and he used to recite John Donne to me. An ambulance-chaser I knew in my newspaper days used to sit outside the emergency waiting-room and read me William Blake. The first I ever heard of either poet! The way I collected my education, my high school having no use for same! Ha-ha. Very funny: I'm dying laughing. Imagine I have to go to work now on parsing and pluperfects, in my old age! Well, to the point, friends! I see you there and I am here and I see something ahead. The choice will come, the choice has come. Perhaps you don't see it clearly yet; but one day it will be as obvious as the cop's club and you will weep by teargas, because it is then too late to choose. Some of you will be in gaol, some will be silent with the silence that grows over a man like fungus; and some will be successes and able to appear anywhere in broad daylight. The choice is already taken out of our hands. Well, anyhow, this is the way William Blake puts it in one of his cloudy epics and I'm damned if I can remember anything else but this; and I'm damned remembering this, anyway, maybe. It goes,

> But Palambron called down a Great Solemn Assembly,
> That he who will not defend Truth, may be compelled to
> Defend a Lie, that he may be snared and caught and taken.

After a pause, there was acclamation. She was forty minutes getting away from the meeting afterwards, for she talked with anyone who wanted to talk with her. Stephen was waiting for her in the car. She got in and they drove uptown. She remained silent.

'Did you wow them?' he asked.

'Were you in the hall?'

'No, I was sitting in the car.'

She grumbled, 'I recited to them a quote from William Blake.' She repeated it. 'They probably thought Palambron was an Indian chief,' she said, laughing. The laughing turned into uncontrollable sobbing.

The Fathers

'I've got my new passport, I'm getting out of here,' said Asa, to his wife.

'I'm on it too: you can take me – or don't you want to?' said Pearl.

'You're not on it. You don't want to. Sure, I'll go – but I don't know where. Will I make friends anywhere else? Like the friends I have in New York? I was born here, they're all my friends here; I'm a union man here; I can't pick up foreign words. Like I thought in Mexico City, when I saw the procession, they said, "*Troubadours, unite!*" but it meant "*Workers, unite!*" '

She said calmly, 'You know one sort of words work everywhere, honey words. What about Jacinta? I thought you were all set to join her in Mexico City. She won't have you, will she? I know Joe is the kind of upstraight man who wouldn't give her her children.'

'I'm going out to get a sandwich,' he said. At the door, he turned, 'Lincoln said, "Hug a bad bargain closer." We'll stick together if you'll go straight. Though it means I'll never get another chance, at all.'

'Oh, you'll hanker, Asa of the hungry heart,' Pearl laughed, friendly. It was in the living room in Asa's flat. A window at the back looked out on the lightwell, court-yard. It was a bright morning, about ten, and the apart-ment was light. At the back there were two exits from the room, one to a living room beyond which was a small entry, with a mirror there reflecting the kitchen; and one to the bedroom next door. On the window of this room was no rag at all, but through the french doors in the living room beyond one could see new ruffled curtains on the windows. Asa had been sitting, half-lying that is, holding a small red-covered book, on a time beaten horsehair sofa under the window; there was a radio on a small table near it, a thin rug on the floor and near the window a large Renoir print, showing chestnut trees in flower and a walk by the river. The french doors were open, one had been kicked in in the two lower panels, and the glass splinters still lay on the floor. Through these you saw that the place was in disorder in the living room beyond; there were valises, a new armchair with price-tag, wrapping and string on it, on a small table a new 'cut-glass' decanter, an unopened bottle of Scotch whisky, and new glasses partly unpacked; two new pillows still in plastic covers, on the armchair.

On the wall in the living room in which Asa had reclined was a photograph of Asa, when a very young man, in a hat, thick black curls peeping out, around a long dreaming scholarly face; there were also a reproduction of one of Cézanne's pictures and one of Gauguin's of the tropics with brown maidens, a record cabinet, some bookshelves, and a duffel bag marked MG for 'Matt Gordon', their son, a young veteran soldier.

When Asa returned, he took off his jacket and shoes

and returned to the sofa to read the red-covered book. Pearl crossed the room to the closet, in the bedroom, to take out a dress, she rejected it, took out another, went into the bathroom (opening out of the other living room) and came out with the dress held against her: 'What do you think, Ace?'

Asa said, 'He's seen you.'

Pearl said with a bluff blurt of laughter, 'I might surprise him. Women are full of surprises.'

Asa turned on the radio and pretended to read his book, his creased face looked like parchment.

Pearl went to the window, took a glass from her handbag, and studied her fair, fluffy hair. 'That new wash you gave me is just right.' Asa looked up, 'You don't want to do it too often, but that way, it's all right.'

'You never liked me but you always thought I was a good looking girl.'

Asa, who had taken off his jacket and shoes, which he had arranged on and under a chair, turned on the radio and read his book quietly. He was a powerful man, tall, middle aged, partly bald, but moving with large harmonious movements.

Pearl snickered, 'I told you I wanted a little loving and I got it. I told you you'd lose me.'

Asa turned the radio on louder. It was playing *Showboat*.

Pearl, arranging a bead necklace before the bathroom mirror, shouted, 'In prohibition days when we got together you were going to the top. A woman expects a man to be a success. At my age she ought to be getting those little comforts. I pushed you enough –'

Asa turned up the radio.

Pearl shouted above the radio, 'We could have gone on from there. But you had the will to fail. I like the good things.'

From the courtyard now came shouts, 'Pipe down, for love of Mike, can it, turn down that radio, for Pete's sake.'

Asa turned off the radio before Pearl had finished shouting and returned to his book, a comic book called *The Bishop's Jaegers.*

Pearl laughed, 'I know why they don't want the radio, they can't hear us, The Gordons at Home, the daily soap opera. We ought to sell it.'

She had come into the room pulling a curl into place.

Asa said, 'I thought we agreed that this' (he indicated the room with his hand) 'was my room. Count me out of this episode.'

Pearl said, 'That was the sofa we bought to sleep on when we first got together. It's kind of old and worn-out. Do you think you can sleep on it? Your feet always hung over.'

Asa remarked, 'Well, anyone who wants to move in will have to buy the furniture.'

Pearl laughed, 'I don't know that we'll buy that sofa. You won't find it very comfortable anyway with Will and me here.'

'It suits me; I like to be alone; and sleep alone.'

'You won't be alone and sleep alone long; you'll end up marrying some widow with two children. Other men's children,' she laughed.

Asa read his book.

Pearl laughed excitedly, 'You'd rather be in love than make good. In Mexico you thought the troubadours were having a strike: it was the workers. You're a troubadour. Not a man: I said I'd get me some real loving and I got it.'

'You never did without anything you wanted, did you?'

Pearl said, 'No. Everyone says my looks have improved lately. Do you think that Royal Jelly you got me worked?'

Asa read his book. Pearl continued, 'Yours haven't you know. Your hair's coming out in handfuls, all the lotions you rub on.'

Asa laughed at his book, a deep ringing laugh.

Pearl said, 'But it doesn't matter, Jacinta's got you where the hair is short; maybe she doesn't want you, doesn't want to make good. You like that. You don't have to make good.'

'I'm willing to made good,' said Asa.

'But she won't take you up on it. You've always liked that sort; and the oddballs, artists with studios. They get in your hair and you like it. Something to live for! Not for me. I like a good time and getting there. No problem child.'

Asa said, 'Why don't you make some lunch? Is your Uncle William going to do the cooking for you?'

'He'll be my husband, not my uncle.'

'I call him your uncle, he is your uncle. It's not my affair if you marry your uncle. I call him your uncle.'

'I don't care for names, I care for facts. We'll eat out in restaurants.'

'He'd better, if he wants to survive. What does he see in you?'

Pearl giggled, 'I could make you stay with me, too, if I wanted to. Don't underrate me.'

He turned on the radio to low music and said, 'Could you?'

The letterbox rattled and Pearl went. Asa said, 'Any mail?'

'From Will.'

'Uncle William writes to his loving niece.'

Asa laughed and read his book. He laughed aloud and said, 'Matt would laugh at this: *The Bishop's Jaegers*. Did he ever read that one?'

Pearl crossed to the bedroom with the open letter in her hand.

Asa turned a page, laughed.

There were courtyard sounds, a cocktail party continued from the night before. A drunk shouted, 'I like women too much, my wife has only girls.' A woman answered, 'Yes, it's a sign you like girls too much.' The man cried, 'I love my wife too much.' The woman answered, 'I like boys better than girls myself.' The man said, 'I got to go, got to go to the hospital to see my wife.' 'She don't need you,' said the woman, 'You done your stuff.' He said, 'I got to go to the hospital, see what's wrong.' The woman shouted, 'There's nothing wrong, sweetheart, you stay here, have another drink.' Stoutly the man replied, 'I got to go.' A man shouted out of a ground floor window, 'Man, you can't go there drunk!' Voices in the courtyard shouted, 'Stop that row, pipe down, Jesus!' and a woman on the second floor shrieked, 'I'll complain to the janitor, I'll get you thrown out, you pack of drunks.'

Asa put his book down, listening gaily; he put his head out the window. Meanwhile Pearl came to the door with her hat on. Asa turned and said, 'Get me a tin of tobacco when you're down. Want some money?' He saw her face. 'What's gone wrong? Uncle Will backed out?'

Pearl said, 'He said he can't come: it's all off.'

'Are you going to see him?'

'Yes, I'll make him explain himself.'

'He's just got cold feet. All men get it. It's nothing. Go and see him.'

'Sure, I know him; I can make him see it.'

Asa said, 'If he won't come round, keep his things' and he looked at the new chair, pillows and glasses.

Pearl gave him the letter, 'What do you make of it?'

Asa glanced at it, 'He don't like me being here, too, he says.'

'I'm going to see him.'

Asa said, 'I'll go to the Turkish Baths. I'll keep my stuff in the boxes at the station. When you sell that sofa, I want the money. I bought it.'

Pearl said, 'I know where he is now, at home. Goodbye.'

'Do you want me to blow? Will you bring him back?'

'No, you can stay till I get back; perhaps I'll need you after all.'

'Poor Pearl! No chance. I suffered too much.'

'I suffered too,' said Pearl, 'Goodbye for now.'

'I'm taking the radio,' said Asa as she closed the front door.

Asa put the book on the radio and lugged both to the little telephone table in the entry. He put two or three valises of different sizes and his son's duffel bag near the table on the floor. Then he extracted the telephone from the heap, put it on the radio and after a hesitation, dialled and said, 'Er, hello darling! Er – how are you? Yes, I got my new passport, everything. Er – when do I see you?' Very hastily he murmured, 'Er – is Joe in? I'll try to get over tonight. I don't know. Maybe, I'll blow. I left my –? I always leave something in your place. What's it a sign of? A sign I want to stay there, or want to come back?' He laughed very gaily and tenderly. 'Er – when will Joe be in? Tell him I'll try and get around tonight. Sure, I'm taking the radio – I can't take the Cézanne – see me sitting on Grand Central with a radio and a Cézanne and a brownpaper parcel? Eh? Heh-heh. I've got a bed for the night, Eighth Street. I'll see you darling,' he said in a very yearning tone.

He sat down for a moment, then went to the bathroom. There was a ring at the door. Asa came out of the bathroom with shaving tackle, brush and comb, put them on the duffel bag, opened the door and took in a telegram. He gave the boy something, closed the door, read the telegram, opened the door and shouted, 'Hey Mac! There's an answer.' The boy returned. Asa took a pencil from his pocket, wrote and offered the telegram to the boy; 'Can you read that?'

The boy read, 'Flying out immediately, Asa Gordon.' 'OK?' 'OK.'

He gave the boy money; added 'Eh, go straight back to the office, will you? That's about my son, he got hurt in a strike.'

'Tough luck, I'm sorry,' said the boy.

Asa started to put things in an airlines bag, behaving confusedly, then telephoned Coast Airlines for a reservation. He was told he had to wait two days. He expostulated, shouted, said 'I'll call back in half an hour; you got to get me a seat; my son's in hospital.' There was a knock at the door. He went and let in Margue, Pearl's sister and Edgar her husband.

Margue was just like Pearl, younger but fully greyhaired, undyed. Ed was a lithe middle sized man over sixty, with dyed hair and looking a few years younger.

'Is Pearl here?' said Margue.

'She's gone over to see Uncle Will.'

'You know then?' said Margue.

'You mean Uncle Will's backing out?' said Asa.

Margue said, 'He came to our place last night and gave us a song and dance: he doesn't want to go through with it: he's afraid of hurting you. He likes you.'

'He thought of that about ten years too late, didn't he? What does he mention it now for?'

'It was just romance all those years; Pearl felt you didn't love her.'

Edgar cackled, 'Love! I don't want love. I want to get a berth and run away to sea like I did when I was twelve years old. I got on a ship in Cape Cod and I never went back there. I'm a Cape Cod boy just the same. I went down to the wharves the other day. I told them, I'm stronger than I look.'

Margue said, 'You'd had a glass: you drink too much.'

Edgar said, 'I couldn't go in scraping those ovens if I didn't have a glass of whisky first. I wouldn't have the guts to do it. When I come out I need a drink, too. I'm half-roasted.'

Margue said, 'It's nice for me. He sweats all night, the bed's all damp and he spent his last vacation three weeks, leaning over the bridge, looking at the water.'

Asa said, 'I've got some rye, Ed; do you want some? No, Uncle Will sent in that Scotch, I'm not touching it.'

Margue said, 'Asa I want to talk to you about Pearl.'

Edgar explained, 'She wants you to stand by Pearl; Uncle Will doesn't want to come here to live.'

Asa said, 'Pearl knows I'm leaving her anyway. I told her long ago, anyhow. This getting in Uncle Will is her idea.'

Margue came up to him and said in the broken soft persuasive voice of both sisters, 'You were always very good to the children, Asa. You can't go and leave them now, in view of the present situation with the troubles about and this a bad section and unemployment. You can't desert your own. You've got to stand by Pearl. She's alone, she hasn't got any money. You know she never saved, she lived off the till.' Margue laughed, 'She was always proud of that. "I never kept accounts, I lived off the till and we're all right, it came out," she says. Ed was always talking of going on a ship, but he wouldn't leave the children; and this week he says he's going to Buenos Aires, but I know he wouldn't leave Jenny to face it. He's proud of his daughter.'

Edgar said, 'The girl's smart, she's the image of me and her youngster is all right; but Robert wants to be a salesman, make quick money; he's a drop-out, he's got some background, could do something better; but a bum, like his father –'

'Edgar, be ashamed,' said Margue.

'He is like his father, that bum you were too smart to marry,' said Edgar. 'And he's got $200 I gave him, he doesn't need me; but Jenny looks to me, she's my daughter, she doesn't have to marry the father of her child or any fella, she's got me; that's different. But where's Asa got to stand by Pearl's children anymore? He brought them up: that's enough. I'd say that's a crate full pressed down and running over.'

Asa went into the kitchen and they heard him at the cupboards.

'Ed!' said Margue.

'Don't Ed me. OK. Why should Asa stand by Pearl's children now? If he wants to go and remake his life? It's not too late for me and I'm sixty-three. I'm going to Buenos Aires next week, you can darn a couple of pairs of socks for the first time in your life as a going-away present. It's not too late for Asa, he's only forty-four.'

'I thought you were going to stand by Jenny.'

'I'll send Jenny money or she can come with the kid and join me. There's plenty of work there: she's a lab worker. She can work there.'

'What about me?'

'You've got plenty of friends. Men friends. I like to experiment you said. I don't mind: stay here, experiment.'

'It's too late for both of you and it's too late for me. Well, maybe it's not too late for Uncle Will.'

Asa came in bringing whisky. 'Here you are. Here you are Margue.' Margue and Ed said 'Mud-in-your-eye,' Asa said nothing. Then he told them, 'Matt's in hospital. Some goon got him in the strike. I just had a telegram. I'm flying out there.'

'Well, you can't go now, till Pearl's problem is settled,' said Margue.

'Hear at her! She's a mother – you wouldn't think it,' said Edgar.

'I'm thinking of my sister. He's always been a good father, I know.'

Edgar giggled and jerked his thumb. 'You and your good fathers!' He winked.

Margue said, 'I have a right to think for my sister, when there's trouble, Asa doesn't see wrong in it.'

Asa said, 'Asa doesn't see wrong in it, but I'm going to get Matt out of that hospital as soon as I can and take him where he won't see the face of a goon for a while; we'll go to Mexico. I'll give Pearl a bit of money, she can get a job, the girl has a job and that's that.'

Margue said, 'I can't understand, when danger threatens, the men run and the women stand their ground.'

Ed giggled, 'Look at Margue standing her ground! What are you standing for? I thought you were taking a honeymoon, a chartered flight to the south of France with the other canasta mamies, looking for romance, a Latin lover.'

'Well I want to get a look at France.'

'And I want to get a look at Buenos Aires.'

'It's not the same. You don't understand what women want: you never did understand me, Ed.'

Edgar laughed, winked at Asa, 'The Dolly Sisters.'

Margue said, 'Pearl and I had a hard time when we were girls. We all lived in one room and when Mother remarried –'

'You mean –'

'Be ashamed, Ed; we should be decent in the home. When Jack came in, there was just a blanket hung between us and the bed where the newly-wed pair were.'

'We all had a hard time,' said Edgar.

Asa said, 'Do you think it would be any good phoning round the hospitals? I don't know the hospital and I don't know if they have his name right; in the strike he used a different name, so he would get his army pay all right. I'll put in a long-distance to Martha – the gal who telegraphed me.'

'You do that, Asa,' said Margue.

Asa went out and began telephoning. Margue said, 'You see, Ed, he is real fond of Matt, like a real father: he always was crazy about Matt. But if anything happens I think we should tell the real father.'

'What sort of real father! Include me out. That real father never put up a cent for the kids and that real father has the nerve to hang around here whenever he wants to see them or on their birthdays, but he doesn't give them even a cake of soap.'

Margue argued, 'Pearl is a good mother, Ed! She got a good man to provide for the kids: that is the best thing a woman can do. What can a woman do if she's left? Pearl got a good father. You see her with the kids, she loves them, see her with them, any time, it's lovely and they know it too. They know about Asa and the real father, but they appreciate what she did for them. They adore their mother.'

'Then why does she tell them Asa's going crazy.'

'She does not say that.'

'She does say that.'

Margue said apologetically, 'But he is going crazy: he wants to go away, he wants to start a new life at his age; he wants to drop his responsibilities. And you can see she's right, he talked about going to Mexico. A woman has to think of her kids first of all. You wouldn't want her to forget them?'

'OK, OK, Pearl's all right, a nice girl.'

'And you know it, don't you? You and Pearl had a bit on the side.'

'Can it,' said Edgar.

At this moment Pearl herself came in the front door. She had a very pleasant ladylike manner, genial, humane, unruffled.

Pearl said, 'What are you doing here? Will just went a bit crazy last night, it's all right now.'

Margue said, 'You made it up? I thought it might just be a lovers' quarrel.'

Edgar sneered to himself.

Pearl said, 'I reasoned with him, told him everyone knows, it's no disgrace, everyone thinks it's natural. He'll be no worse off, he's not bound down, we'll get married later maybe, he might as well take a chance once in his life, we always suited each other and I told him Asa's moving out, got his bags packed. Will will have a real home, not that little dark basement room he has.'

Asa returned from the telephone. Edgar said, 'You moving out?'

'To the Turkish Bath. My shirts, I'll keep at the laundry. They're used to me.'

Edgar said to Pearl, 'Do you know your son Matt's in

hospital, kicked by a goon?'

Pearl said, 'Crazy guy, where did they kick him? What's he doing in California? I told him it's quieter here. You better go out there Asa, see Matt.'

Ed said, 'There's a mother for you. "Fly out Asa, not me. I've got to hang up a new curtain." '

Pearl said seriously, 'What can I do? Asa knows what to do. Is that why Asa's on the telephone?'

'He's fixing to fly to the hospital.'

'Yes, that's a good idea. I'll send Matt something he'll appreciate.'

Margue said, 'You really fixed it up? Will means it?'

Pearl said, 'Men are always funny about taking up with you; it makes them nervous. They're afraid of something. Just get them to cool it.'

Ed sneered. Margue said, 'Why I wonder is it? We take a chance as much as they do.'

Pearl said, 'Men are always thinking they might meet the right woman, we're more practical, there's no right man, we're not such dreamers.'

Edgar said, 'Dreamers! I was on the beach, I met Margue your sister, at Atlantic City under the boardwalk. I went out in a boat with her, we stayed in a place overnight and the next day we went back to New York together. Then a few months later, she's pregnant, we got married. That was a funny dream all right.'

Margue said, 'You're not right to talk about me that way to the family, Ed. I stood by you all these years, I'm your wife; and it hasn't been dreams for me; it's been tough all these years.'

Asa rushed in. Pearl said with sympathy, 'What's the news, honey?'

Asa cried, 'Matt's gone. Fractured skull: he never came round; he came to – for a minute –' he looked round, sank down, lowered his big wild head.

Pearl said, 'Matt! That's crazy! Such a lovely boy! You knew Matt.'

Asa staggered up and went to her: they embraced and consoled each other. Then Asa broke away roughly, 'I'm going, I'm going down to the airlines: they'll have to find me a seat.'

Edgar went out to ring up the airlines. Asa said wildly, picking up the red-covered book, 'I'll take this along and I'll read it on the plane and I'll laugh where Matt would have laughed. I'm going to see him. I won't laugh when I get there. I'll find out the goon and I'll break him. I'll crack his skull with my teeth. I'm going to get him.'

It turned out that the funeral was in three days, there were no seats on the planes, all priorities.

'You can't make it, you can't get there in time,' said Ed sadly.

'I'm still going, I'll tell them to freeze him. I'm going to take him with me. I'm not going to leave him there, where they killed him. I'll take him with me to Mexico. I won't bring him back here. I want to be able to go and look at him.'

Pearl had gone to the telephone to tell Jake the real father, her lover when they all were young. She came back to say Jake wanted Matt here, he wanted him buried here. She said maternally to Asa, 'After all, Asa, he has a right; he has a genuine right. He's the father.'

Asa got his hat jammed sideways on his head, he picked up the packed grip and dashing zigzag like a bumble bee, he rushed out of the house, crying, 'I'm going. I'll take a bus. I'll bum my way. I'm going to see Matt,' and he left.

Pearl got on the phone again and had a long soft consultation with Jake. They decided to do nothing. They had both known Asa from childhood. He would get out there, then would telegraph his grief and his whereabouts, telephone and do what they wanted, bring the boy back.

5   *Post-war Europe*

The Captain's House

The old cavalry town of St Germain-en-Laye is on the edge of a cliff above the Seine – Paris can be seen in the distance.

On the other side is the forest.

There are palaces, villas, gardens behind stone walls; there are wide stony streets.

The young couple went there early in spring to avoid Paris, where they had friends; and went to the first house-agent they saw, near the station. She said they would scarcely get private rooms now, because the season was beginning and the French and American officers had taken all the rented quarters.

She was a young woman, efficient, with abundant soft dark hair. They hesitated. 'The hotel in the market-place is very noisy.'

After looking at them again, she said, with a disturbed gentleness: 'There is a place; but you must stay three months and pay in advance. There are two rooms in a private house, in private grounds –' She paused, thinking of it, and they imagined a long park with a white manor house and two or three old trees blotching the view.

She began to tell parts of a story: 'It belongs to Captain Voisin; but it was his wife's. The countess died a year ago, in spring, very suddenly. She was young, quite young, only about forty, with black hair and so charming.'

While they made arrangements and paid, she could not help going on with the story; it escaped from her lips.

'It was such a terrible blow – she came home, she went to bed, and in three days she was dead. The house is too big now. He has only his daughter with him; and she, the countess, had the money.

'He was an officer in a Spahi corps, when she met him, and she did not mind that he was poor; he did not even own his own horse. She left the money to her daughter, who is engaged to marry; and she left the house to him.

'He is so pleasant, so kind and gentle; and he misses her so badly. He often comes in to see me.

'The countess sang beautifully. The house was full of music. You could hear her singing from the street. The house was never silent for a moment. You can imagine how he feels it!'

Long after they had arranged everything and she had telephoned the captain, she kept them there to tell the tale.

'He was broken with shock and grief. He had in two doctors from St Germain and a specialist from Paris.

'She died and he sued them for neglect. He spent all his money on the suits.

'Everyone pitied him; and he did not win.

'He is respected in town and the tax inspector and rates collector have given him time. But now he must let rooms in the house, to pay.

'You will really like it,' she continued in a friendly,

almost pleading manner. 'If you stay longer, the captain will be pleased. Because he needs the money, he really needs the money.'

The main road to Versailles runs through the big market-place and turns at an angle near the forest. This is not far to walk, but it is already in the suburbs of an old royal town that has been occupied by armies, French, German, American, in war and peace.

There are high-walled houses, a merchant's yard with hay, potatoes, wood, stables with reeking litter, old walls broken into for a small hairdresser, bootmender, grocer; cafés, some with queer décor, some frequented; a shuttered villa which is brilliantly lighted at night.

On the gate in a tall overhung fence is the notice, *Chien méchant*, beware of the dog; and the dog barked when they rang the bell.

Instantly cries like bells rang out behind the fence, 'Yac, Yac! Yac! Yac!' A soft-faced girl with long hair, an apron, house slippers, opened the gate.

'Madame?' they said. She giggled. Behind her, a large Greenland dog peeped out into the road. There was a flight of five steps to the front porch where, under the glass weather-fan, stood a tall man of sixty, of surprising beauty.

'Yac, these are friends!'

The dog slunk round and about sniffing.

Out of the hall rose a flight of polished wooden stairs, lip-curving down like petals. The Germans took their carpets, said the captain and he had not been able to replace them. 'But we keep them waxed!'

The German officers lived here in the early forties and allotted the attic floor to the captain and the countess.

The officers took their bed-linen, table silver and the best pictures, but they gave them others of poorer quality;

'otherwise,' says the captain, 'the Germans were very correct.'

They built a bomb-shelter at the end of the garden and said the captain and his wife might share it with them in a raid. The shelter is still there and looks like an underground tomb.

The captain and Marie-Lou the maid are joyous bringing up the baggage and he hangs a mirror in the slot of a room to be used for bathroom and kitchen, saying, 'That is for your shaving, sir.'

'I go to the barber's,' says Aldo.

'You are wrong sir.'

'Where may I wash?' says Laura.

This seems unexpected. He thinks and says, 'I'll go to the attic; I'll get you my wife's.' And he does go, and returns with the china and then with the washstand.

'These belonged to the countess,' he says, with wondering joy and pride, as if thinking again of his great luck.

Afterwards, he hesitates in the doorway, and says, embarrassed, that he will not report their stay to the police, for he would have to pay a tax; so he begs them not to tell anyone where they are staying and to get their letters at the *Poste restante.* This is agreed to. He is pleased.

Meanwhile the captain says several times, with a delighted expression, 'When my wife was alive, the house was different. It is sad and quiet now; but then it was filled with song. My wife had a lovely voice and she sang from morning till night.'

To live in, the villa is not sad and quiet. Anne-Rose, the captain's daughter, and Marie-Lou, the servant, try to fill it with song for the captain's sake. Marie-Lou's four-year-old daughter, Lilette, also sings like a skylark, faint and persistent.

They even try to outsing each other, Marie-Lou with a

sweet full voice using operatic and classical music and Anne-Rose, tuneless, singing ballads, folksongs and popular hits.

Marie-Lou is a slender weak girl, lightminded, touchy, overworked. '*Je suis bizarre,*' she says to them, 'I'm a bit odd.' '*Je sais que je suis bizarre, j'étais toujours bizarre.*" She is a relative of the countess and from a northern province; an unmarried mother.

The young tenants cannot bring themselves to call her Marie-Lou as if she were a servant, nor mademoiselle, because she has a daughter; so they politely call her madame, which displeases the countess's daughter, herself mademoiselle.

When they cross the hall downstairs to go out, Anne-Rose makes a point of calling out, 'Mademoiselle' though in general she calls her cousin Marie-Lou; and when they cross the hall at dinner-time, she jeers through the dining-room door, 'Ma-daame, Ma-daame!'

'Must I say Mademoiselle to a mother? I cannot,' says Aldo. 'Besides the Chamber of Deputies is considering whether all women shall not be called either madame or mademoiselle. Because many women suffer from these status titles.'

Marie-Lou's work is never done, and she is not paid, except by Aldo; this is in the agreement.

One day she stands dejected by the staircase.

'Are you ill, Madame?' says Aldo gently.

'I have cut my hand with the breadknife.' She shows a clumsy hasty bandage drenched with blood.

'Have you seen the doctor?'

'No, no. There are no doctors here.'

'What you need is an electric floor-waxer.'

'Not here, not here,' she says, mocking.

She has a sweet French and is a well-educated girl; but

there is something flimsy and out-at-elbow about her.

She has a pleasant voice, when singing, but there are days when she shrills and screams songs all day; even Beethoven's 'Ode to Joy' is screamed at the street.

'It is the turn of the moon,' says Aldo; 'my mother had a girl who did that.'

They find her in tears, polishing the lowest step, as they walk down. Aldo is cut to the quick, to think she must work for them, too.

'Even one girl like this is enough to condemn a society; if one idle girl and the captain, kind as he is to her, can potter about all day and trifle while they enslave one human being, then that society is condemned.'

He is impatient with the mannerly captain. Though it is spring, they go out in a shower of hail and come home cold; there is no heat in their rooms.

In the morning Lilette comes into the tenants and sings to them,

> 'Dors, ma Lilette, dors, ma mignonette,
> Quand tu auras vingt ans passés alors tu vas te marier
> Avec un homme sage, qui fera ton ménage,
> Avec un homme de Paris, qui fera ton petit lit.'

'Who taught you that sweet song, Lilette?'

'The good sisters taught me at school.'

She dances and waves her hands, she places her feet in and out. When they meet the little leaning nun with her infants' class in the street, she has a warm smile and the little children say, 'Bonjour, Monsieur et Madame.'

One morning Lilette brings them a statuette.

'This is for you; it is God.'

'The baby is God?'

'No, it's all God.'

'No, the baby is God; that's his mother.'

She looks at it thoughtfully, carries it back with her to work it out.

Often Marie-Lou takes her to school, but if it rains or Marie-Lou has her bad toothache, or her hand is bad, then the captain takes Lilette in the car; and he goes for her every afternoon while Marie-Lou is making dinner.

When he goes for Lilette, he changes his gardening clothes, puts on his gloves and hat; and when he brings the car back, he gets out in haste, goes round into the road, opens the door for Lilette, hands her out and escorts her to the gate.

Lilette is coquettish with him, sometimes dainty, sometimes rough. He stands quite still and lets her beat him on the haunches or try to push him down into the dirt.

Whoever stands at the gate must call, 'Yac, Yac!' and Yac answers 'Warf! Warf!'

At once people in the house shout, 'Yac, Yac! Yac!' and Lilette running in the garden, calls out, 'Yac, bad dog.'

When the tenants come into the garden, Yac stands up, puts his claws on their shoulders and licks their faces. He kisses them all over frantically, huffing and puffing with excitement; his slender black wolfish head hangs above them, showing his white wolfish teeth, his tongue hanging out.

He tries to walk along with them on two feet, kissing. Aldo does not like this at all; he does not think much of animals; but if he pushes him away, Yac becomes wilder: he thinks a game is beginning. Though so large, he is only seven months old; he thinks like a child.

Anne-Rose, the countess's daughter, is engaged to Charles-Robert, who comes on his motor-bike every evening; everyone calls him Charles-Robert.

On Saturdays, Yac, too, has a visitor, his sister Teet-Jeanne, a small black Greenland, who is brought by a little boy, Freddy. Yac and Teet-Jeanne run round and round, play hidings; they bite and wrestle and laugh.

Anne-Rose and Charles-Robert stand by the motor-bike and laugh and fondle. Freddy and Lilette run up the garden. The captain smiling, stands about awkwardly, very pleased. Aldo and Laura look from their upstairs window at the forest.

The forest is beginning to sigh and rustle, for evening is coming. There is a palace opposite, behind a high garden wall and behind old chestnut trees; but they can see in.

In the palace are workshops. There in the week, women and girls paint raincoats. Through the windows of the palace in every room, in the drawing-rooms, the dining-rooms, the bedrooms, in the hayloft and the attics of the stables, where once the men slept, there can now be seen beautiful raincoats, in every paintbox colour.

They come out of cases, they are stretched on long tables, they hang in the hayloft on racks, they are packed into separate cardboard boxes with tissue paper, downstairs; and on Monday they will go away again in trucks.

All the fruit-trees, the nut-trees, the flowers of the palace have come out in leaf and bud. The girls, women and men have gone home. The wind in the forest is coming from the east. It turns over the heads of the trees. The forest is beginning to roar.

Yac's father and mother, two small Greenlands, are taking a walk in the forest.

There are beds of violets, and many kinds of low spring plants and many old trees covered by ivy, which has smothered and split them.

Here and there by the paths are depressions once hastily dug; men lay in those hollows, living and dead. There are riding-paths down which ride men and women in coloured jackets on shining horses of magnolia, chestnut colours.

There, along the path by the hospital's gnarled wall come girls and women in white hoods and white shoes;

they have big clean faces and bright eyes; free among the trees and singing.

Yac's father and mother bark at the horses, the fluttering ivy, the lizards in the violet-beds, the singing nuns. Yac hears them and calls to them, 'Yac, Yac! I am Yac, Yac!' But Yac's parents take no notice of him; they have forgotten all about him and Teet-Jeanne.

Marie-Lou lays the table. Anne-Rose is sitting embroidering a tablecloth. Upstairs, Lilette is weeping.

The captain rouses himself from his chair, he takes the stairs three at a time, but softly.

'What's the matter, my darling?'

'I can't have dinner, because I must put my things away,' says Lilette.

The captain bends to the floor, curls his big hands over the doll's furniture and puts it all in the doll's house.

Aldo is angry with the captain because there is no heat. Aldo says, 'Yes he is nice to Lilette, treating her like a granddaughter, but the little pious stories always have a kind old retired gendarme with a dainty little fury he loves; that doesn't make him less a gendarme.'

'Old Kasper and little Wilhemine,' says Laura.

'I must make dinner because Marie-Lou's hand is too bad,' says Anne-Rose. 'So what will it be – oeuffs, poached, fried, boiled, scrambled; any kind of oeuffs?' She was in England during the occupation, as a little child, and now she thinks it amusing to speak an English kind of French.

Aldo and Laura take Lilette out for the afternoon. They go to a teashop, order a plate of fancy cakes, ice-cream and lemonade. But Lilette refuses them all.

'I cannot eat any of that, because I have decayed teeth,' and she shows them – little rows of broken brown teeth, like bad dock timbers.

On the way home, they buy her what she points to, a

boy bridegroom and a girl bride standing together; but at home Marie-Lou is shocked. She takes them away from her and wraps them in muslin. Lilette must keep them eight years, till her First Communion.

One day because of the ashes still steaming and glowing, the dustmen do not collect the rubbish and the next day Yac has taken it in hand. He has spread it all about the garden, not failing to pick our choice items, like Marie-Lou's bloodstained hand bandage, which he spreads out on the cellar steps, while he takes other finds to his kennel.

'Oh, this dog is the plague of my life,' says Anne-Rose. 'He must be trained.'

Now Yac is tied to his kennel. That day, the house, the suburb, ring with his sorrow. Sometimes he yelps so sharply that people pitch out of the house, shouting, 'Yac has hung himself on his chain.'

Lilette creeps into his kennel with him, hugs him and talks softly; and for a while he is quiet, but his shouts do not stop till nightfall. 'Oh, let him off the chain!' No, no, he must learn to be a bad dog. This hugging and kissing won't do for a watchdog.

The tenants are sorry. Each night they make for him a meat patty and take it down when they go out to the café for coffee. 'We must not forget Yac's hamburger,' they say.

'Yac's hamburger, Yac's hamburger,' jeers Anne-Rose, when they pass through the hall. She does not like the young couple; she is afflicted by the presence of tenants in her home.

They go to a café near the castle and the station. St Germain is now a very lively town: it is full season.

The waiter in the café has become used to them.

He likes men only, well-dressed Frenchmen only. A

pink and clownish face, red waving hair, he goes 'tt-tt' when he sees shy, shabby or foreign people in the café.

He stops, stands, watches them at the door, tries to will them away, even if they have seated themselves before he sees them, even when they are decent lady school-teachers or foreign tourists, well-to-do Spanish or American.

He does not like anything eccentric. He might 'tt-tt' Aldo and Laura too, but he likes Aldo.

So, when he sees them, he smiles and makes not the slightest difficulty about taking off Laura's coat, though he prefers Aldo to do it.

He likes a few friends and is a very nervous touchy man. Still, he gives splendid service; he's swift, neat, efficient, perfection. He is saving up for a fine café of his own, and Aldo discusses it with him.

When Aldo and Laura return about eleven, in the front hall lies a large black blot which remains silent but wags its tail; and as they advance with caution up the waxy stairs, it jumps up and, bounding awkwardly after them, kisses them.

He sneaks up after them, in silence, understanding the mystery, Night; he creeps to door after door snuffling; and though he is supposed to lie on the mat in the hall, when all are asleep he lies on the landing near his people.

One day Aldo slips on the bare polished wood, falls downstairs and bumps his head. The captain helps him to his own sitting-room, places him on a couch and speaks cheerily.

'It will be nothing, my dear sir – just a bump. Don't worry about it; a little rest and it will come right. I'm an old soldier. In the cavalry we were always getting bumps and bruises; but at the most, a few days in bed and then right as rain.'

He talks about the room, to take Aldo's mind off his trifling misfortune. There is a picture of the hero of Verdun and of Vichy, the old Marshal Pétain, of his Holiness the Pope, and framed also, the Pope's blessing on the captain's marriage with the countess and the certificate which makes the captain a Papal count.

'I am not a real count, you know,' he says honestly; 'I am a count by courtesy.'

There on the walls are swords, daggers, 'heroic cutlery' as Aldo says, pictures of guards mounted, lines of cavalry, and the captain in Spahi uniform, tall, young and the gift of beauty in his empty face.

He at length helps Aldo up to his own room and there for some days Aldo lies suffering.

Laura asks the captain for a doctor: 'Perhaps my husband has broken a rib.' The big man is frightened. 'But I can't ask the doctors to come; in this town they won't have anything to do with me.'

'But they would come to us.'

'But if they came, they would see that I have tenants; they would want their money. They wanted me to sell this house, do you know that? When I must leave it to my daughter. Please do not call for a doctor: no, no, it is out of the question. The gentleman will be all right.'

'Can we get a doctor from Versailles or Paris?'

'No, no, it would become known. I assure he will be all right. It is just shock. I know all about these little accidents.'

'If he will not, let us wait,' says Aldo, depressed. He lies in bed for several weeks.

It is cold, for they face north. All day long Yac howls, shrieks and yelps. The girls sing and outsing. When Aldo gets up, they go into the dusty boxroom for a ray of sun.

Marie-Lou, Lilette and the captain visit the sick man.

The captain makes conversation.

Aldo says something about Russia, the captain chatters away: 'The German officers when they were here, told me how barbaric the Russians are. A major had a Frenchman's finger in cottonwool in a box. I saw it myself. The Russian had hacked it off for the seal-ring – and not much of a seal-ring. But it was found on one of them and brought back by the Germans. With my own eyes, I assure you, sir.'

When he goes, Aldo is furious. 'What an imbecile! You can buy them in the tricks and jokes stores, such fingers.'

At length, Aldo goes to a doctor in Paris. 'Ah yes,' says the doctor, 'I know those stairs. Throughout Paris, when the Germans left, we had those stairs; you could not dissuade the housewives.'

On the way home, Aldo stops at the agency to give notice. When he reaches the villa, the captain already knows and says, deploring: 'I thought you would stay another three months; I thought you liked it here.'

'You see, we must go to Paris to see our friends; we need friends.'

The next day, the captain asks them down to the back-garden, sunny and full of flowers.

'I want you to meet my old friend the Countess Delamare. She lives not far away. I frequently go and have tea with her; in the afternoons. She wants to meet you and perhaps you can visit her, too. For tea, in the afternoons. You will have friends here.'

There stands the countess, a tall, fleshy woman of about sixty, in a long, dowdy dress, and she gives them a wizened frolic glance. She shakes hands and says, 'Perhaps you will come to call on me some afternoon,' and almost laughs, for she knows they will not.

The captain however, delighted, is like a boy let off punishment. Afterwards, he says to them, 'I am not very good at things; my wife did everything and always knew what was best. But the Countess Delamare gives me good advice. You will like her: she is very entertaining.'

'Thank you,' they say.

Anne-Rose is restless. During the transport strike, she found an excuse to go to Paris, riding pillion with Charles-Robert on the motor-bike. There she stayed with friends in the fashionable Sixteenth Arrondissement, doing office work as a volunteer against the strikers; and now she has gone again, to stay there till she marries in the fashionable church in which her mother was married.

The captain is very merry. He dines every evening with Lilette and Marie-Lou. Decorously, he keeps the curtains of the dining-room open so that anyone may glance in. They sit long at table and there is continuous gay talk, singing and fits of laughter.

Marie-Lou is quite different, sounder, stronger. But the time has come for Aldo and Laura to go. They say goodbye to the agent. She is polite to them in a reproachful tone.

'It was the accident chiefly,' they explain. She watches them, standing there in her soft dark dress, with her arms drooping against her thighs and as if she stood behind the fine black gauze used by photographers.

'The accident?'

'We could not get doctors. The captain would not send for them.'

'But you see –' and she begins to tell the story, as if they had not understood and would now relent.

Yac, Yac

The house is on the edge of town near the forest. The highroad runs past the house with soldiers, guns, horses and tanks; and in the early mornings with trucks and carts carrying vegetables, fruit, cheese, meat for the town market.

The house has a high fence and gate. On the gate is a sign, *Beware, Bad Dog.* When anyone stands at the gate, the dog barks; 'Warf, warf, warf!' Then you shout, 'Yac, Yac, Yac!' People in the house also shout, 'Yac, Yac, Yac!' and a little girl running in the garden, calls out: 'Yac, bad dog.' You ring the gate-bell. Marie-Lou, a maid, a pretty young woman with curls on her shoulders, comes out in apron and slippers and opens the gate. Yac tries to hide behind her and look out into the road. Yac is a stove-black Greenland dog, a puppy only seven months old, but very, very large. He knows that he is a puppy. He does not know that on the front gate they tell you to beware of the bad dog. He is not a bad dog; he is a very good dog. When you come into the garden, he stands up and puts his front paws on your shoulders and licks your face; he kisses you all over frantically, his slender black wolfish head hangs above you, he shows his shining white wolfish teeth, his tongue hangs out, he huffs and puffs, he dances and whines and grumbles with excitement. He tries to walk along with you, on two feet, kissing.

The house is white and between the front windows, two on each side, are steps leading up to a platform and the front door, over which a glass weather-fan projects. There stands the count-captain. 'Yac,' says the captain, 'this is a friend! A friend, do you hear?' Yac, with his tail and ears lowered, sniffing everywhere, slinks around and between your legs. He jumps up and sniffs your chest, your arms, your neck. 'Down, Yac.' Yac slinks about. Yac belongs to the count-captain, but he hopes he belongs to Lilette. Lilette is a little girl, four years old, with long curls on her shoulders and her mother is Marie-Lou. Her father was a soldier who is long gone and perhaps long dead.

Yac has a sister he sees once a week on Saturdays. This sister's name is Teet-Jeanne. Teet-Jeanne is brought to visit once a week by a little boy called Freddy. Yac and Teet-Jeanne run round and round, they chase each other and bark, they bite and wrestle and laugh at each other. When Freddy takes Teet-Jeanne home, then Yac is naughty. He barks after Teet-Jeanne all the way home; he can hear her going home because she barks back at him. When she gets home, she barks, 'I am home.' And Yac barks, 'Come back, come back!' 'I'm going to eat now,' Teet-Jeanne barks. 'Oh, she's going to eat,' barks Yac and he begins to cry. He barks and howls. Older dogs in other gardens, talk to Yac. They bark, 'Are you lonely? Cheer up!' or 'I'm lonely, too.' But Yac very often takes no notice; or else he answers the other dogs and then he begins to cry again. 'Teet-Jeanne! Teet-Jeanne! Oh-oh!'

Everyone in the house shouts, 'Yac, Yac, Yac!'

There are people living upstairs. They shout, 'Yac!' There are Marie-Lou and Lilette living in the attic. Lilette runs to the dormer window and calls out angrily, 'Yac! Bad dog!'

For a moment Yac is quiet; then he thinks of his troubles and because he is so young and so small, he begins to cry again. He is not really small, but he thinks he is small.

The captain's wife, the countess, very pretty and very kindhearted, is in her studio on the second floor, where she is painting and singing. She stops singing and she calls out, 'Yac! Poor, poor Yac!' But Yac takes no notice. 'Yac!'

'Yac!' says the captain downstairs. The captain is sitting in the backroom which has a glass wall and is full of light; he is waiting for them to start cooking dinner. Beside him, his daughter Rosalie is sitting in a chair and embroidering a tablecloth, for her future home. She is engaged to a boy called Charles-Robert, who comes every day on his motorbike. Everyone calls him Charles-Robert. They are going to be married in the smartest church in the smartest quarter of Paris; all because of the countess. Rosalie speaks a peculiar French. They sent her to England during the occupation and she now thinks it better to speak an English sort of French.

'Oh, this noisy dog is the plague of my life,' says Rosalie; 'he must be trained.'

Upstairs, the countess is singing again. Marie-Lou, in the kitchen, begins scolding Lilette; 'You won't get any dinner till you tidy upstairs.' Lilette, sniffing, climbs the stairs, hanging on to each banister.

The people in the attic are looking out of the windows at the forest. The forest is beginning to sigh and roar gently, for evening is coming. There is a palace opposite, behind a high garden wall and behind thick chestnut trees; but from where they are, they can see in. In the palace are now workshops. There are women and girls who are painting raincoats. Through the windows of the palace, in every room, in the drawing-rooms, the dining-rooms, in the bedrooms, the halls, and in the hayloft and attics of the stables, there are now beautiful raincoats, in every paintbox colour. They come out of cases, they are stretched on long tables, they hang in the hayloft on racks, they are packed into separate cardboard boxes with tissue paper, downstairs; and they are sent away again in waggons.

All the fruit-trees, the chestnut-trees, the flowers of the palace, have come out; you can see them and the coloured raincoats. It is evening now and the girls and women are going home. There is a wind in the forest coming from the east. It turns over the heads of the trees. The forest is beginning to roar.

Yac's father and mother, two smaller Greenlands, are taking a walk in the forest. There are beds of violets, and many kinds of low spring plants, and many old trees covered by ivy which has smothered and split them. Here and there are depressions once hastily dug, when French-men hoped to stay the Germans as they advanced; men lay in these hollows, living and dead. There are riding-paths down which ride men and women in coloured jackets, on shining horses of all horse colours. There, along the path, by the hospital, are girls and women all in white, with white hoods and white shoes; they have big clean faces and bright eyes; they are singing. Yac's father and mother bark at the horses, the fluttering ivy, the lizards in the violet-beds, the singing nuns. Yac hears them and he stops crying; he answers back, 'Yac! Yac! I am Yac, Yac!' But Yac's father and mother take no notice of him; they have forgotten all about him and Teet-Jeanne.

Marie-Lou lays the table. Rosalie, the daughter of a countess, is sitting still, embroidering a tablecloth. Upstairs Lilette is crying. 'What is the matter, my little treasure?' says the captain's wife. 'I can't have dinner because I must put my things away,' says Lilette. The captain's wife helps Lilette to put all the furniture back into the doll's house. 'Now go and give Yac his dinner,' says the captain's wife; 'Yac is crying because he is hungry.'

The captain is an old soldier. Once he fought in the desert, rode on an Arab horse, wore an Arab costume. He was tall, fair, with large bright blue eyes and everyone called him *Un beau gendarme*. He owned nothing at all, not even his Arab horse; but he was so handsome, so gay, so loving and gentle that the young countess felt she could marry no one else; and by courtesy he too achieved rank. The family then arranged it that he should become a real count in his own right; and there it hangs on the wall, a document proclaiming that he is a Papal count. He shows it to the tenants and he is very pleasant about it; he tells the whole story truthfully. 'I am only a count by courtesy, as it were.'

The tenants, going out after supper, to sit in a café in the town, bring down what they call 'Yac's hamburger'. It is made out of giblets and other remnants of the chicken they ate. They go through the hall saying, 'Here is Yac's hamburger.' Rosalie at table roars with laughter, 'Here is Yac's hamburger.'

Yac, alas, is now chained up all day, to teach him to be a bad dog; this will never do, this kissing and hugging and dancing that he does. So he moans and shrieks; his wretchedness flows out over the neighbourhood. He stops moaning to hide the hamburger in the back of his kennel. When the tenants return, it is very late. They let themselves in with two keys. In the front hall, on the linoleum, is a large black splotch, which remains silent, though it wags its tail; and as they advance towards the stairs it jumps up and overtopping them, kisses them. That is Yac, the housedog, now trained to mind the house. He sneaks after them up the stairs, but in silence; and after everyone is behind doors he, in silence, understanding the mystery, Night, creeps to door after door, snuffling for reassurance; and though he is supposed to lie on a mat in the front hall, when all are asleep he lies on the landing near to his people.

The Hotel-Keeper's Story

If I knew how to write, I would write a book about what happens in the hotel every day. Not a day passes without something happening; some days too much happens. Yesterday afternoon a woman rang me up from Geneva and told me her daughter-in-law died, died yesterday. The woman stayed here twice and came to see me several times. We became friendly and she confided in me although I always felt that I didn't know the truth about her, whether she was divorced and remarried, or otherwise. I knew her before her son was married and I always felt she had a secret or trouble, for she used to telephone me crying and saying she must talk to a friend and I was so good to her. I was looking for a friend too and I still am; for I never had one since I lost my girlhood friend who married a German exile and is now living in Berlin; but this woman was not really my friend. We did not tell everything to each other. My girl friend Elsa and I never had any secrets; we laughed and we talked – and when her parents put her out of the house because of her affair with the German, she came to my place and had her baby there: and that was the happiest time of my married life; but of course she was in trouble then, and had other things to think of. When you grow up and marry there is a shadow over everything, you can never be happy again. How happy you are as a girl, going out with your friends and always laughing! Besides, you understand I have the hotel to manage, the marketing to supervise, I do most of it myself; I have the menus to type out, the servants to manage; I have to settle all the troubles with the guests; and then I must talk to them all; anyone who comes here and stays for a few months or for the winter season, feels that we are his friends. Still, if anyone needs me I must talk to them mustn't I? This woman used to telephone me every day during her son's engagement and early married days when he left the house for his bride's house, and then for a few months I almost forgot about them. Then she telephoned me and said that her son and daughter-in-law had moved in with her, and she was laughing and crying, nothing so tragic and so beautiful had ever happened to her; and then she began to telephone me every day again, telling me all that went on with the young couple in the house. I don't know what went on; she would be laughing and crying, and it was never clear except that she talked so much about unhappiness and happiness, love and misunderstanding; and I began to try to miss her telephone call. It is not only the accounts but my little boy takes up my time; I must go out in the evenings with Roger when he goes on drinking parties; and then I am obliged to study French and English; and then I felt it was all useless, I had not the time and I felt there was something weighing on her which she could not tell me. Yesterday, when I head her voice I felt a blow on my heart; she was crying and she said something terrible had happened and she must tell me the end of it before she called the police. It was very confused for she was sobbing and exclaiming and yet she said it had to come to that and I think she said that her daughter-in-law was dead and her son had gone away and left her. But it may have been that her son was dead too, or that her son was dead because she had killed her daughter-in-law; and for a moment I thought she said that her son had killed his wife. But I kept hearing, 'This horror, this abomination' – and what was it? It occurred to me afterwards that it sounded more like an accident or that her daughter-in-law had committed suicide. She spoke in French so hurriedly and my French is not very good. I have not had time to look in the paper this morning; and then I have always had a suspicion that I don't know her real name now. You can see how close we get to people and yet we stay right outside of their lives. We know everything and very little. We don't enquire too far and we keep silent on many things we guess. The police are there to do their job; we do ours: we work together and respect each other, because each keeps to his function. The police are our friends and we need their help.

Yesterday morning I had trouble with that dark fat man you may have noticed the whole of last week in the dining-room. He took double helpings at all his meals and had three decilitres of wine with each meal and his breakfast in his bedroom. He came last Thursday and asked for a room. I quoted him four francs fifty, the usual price which is written up over the gate, and yesterday gave him his bill, at twelve francs fifty complete pension plus the wine he had drunk and service extra, the usual thing; but he said I had quoted four francs fifty all-in and he would only pay thirty-one francs without even the service extra. Besides he said he had no more money except for his fare on to Berne where he has to go for business. 'I don't care about that,' I said, 'you must pay for your meals and wine. Besides I know you have much more money than you say; you probably have two or three hundred francs in your wallet.' You see we get used to sizing people up. I had already thought I would have some kind of trouble with this man although he was quite quiet; but I felt sure he had some money and we can do nothing until it is time to present the bill. I was ready for him you might say. He spent two hours arguing and took his wallet out to show me he had only fifty or sixty francs; he called me a robber, a thief, a liar and said he would send for the police. 'Send for the police, I shall be glad of that,' I said. But I had already sent Jenny for the police. It is a good thing, a blessing for me that they are only just down the street: they come in four or five minutes any time I send for them. They haven't much to do and they like the excitement, too. Well, they made him pay and sure enough he had over two hundred francs in his pocket! They went over his papers, and there were some details he didn't want known – that, however, is neither here nor there – and he went away quite quietly in the end to the bus-stop with the gendarme who put him on the bus for the station.

As for that short fat man who is always on the stairs, and who is at present in numbers five and six, he is the Mayor of B., the Belgian city. He is a funny customer, I never had one like him. He makes us all laugh and he is a little hard to handle but so good-natured that I don't mind; besides he keeps the servants in good humour. He came on Tuesday two weeks ago in a Belgian limousine with a liveried chauffeur who put him down with two leather bags and a shopping-bag outside the hotel and drove off. He was quite negligently dressed, in old sports clothes and a worn felt hat just as you have seen him. He said he stopped at our hotel because of its name, *Hotel Swiss-Touring,* he wanted a hotel, he was in Switzerland and he was on tour; and he laughed. He said he must have the best room in the house, but there was only a small one vacant then on the second landing where the best rooms are, so I said he could have that and take the large double room as soon as the Russian family moved out. It was then he told us that he was the Mayor of B. and that he had come here for treatment because he had been over-worked and been having too good a time after work; high living and high thinking, he said. Then he said he had got very nervous under the Germans and that as he was in his fifties now he could not stand things the way he could when younger. He not only filled out all the required details on his police paper but he wrote in, 'So-and-So, Mayor of B., Belgium,' and made several additions, things not required by our officials. 'Perhaps they require that in Belgium,' I said to Roger. But Roger said no. 'Well,' I added, 'perhaps the Germans required that and he has got it on his mind; for he keeps talking about the Germans.' But Roger coloured and declared that the Germans did not make people fill out nonsense. The Germans are a modern, orderly people whose only object was to bring backward countries up-to-date and to pre-vent the disorder malignantly stirred up by the commu-nists. Roger at one time worked in Germany, and has pleasant memories of the Nazi days, for he was butler to one of Hitler's generals at one time. I can't help teasing him about it; 'You're French and you're Swiss,' I say, 'and you love the Germans, while I'm German Swiss and I hate them. Why is that, Roger? Because I understand them.' And I can't help telling him that his father was only a farmer, while mine was a government official and that I always lived in the thick of such discussions and so I know what has been going on all the time. 'Isn't it a shame to have the chance of being neutral?' I ask Roger, partly teasing and partly serious. 'A shame to be a partisan and of such wicked people as the Nazis?' This makes him very angry and upset; the first time I said it in the first year of our married life, he left me and went away for three weeks without giving any sign of life. It's a strange thing how this insults him, for underneath, at heart, Roger is a decent man and reasonable. But you know the Germans have left deep marks on everyone's heart and mind in Europe; they have burned themselves in, for better and for worse, and so it will be for a long time. Well, I get too much of it, and I can't help giving some of it back, though I am very good-natured and in my business cannot offend people.

At first the Mayor took his meals in the dining-room and was very affable. He went from table to table making friends and talking about the weather, even inviting people to his room to have champagne, but after a few days he began to complain about Germans in the hotel. One evening he had just begun his meal when our two Dutch ladies walked in; and he got up and came straight to me in the office with his serviette in his hand and quite loudly and rudely said he must finish his meal in his room, that he refused to sit down with Germans. I explained that they were Dutch and came to us every year. But he has eaten his meals upstairs ever since. I cannot make up my mind whether he objected to the Germans in his country; or whether he had too much to do with them. He twits us and harps upon the subject and I wonder if he does not do it to get a rise out of me too; for he must know from my way of speaking French that I am

German Swiss. Then, for instance, he came upon me speaking German to Jenny and he said to me, 'Who is that German woman?' I was quite firm with him. 'She is a Swiss girl and my housekeeper,' I said.

And what did he do? I had to laugh even so. Lina and I laughed together. Lina the chambermaid, not the kitchen-maid, came down laughing you see, and saying, 'Here is an official communication from the Mayor of B.' It was a little cotton hand-towel with our name embroidered on it in red, *Hotel Swiss-Touring Ouchy*. He had written all round the border and then on the towel and in such a way as to keep on including the embroidered name in his message:

> It is no wonder that the guests of the Hotel Swiss-Touring Ouchy use your skinny little hand-towels for writing notes to the management of the Hotel Swiss-Touring Ouchy and letters to their friends, for in your German starvation hotel you do not provide good writing paper for the guests of the Hotel Swiss-Touring Ouchy and they are going to be always obliged to inscribe their letters, papers, documents, bills, receipts, memoranda, diaries and last will and testaments on your little skinny hand-towels. Take notice for if you do not I am going to do my writing on your hand-towels, wash-cloths, floorcloths, mops, window curtains and bed-sheets; and I shall even use the counterpane. Notice to the German Hotel-keepers! Provide paper for guests, even in the little back room. Document Two. So-and-so, the Mayor of B.

You can imagine I kept it; and of course I charged it in the bill, as well as the cost of a tablecloth and a traycloth which he likewise wrote complaints upon and sent down to the office to me, numbered like all the rest of his written statements. You see his police paper was Document One. There was no nonsense about him, he understood everything and was very witty, saucy, sarcastic about things. He has his wits about him; and I'm quite sure he has been someone important all his life and is used to doing just as he pleases. I expressed this idea to Roger but Roger was still furious about the German question and he replied that he was just like all Belgians and now I could see how necessary it was for the Germans to walk in and bring up-to-date this old-fashioned, medieval, fantastic society. 'Well, then, we must invade all other countries and teach them hotel-keeping, banking and how to make watches,' I said laughing. But at that Roger shut his mouth tight and went out into the town to join his drinking friends. Well, that is a thing that used to make me cry and gave me headaches but now for the most part I laugh and I am getting to like my life. In fact, this is my life, the hotel, my little boy, and Roger and I look back to the days when I was a girl and think, 'How did I get on without all this? What did I do all day?'

The Mayor's other documents were all kinds of things, postcards of the lake which he gave me to post in dozens; and some which he posted himself to me. One of them is so funny that I kept it to show people. It is addressed to me, Madame Bonnard, Proprietress, Hotel Swiss-Touring etc., and has a number like all of them, Document 89. I do not know if it is really 89. He says he keeps the more important documents, his own notes and his diaries himself. It is written all over in a very good hand,

Madame Bonnard, my damn Bonnard, bonart, bon-narr, bonnarrish, anyone who wants to visit your hotel can apply to me, the Mayor of B., and I will recommend this hotel, like all the Germans it contains, sweet little Germans, sweet dirty Germs, down with Germs, down with Germans, why do you have Dutch-Germans and Swiss-Germans in your hotel? Your hot-hot-hot-hotel, not-hot-

hotel, down with Germanisms, down with Hotelism. Madame Bonnard is a very good German, a, b, c, d, e, f, ach-german, boo-german, cousin-german, down with german, and the german, foul german, germ-man. Come and drink champagne with me, germadam! Document 89. Sgd. Mayor So-and-So of B. Belgium.

And after that every day, ever hour, the maids and the servants brought me messages from the Mayor. And what do you think is the latest! He has numbered all his clothes. He took them all out and spread them about the floor, the towel-rack and the bed with a number pinned to each one and he has given chances in the lottery to every one of the servants. The guests have refused them; but he went out at night and posted a numbered piece of paper to each one of the guests; and the Dutch ladies and Jenny the housekeeper and myself got two each because we are Germans, he says; the Germans know how to strip people better than others and so we have two chances in the lottery; then he will be naked, and he will have to stay all day in his room and drink champagne. That is what he says. In the meantime, he goes of course to the specialist who is giving him shock-treatment so he tells me, of one thousand volts a time; a little more, says he, only one thousand and two volts and he would fall down dead. He needs the champagne as a pick-up after the treatments. And besides this he has taken a season ticket to Zurich and another to Geneva. He actually does go to those places. I have seen lawyer's letters from Geneva and Zurich addressed to him, So-and-so, Mayor of B.; and one came to So-and-so, Mayor of L. I said to him, 'But you can't also be Mayor of L.' He said, 'L. is a fortress city, it is built to stand against the dirty Germans and next time the Germans come visiting I am going to be Mayor of L. and I will show them tricks.' All this is rather strange, I know;

and yet the man is doing business here and I suppose it is just the result of his nervous breakdown and his champagne. He crosses the frontier for example nearly every day and brings back champagne from France. He does not even hide it. I suppose he gives some to the frontier guards. And then he buys it here and offers it to everyone; and he said to me,

'Madame German, I have brought you a whole crate of champagne and we will toast the régime in it,' but it was only a toy crate of liqueur chocolates in the shape of bottles, you know, so I was able to accept it. In all he does, he shows a very good heart; and he pays his bills not only promptly but generously; and gives presents to all the servants. Naturally I have had to stop them drinking champagne. All this gives them something to think about. They are much more cheerful at present. I should not mind at all his little jabs at me, if it were not that he touches on this very sore point of nationality; for I have more than my hands full with a Swiss-French cook who thinks very highly of himself because his grandfather worked for the La Harpes who as you know were at the Russian Court; an Italian kitchenmaid who came here almost barefoot from her mountain village, and a German-Swiss housekeeper, to mention only three of them. All these dislike each other. The cook is nervous like all cooks and really would love to poison the others. The Italian maid feels she's despised, and Jenny is a poison-pen writer and when things don't suit her, she goes on the rampage and drinks vermouth in her room. Still I know more than I used to and when they are too troublesome I threaten to send for the police. That dampens their spirits; they all go quietly back to work.

Well, as for the Mayor, I suppose he will settle down. He intends to live here in Switzerland. He is negotiating the purchase of several large properties in Geneva, some businesses in Zurich, and he is just about to buy the *Hotel Lake-Leman,* the one with the palms near the casino you know. I had no idea it was for sale. But the Mayor found out immediately. He has been over there for the past week, has inspected it from top to bottom and he is ready to conclude the deal. If he buys the hotel I suppose he will settle down in this town. You see he has taken a great fancy to my little son, Adrian, even though he is only three years old. Adrian is very forward for his age I know and very engaging, naturally charming like his grandfather. He spoke and walked much earlier than most children and has a wonderful gift of doing imitations. Perhaps he will be an actor when he grows up. All you have to do is give him a piece of lace or a shawl and he will spend hours, the whole afternoon, talking to himself and impersonating things. Sometimes he is a lady, or a dancer, or the Mayor, or Mrs Trollope or a fisherman; and all with a scarf, a piece of string! Mrs Trollope's husband, Mr Wilkins, told me that in his experience, hotel children are very bright because they are brought up in mixed society from the very beginning and have none of that shyness which is at the bottom just uncouthness. The Mayor of B. says he will stay with us, then; and he is giving the *Hotel Lake-Leman* to Adrian because he has fallen so much in love with him. Naturally, I refused and so did Roger; but the Mayor is very pressing and has already given me a document promising the hotel to Adrian. We cannot take it – how can we take property of that value? And I pointed this out to the Mayor. I even said, 'What will your heirs think? What will they say?' 'Then,' he said, 'since you are so scrupulous, so honourable and so businesslike, I will just give you the hotel in trust for Adrian, or for myself, and you shall draw the benefits and I will pay you a management fee, and I will retain the property in my name. Will that suit you?' But we still have not decided; for it does look strange, when we have known him such a short time. Roger even wonders if the funds are his and insists that we must employ a detective to discover the origin of the funds; for he does not believe that the Mayor is simply good-hearted and has fallen in love with Adrian as I do. But the Mayor told me himself that he is so happy here and we are so good to him that he wants to live here for ever and never go back. He says he is very tired, he has lived his life and now he wants to retire and live for ever in heaven on our beautiful lake. There is nothing uncommon in this. So many people do it. In our hotel there are half a dozen retired people who want to do just that. 'Very well!' says Roger, 'but he mixes up the Germans too much in his story and we must find out where he got those funds and what right he has to them; and whether he has not simply absconded with funds; perhaps he is an embezzler, a thief.' And Mrs Trollope, who is very sharp in money matters, said to me: 'Telephone to B. If he is such a well-known person nothing could be easier. Telephone to the Town Hall, X.B., or let Mr Wilkins.' But we have not done it yet. We have no right to meddle in our guests' affairs. Let him stay here I say and do his deals which have nothing to do with us, and if he presses the *Hotel Lake-Leman* upon us, we will get a lawyer to look into it. If a lawyer says it is all right, we are safe from legal pursuit.

I was walking over to the movies only last night with Mrs Trollope when we passed the Mayor of B. outside the *Hotel Lake-Leman;* he was there without a hat and in a very unconventional costume as usual, for that is how he goes everywhere even to France and Geneva. He saw me and came up excitedly, not even noticing Mrs Trollope, and he said; 'It's done, it's done, just as I told you. It was all fixed up, signed, sealed and delivered forty minutes ago; aren't you glad of that?' So I smiled at him and talked with him a while and went on to the movies with Mrs Trollope, for it was getting late. 'Who is that?' said she. She had not seen him at first and lately he has been eating in his room. In the intermission I told her all about him. She listened to me eagerly; but she said, 'I suppose he drank and made merry with the Germans and now he has gone mad.'

A Household

The Swiss City of Basle is on the river Rhine at the head of that trade route which is effectively closed by the Falls of Schaffhausen, some distance above. Basle stands on a tongue of land between the German and French frontiers. There is a small green park called the Brüderholz over which the warring nations sent stray shots during the last war.

Before it enters the city the Rhine flood passes green fields, low hills and orchard valleys: below, it pours towards the electric station of Kems where it enters and rises above a strange moon hollow, easily flooded. After that, bearing boats and barges, it goes down to the German Rhine cities and ports, and on to Rotterdam, nine days away.

The city's Rhine Bridge crosses a narrow gorge through which the river gushes between strong piers, deep boisterous waters, threaded like bundles of green reeds; and in this water can be seen turning and diving, pale long soft forms – they look like Rhine maidens; they are large salmon.

Little Basle lies low on the right bank: beyond it, a deer park marks the fringe of Switzerland. It is sullen in summer with thick-leaved old trees that do not let the sun through and with the gloomy bellowing of stags. Beyond this, also marking the German frontier, a funeral place, lifeless, soundless, neat, with pale inhuman lawns. Then, a barrier, a low bluff and Germany. Beside, not far away, the grass-edged river rides, broad and fast; square salmon nets are fixed between the trees, ready to lower.

Basle is a rich, scholarly, strong and independent city, a fort of peace and plenty standing in the war-savaged treasury of Alsace.

Mulhouse in Alsace is a sister city, twenty miles distant, some forty minutes by train. People living near the frontier have border passes and cross without trouble. During the war the frontiers were closed; but when peace came, French people would visit Switzerland to get extra supplies. Switzerland itself was rationed at that time and the amount each visitor could take out was limited. Still, there were fats, flour, oranges, milk, coffee, and wine which could be spared. Besides their marketing the French visitors would often have a meal in a cheap good restaurant; for instance, the *Lälle König*, the *Lolliger King*, at the Great Basle end of the Rhine Bridge. The Lolliger King looks out above the door and to signify that meals are ready, his long fat red tongue begins to roll between his red lips and his big black eyes turn round in excitement. When he stops, eating is done. In between you hear the waitresses calling, *Guten Tag, Bonjour, Monsieur;* and at the end their peculiar Basle goodbye, *Auf Wiedersehn, Adieu, Merci, maintenant.*

Though war and occupation were some years behind them, times were still hard in France. Mrs Poupon, a houseowner in a suburb of Mulhouse, and her tenants, Mr and Mrs Legland and Mrs Levasseur, came to Basle every Friday or Saturday by train. They were all middle-aged. Mrs Poupon was an alert dark-haired woman, with the self-contained, courteous manner one sees in cities: Mr Legland was chief accountant for a large Mulhouse firm. Mrs Levasseur had only her widow's pension and did housework for others. Mrs Poupon, also a widow, lived on the rents and sometimes cooked meals for her tenants. During the hard times of the occupation they had had to pool rations; they had sat at one table, been warmed by one fire; and in spite of differences of opinion and character they had become close friends.

They had now returned to eating in their own quarters; but still did their marketing together.

One Saturday morning Mrs Poupon and Mr and Mrs Legland started out, leaving Mrs Levasseur at home. Her married stepdaughter was coming with her husband, for lunch. Mrs Legland, a heavy, awkward woman of fifty-five, with white hair, and dressed for shopping in black skirt, white blouse, a large black hat, turned round in the hall as they were bustling out loaded with shopping bags, and said to Mrs Levasseur, 'Why don't you tell your stepdaughter and her husband to come with us to Basle? We can wait. We can take the next train. They could see the country and bring back extra rations. Think! Six half-litres of oil, or say, one litre of oil and four pounds of butter, six loaves of bread, six bottles of wine! Don't you see! And think of all the meat and vegetables! Two bags apiece. As it is we're out of your usual *tolérance* [food allowance].'

Mrs Poupon said they did not need all this; they could easily manage for the week. 'I am sure Mrs Levasseur wants a quiet time with her little family.'

In the train Mrs Legland, sitting erect, stretched her legs, looked at their bags in the net above their heads and said she was sorry the Levasseur family had not come. 'Above all the butter,' she commented: 'it is a loss, a real loss. One can make too much of members of the family. Or she could have left them to rest, while she came with us for her share. She need not have waited for lunch at the *Lälle König*. You know, she treats her stepdaughter like a daughter, just like a daughter. But you can tell from looking, I think, that she never had any children. Why, we do not know.'

'Mrs Levasseur has a very motherly attitude towards her daughter,' said Mrs Poupon. Mr Legland, fat and slack, rested in his corner and watched the landscape with a faintly pleased expression.

'Ah, you don't know what I mean,' went on Mrs Legland, 'you yourself never had any children, why we do not – you have been lucky in a way. The bigger they are, the bigger the troubles! And you with that beautiful house on your hands. You are lucky, Gertrude; you are lucky; very lucky.'

'But I must work with all my luck.'

'Ah, yes,' said Mrs Legland thoughtfully, 'you have the house, the furniture. Of course, you paid off the mortgage with that cash legacy and that wiped that out; cash in hand – you have the rents. Still, you must work. Yes, but the furniture! Think of living with it, owning it! That is remarkable luck. Have you brought some work? I have brought the table-centre you knitted for me.'

'I have brought some handkerchiefs,' said Mrs Poupon.

Mrs Poupon worked all day at embroidery and lace. They all kept their eyes and ears open, in Mulhouse, in Basle, hoping for someone with a daughter to marry, who might give Mrs Poupon an order for the trousseau. She did work for the shops; and they kept a lookout for tourists in Mulhouse and Basle: there were very few in either city. Mrs Poupon's work was fine and regular; her petit-point and drawn-thread work suited modern taste; the rest, exquisitely fine knitted silk lace and handkerchiefs with tatting, belonged to old-style households.

The Mulhousers did their shopping and went to the *Lolliger King*. They felt happy as they sat in their usual leather-seated booth with the polished table between them. On one side the tall windows of different coloured panes, a little below street level, looked out on the midday street, the traffic going towards the Rhine Bridge. Above was the painted and beamed ceiling. On the other side, some empty seats: it was a booth for six.

Mr Legland, pale, short, obese, in an old black suit of provincial cut, sat silent in front of his cloudy absinthe. Halfway through his second drink, he began to smile at Mrs Poupon's demure jokes.

'I really think Mr Legland drinks; yes, he drinks,' she said to Mrs Legland.

Mrs Legland sat up straight; she smirked. She was a plain provincial woman. Mrs Poupon had travelled a bit and she was a landlord. The friendship pleased Mrs Legland.

'You must not drink too much,' she said to her husband, her eyes wandering round the room.

He smiled and took a swallow, 'Oh, Saturdays! I waited for this.'

'Yes, he loves to drink, he loves to drink,' said Mrs Legland with a quick ray of fun. 'That man, he loves his drink! If we weren't here, Gertrude, three or four; more – he couldn't stop!'

'Well, the money would stop me,' he said smiling.

With their meal they had wine. Mr Legland said wine

would not mix either with his meal which was hard-boiled eggs in white sauce ('very filling and settling and cheap,' he said), or with his absinthe; and he wanted a third absinthe. 'I am allowed that on Saturdays.'

'Let him have it; let him gorge himself,' said Mrs Legland, her eyes sparkling. She ate fast, ate a lot, changed complexion and character: she had soup, steak, cheese and fruit with cream. She became bossy, patronising, genial. 'Let him have what he wants; he's enjoying his food; he likes it,' she said loudly; and tossed her head, in her health and strength. She surveyed the bags of food. 'I wonder how Mrs Levasseur is getting on with her so-called children! Well, no matter. She was a good stepmother to her and she intends to leave her her furniture; so she told me. They will have enough. They couldn't take more. They'd have to move. "I am not her mother," she told me; "but I feel like her mother." Of course, anyone can see whether a woman has had children or not. There is a way of looking and talking. What a pity, Gertrude, that you had no children! But perhaps that is your usual luck. Who knows? Who knows how they will turn out? No children are better than bad children. You are obliged to leave them something and you worry. They will send the lot to the auctioneer's and be in debt, too. I can congratulate myself upon my boy and girls, settled and always considerate and grateful. I can congratulate myself–'

At this, for some reason, she looked at the couple which had come to sit at the table, after asking permission, in French. They were speaking English and had just made a joke in German. The restaurant was crowded; it was the rush-hour. These two, younger by ten years than the Mulhouse friends, were Rhineland types. They were also carrying shopping bags of comestibles, wine, too. He was short, stout and dark, young, healthy, with beautiful eyes, hazel fringed with black, and a wide mouth, a snub nose. The wife was a type you also see locally: sandy, tall, bony. Mrs Legland, after studying the shopping-bags, moved her shoulders and her eyebrows significantly. She meant, Are they Germans? Everyone knew there were Germans in exile in Switzerland. Mrs Poupon looked, and shook her head. Yes, yes, signalled Mrs Legland, in the sudden silence. Mrs Poupon shook her head, Never, she meant. For long years they had dealt in silent conversations.

The strangers of course looked up. He was palefaced as Mr Legland had once been, a healthy pallor, roundfaced with bright eyes full of life; and he was dressed in a blue suit of English wool. All their eyes were on the man when he looked up. He smiled and said at once, in good French and much as they spoke it themselves, 'Are you from France? I spent many years in France. Where are you from, may I ask? I think I saw you with another lady on the Rhine Bridge last Saturday. We live here in Basle.'

'Yes, we were there,' they said excitedly, 'we always come to the *Lälle König* on Saturdays.'

'Yes, so do we. The food is good and cheap and we don't get enough at the pension where we live.'

'Ah, you live in a pension,' said Mrs Legland.

'Yes, foreigners you know are not allowed to rent flats in Switzerland at present. On account of the Swiss returned during the war.'

'Ah, naturally, pension food,' said Mrs Poupon.

'The lady has to send her son through college and he is now only four years old. She has quite a time to save up. "So I must take it out of their bellies," she says frankly, "Mr Parvis, I am an ogress of course, I am the wicked paunch-pinching pension-keeper." That is my name,

Parvis. This is my wife. We are Americans.'

The Mulhouse family explained that they were shopping there. 'But we can't take all we want,' said Mrs Legland. 'We're restricted in the money we can bring in and in what we can take out: there is a food allowance called a *tolérance*.'

After a while, the American asked to be allowed to buy them another carafe of wine and another absinthe for Mr Legland. They accepted. Mr Legland drank and began to talk. He sat up; he looked younger. 'We're from Mulhouse – it's a pleasure to be able to come to Switzerland. It's a pleasure to be able to cross the frontier freely, as we used to – at one time the frontier seemed inaccessible.'

'One can't say that,' said Mrs Legland. 'It was always in the same place.'

They had an animated talk. Mr Parvis's grandfather had come from Strasburg. He talked to them about Alsace. 'Everyone knows of its wealth, that it is worth fighting for; and the ebb and flow of peoples, from the Mediterranean to the North Sea and the Baltic, and the curious fact that it has retained its identity, its unity–' He said he adored border cities. 'Rémy de Gourmont says the meeting place of cultures is the cradle of civilization: Mulhouse, Basle, Verona, Warsaw, Berlin –' They sat there a long time and Mr Legland had a fourth absinthe. One could see the kind of man he had been once, before being overwhelmed by fatigue and fat.

And then they pricked up their ears. Mr and Mrs Parvis had a daughter. 'My daughter is in Paris now: she worked for the French Government in exile; and now she is working for a film company.'

These words were strange to the Mulhouse people: 'the French Government in exile' – it was as if they had been deaf and were hearing faint sounds now. They digested these slight sounds; but Mrs Legland said hastily, 'Is she thinking of getting married?' And they began to show the linen-work and lace. Mrs Legland offered her card:

> Mr and Mrs Antoine Legland,
> 71 Faubourg Street,
> Mulhouse (Haut-Rhin).

'But she is the owner,' said Mrs Legland: 'this is Mrs Poupon. It is her house. We all live with her. The woman you saw last week was the other tenant. She is missing her *tolérance* today because she is entertaining her stepdaughter. She adopted her. She is really a foster-mother, but we say stepmother. She treated her like a mother, although she never had any children. But she seemed to have the instinct. Still one can tell that she is not the mother. In fact, my children are the only real born children in the house. They are grown up now and married; and people say, "What was it all for?" But it is better to have had them.'

She said all this and much more masterfully and genially, as if it was something they should know.

'I expect we'll see you here next week,' said Mr Parvis. 'My wife likes meat and she doesn't get enough in the pension. When she can't drag around any more, I bring her here to eat something.'

On the way home they chattered endlessly about the meeting. Mrs Poupon said, 'It's strange that we've been coming here for years and this is the first time we've met anyone.'

Mr Legland said the man was very intelligent and he'd like to see more of him. 'An open mind and he knows as much as an educated European. Most Americans know nothing.'

'But after all, he is not an American, but one of us,' said

Mrs Legland. 'The family is from Strasburg. But why are they here? Think of the opportunities for making money in the United States. Surely if he were really American he would be there.'

'Perhaps the wife is ailing.'

'But sick wives go to the mountains: there are no mountains here.'

Mrs Poupon said in a low voice, 'Perhaps he has business here.'

'No doubt he has his reasons,' said Mr Legland firmly.

They were all silent for a few minutes, reflecting, and conversing in silence as they had learned to do.

'Well, if I didn't know I'd say the wife was German; and perhaps it's on that account,' said Mrs Legland.

'There are plenty of Germans in America,' said Mr Legland. 'And what does that prove?'

They all met the following Saturday and became so friendly that they promised to look out for each other each weekend. Mrs Legland began to dress up for the visit and Mr Legland brightened. They often laughed at home now, repeating what their American friend had said; and they told others, 'Our friend, the American, who has a very lively mind, says–'

One Saturday, Mrs Poupon, the houseowner, did not come, but sent Mrs Levasseur in her place. Mrs Poupon had had all her teeth out and was waiting for dentures; also, she had not saved all the necessary money yet and had to economise.

'Yes, though she is lucky, cash is usually rather short,' said Mrs Legland: 'she has the rents; but they barely cover expenses. What a house though! And furnished in wonderful taste and richly.'

There was great talk of the children, the house, of Mulhouse; but all the time Mrs Legland was inattentive.

Suddenly she said, 'Oh, I wish you could see it, Mr Parvis. Mrs Poupon has had great luck. She inherited beautiful furniture, very beautiful. Each time I look at it, I think, How beautiful! What luck!' She looked at the other women.

'Yes, it's nice,' said Mrs Levasseur, who polished this furniture. Mrs Legland continued, 'So much! And was no relation. She merely worked for the woman, as companion to an old woman with no one to leave it to; no husband, no children.' After a pause, in which her thoughts were away in Mulhouse, she continued, 'Just to get it out of friendship. Well, it can happen. But what luck! She has had two legacies, you see: that is real luck. And I believe there was a third, long ago. Remarkable. You should see that house, Mrs Parvis! She owns the house; she owns everything in it – but your bit of furniture, Mrs Levasseur. And of course, she owns that nice backyard with the fruit-trees. From that we make kirsch and peach brandy, every year, first-rate. And the – the crystal, the tablecloths – a bedroom set, Mrs Parvis, every bit hand painted with fruit and flowers.' She paused and became lost in thought. Suddenly, she came back, opened her large handbag and drew out a clean handkerchief worked with drawn thread and embroidery.

'Look at it!'

'It's beautifully done.'

'That's her work. Now, Mrs Poupon sent it to you, for you to have for your kindness; and also for you to see how she works. So that if your daughter marries you may like to give her a dozen handkerchiefs; or Mrs Poupon could undertake the trousseau. Or anything. You should see the house, Mrs Parvis. She owns the house; she owns everything in it; and the entire house is supplied with doyleys, chairbacks; towels, tablecloths, napkins and curtain fringes, linen hemstiched and embroidered by herself for her own wedding, with the initials; and a suite in petit-point, a firescreen – she can do anything! You won't see such stuff anywhere. Imagine coming into it all, I've never seen the like. That house is perfect. One couldn't ask for anything more. Ah, if your daughter were thinking of marrying.'

She looked Mrs Parvis up and down keenly, but no answer was made; and Mr Legland, who now felt more at ease, put in, 'And how is it at your pension?'

Mr Parvis exploded into talk, while a delighted expression crept into every part of Mr Legland's face. For a long time he had been the only man in a household of women.

'Why on earth do all Europeans imagine that Americans are Tories, oppressors, conspirators, no-good tramps: why am I supposed to be in favour of everything evil, rotten and tumbledown in Europe? People decide that I am a bastard without asking me,' said Mr Parvis uproariously. 'Everyone knows there are a lot of people living in Switzerland who can never cross the German, the French or the Italian border; but why the devil are they shooed on to us? At the same time I can't go to Frau Bolte, the pensionkeeper, and say, I don't like the smell of this innocent Luxemburger who says he escaped from the German army in time or I don't like a hair of the head of this engaging young German girl who loves the Americans in Berlin and defends the airlift. I ought to, but I can't. All the decent people in the pension are beginning to look at us sideways. We had two decent young French Swiss at our table and Frau Bolte shifted them so that we could get an earful of nagging, leading questions and propaganda.'

Mr Legland laughed; the ladies said nothing. Mrs Legland had gone into one of her daydreams during this speech, which seemed to her political, and in the silence which followed, she awoke, exclaimed, 'Oh, I wish you could see the house and the things she has done! What a house! Complete from attic to cellar: one couldn't ask for another thing. For instance, there's a beautiful embroidered cushion in colours, a whole picture, a copy of an oil-painting done in the right colours in petit-point – exquisite! I see it every day. I go up to look at it. Of course we're friends. But I can't get used to it. The question is to see it, to see her work.' She fell into a reverie again while they talked; and awoke again to say, 'Yes, it's a pity. You ought to see the house. Don't you think we could manage it, Mrs Levasseur? Could you come to Mulhouse?'

The Americans accepted.

There was excitement in Faubourg Street. 'Let us ask them to lunch on Bastille Day. I never did believe they were in hiding in Switzerland: they're too frank.' 'But why don't they live in France then?' 'Well, we ourselves have to go to Switzerland for food.' 'Yes, it's no fun here at present.' 'Yes, until the storks come back, our luck is out. They've taken our luck to Poland.' 'Have they brought luck to Poland?' 'Well, they're Alsatian storks, not Polish.' 'All that is just superstition, it's the bombings and the fouled water.' 'We ought to build stork nests on the factory roofs.'

'Two or three storks have come back,' said Mrs Levasseur.

'Do you think they will bring the *tolérance* with them?' said Mrs Legland.

'You can't ask guests to bring food,' said Mrs Poupon.

'Still, I am sure they will. Americans are so generous. Always offering my husband drinks. You miss that, don't you, Antoine?'

Recently, Mr Legland had not been able to go to Basle.

They were reconstructing the station and the waiting-room could not be used. While the women shopped he had liked to sit in the waiting-room and doze. He had bladder trouble too and had been unable to find the new way to the urinals.

'Yes, he misses the absinthe,' said Mrs Legland: 'perhaps we should get him some.'

'It's better for him to miss it. You know the doctor said it was really bad for him,' said Mrs Poupon in an undertone.

They were standing in the kitchen in her flat. This kitchen opened on the landing and Mr Legland was sitting, doors open, in a room underneath, working at accounts.

Mrs Legland stared ahead of her out of the window, at the stretch of yard downstairs. There were signs of the country here. Beyond a grass patch where they dried the clothes, were mature fruit trees in good condition. There had once been a large orchard here. Beyond was a small field belonging to Mrs Poupon. It was rented at present. A bay stallion grazed there after work and in the week-ends. When Mrs Poupon took him food on a chipped enamel plate kept for him, he came trotting eagerly, lifting up his big feathered feet as he did when running over the stony streets of Mulhouse with coal and wood. Mrs Poupon even bought a little oats for him. Mrs Legland worried about this; it came off the rent of the field surely.

'I beg your pardon,' she said to her friend.

Mrs Poupon repeated, 'Do you think you should put brandy on the sideboard down there, where he can get it so easily? The doctor warned us about accidents.'

Mrs Legland said carelessly, 'Well, with his work – at night – the extra work – it's so profitable you know – you see I have pity on him, he's so greedy – loves to guzzle – he loves it so.' She laughed, gloo-gloo, like water in a pipe. She was proud of his extra work also. They were comparatively well off; in fact, they made things easier for Mrs Poupon.

'Think how well we managed a few years ago,' she said regretfully but in high good humour, too. 'All of us pooling our rations: and how you cooked! It wouldn't be a pity to see that again: it was a good plan.'

'Mrs Levasseur has her little family; she has her hours,' said Mrs Poupon.

'Aren't there others? Yes, it was a very good arrangement,' said Mrs Legland restlessly. 'Even my husband had to do his work up here, to get the warmth.'

'He needs the room,' said Mrs Poupon.

In the little room where he now sat, an inner room that could not be seen from the staircase when the doors were closed, Mr Legland had a safe, a table, a chair. Here he had always done night work, secret work, even during the occupation. Here he made up and kept the second set of books which gave the true position of the factory; and neither the occupant nor the tax inspector had known it. He had always received a bonus for the work and for his constancy. During the occupation he had run other risks; but he had kept his head and got on well with the Germans. Now, when he was very ill, old before his time, oppressed, tired, on sick leave, another accountant brought him the books and papers to check and left them there; and he worked on. Handing it over would be a ticklish business. He liked to be alone with his work, and after his work was done he would lock the private room, take an armchair from his dining-room and sit on the little balcony on to which it opened. Since his illness, this had not been allowed. No doors must be locked and he must not sit near the low iron railing of the balcony. Instead, his wife or Mrs Poupon helped him to his own dining table, only a yard or two to move; and there he sat, collapsed in his carving chair. At his left hand always stood a small tray with a carafe of red wine and a glass which his wife filled for him when she went by. He had no friends, although he was affectionate. Mr Parvis was the first friend he had made for many years. But the letter which came ten days before Bastille Day said that Mr Parvis expected someone on business, an American acquaintance who was flying out of his way to see Mr Parvis and would be there in mid-July. Mrs Parvis alone would keep the appointment with them.

Two of the women, Mrs Levasseur and Mrs Legland, made a special trip to Basle the next Thursday, found the pension, a place for students and low-paid office workers, in Plough Alley, and at the end of a narrow hall, on the mansard floor, they found the American couple in a small room with one window, two cots and a wooden table. The two women, out of breath, sat on the two chairs and the Parvises sat on the cots. On the table was a scientific translation they were doing for a publisher.

Embarrassed, the women carried out their mission and begged Mr Parvis to come.

'Mr Legland is looking forward to it so. He cannot leave the house any more. He has had a stroke – too much self-indulgence, yes, we expected it –' put in Mrs Legland with her throaty laugh, 'and he can only sit at home and do extra work. And Mrs Poupon is getting her new teeth specially for your sakes.'

They were having bad luck, said Mrs Legland. They could now only get two *tolérances* every Saturday. 'Mrs Poupon,' she continued, brightening up, 'is very lucky; a perfect housekeeper, too. You will see the furniture when you come,' she said earnestly to the man, talking breath-lessly, 'the beautiful furniture. There is too much, too much for the house; you'll see. But beautiful! What a treasure! A sideboard of walnut and a table of flame walnut; and a set of chairs covered in petit-point. As for the bedroom suite and bedroom china – you never saw such a house! It's a perfect joy. Too much, but you couldn't store such stuff. One can look and look, look and look.'

'Yes, yes,' said Mrs Levasseur, coolly.

They stayed only a few minutes more; but Mrs Legland continued pressing, 'Heavens, what a feast! We say shortages, but when you have seen how we live! Mrs Poupon manages wonderfully. Yes, it's a true pleasure to live in that house. She could manage for six or eight just as well: she takes pleasure in it. But it must be seen. You know a great feast is in preparation in your honour. Yes, you are coming, aren't you? I know you will.'

The women were embarrassed at being received in the poor bedroom. The Parvises lived abroad, hence must have money. What could it mean?

'Swiss prices are sky high; of course they could live better in France, say in Mulhouse,' said Mrs Legland.

'Oh, he will come,' said Mrs Levasseur.

'Oh, I'm certain he'll come and bring a bottle of absinthe for my husband. He loves to see him swallow it. Oh, he's a drinker, Mr Legland: he loves the stuff.'

But Mr Parvis was not anxious to go to Mulhouse. The household did not interest him; and his shoes were worn out. The fare and the cost of the food to be taken was a consideration too. It was true that his family was from the Rhineland; but for that reason he did not like the district and was tired of Rhineland associations. He belonged to the group that adores Paris. He bought absinthe for Mr

Legland out of kindness; but a man full of drink seemed to him temporarily a madman. The only thing at all was to spend Bastille Day in France, after so many years of her oppression; but then came in again the price of shoes in Switzerland. 'I'm sorry I can't go to Mulhouse, in a way,' he had said to the ladies. 'It's the *patrie* of Alfred Dreyfus; and there the Dollfuss-Mieg Company made the first European experiment in paternalism, workers' dwellings, the original company town. Mulhouse is of interest to women all over the world. My mother always sent me for DMC 40 white. But I understand the arcades were smashed by the Germans.'

'By the British,' said Mrs Legland automatically.

On the fourteenth of July, Mrs Parvis set out with two bags of food, tied with tricolour bows. There was a strike of customs and railway clerks that day. What a pity! people were saying; we could have brought more than the *tolérance*. Railways office workers, angry at being disturbed, angry that they had to scab, were sending them through quickly at the customs barrier. 'What are you taking out?' 'The *tolérance*.' 'And what is the *tolérance*?' An enumeration: and then, 'All right, go through,' very irritably.

A Swiss family of fat people began to eat from their baskets as soon as they were on the train, although it was only half-past nine: 'second breakfast,' said they, in Basler German (an allemanic dialect). They looked several times at the tricolour bows and at the woman with the bags. 'She's not German then?'

The Mulhouse station was a big airy one, new-built since the war, still surrounded by ruins. Here was Mrs Legland looking wonderfully smart in summer pink and a big pale straw hat. She was preoccupied as usual, as if she had somewhere else to go, had not wanted to be there.

Yet she was very cordial.

'Where is your husband? Why didn't he come?'

'His business friend arrived.'

Mrs Legland was most uneasy. She looked around the station. 'There's another train in soon; let us wait.' After a while, she continued, 'Well, perhaps he will come later. There are several more trains before lunch. He will talk to his friend, finish with him and come, I know. Lunch won't be till three o'clock. What a pity he didn't come! She's made a beautiful lunch, a *coq en pâté, fruits rafraîchis,* lots of things, a real feast. During the war, with her we didn't suffer. We all ate together: there's so much more for everyone.'

They boarded the tram which started at the station and while they were waiting for it to start, she looked over her shoulders, down the streets, said restlessly, 'What a pity your husband did not come.' She bought the tickets. 'What train are you taking back? Don't you know? Oh, you must know. Of course you could return by bus. Have you a return ticket? Of course, your husband could come by bus. Let's see: you almost have time to go back and get him. Ask him to come. Well, no; but you could send him a telegram. He could catch a later train. A wonderful spread! What time are you returning? Oh, what a pity!'

Meanwhile, with wandering thoughts and anxious talk, she stared at the bags of provisions brought by the visitor. Mrs Parvis laughed and said, 'I could take the train back. I could leave these bags with you.'

'Yes,' agreed the lady, her thoughts wandering, 'and bring him back.'

'Should I get off and look at the trains for Basle?' Mrs Parvis peered through the window at the timetable posted up on the station.

'I don't know, perhaps,' said Mrs Legland, vacantly,

most uneasy. 'I was sent to bring you home. Mrs Poupon couldn't come, she is cooking such a feast.'

The tram started. Mrs Parvis said cordially, 'I brought these two packages for you: it's really nothing. I could bring only the *tolérance* and a few things.'

'Yes, yes, I thought you would,' said Mrs Legland uneasily. 'People always do, coming from Switzerland.'

'It's a pity my husband could not come: he could have brought more.'

'Yes, yes, I know. I thought of that. But he might come still. I know he meant to bring them.'

She pointed vaguely to things in the city, 'The war – the British blew those up, we had raids after the Germans left,' she said absentmindedly.

They got out where the suburbs began and walked some distance through stony bystreets and down Faubourg Street, a grey paved street with low houses. They came to the front door of a small three-storey house with two iron balconies. A large faded French flag hung from the first floor balcony.

'Ah, the flag,' said Mrs Parvis with emotion.

'Yes, it's an old one: it's not new. It was in the attic.'

There were a few flags about in the long drab street.

Mrs Legland cheered up as she put her key in the door. She chattered, she smiled and became younger. 'The names are on the doors, everyone has his nameplate. My husband's at home, but he's probably asleep,' she tittered. 'You'll see him at lunch if he can get upstairs. He's not allowed to move; no stairs. Mrs Poupon lives on the second floor and we on the first. My husband had a stroke. The doctor said, Not too much food or drink. He loves his tipple; ha-ha. The doctor said, No brandy, no rich food. He doesn't care: he doesn't care!'

They went up the polished carpetless stairs of the

narrow house. On the first landing two brass plates on two doors, said, Mr and Mrs Antoine Legland. She opened the door of the balcony room and they peeped in.

'Here is Mrs Parvis. Mr Parvis is not here, but he will come later.'

It was a darkened room with tall heavy furniture. Mr Legland, in the same black suit and very pale, was sitting collapsed in a highbacked armchair. After a moment, he turned his dark-eyed face towards them and they went in.

'Don't get up; how are you?'

'I'm not very well. Forgive me for not rising.'

He lifted a flaccid hand. There was a painted bowl containing flowers on the knitted lace centrepiece; and at his left hand stood a carafe and a glass, on a silver tray. The carafe and the glass were each half full of wine. Mrs Legland said with a gleeful smile, 'You had a little, eh? You keep it up, don't you? Perhaps you'll come upstairs for the eating and drinking? Would you like anything now? A little more wine. I'll pour it and then we'll go.' She did so, saying with a gay smile to her visitor, 'Not supposed to, but this is the Fourteenth. You must rest, take it easy, my dear,' she continued to the man. She opened the window and threw wide the shutters, showed the faded flag. 'He likes that: he wanted to hang it out himself! You can take it in, my dear. Well, we'll see.' Then she opened the door behind the man's chair and showed the small workroom. On the table was a pile of account books bound in marbled paper. 'He's entrusted with confidential work, and it's profitable. It's all right my dear man; no one will talk. We're going upstairs for a chat. Now doze off. There's brandy in the sideboard. That's for later. On the Fourteenth it's different. Besides, you can't get to it. Ha-ha. I'll come for you.'

'If I can walk up there,' he said amiably but faintly.

She opened the door wide. 'There! How good it smells! You've no idea what is being prepared upstairs.'

'I do know,' he said.

'Ah, your mouth's watering. You'll eat. What a feast!'

Upstairs, Mrs Poupon was in her apron in the kitchen. 'You must really excuse me; I am the cook,' she smiled pleasantly, showing her new teeth.

Mrs Parvis put her bags on a kitchen chair as she went through. Mrs Poupon turned away her head and said nothing. 'There,' said Mrs Legland, 'there is Swiss food, only one *tolérance;* but there are good things there!'

Mrs Poupon overlooked this remark. She came in without her apron to offer *bénédictine,* 'Have you ever had *bénédictine* for an *apéritif* before? We drink it that way and have got to like it.' The women laughed; and after a little Mrs Poupon went back to her stove.

Mrs Legland remained and began pointing out the things she had so often described. 'Some more *béné?* I am saving myself for lunch. What a lunch! You'll see. Would you care to look at the furniture while I'm helping? And there's the bedroom. Please go and look, above all the hand-painted china.'

She went into the adjoining room to set the table and once more she became fitfully attentive. She stood in the space between the rooms and began again about Mr Parvis, repeating all that she had said and saying they might telephone him. 'Then you could go by a later train, have supper here: we intended that if he came. There is plenty, a veritable Lucullan feast, great platters, wine, liqueurs, plenty,' she said softly in one of her moments of warmth. She took the visitor to the balcony and they looked down on the flag which hung windless.

'An old soldier with battle fatigue,' said Mrs Parvis.

Mrs Legland did not catch this, but Mrs Poupon began

eagerly laughing, 'Yes, an old soldier; that's what it is; it looks just like that.'

Mrs Legland said, 'Soon I will bring Mr Legland up: then you'll see just how he is now. He's not permitted to do anything, even eating, even eating.' She found this funny, like a child.

In the street a starving fox terrier was wagging his tail outside a little house, a mere cabin in a garden, in front of which he had found a dry and meatless soup-bone. A hungry cat came up and stood under the 'old soldier'. Seeing this, the terrier ran up, too.

'The animals in the street smell your cooking,' said Mrs Parvis.

'Yes, I feed the poor things,' said Mrs Poupon, running and throwing some scraps into the street. The dog and cat began to eat. 'You see, they are used to me!' Mrs Poupon smiled and sat down. 'You will eat soon, too.'

They began to talk about Basle and what luck it was when the frontier was opened. For a few years after the occupation France suffered a great hunger. Most country people had homebaked bread, but it was hard as baked clay, very often, and yellow, grey and even an unhealthy black. Everyone was hungry: people ate strange things; some people developed food manias.

'You would not see a horse or a cow in the fields,' said Mrs Poupon. 'They are just beginning to appear in proper numbers; they have been apportioned. I like to look out my kitchen window and see a horse, though it is not my horse.'

'Oh,' said at last Mrs Legland, sitting on her chair, restless, tense, looking uneasily to the side, 'we did not do so badly under the Germans. They had bad luck. They had bad crops, very bad crops for two or three years, three or four years of bad luck.'

'You can't plough fields with bayonets,' said Mrs Parvis.

Mrs Legland did not apprehend.

'The Germans took the cows,' said Mrs Poupon. She watched the visitor brightly.

Mrs Legland, following her own thoughts, was swelling, becoming stuffy, proud. 'No, we didn't do so badly! I used to get an extra half pound of butter every week – that helped! They were not so bad if you didn't bother them. They were good to you. They had sense. They didn't punish those who minded their own business. They were there. Nothing was gained by making trouble. Innocents were punished. They were the government, just local officials. One must understand. Witness me. I got an extra half pound of butter every week. So you see they had the butter. They had to have some way of disciplining people. They gave me other little things, too. And others, too.'

Mrs Legland had stopped shifting and for the first time spoke forthright, and with conviction. 'Half a pound of butter and other things,' she repeated; 'and we all benefited.'

Mrs Poupon went to a bookcase which was part of the walnut suite and took out a large presentation volume. 'I want you to see this.'

'No, no, Gertrude.'

'This is the golden book of patriots from the first world war, when we returned to France, the resistance, you would say now; the liberators. My husband's name is there.' She put the book down and pointed, *Georges Poupon,* with the decorations, and a little cross to show that he had died.

Mrs Legland was extremely embarrassed, half rose, put out her hand, 'No, no,' she murmured, as at an indelicacy.

The visitor was delighted. She made some comment and seeing the harm was done, Mrs Legland said, 'And she has a pension too as a result: no harm in that.'

'This would please my husband,' said Mrs Parvis. Mrs Poupon smiled.

Mrs Legland grumbled, 'People didn't understand. They were not masters of their fate: luck was out. They wanted to please. Many people got butter.'

They talked: about how the storks had deserted them: about the richness of the country in good times; about the river Rhine; about everything that had already been said.

At ten to three, Mrs Legland went downstairs for her husband. 'I don't know,' she said, merrily, reluctant and longing, like a schoolgirl, 'he shouldn't, but he'd hate to miss such doings.'

They fitted him into an armchair where he rested his obesity on the chairback, the arms of the chair. 'Excuse my sitting down first,' he said.

'Where is Mrs Levasseur?'

The women exchanged glances. 'Oh, she had to be out today: she has other interests now. She prefers her own quarters. She cleans the house for us, you see. Quite willingly. We're very friendly, but we don't live together as in other days.'

It was an extensive, a generous and rich meal. A French-cooked meal with some Alsatian specialities added, a platter of cold meats, sausages and *pâtés;* and later, the brandy and kirsch they had made themselves, very strong, pure and good. Meanwhile the radio played music and fanfares from Paris where the parade was going up the Champs Elysées. Mr Legland ate and drank and smiled at the music; Mrs Legland was silent over her plates.

'It reminds me of old days – when we lived in Paris.

We lived in Paris many years,' said Mrs Parvis.

The man said gaily, 'I marched there once, after the other war: our regiment marched to the tomb of the unknown soldier.'

'Do you know what that is?' asked Mrs Legland.

'Oh, yes,' and the visitor began to talk about Paris, so far away to them, the capital of their country, but to them somewhat alien. They listened in an odd silence. Many questions with debatable answers ran through their minds, incidents kept secret and that no foreigner should know, ideas long unsaid. It was strange this foreigner rejoicing at the freedom of their country. They wondered what meaning it had.

'Would you go back?' said Mrs Poupon.

'Oh, we will go back some day.'

It was strange, because the woman had never spoken. Mr Parvis, to entertain them, had talked about Alsace and Lorraine, their rich and ancient history and all the economic meaning of it, the peoples who had lived there and the future of the country; independent or as a part of France – what policy? And they had taken his love of France for a love of Alsace; but now it was clear that this couple would never leave Basle for Mulhouse: they were going to leave it for Paris. And it was the stranger because Mrs Legland had got it firmly planted in her head that somehow they were Germans, *'Allemands de chez-nous'*, and would be happiest there in the rich, cozy, quiet life of the province.

The women were silent; but the man smiled, joked, laughed. He had known all along. He was drinking a lot of wine and now that the coffee had come, he sent down for their Dambacher, a splendid local wine and for kirsch and brandy. He was given some of each, 'the *tolérance* for the Fourteenth' and the wines and spirits had given him life. He drank, flushed, his eyes sparkled and he spoke with authority to the women. 'Bring up another bottle of Dambacher first,' and he described the quality of the local wines, the beautiful hill of Dambach, 'You must see it, there are many such hills and they have beautiful vineyards, each one its own wine. I can see you really care for wine; and that being so, it is worth the trip.'

'If I ever make money,' said Mrs Parvis, 'I'll travel round France with the seasons, tasting the wines; that is my dream.'

They laughed. This went on for a long time and at length Mr Legland said, 'No, I can't manage any more. I must sleep. Help me down.'

'Later,' said his wife, 'we'll have something, tea or coffee: you'll have some of that, with cake.'

'No, no, not now.'

Mrs Levasseur had appeared in the kitchen and Mrs Poupon went to help her. Mrs Legland was left to entertain. She was in a good mood. 'It does not look as if Mr Parvis will come, does it?' And at once she began upon the amenities of the house. 'If my husband does not survive long, what do I want with a three-room flat? I could easily move in here. And there's a room on the landing. I would ask for nothing more. Think of living with this furniture and this cooking! Every day. Yes, of course. He's in a very bad way; an accident could easily happen any time. For example, the doctor said, "Don't let him sit near the railing, it's rusted and old." Suppose he collapsed against the railing. Yes, it could happen in a moment! Think of living in this splendour! And then of course the flat downstairs would not be needed. Oh, we will manage everything beautifully. Now you must take a bottle of kirsch to Mr Parvis. You said yourself how good it is. He will see. And when he hears –'

She leaned forward, her eyes sparkled, she was slightly flushed, engaging, 'Now you have seen the house, you can tell him everything.' She began to show it all piece by piece: they toured the flat again. 'Ah, what a pity he couldn't come! Well, tell him in any case –'

She walked about, distracted. 'The doctor said, Any time, in his condition. Keep the windows closed. One can't watch all the time. Yes, here you live like a *coq en pâté* as your husband said, like Gott in Frankreich.' As she said the forbidden German, she laughed in her throat. They had tea and Mrs Legland ate hungrily, though no one else did. The food went to her head and she talked as before. When the meal was over they prepared for the station. On the way downstairs, Mrs Legland opened the door of her dining-room to show the man in black, motionless at the table.

'Goodbye, Mr Legland!'

He did not move.

'Mr Legland! Mrs Parvis is going now. Don't you want to send a message to her husband?'

The man began to turn. His face came round a little. 'I'm afraid I won't see him again. Please say goodbye to him. *Au revoir!* I must stay here,' he said faintly.

'Yes, his bit of work is all he has strength for,' said the wife.

Just before the door closed, a faint voice was heard, 'I should like a little brandy Marie, so that I can work.'

'Oh, no, no,' said Mrs Poupon in an undertone.

'He must work,' said the wife; 'there, I shall put it on the sideboard again so that he doesn't get it till he gets up. And the window is open; you can see the flag!'

They walked away quickly, very lively.

Mrs Parvis looked back and they all turned. 'I am looking at your flag. It must be reviving.'

'Yes,' said Mrs Poupon.

Mrs Legland laughed, 'I thought you were looking back to see if my husband was looking out. The doctor said, 'In his condition, at any time'; for instance, he might fall off the balcony. One must watch all the time.'

After the Town Hall, they took the tram and spent some time in the new waiting-room, surrounded by homing holiday travellers. 'What a pity you didn't bring the kirsch,' said Mrs Poupon; 'I ought to go back for it.'

Mrs Parvis said no.

'Oh, my husband will drink it up,' laughed Mrs Legland.

'I think if you'll excuse me, I'll take the tram back,' said Mrs Poupon: 'I feel concerned about Mr Legland.'

'Oh, he is probably working; or he may be taking the air,' laughed Mrs Legland.

'No, someone should.'

'Well, go then,' said Mrs Legland. As soon as she had left, Mrs Legland in an undertone, almost a murmur began again about the wonderful furniture and about her living with Mrs Poupon. 'It would be very convenient.'

At last the train came in, and old odd train with windows stuck and bulging sides, like the old carriage-work, an antique in use in the shortage of rolling stock. It was the Basle local. Goodbye! Till next week!

But the Mulhousers did not come the next Saturday. The Americans never saw them again.

The Woman in the Bed

It was an afternoon in spring: the hotel guests were walking or resting. Mr Robert Wilkins was stretched out, in his little room fronting the Lake of Geneva, on a lounge chair in the sun, before the open window; and through the communicating door, he could talk to Mrs Trollope, who lay on her bed, with cushions underneath her head and hips. She had spread out on the windowsill and carpet trails of breadcrumbs, made from the white rolls she had brought up from lunch. She kept the windows open, the curtains apart, so that the sparrows could come in, picking up the crumbs as far as the chairs at the edge of the dais, where she had trained them to sit. She remained motionless, with her black curly head twisted sideways, waiting. With her black eyes wide open, eyes blackrimmed as if traced with kohl, she watched the fat sparrows look, call, comment, hesitate, hop, enter and fly eventually as far as the edge of the dais. The dais was built under the window to accommodate an invalid chair for a sick guest. She was careful not to make a move. Just the same they knew she was there and looking and they were never at ease.

About four o'clock Mr Wilkins called to her, 'Lilia, there is a knocking on my wall.'

Mrs Trollope replied, 'Oh! that must be that poor thing, Miss Chillard. I sent a message that I would go in at teatime and you know I meant to take her dry biscuits.'

Mrs Trollpe got up cautiously, but the birds flew. She slipped on her shoes, tidied her hair and went out quietly, looking back to see if they would return. As soon as she went out, they would return and behave in a different manner, free and quarrelsome.

About a hundred yards down the street was a cake shop which she and her Swiss friend, Madame Blaise, always patronised. There she now bought two hundred grams of dry biscuits.

When she got back to the third floor, where the smaller rooms were and where they lived, she went into Mr Wilkins' room to show him what she had bought and to give him some chestnut creams, which he liked to have with his drinks before dinner. He said to her:

'Lilia, please do make haste. That woman has been knocking on my wall for half an hour. I think she expected me to go in. I called out, I can't come in. I am a man and I am in my underwear.'

'Robert, the poor thing's sick and she thought it was I'.

'I wish I could believe that.'

'I won't stay here and listen to your jokes in bad taste.'

'No one laughs at jokes in good taste.'

'No one but you laughs at your jokes anyway.'

He said calmly, 'No wonder everyone takes us for husband and wife.'

'To that, Robert, I am not going to say anything. You know only too well what I think and you are trying to provoke me for your own amusement.'

'Wake me up about five-thirty, Lilia, we'll have our drinks; and don't invite that woman.'

'Oh, the poor thing! She makes my heart bleed.'

'I trust she is not going to make our pocket-book bleed. Be careful, Lilia; don't commit us. I shall give her nothing and I will not allow you to give her anything.'

'You are hard-hearted, Robert: it is your years in business.'

Lilia was smiling slightly, just the same, as she knocked at Miss Chillard's door, number 27; but she was concerned and sympathetic when she saw the woman in the bed.

This was a woman they had met some months previously at this same hotel. At that time Miss Chillard was travelling with an older woman of humble manner, like a poor companion or paid toady. This companion would come down to dinner as soon as the bell rang, would take her soup eagerly and then wait for Miss Chillard. If Miss Chillard did not appear, she fidgeted and sometimes went upstairs to fetch her, but Miss Chillard, brought down like this, remained distant, did not speak to guests or servants; and the short meal was conducted in a miserable silence.

Then for a few nights the poor companion would eat her soup and meat dish with a hearty appetite, look friendly at the other diners, speak to the servants, and she might be joined by Miss Chillard for dessert. Miss Chillard never ate soup or meat, she had a special dish of eggs perhaps, and took few sweets. She often finished her meal earlier than her companion, when she would sit with an air of rebuke. Sometimes Miss Chillard in her highbred insulting English voice, spoke thus:

'Perhaps, thinking it over, you had better go on. You

can do nothing for me. I shall try to get a position *au pair*. I'm sure I don't want you wasting any more time and money here.'

Otherwise, Miss Chillard spoke to no one, except rarely to the servants and to them she spoke in English, though she understood French and Italian; but she would not put herself on their level.

Though Miss Chillard was tall and gracefully built, she was underweight and her shoulders deeply bowed. She had many certificates from foreign doctors and she was always sending these home, that is to England, to prove to the Bank of England that she needed to stay abroad and to receive money abroad.

It was at a moment when she was short of money and she thought of getting a place *au pair,* that she had spoken a few words to Mrs Trollope. Mrs Powell, an elderly American lady, a great gossip, had reported that some months ago she had seen Mrs Trollope wheeling an old invalid in a distant part of the Montreux district, in Vevey, in fact, as a hired attendant, and the hotel-keeper Mr Morin had explained that this was while she was awaiting her funds from England.

Mrs Trollope and Mr Wilkins, cousins as they said, were transferring all their funds in England abroad. It had to be done at a certain rate, so many thousands a year. Miss Chillard found this out; that Mrs Trollope was rich and had also been a victim of the regulations of the Bank of England.

Miss Chillard's companion left for England. It then appeared that she was Miss Chillard's mother. Two days after the mother left, Miss Chillard, with what remained of their funds, left for Zermatt. That was the previous year. But now Miss Chillard was back at the little hotel and was on her way back home. The Bank had turned down all her applications.

Mrs Trollope was startled by the terrible change. In the sagging bed, propped up by several large pillows, lay a tanned bony virgin martyr, with roving eyes in deep hollows. Her fair hair was scattered about the pillows, a loose low nightgown with lace inset showed her emaciated neck, bony chest, the wide-set weakened breasts. But the neck had been a column, the chest, broad deep and strong. There was still a marked beauty in this disorder, a high-spirited selfish temper. Lilia was distressed.

'Oh, dear Miss Chillard, how are you? You don't seem well. Have you seen a doctor?'

Miss Chillard said she had seen two. Mr Morin, the hotel owner, had brought one and some dear friends from Vevey had sent another.

'They would do anything for me.'

She was worried. Expenses were high and she must pay the doctors. She had left all her luggage at Zermatt, because of an unpaid bill. She had not even paid Mr Morin her previous bills, and had left luggage here too. But she had always expected the Bank to allow her to have her money. The Bank said what? She could go to places in the United Kingdom, like the Peaks or Scotland, places quite useless for her. They were sending her home to die, in their tight-fisted ignorant way. She was half dead now. She had many friends and hotel-keepers who knew her and respected her in Zermatt and elsewhere. They really adored her, but she had been obliged to leave them, too, without paying, having only a little left, and that to be kept for the doctor.

'I am worried about you, Miss Chillard.'

'Do not worry about me, Mrs Trollope. I expect

another doctor now. Dear Madame Blaise is sending me one. Her husband is a doctor and they have friends here. People are always so good; but that man next door pretends he does not hear me knocking and I am so afraid I will die in the night.'

'Oh, no. That is my cousin, Mr Wilkins. He is rather shy with women. But he will always call me. I am right in the next room. I can even hear you if I leave my door open.'

Miss Chillard looked at her with scorn. She lay still in bed; her blue eyes burned. Her two or three valises stood about on the chairs. She asked Lilia to get her several things from them, a teapot, packets of tea and sugar, some talc, some perfume. She spoke clearly and in detail and Lilia found everything; yet Miss Chillard seemed nervous. Lilia thought, Oh, poor dear, how poor she is; and she thought she should explain to Mr Wilkins what it must be like to be chased out of one hotel after another, invalid, unable to pay, and yet with money of her own, disgraced and disinherited for no reason: one of the miseries of these days, the rich turned tramp by a government which did not care for the rich.

'Just as I was myself, Robert, till my money came through,' she would say. How she had puffed on those streets round Vevey, thickset, heavy, on her high heels: and how she had been treated! She said to Miss Chillard,

'Won't your mother be glad to see you? Won't it be better for you, after all, on your lovely Devon farm, in the country, having good food, better than this hotel food, which you do not take to? Now tell me what you had to eat today? Can't I get you anything?'

The afternoon sun, hot, brilliant, poured at the window, though it could not get in. The window was closed, the heavy winter curtains were drawn. It was already sunset in the room, though for a long time yet the light would flower on the lake outside, till its flowering drew together and became a pillar of fire from shore to horizon.

'There is something, if you would be so generous, just get me two ounces of water biscuits. I saw them before when I was here, rather sweet with scarcely any flavouring. I have the name somewhere. I shall look for it. I shall make my tea and that is all I really want. And if you would get me my medicine. My purse is in the corner of the blue valise, no, not that one, the one in the corner,' she ended sharply.

'Oh, but dear Miss Chillard, I brought you some dry biscuits, two hundred grams, the sort you like.'

'Oh, how good of you, how lovely of you. But I cannot really eat. I shall keep them for the servant Luisa, as I have nothing to pay her with and I expect she will be glad of something to eat.'

After a few more words, Lilia left Miss Chillard, went to her room and spoke to Robert through her open door.

'But of course, Robert, I am not sure she would not be a world better if she ate some soup and let in a little sun. It was very lovely of Mr Morin to give her that corner room with the balcony, when they know she has not paid. There are good people. But I should have got her water biscuits; I made a mistake.'

'Well, get her a few and see if she can digest those, before you buy half of pound of the things,' said Robert.

'Robert, there is one thing that comes out and that is your country origin, that grasping strain. You are so much the poor boy who made good. One must look at every penny. When a poor English woman is here and cannot eat anything, it is no harm to make her feel a little happier. And she needs her medicine.'

'Get her her medicine and get her one hundred grams of biscuits. She won't eat them. She is just employing you.'

'You know, Robert, I must have something to do. The thing about our lives now, living abroad, retired, is that I am completely useless. I wish I could go and help peel vegetables in the kitchen. They don't like to do it. They quarrel: "Is it the day for the Italians or the Germans to do it?" Gennaro took a knife and Franz took a meat chopper yesterday about it. I would love to do it. I'll ask Mrs Morin.'

'No, please Lilia. Go and buy the biscuits, every day, if you wish. If you must play the good Samaritan. I think she's leading up to a touch.'

'You do not see that a person can be sick without a profit motive and a person can be kind without a profit motive.'

'Now, Lilia dear, make haste and get the water biscuits. You would give away your last shilling and it's a good thing I am here to see you do not.'

A little flushed, Mrs Trollope went along the street to get the medicine and the biscuits. When she returned, she was a little surprised and embarrassed to find two strangers in Miss Chillard's room, a French couple trying to speak English to the invalid.

They were poor French tourists. The woman in a black basin hat and a grey suit had a nervous face. She was offering a small bottle of liniment to Miss Chillard and Miss Chillard said to them in English that she needed vitamin A and not liniment.

'My fingers are so cold, I wish you had brought that instead.' She turned to Mrs Trollope and said as to a servant, 'Do please explain to them. But don't refuse the liniment, take the liniment. I don't want to hurt their feelings. It probably cost them a franc or so. I shall ask the Italian maid to rub me. I might get back some feeling into my legs and arms.'

The French husband, in a worn striped suit and painted shoes, had brought some chocolates, which he had already put out of the way on the table. The couple murmured good day to Lilia, but looked at her with such reticence that she felt that she had intruded. Perhaps the three shared a secret. She excused herself in her correct high-school French, after putting the biscuits on the bedside table and saying,

'Are you quite sure I can't make tea for you?'

Miss Chillard said, just as if the French people were not there:

'Oh, no, thank you. I am trying to explain to them what I want, but they don't understand. I met them at Zermatt and they were very good to me. They want to do something for me, but they don't know what I want.'

She lay back on her pillows with her bosom exposed. In her exhaustion she had not moved, not to take the gifts, not to draw up the sheet, tighten the neck of her gown or touch her hair. She lay there immodest. Yet she had a silver hand-glass lying beside her on the bed, next to the wall.

In the eyes of her visitors was their knowledge of what she was, so much in need that even her skin had to have its say, come and look about, waiting for the eyes of love; and the woman herself was so used to her trouble that she was almost without understanding of it and exposed herself thoughtlessly before all – men, women, doctors, tourists, friends, strangers – and this was a relief. A drinker will first of all conceal his drinking and then drink before everyone, not caring and soon not knowing. She had certainly at one time had beauty and health. The visitors were ashamed.

'You must eat, pills are a bad substitute for food,' the French couple were saying.

There had been no introductions. Mrs Trollope left them in the room. Shortly afterwards, she heard them on the landing. She looked out to ask them a question, but seeing them dubiously and dowdily standing together, heads down, deploring something, she withdrew. After a time she returned and said to Miss Chillard,

'If you feel faint in the night, knock and I will surely hear you. I don't sleep very well myself.'

'Oh, thank you very much. I think I should rather rouse the nightman; Charlie is very kind.'

'Oh no. You know Charlie is also the porter. He sleeps on a stretcher in the office. There is no nightman. Please call me. He needs his sleep. My cousin's room is next to yours.'

'Yes, I know,' said Miss Chillard.

Mrs Trollope felt unhappy. She did not like to say Mr Wilkins was her husband: she did not like to explain the relationship. Miss Chillard, since girlhood a guest in foreign hotels and pensions, surely guessed, like others?

When they were having their rum and vermouth, Lilia said to Robert:

'We are English. Shouldn't we do something about poor Miss Chillard?'

'She has managed to the age of thirty-five without us.'

'But it is different now. I feel for the honour of the English on the continent. We used to be welcome; now we're not respected. It is the unpaid bills and the low allowances.'

'Frankly, Lilia, what honour do you think the English

have ever had on the continent? We English have always been mocked, out of jealousy or out of contempt. I shall not think about it.'

'If she raps in the night, let me know.'

'I shall probably not hear a sound.'

'I am afraid she is really sick, though,' said Lilia.

'If she dies, what difference will it make to you, Lilia?'

'You make friends quite easily. Your friends don't see you as you are, a stony-hearted man.'

He drank his second vermouth chaser with a smooth face. Then Lilia said,

'Well, let's take our rest now. We have this dinner with Doctor Blaise and Madame: and that reminds me, Robert, we must take out the Pallintosts.'

'I know; I think it is a bit stiff, when the Pallintosts only came here to sell me a car. I shall take it off the commission.'

Lilia went into her room and shut the door. Immediately, she heard a knocking on her wall. It was Madame Blaise's signal. Lilia's face fell. With a sigh, she opened the intervening door and went in to Madame Blaise. Madame Blaise addressed her in the upstage voice that came to her when she had been taking her pills.

'Lilia, what have you been doing? Come and arrange my hair for me.'

Madame Blaise seated herself before the wooden table on which was a large square hand-glass of her own. She had spread out her toilet articles, all in heavy silver. She handed the brush to Lilia, saying,

'Hair first; then we can try another make-up.'

Madame Blaise was a tall heavy woman of German type, with blue eyes and white hair.

Mrs Trollope set to work. It was a long job. They tried the thick straight hair this way and that. Madame Blaise never went to the hairdresser, for fear of catching cold, and she did not wash her hair, except in midsummer, for the same reason.

Doctor Blaise, a French Swiss, brisk, elderly, dark-haired, with his amused smile, kept coming in from the double room at the corner of the building, which was kept for him in the week-ends, when he drove over. The Blaises had a villa on the other side of Switzerland, near Basle, where Dr Blaise had his practice. Dr Blaise teased the two beauties, as he called them.

At six-thirty they all passed through two doors into Mr Wilkins' room, where they had rum, sugar, lime-juice and vermouth chaser; and then they went out to dinner uptown in Lausanne.

In the morning early, Robert looked in at Lilia's door to say that the woman next to him was rapping on the wall again. At this very minute, Madame Blaise, hearing their voices, rapped on the wall.

'Liliali, Liliali, come and talk to me.'

'The hotel's full of poltergeists!' said Robert.

Mrs Trollope sighed, groaned. Robert said,

'I'm going back to my charts.'

Each morning he amused himself for an hour or so by making charts of the ups and downs of the stock and produce markets.

Lilia said, 'Oh, it is a bother. My heart beat all night to suffocate me and now I must talk to these women. I know they are sick, poor things.'

'You encourage them. I am not going in to them in my dressing gown,' said Robert, mirthfully coy.

Mrs Trollope rose, brushed her hair. She wore an old fashioned high-necked pink flannel nightgown with scalloped cuffs and collar, such as she had worn in the convent school. She put her striped flannel dressing-gown on and went in to Miss Chillard.

'Oh, dear Mrs Collop, I had such a wretched night, but I would not call you: and I wonder if you would mind putting out my tea-things. I cannot bear the tea they send me up.'

'I sympathise; their tea is awful. I had got into the habit of going down and getting my own hot water. But Madame Morin takes it personally and says I must send for the servants; that is what they are there for. I said to her. "Poor things, they have enough to do." But since she made an issue of it, I am now obliged to ring. If you like, though, I shall go down now and get you some really hot water. But give me your teapot.'

'Oh, how very kind. Thank you so much, but I think I shall wait for the waitress. What I was going to ask you was, would you mind finding me my Shetland bed jacket. I am afraid I am a little décolletée in this nightgown, and the doctor is coming. I simply can't get up and go through my things. There, if you wouldn't mind, in the green valise.'

The same thing happened. While Mrs Trollope was going deftly through the green valise, though she followed directions, she was afraid she was being closely watched. She thought again there must be money in the case. She flushed. She found the bed jacket almost at once. She said, 'Don't you think you should get some fresh air? It's such a lovely morning.'

'With my trouble I can never trust the air. Perhaps, later on. But I am so weak – you see, Mrs Collop – I cannot eat anything. I got up last night, fell on the floor from weakness and spent the night on the floor. I am dirty on one side, that is what I want to cover up. I am not strong enough to wash.'

Mrs Trollope offered to wash her, gave various counsels: to get up, to sit in the sun, to drink some broth, a little wine. Miss Chillard could not do any of these things.

As Mrs Trollope went on talking, the women studied each other. Miss Chillard's eyes glittered speculatively and with mockery in her wasted face.

She was a real beauty, how did she miss? thought Mrs Trollope. These English girls wasted their lives by never stepping outside a small circle. She must have been a spoiled child, perhaps the beauty of the family, waited upon by mother and everyone. Something had turned her into a hypochondriac. Was it possible that she had never had a lover and was suffering from this hopeless, lingering and wasting disease?

Miss Chillard watched her with a bright look, very close to a fine malicious smile, like a cat watching your face before it makes a pass at your eyes. Mrs Trollope knew something of what she was thinking: 'Is she an Eurasian, and that is why the man won't marry her?' Miss Chillard ended by smiling within, the inward smile of the deducing cat. Lilia thought to herself as she plumped up the pillows, said the sagging mattress should be changed, said the winter curtains were too heavy, that the heating was insufficient and that Miss Chillard must ask for an electric heater for windy evenings. She thought that perhaps Miss Chillard's illness was self-induced, a protest against the cruelty of fate. Miss Chillard was a brave malingerer-errant who was not afraid of homelessness; and who knew enough about people to cast herself on the mercy of hotel-keepers in foreign lands. Who would lead such a life? But what life was she herself leading? Miss Chillard said she could not live anywhere but in Switzerland; in Switzerland only did life have meaning. What did Switzerland mean to her but a series of closed small bedrooms? Her back ached, yet she passed her life on her back, looking up at the ceiling, waiting for the doctor, for a charitable stranger, who was only a servant to her: and yet she had this passion, as if some passerby might have the torch she could seize.

Mrs Trollope stopped speaking, without finishing her sentence, overpowered by Miss Chillard's strange unwavering investigation. Miss Chillard spoke at once, saying in a bright elegant voice that she was obliged to wait here until she heard from the Bank of England; and she spoke as if the Bank of England was no more than the family solicitor. The Bank of England had made difficulties for her, she had sent them over so many certificates, French, German doctors' certificates, in case they thought the Swiss doctors were simply drumming up trade; and it had got her only a few short stays, a few pounds. Now she was afraid she must go home. She picked up a copy of the *Daily Mail* and read aloud a paragraph she had been studying. It said that there might be some momentary relaxations of currency control for certain cases, to enable the English to visit Switzerland. It made it appear that the Swiss were doing badly without the English visitors.

She ended, 'But that is just newspaper talk. I have experience. I must travel to England, I am afraid, in a few days, in my condition, because I cannot pay here. I do not know how I shall manage it. Well, I am keeping just that sum, to travel third class, sitting up all the way. It must be done. The Bank says I must go home. I have told the Bank over and over again that Switzerland is necessary to me, but they will not listen to reason. They make rules and everyone must conform. In a Labour Government I have no connections. In fact, they go out of their way to disoblige people of our class.'

Mrs Trollope agreed with her. Miss Chillard continued,

'I must live here on the good nature of the Morins and other people. I shall not have a penny to tip the servants. I have telephone calls to make to people I know in Les Avante, La Tour-de-Peilz: they are devoted to me, but I cannot pay for these telephone calls. There were some people in Pontresina last year who were so lovely to me, they decided to take the servants in hand themselves: they paid them to look after me. They were so sorry for me when they saw how I worried. They brought me cream and sweet pears, they were divine. There are kind hearts.'

Mrs Trollope said, 'Oh, do call upon the British Consul, surely he will help you. I met him. He is just a pleasant middle-aged gentleman anxious to help, he's like a friend.'

Miss Chillard said in her cool sweet voice, 'Oh, I don't think so. Not yet. I should not like to bother him. What must he think of someone like me? I am in an embarrassing situation. Here I am lying in bed in a foreign hotel running up debts of all kinds. Even if I get to England, how am I going to get money abroad to pay them here?'

'Oh, surely the consul can make some recommendations!'

The sick woman said indifferently,

'Oh, I have cheated hotel-keepers before this. I don't feel myself responsible. It is the Bank that is responsible. And then think what the Swiss got out of us in the past. We made them rich.'

After a pause she added, 'I am so unwilling to go out of Switzerland, because I am afraid they won't let me in again. I am rather a suspect.' She moved her shoulders prettily and gave a luminous smile.

She continued, 'They must know my brother-in-law was here a few days ago to take me home and I refused to go back with him. I want nothing to do with him. One has to be careful in a family. I said, "Go back without me: if you want to help me, help at that end." You see he married my sister, not me: I have no interest in him. I made that quite plain. As far as I can see, the Bank of England is simply enriching doctors abroad. Instead of one, I must have four or five certificates, and then it is no good. It seems to me strange that the Bank bows the knee to a Government like that.'

Mrs Trollope said, 'Oh, naturally, we are all miserable with the Labour Government. I am English to the backbone and I cannot bear to see the country in the state they have brought it to. It's natural to want to live abroad.' But she was uneasy and made an excuse to go.

After she and Mr Wilkins had eaten their breakfast, they dressed and picked their way across that part of the esplanade by the Nautical Club. It was now being repaved, using one large and one small Walo-Bertschinger roller-tractor; these were running over and over the road. They called them the Walo Dragons or the Walos: and every day they went to observe them.

'It amuses me. I am glad there is something to look at,' said Mr Wilkins.

'About Miss Chillard, do you know, Robert, I feel uneasy. I don't like the name of England being dragged down by these people. I am ashamed to say it. I am sure she is really sick but I have the idea that she is a bit of a fraud, too. I don't know what foreigners think of us. It gives us a bad name.'

Mr Wilkins said, 'I shouldn't worry about that, Lilia. You know we always pay our bills. Mr Morin knows we have money at this moment in his safe, five hundred Swiss francs, as you know.'

Mrs Trollope, still nervous, said she did not see the sense of this either. For one thing, the money was really hers and there it was in the safe with Mr Wilkins' name on it.

She said, 'Supposing you went to Geneva or Basle about this motor car, Robert, and I suddenly needed money. Mr Morin' – she said Morin in English – 'would be within his rights to refuse me. My name should be on it too.'

'What emergency could possibly arise? You know Lilia, we are living abroad; we must be careful.'

She said in a lower tone, 'You know I lost a hundred-franc note out of my purse and I have not found it anywhere. I don't like to accuse anyone; it would make trouble. And we don't know it is the servants. My experience is, it is not the servants, usually.'

'In the East, Lilia, we trusted our servants; and we had reason to, though we did not speak the language.'

'Oh, Robert, I am tired of being with people who don't speak English. How strange it is, I say to myself, that they can speak French all their lives and not a word of English. What I mean is, I wish I could speak to someone. I don't think it's natural, Robert, never to speak your own language to anyone.'

'Madame Blaise speaks English.'

'There is a very suspicious-looking man on the fourth floor who is always sneaking about and carries a satchel. I don't like his looks: and we always leave our doors open.'

'The one we saw in the Café Royal? He is the accountant.'

'I should rather suspect him than the servants.'

'What about Madame Blaise or Miss Chillard?'

'Oh, Robert! How can we suspect our own!'

'Well, Lilia, I can't see myself locking our doors. We never locked anything up in the East.'

'I always leave my big handbag standing there on the chair. It would be easy, but how can I lock things up? You are right.'

'What a funny day, Lilia! Sun, wind, rain and cloud.'

'Mr Blot, the taximan, says it is marrying weather. They have a proverb here, marry on a day with four weathers, then the marriage will weather all things. I wish we could be married. I see no sense in our remaining this way. Whom have we to please? The man in the police office called us Romeo and Juliet. When I came in he said, "Here is the ripe Juliet." And we are in our fifties. It is absurd at your age to be tied to an old mother and four sisters, maiden ladies in their fifties and sixties. And you don't like them. I send them Christmas cards, and you always say, "Don't, they don't appreciate it." I know they don't. But it is for family feeling.'

'I promised Mother not to marry during her lifetime.'

'But she is in her nineties, deaf, blind, and she can hardly drag herself about. And you don't believe in a personal god.'

'Just the same, I swore on the Bible and Mother is still alive.'

'Do you think that it was right of your mother to make her daughters promise not to marry? Look at them now.'

'You see, Lilia, that is not the question. The question is, did they promise? And they did.'

'They have suffered: that is why they are so narrow.'

'How do you know? That is pure romance. I have been very happy.'

'With me.'

'Yes, with you. So no one has ever suffered. The girls have kept it from Mother that you and I are together. No harm has been done.'

'Oh, really, Robert, you don't belong to this world. My children are married themselves, now; and they are very unhappy at the way we are living. That does me harm.'

'You forget, Lilia, that they are Mr Trollope's children.'

'I don't forget that. I don't forget that you were a good

father to them. Like a father, and they loved you. And now what can I say?'

'You say I don't understand the world, Lilia. I believe I am very well acquainted with the ways of the world. I think you will admit I have managed our little affairs very well during the last twenty-five years. We have brought up your children and spent our lives together and not a soul has suffered. I am known throughout the rubber world as an exemplary bachelor. I am respected. So are you. And out of respect for us they look the other way.'

'If you believe in example and respectability, why don't you marry me, now that we are retired? We are living abroad! Your mother need never know.'

'My dear Lilia, I never promised to marry you and you know why. When Mother is gone, it will be time enough.'

'If there was some money to come to you from her, I would understand it better,' said Lilia.

Robert laughed frankly, 'Oh, perhaps the old girl is hanging on in the hopes of inheriting from me, now. I control all the money in the family, even yours,' he put in, teasing. 'But I fancy I shall disappoint mother.'

Lilia took a little Swiss handkerchief out of her handbag. She wiped her eyes and wrung her hands in it. 'Oh, if I could only say what I feel.'

'Do not try, Lilia, or you will be just as troublesome as usual.'

Lilia cried out, 'Oh, what is the use of money when it is no use? Our money is impounded and we are in jail because we must stay with it. Will our money do better in Tangier or New York or Bogotá? Then we must live in Tangier, New York or Bogotá! I can't go to England to see my girls unless they pay my fare and so I am a pauper and not rich. Did Mr Trollope leave me all his money for that? I'm not a pauper, I have money. I'm a loving mother and my girls love me. So much calculation is not healthy. I can do it as well as you, Robert; but I do not lick my lips over it as you do. It is a dead end. I'm humiliated. I can't spend money and there are so many things I can't do. You've tied it all up to earn more money. More tied-up money. Suppose you live till ninety-three like your mother and we go on to Davos or Casablanca or Nice; all places I don't like? We live in the cheapest hotel in town. We're shabby people; I mean shabby lives. We don't have money; money has us. And what does it do with us? Nothing. I wish you were not so efficient, Robert. I wish money and I were free. And then if you allow me to buy something, it is just a gold watch or a diamond ring – investments, that is all.'

Robert said indulgently, 'Lilia, you are a child and always will be. Just leave these little problems to me; I am accustomed to them. That is one of my functions in your life and I am glad to be of service to you.'

Lilia said, with a rain and mist of tears in her black eyes and on her face, tanned and dried by oriental suns, 'But I want to be free. Life seems very small to me this way; and what is Mrs Morin and what is Madame Blaise? Are they my old friends? If we can't go to England let us go somewhere where English is spoken. Madame Blaise says she has plenty of contacts in the USA. She put property there for her German friends, in her name, during the war.'

Robert laughed. He had a pleasant laugh, pulpy, musical. 'And never gave it back, I expect,' he said.

'Your idea about a long walk is no good at all for my back. I am going home to rest before lunch,' said Lilia.

'Very well, Lilia: but it is your own fault. Two good plates of soup at lunch, no meat, plenty of salad, no coffee and you would feel well.'

He took Mrs Trollope to the hotel and then went on to

discuss the day's prices with the clerk at his bank. He sometimes made the rounds of the banks, arguing about currency and stock exchange prices, for his amusement.

At lunch time, she said she was not hungry. Robert replied, 'My mother always said, those who do not wish to eat, need not eat. Those who are hungry will eat.' He went down.

She had slept better since she began doing a crossword puzzle at night, on Robert's advice; but it did not always work. She would hear, on one side, Mr Wilkins, deeply asleep, since eleven; and on the other the sleep-mutterings of that strange cocoon, Madame Blaise, wrapped up in her stifling room, in her blankets, dressing-gown, shawl and all the rest. Where was there anyone normal, busy, jolly, such as Lilia and Robert had known in Malaya in the old days? Then she had had many real friends. Their love affair was known and respected, and Robert was not regarded as a bachelor but as a man almost married: and behaved so and liked it. He had treated Mr Trollope's daughters as his own and the girls had loved him. Their friends, even people they did not know, spoke complacently of 'Robert and Lilia'. She had known happiness.

She thought of slipping out of the hotel and taking a walk by herself. She heard Madame Blaise making the noises preparatory to going down, and presently she came through the intervening door.

'Lilia, Lilia, come down, dear, for lunch. You know you are hungry.'

She was hungry, even for the thin potato soup the German cook had prepared. The new French cook had not come yet.

Madame Blaise wore her usual outfit for the dining room, her old brown felt hat, trimmed with a fur band, her brown wool dress under her fur coat, her gloves and handbag, with new fur boots, rather smart, halfway up her calves, and under them thick brown stockings.

'Gliesli, dear, I am not going. I am too unhappy. I cannot face another meal with Robert hidden behind the *Times* or the *Financial Times* and myself looking in that big mirror. I can see what everyone does. I can see Mrs Powell, that woman from Savannah, making a big half-circle to avoid saying good day to me.'

'Why should she? Don't be foolish, Lilia. I need you, I have promised Dr Blaise to go back home to Basle and I am very worried. I am going to die there.'

'Gliesli, Mrs Powell avoids me because I am not married to Robert. We have no friends, Gliesli, you are right. You and I have no friends in the world but each other. You have a son and daughter, I have three daughters, but now they are leading their own lives, their love has turned from us; and that must be. We are on the shelf. And apart from that, I cannot face Robert again. My heart has turned against him. I am not angry with him. There is something there,' she said, pressing her heart, 'which would never allow me to do that. But now I must leave him. My own children loved him. Now my children say, where is your self-respect? I never thought of self-respect; I thought only of Robert. But now I can see he does not think of me. I tell him I am suffering; and he says, "What sufferings have you? I am looking after your money: our old age is taken care of."

'I suppose I made a great mistake: but I would make the same mistake again. He told me he loved me; I loved him. I am glad I had that. I can't imagine my life without that love. Everything almost melts away when I think of it. And often before this, Gliesli, I meant to go away from him, to teach him a lesson; but I couldn't. If he loves me, Gliesli, why must he tell everyone, she is not my wife, she is my cousin? Why does he send me ahead of him into hotels, to engage the rooms in my name, so that he comes in afterwards almost as my lodger? When no one cares at all? He only makes us conspicuous. I have laid my head all these years on a stone. I cannot go down and hear him say, when he lays down the paper, "You see Lilia, how right I am when I want you to transfer all your money." And Gliesli, because he can work on my feelings and I have no plans, and the children are provided for, he is slowly engulfing all my money.'

'Come down, Liliali, I am famished.'

'Gliesli, he has broken my heart. In the end, Mr Trollope proved my only friend; but only when he left me for a Malayan woman and gave me the money for myself and the children. Ah, Gliesli, my heart is crumbling; there is nothing there to prop it up. I am not going down, Gliesli, to see Robert taking his two soups behind the newspaper, while I watch this sad lot of scarecrows in exile, in the looking glass. We might as well all be barefoot.'

Madame Blaise said, 'Well, I must go down: I am hungry. If I don't go now, that dirty little peasant whore will find some excuse for bringing me cold soup with her thumb in it, and I don't want to argue today. The doctor gave me my medicine. Why don't you take it, Liliali? You would not have the blues.'

'You know I will not take these things,' said Mrs Trollope.

'Why don't you and Mr Wilkins come home with me to Basle and see what my husband is preparing for me; and what Basle is like, such a cave of trolls – do you know they have a staircase called Deathdance Stairs? I shall slip on it, never fear. My husband's a troll. I must go or my husband will not give me any more medicine. I must be

looked after, he says. So he has got me back. I know what
he wants me for: to kill me. If you were there, he would
not dare: or you could be a witness and do for him in the
end. Oh, but never mind. I shall give him a nice chunk to
swallow; let him choke on it. For I am sure he is sleeping
with that ugly old creature, my servant Ermyntrud, a
trolless. I shall leave her all my money but only on
condition that he marries her.'

'Oh, hush, Gliesli!' She could hear Madame Blaise
laughing on the way down-stairs.

Robert brought nothing up to her from lunch and did
not ask after her health. He merely mentioned that Mr
Pallintost seemed anxious to sell the car and he, Robert,
thought he would go to Geneva to see it, that afternoon
or the next morning.

Before he took his nap, however, Robert said, 'Lilia, do
go in and see that woman who is knocking on my wall.'
Then before she left him, he said in a clear business tone,
'Lilia, I went to Mr Morin and got him to put your name
on the packet in the safe. If that is what is taking away
your appetite, I know you are a child and must be
humoured.' She looked at him, about to say something,
but did not. She went in to Number 27.

The previous afternoon, Miss Chillard had gone out in
a car, brought by her French friends, to La Tour-de-Peilz.
During her absence, Roger Morin, the hotel-keeper, had
done an incorrect thing. He had gone in, opened her
cases, and found a good deal of money in them, enough to
pay her bills. When Miss Chillard returned about seven
and asked for her dinner, he took it to her himself and
told her what he knew. She was indignant and, in fact,
what he had done was against the law. She now explained
it to Mrs Trollope.

'That money is for the doctors. I am going back to

Zermatt if I can. That is the only place on earth I have been happy and there is only one person who understands me and makes me want to live. He said, there is hope for everybody. He is a doctor there. It is for him I am here. If I cannot pay him, I cannot go; and if I cannot go to Zermatt, why hang on? I am dying now. Why do they grudge me a few months?'

But Mr Morin had said, he had to live, too. He had to pay ten per cent of his gross, every day, daily that is, to the former owners. These were the hard conditions he had been forced to accept, having no money when he started. If Miss Chillard did not pay him, he would send for the consul and for the police.

Mrs Trollope said she had an appointment at the tea shop with Madame Blaise, but she would come back in the evening. Miss Chillard said, 'I shall be in jail by then. I did not know the Swiss could be so sordid. The English have always been their friends and built up their business.'

Mrs Trollope went back and told Robert she must have the packet of money from the safe. 'You must get it for me. It would look odd if I went and demanded it on the very day you had my name inscribed on it.'

'Oh, I am busy; I have not finished my charts.'

'I am not going to go on paying the hotel bills until I get that packet. I cannot think what possessed you, an honourable man as I know you to be, to put my money in the safe with your name on it.'

'You know why; to prevent your spending it foolishly.'

'I accept that. But give it to me now. I am going to see Madame Blaise and we are going to buy some rings. If you do not, Robert, I will not buy this car, which you are calling your car.'

He was astonished. He went downstairs with her.

They opened the safe and she got her money. Robert asked her for a receipt; but she refused. 'A receipt for my own money?'

'Well, I hope you will not be foolish, Lilia. We have everything in common. It is my money too.'

At this, she flushed and said, 'I am late already.'

As she was leaving, he snickered and added, 'Well, I know it is my birthday soon.'

Mr Wilkins began to get ready to go to Geneva with Mr Pallintost. He murmured thoughtfully to himself. This little habit had grown on him. If she mentioned it, he would sit for a long time in a chair, calculating, but holding his mouth.

Lilia and Gliesli did not buy anything, though they visited several jewellers in and around the Place Saint-François. Lilia came back with the money still in her purse. She said to Madame Blaise,

'I am glad I bought nothing, Gliesli. If I gave him that cigarette case, at which he keeps hinting, he would not believe I am dissatisfied. I must get away. It will be a wrench, but this is agony; I am living in disgrace not for a principle, not for love, not for anything. I would rather give this money to poor old Charlie, with his back broken from carrying trunks about, or to Clara, or Luisa, or a beggar in the street than to Robert, who takes it without gratitude; because for him, it is his, on account of his cleverness.'

They went and sat on a bench on the esplanade, facing the lake. Sparrows came round their feet. Mrs Trollope said to them, 'I am sorry. I did not think of you today.'

The two ageing women sat there, their wrinkled and puffy hands clasping. At that time there was a fad for coloured rings. They both wore many thin rings set with tiny precious stones, along their fingers. It was like buds of flowers and leaves on winter branches, unexpected, exquisite and like an expression of inner life.

Madame Blaise began to talk about her son who was wasting time in Paris; she wanted him to go to America where she had money, to go to a dude ranch.

'He might get killed there,' said Lilia.

'I'd rather see him dead than married to a woman,' said Madame Blaise. 'I'd rather see him a sodomite in red boots and lipstick than married to a woman. He's twenty-nine and I've kept him; he's mine.'

Lilia was tired and trembling. Madame Blaise read to her a letter from her son; a letter she had already heard twice. Lilia began to think of Miss Chillard. Supposing she, Lilia, did what Robert wanted: brought out and tied up all her money. Supposing that then he died – a forbidden thought – and left the estate so that she was almost helpless. He was capable of it, she fancied. He liked to think of his cleverness; he was comical, impish; he might leave it to his sisters, or in trust, inextricably bound. Supposing she ended up like that, with her little aches and pains, in a narrow hotel room, despised and harassed?

'I cannot breathe properly today,' she said to Madame Blaise.

'It's the *föhn* coming: I shall be glad to miss that,' said Madame Blaise.

She was now studying photographs of her son in front of the large villa near Basle; with a new car, with a horse. How foolish she had been, thought Lilia. For an instant Robert appeared to her as a stranger. Who was he? What was his secret life? What did she know about men? What do women know of men, who run the world and do as they please? She had a terrible choice to make, between Robert and a sort of freedom, between a wandering old

age tied to currency rates, prices on the exchanges, and
that homeland in which she was a stranger, perhaps even
'a coloured person', she who had been a beauty in the
East. And if she married Robert she would be worse off;
have no voice at all in her affairs – a slave.

If she went back to England now, she could repatriate
the money she had brought out, explain it somehow. She
could live in Knightsbridge, get up, not too early, have a
little trot round the pleasant shopping streets, go to the
races, have a drink in a bar with others like herself, be
welcome to her children and grandchildren, taking gifts,
buying a French dress, going to dances in hotels. She and
Robert loved dancing; that was one of the things that still
kept them together. Her heart sank. She and Robert
loved each other.

'We are one flesh,' she had said to him once, with deep
emotion.

'And one fortune,' he answered quickly, embarrassed.

She said to herself, 'It is only too true. What am I to
do? My life is wasted.' She walked Madame Blaise to the
tea room, made an excuse and went to the church; and in
front of her saint she prayed for a long time for guidance,
and for help for Miss Chillard. As she knelt there, she
heard money clinking somewhere and she thought of the
money in her bag, the packet from the safe.

'I will do one good deed; and perhaps I will be forgiven
for leaving Robert.'

She went back to the hotel and although she heard
Robert calling her and Madame Blaise rapping, she went
in to Miss Chillard.

'Miss Chillard, I have had an answer from my saint and
I am going to give you the money to go to Zermatt. If you
get there, can you manage?'

'They can put me out dying at the station. I do not care

once I am there. For me that is the only place on earth. It is heaven to me.' She put out a hand to thank Mrs Trollope, or perhaps to take the money.

Mrs Trollope went down hastily to study the timetable and then went to get the ticket. There was a train going through the next morning early. She consulted old Charlie about getting Miss Chillard to the station unobserved. The hotel-keeper was glad to help, for it looked as if Miss Chillard might die there, in the hotel. Mrs Trollope ate some dinner, did her crossword puzzle and appeared her usual self. She went to sleep early.

At one-thirty in the morning Robert knocked on Lilia's door. Lilia was to wake Madame Blaise to answer the telephone call from Paris from her son. Madame Blaise bundled herself into several extra pieces of clothing, a wrapper and her fur coat, tied a scarf round her head, with her hat on top of it. While dressing she shouted at Lilia, who was helping her, that Lilia had no thought for her at all; she knew that Madame Blaise's grandmother had died of tuberculosis yet Lilia thought of nothing but her own selfish whims: she was a tiresome little woman, a hotel pest, and Madame Blaise did not know why she had left her beautiful home, not cold, like this death-trap, but heated, like a hothouse; not packed with hotel vermin from the mountain, ignorant peasants, but full of efficient servants, where everything was done for her, hand and foot. Why had she come to live with ridiculous English exiles in the cheapest hotel in a seedy French-Swiss resort? She said to her husband who had come in from his room, 'You are French-Swiss too, and absolutely intolerable, dirty and inefficient. And the French and English are a fallen nation. And you know it too, Trollope and Wilkins, cousins who sleep together, or you would not be hiding here like misers, insects that you are, lower than the hotel vermin of whom you make friends. Rich people and grudging every penny, going shabby. There is a woman who is ashamed to look her daughters in the face! My son is my slave!'

'Come to the telephone, Liesl,' said the doctor.

She said to him, 'And you, Blaise, you want to expose me to the cold and you grudge me every penny. You push me out of sight here in a rubbishy little pension, so that you can eat and drink all you please and sleep with the trolless Ermyntrud.'

'Come on, Liesl!'

'I will go. I think it will be better if I do go home. I am rudely treated, I sit in the dirt; a woman like me.' She picked up her crocodile handbag to take it with her, put her hand into it and suddenly pushed her closed fist at Lilia.

'I present you with five francs. Perhaps you will come home with me and push my chair for me?'

She went downstairs. They heard her coming up a few minutes later.

'I am shivering, Blaise, it's terribly cold. I'm freezing. I'm utterly wretched here. I must go home.'

The doctor said goodnight to Lilia and Robert in his affable way, with an odd twinkle and a sharp stern sidelong glance which was often an expression of his.

Mr Wilkins said, 'What a comic! I have a most disagreeable impression.'

Mrs Trollope was in bed, crying 'And all because I did not take her to tea! It was my turn. She is greedy; people are greedy.'

Madame Blaise knocked on the wall and called, 'Let people sleep!'

Lilia wept.

The result of all this was that next morning very early,

Madame Blaise, in high spirits again, with her pills, went off with the doctor in his car to the house she had quit seven months before, after swearing never to set foot in it again. Lilia helped her dress and pack and went down to the gate. When she left, Madame Blaise kissed Lilia, took her by both hands, begged her pardon,

'I was tired and nervous and frightened, the doctor had been roaming round his room all night and I thought he was going to kill me.'

The doctor laughed.

'Lilia, I shall write to you every day. Now mind you write to me. Forgive me darling. You are my best friend. Remember, it is your duty. I impose it on you. You must live for me when I am away, for I shall be lonely without you. Remember, you are my confidante, you know everything; what a waster my son is – you know about him,' she said, pointing to her husband. 'I adore you, Liliali, and if I do not write you must come over at once to Basle and find out why. It will mean I am in danger or dead. Send me a telegram and you can come any time. We will sing *Happy days are here again*.'

Madame Blaise left her so.

Mrs Trollope did not like the parting. She told Mrs Morin that the old lady was overbearing and impertinent, 'But I forgive her, she has so many troubles and she is afraid of her husband.'

'Oof, I am glad she has gone; and now Clara must start on her room,' said Mrs Morin.

Miss Chillard, supported by the Morins and Mrs Trollope, was just able to walk out of the hotel to the taxi taking her to the station. Mrs Trollope said to Charlie, the porter, 'I don't know how she'll make the long trip to Zermatt.'

'Well, she says it's heaven there; and if she passes out in the train, she'll think it's Zermatt.'

They found her a compartment, with a few other passengers going to Zermatt, and they put in her bundles. She said, 'This is what I wanted. I never believed it would happen.'

'Goodbye, goodbye,' they called.

She did not answer.

'What a card! What a pair of cards we lost this morning,' said Charlie.

'I wish I were going too, Charlie.'

'Well, go then!'

'Yes, I will. I'll send a telegram to Madame Blaise. I'll go this afternoon while Mr Wilkins is in Geneva.'

Mrs Trollope told the hotel-keeper that she was going, too.

'Mr Wilkins will pay the bills from now on.'

She added, 'If Miss Chillard is going to heaven, I am sure I am going to hell, for that is where Madame and Doctor Blaise live. But she is my only friend.'

'Are you really leaving him?' said Mrs Morin, friendly.

'Yes. I think he wants me to. He doesn't know it. He is not hard-hearted. But he was always a bachelor and I was always a married woman.'

When Mr Wilkins left with Mr Pallintost for Geneva, she packed and Charlie helped her to the taxi.

He came back in, a tall broken old man, bent and walking crabwise. He laughed.

'Well, she's a trick, a real circus turn,' said he.

The Boy

Her name is Fifi, Fifi Mercier, but she says she is called La Grande Fifi; and that is what we call her among ourselves. If you meet her on the hill, on the street, out shopping, you see in the distance a stout active little lady, in her middle fifties, with a broad pretty face, untidy white hair, dark eyes, a ready smile. She wears an old blue dress, with a peep of petticoat behind, cotton stockings and canvas shoes.

This is what she looks like; but you don't know her. She is a romantic figure. She runs a students' boarding-house on the stiff Lausanne slopes, in a decent middle-class house, where there are some quiet families. But on the ground floor is a retired postman in poor health, who thinks everyone is a German; and on the top floor is a woman who causes traffic congestion on the stairs, especially on market days. She is a witch-doctor, who cures farm animals at a distance, if the farmers bring her a knot of hair or bit of hide; she cures and protects from sickness and evil by swinging a watch. She makes good money and the farmers swear by her: 'If we did not have her, all the animals would die of foot-rot.' The witch makes better money than La Grande Fifi, who is so worried about taxes and rent that she has bad dreams. She dreams that her lodgers are sick and go to the kitchen to heat some milk and barley-suger (a cure for coughs). She dreams she sees them there and says, 'You must pack, I have to go, I am turned out for not paying the rent; I am sorry for you when you are so sick.' This is her worry. She has four students, and a married couple who do their own cooking on a picnic stove in the handsome large washroom. The students eat with her in the dining-room; their payments are irregular but they do their best.

There is one other border, not a student, whom she calls the Boy, *le petit*. His name is Mr Bernard, 'a very young man,' she says; and then she adds that he is thirty-three years of age. He has a pleasant room, a girl-friend who visits him; and he has a mini-piano – he plays well. On Sundays he plays the organ at church. His girl-friend, Miss Corelli, does not visit him often, and then only at lunch-time. 'Really I can't tolerate that – have you ever seen the like, a girl visiting a man in his rooms? I must watch the morals of my house,' says La Grande.

The Boy does not seem troubled about it himself. He has been in Fifi's boarding-house eight years and has been engaged five years. His fiancée is a tired-looking blonde who works in his office; he is an accountant. Last year Fifi had to show her landlord that her accounts were in order. They were in order, because Mr Bernard takes care of them. Now the landlord writes to Fifi, 'You did not answer my letter asking for certain information.' What does that mean? It means he is trying to evict Fifi; that is why, for one thing, she has to be strict about morals. So she tells Mr Bernard and the students.

The Boy is tall, dark, good-looking, languid; and in winter he has a cough. She turns off the heating at the end of winter, as soon as she can, to save; and then the Boy stays in bed, partly sick, partly malingering, in protest.

'I shall call the polyclinic doctor,' she says.

'Oh, no, I must have a private physician.'

'I must tell you I called the polyclinic doctor anyway. Who is going to pay for the private physician? I, you think? My dear, you are crafty, the son of a peasant and you are crafty like all peasants. The fact is, you must go to the polyclinic and ask for an X-ray.'

Le petit stayed in bed with a pain in his side and then got up and went for a motor-ride all the afternoon. When he returned she said, 'Now you must go back to work, you are not serious;' and as soon as she said this he went back to bed.

'I don't know what to do with the boy,' she complained to the married couple. 'He has been sick for two years; and he has such habits. He drinks whisky and gin in his room and goes out at night playing poker for money. Sometimes I drink with him in the dining-room, to keep him in. Some days he will say he is cleaned out, he hasn't a cent; and the next day he comes back with money. He is an accountant, a man in a position of trust. Where does the money come from? I know it is a stage in life, and he lives alone in a room; but perhaps it won't get better, it may get worse.'

She worries for another reason. People who have lodgers must have a bedroom for each one in the house; to sleep in the living-rooms is against the law. But La Grande Fifi has no room of her own and sleeps in the dining-room on a couch. When the last meal is finished and the students have gone to their rooms, and the kitchen settled, she makes up her bed there, with sheets and a blanket; and there she goes to bed. But she does not lock the door.

The Boy takes her out once a week to the movies and comes to her room every night. He cannot sleep unless he has told her everything that happened during the day. There's no harm in the others hearing voices there, for it is the dining-room, not her bedroom; and she is not undressed, only resting her legs.

She is often so tired that she wishes he would not. Sometimes you can see her, sitting up on the couch, in her white hair and white high-necked flannel nightgown, a shawl around her shoulders, waiting for him. She hears him come in the front door: 'Paul!' 'Yes, Mamma!' 'Come in here, darling: I'm sitting up for you.'

'Poor Mr Bernard, you are a mother to him!' people would sometimes say, and she would reply: 'Oh, I am better than that. His mother is a very strange person, eccentric, a queer type; she would not listen to him nor understand what he needs. One must be sympathetic with young people. He left home and came to me – eight years he's been with me. We have grown used to each other.'

The Boy is her lover. He goes to her room three or four times a week and stays there, only returning to his own room in the early hours. Still, while being frank about their relation, for the sake of decorum they also pretend that it is not so. La Grande Fifi is happy about it and proud of it. At other times there is trouble. Mr Bernard on occasion breaks with her; he even leaves the *pension* and goes on a business trip – that is, he goes to another *pension*. But he returns. The fact is, Fifi's son, who has a room in the *pension,* makes trouble about Mr Bernard. Michel is a dark thin self-contained man of twenty-eight. He has her name, Mercier, a common name; and at first no one thinks he is her son. They even suspect he may be her lover. He sits in the kitchen very early, in his pyjamas and gown, making his own breakfast; he leaves before the others are up. He often eats his dinner at home, but not always, and he is often away.

Eventually she may say: 'This is my son, Michel,' and it is clear she is proud of him. Michel sometimes nods and moves away with an odd gait – soft, and as it were clinging to the floor. After the introduction he acknowledges no one.

Sometimes she talks about Michel. 'I have relatives in Paris, they are rich and because I am poor they do not want to see me. I was there once and they wanted to marry me off; they brought along a middle-aged man. "I am not in Paris to marry," I said, "I am here for a holiday." Now they don't want to see me, *ils ne causent pas!'*

She explains that once she spoke French very well; Paris French, not Swiss French, which is called *français fédéral* for a joke.

'I once had many books,' she says. 'I don't read much now, only when I'm lying down resting my legs. I know it isn't a good thing. You see, I once lived lower down on the lake side. I gave all my books and my son's prizes to a bookbinder there; he was my fiancé. I had a room to let and he lived in it. I quarrelled with him, I put him out the door and he took away all the books and my son's prizes. Now it is as if my son never had any prizes. My son was learning bookbinding with him and then he gave it up. But he does not care much; he is always on the mountain.'

Once she had a quarrel with her son very early on Friday morning. 'You *must* stay,' she said. 'I am not staying. I'm going on the mountain.' 'But what shall I do? They are coming to see you, Michel.' 'I have no interest in it. They are wasting their time. I shall be on the mountain. I want to try the rope.' On this one occasion he hangs about the front door for a few moments and talks to the boarders. Mountaineering is expensive. He has saved up and bought a new nylon rope, very light and thin. He shows the rope to Mr Bernard and other boarders before he goes; and he smiles slightly, quite pleased.

But La Grande Fifi is very sad in the evening and in a low voice confides in Mr Bernard; she cries too. 'The poor girl telephoned from Geneva and wanted to speak to him, but he was away. I said to her, "Claire, he is on the mountain, he is not here." She is Michel's girl and I am very willing for them to marry, I like her; but he doesn't want her any more. He thinks of only one thing. He is obsessed.'

The next day, Saturday, the parents arrived from Geneva with their daughter Claire. They sat in the kitchen for a long time talking. Fifi was not against her son, particularly; nor very much for him. 'I ask him, I keep asking him about the marriage. He says, "It's a nuisance," and goes off. He does not want anything but the mountain. I am very sorry.' 'Oh, we know how it is, Madame.' 'I am really very sorry.' 'Oh, we know it isn't you, Madame.'

It is a dry, acid, restrained scene, with helpless people; without passion, unfortunate. 'Nothing can be done, he won't change. And what sort of a husband would he be, always on the mountain?' 'Yes, yes, but just the same, it's trying. She was promised marriage.' 'He will never marry. He told me so. "I have another interest," he said.

The Boy is away on holiday; that is, at another *pension*. But after two or three days he begins to telephone her, in the evenings. Once he even telephoned her at lunch-time, when she was busy serving a meal to the young men who had to return to work and classes.

In the evening the Boy again telephoned and they had a long talk. She, too, had things to tell him. 'Really, Paul, I don't know what you're doing there! I don't ask where you are. It is your own choice. Paul, you know my two old men, with the farm and the vineyard? Yes, I told you, my darling. It is a really big country place, away out; they are wine-growers, really big with an extensive vineyard. Ah, I could have been there myself. I was there every summer. One of them is eighty years old, but hale, active; and the other has been in bed for a year. He's paralysed and can't even eat or drink by himself. He stammers. I could have married the healthy one if I had wanted to. What do you think has happened? It is the hearty one who has died! It is a shock to me, Paul. He died suddenly with pneumonia and with winter coming on. The other one is in his bed, still alive.'

She listened to *le petit* on the phone and said, 'But, my son, they were – well, they were brothers – you might say, of a sort. Now, he will dismiss the housekeeper and sell the vineyards. Of course he inherits. You see the kind of thing that happens to me? At one time the healthy one had the reins and if I had married him I would have had my share . . . Well, Paul, you must do as you wish. I am not one to give advice. People must work out their own fate.'

'Ah,' she says today to the students at lunch, 'in the next room, the room now rented to the married couple, was once a professor. I think perhaps he was a little mad. He was forty years old and gave lessons at home; he did not go out much. He got up every night at two o'clock and walked up and down, pulled out his trunks, arranged things, made noises, and then went out to the railway station. "What do you do at the station?" I asked. "I enjoy going to the station," he replied.'

'But he didn't like it here. He used to complain, "What kind of town is this? All roofs. Wherever you look, you see a roof." He pushed a table against the window, so that he would not look down at the roofs. I was afraid to go in there. He made passes at me. I found him here – in my dining-room at eleven at night. You know I come in here to rest my legs, until everyone is in, and sometimes I fall asleep. I had not bolted the door – why? I was just waiting to go to bed.'

The fiction is that she sleeps in what is really her son's room.

' "What do you want here?" I said. He made certain proposals to me. I said, "Go away! This is a house full of young people; we must think of their morals." Sometimes I found him here when I came in from the kitchen to rest my legs. He went to Paris in the end and sent me a letter asking me to go there, too. I'm not a young girl to do unconventional things. Think! But I could have been in Paris.'

The Boy came back to her presently and there was bustling and buffeting at night in the dining-room. There was talk, laughter, weeping, expostulation, night-life. Later on, Mr Bernard went back to his room. For a while he seemed to be punishing La Grande Fifi. He invited his girl to come to his room, and when Fifi scolded him he threatened to go back 'There'. Where he had been was never mentioned. He, too, was scrupulous not to hurt her feelings about it. He would say, 'When I was – somewhere, recently . . .' and 'Naturally, in some other places conditions are different!'

They spent long evenings together. She was glad of

him. Her lease was nearly up and she was afraid the landlord would ask a higher rent or find some excuse for putting her out. Michel, her son, was seldom home, usually just to eat and sleep, and in the weekend he would again be on the mountain. If his mother talked to him, he said nothing.

But Fifi and Paul talked of nothing else. 'What will I do if they put me out? Where will I live? And you, too, Paul – where will you live? Will you go back to your mother?' 'No, never.' 'You'll get married, I suppose; you'll marry that girl who comes here? It's high time isn't it? You've been engaged six years,' and Fifi would laugh. 'No, no; she wants to get married, but I haven't the money.' 'Will you go back – over there – where you were?' 'No. I don't know what I'll do.' One evening Paul came in very much exited. He talked all through dinner to all the other lodgers. He went to his room, played the piano a little while Fifi washed the dishes and then she came to his room and they sat there talking it over.

'I can make money, Fifi, we'll have money. You won't have to leave, even if he does raise the rent.' 'But supposing he finds out about my sleeping in the dining-room?' 'No, no, you say you sleep in your son's room.' 'But supposing Michel is here? You know they sent someone already, unexpectedly; and there were Michel's mountain things. "They are my son's," I said: "he keeps them with me for convenience, but he lives up the mountain." So I got away with it. But people talk. I can't sleep, my darling. I dream we haven't any of us a roof over our heads. The others, too. It is a responsibility. I offer people a roof; I try to make a family life for them.'

'Leave it to me, my dear,' said *le petit*. 'This scheme of mine will make money. I'm a businessman, aren't I? I know the inside of business. I am an income-tax accountant, I know all their secrets; nothing is hidden from me. Now you know, Fifi, my brother is still living at home. He has no go in him. But I left my mother ten years ago and after two years in – another place – I came here and I liked you as soon as I saw you. So leave it to me; your fate is my fate.'

They had a warm eager talk and he told her what he had not been able to tell at the dining-table.

'I met this Italian in a café; I knew him from living over there. He came to me and said that astrakhan skins are being sold dirt cheap because the boom is almost over and astrakhan is going off the market, with all the nylon furs coming in; and then they are going to sell coloured astrakhan, the black skins won't be saleable. There's a chance now to make a big profit, people will be greedy for the skins; they'll pay any amount because there are plenty of women who want just that, an astrakhan coat and can't afford it.

'So you see, though the smart markets won't want them, everyone else will and I can unload them in some country, say, Canada or England, where they are not very fashionable, or even Italy and Spain and Greece, where the winters are cool enough. My friend has friends and they will help; and it doesn't matter about the export licences, because we will smuggle them in.'

'Smuggle? Can he do that?'

'Well, my friend can't smuggle them, but he thinks what we can do is smuggle them in in automobile tyres. It is something he heard of. We will have to make some connections.'

'But Paul,' she said, worried. 'You know people were picked up last Christmas for smuggling all sorts of things in tyres and now they examine all the tyres at the frontier.'

'We must manage it somehow. Tyres are one of the few things large enough for smuggling skins. Well, if that doesn't work, we must try some other way.'

'Couldn't you try a legal way?' asked Fifi.

'The difficulty is, I am not a registered business. I have no permit and there are the exchange regulations. We must bypass them all. But a businessman can find a way. The first step is to get rid of the skins. Legally, my dear Fifi, you can only export merchandise actually made in the country – for example, Swiss watches; and astrakhan is not of course a Swiss product. And then you could export by exchange, import from Italy some Italian product of the same value. This question of bills and values can be fixed up through friends. Yes, I have been thinking it all out. It will be done and then I'll be in business on my own. You cannot make real money as an accountant. I work hard, I have a good position, but those businessmen make more with a hand's turn than I make in a year. It's the ingenuity which is rewarded, you see. And rightly, I hold.'

'Can't you get on the business register?'

'No, they poke their noses into everything. Later, yes, when I have money to set up business. Then Fifi, you won't have to worry. I'll look after you; I'll set you up in a *pension* – anything you like. I'll buy you a farm. But *you're* in business; you have a business permit. Why can't you do it?'

'My dear child, I have a permit for a boarding-house; and then they're always inspecting me. Look at those people I allow to make meals in their room; I'm not sure that it's legal. It worries me at night. And you must not use your room as a business office, it's not allowed.'

'What will I do? I mustn't lose this opportunity. Well, I had better tell you – I have already bought those skins. I used up all my savings and I borrowed money at work and from a moneylender, because I'll get the return. But they're valuable; I must have somewhere to store them. He's delivering them today. I told him to bring them here.'

'Oh, no. You'll get me into trouble.'

'I have no money to rent a store-room. I haven't a penny. I've mortgaged my salary in advance. What am I to do?'

He began to weep. La Grande Fifi, a soft creature, took him in her arms. He looked worn, his persistent cough became worse; he caught cold in the corridor at night; and every evening he sat begging and cajoling her in the dining-room until time for bed. The Italian, he said, was anxious to get rid of the skins and insisted upon his receiving them.

So she agreed. One lunchtime he came up the stairs three or four times carrying long heavy cardboard boxes which he deposited in his bedroom. They gave out a strong smell of dead skin and preservative. This led to two weeks' hysterical talk between Fifi and Paul. Everyone in the *pension* knew about the proposed deal, the smuggling, not to mention the self-advertisement by the skins in the bedroom.

But the Boy arranged to barter the skins for Italian ceramics. He now received regular business letters at the *pension,* to Fifi's constant worry, and spent two or three Sundays typing his replies. He explained everything to calm her and said, craftily, 'My mother would never allow me to make money; she does not understand life, she is, as you know, an eccentric. And though she is your age' (a fact admitted between them) 'she has no experience of life at all. She doesn't understand a plain commercial undertaking.' Fifi was pleased – but her *pension* was her livelihood. His business letters were simple, his telephone conversations naive; and what with the foolishness of poor Fifi, who related her troubles, and poor Paul, everyone – the satirical and incredulous students and the lodgers – knew all that went on.

One weekend Paul spent sewing the skins up in gunnysacks; he threw away the cardboard boxes. On another weekend he was mysteriously absent; a doomful quiet hung over the *pension*.

When Paul returned on the Monday it was to mourn. He had tried to cross the frontier to Italy with a gunnysack full of skins. He was with his sister, who had already lent him all her savings, about 500 Swiss francs. On top of the skins they had placed a few ski-clothes; but how strange it was to take ski-clothes across in a gunny-sack! And then the smell! At any rate the skins were at the frontier waiting to be redeemed.

This being so, *le petit* wrote to the man in Italy: 'I find it impossible to export the skins straight out, so we must agree to a barter. Please let me have a list of the ceramics you intend to send me. I enclose the valuation of the goods I want to send you.'

The value of the skins was given, of course, at much below market value. The importer at once replied: 'Your merchandise is shown to be not enough; it is not what I expected. You have not shown a proper valuation.' (But *le petit* had been told that Signor Gino 'would understand'.) 'To transact this deal you must send more merchandise.'

Paul now borrowed another thousand francs from a moneylender and bought more skins.

La Grande Fifi was deeply disturbed. One of her lodgers had developed a winter cough; she gave him her recipe, barley-sugar in hot milk, and this did quieten him for a while; but then another lodger developed signs of heart-strain. Running up and down the steep streets of Lausanne four times a day does not suit all bodies. She did her best for all; and when the long day was over, she had to sit up every night with Paul talking over the tangle he had got into. Sometimes he cried and sometimes he exclaimed, 'But that is business, my dear Fifi; business is a headache. If you haven't the stamina for a little obstacle like this, you can't make money.'

'But supposing they find out, with all these letters and telephone calls, that you are using one of my bedrooms for a business office? I shall get into trouble.' 'What am I to do then? Do you want me put out in the street? Are you going to be like my mother, just criticising and never helping? See what happened to my elder brother – he is still at home, under her thumb; he will never marry now. He lost his girl. He did everything Mother said. "Get rid of the girl" she said, and he did. He wanted to go into business, too. She wouldn't let him; she told him he was just a routine brain, a mere clerk. He never got away. Are you going to be like that? I thought you understood me and were on my side.'

Then he would weep and she would comfort him. She did not know what to do. She did not want to lose him; she loved him, half as lover, half as mother.

At last permission was received. He was allowed to exchange the astrakhans for Italian ceramics, which would be coming in as barter, in twenty cases. In the meantime he had written to Berne, to Washington, D.C., and Montreal, about selling the astrakhans and about import licences. He found that he could not take any risk himself nor sign any bills of lading or undertakings, having no business permit, but that the Italian merchant had the necessary authority.

'It is all right,' he said, taking a leap as he came into her room that night. 'All will be well. The Italian will of course take the risk. He is a friend of my friend here, the Italian in the café, and they are very anxious to get hold of those skins.'

'If the skins are so good why not sell them here?' said she.

'Try to sell furs in Switzerland!' said he. 'It can't be done. Besides, I have this information privately. It's a quiet little deal. It's very simple, Fifi. You see, you don't understand business. I am not in business, that is why they won't allow me to do it, but they are willing to treat with me: they see I have a business mind.'

The month ran out. Paul obtained a further renewal of his option by assigning the furs. Another month passed. He then tried to resell the furs, as Fifi advised. But the furs he bought for 1200 francs, the dealer now said, could not be resold for even 200 francs – they were rubbish; and overseas, the fad had passed. Paul was excited by all this activity; he was still in business. He kept carbon copies of his letters and at night read them to Fifi. Sometimes he said he was dealing in private matters which could not be breathed even to her. He was self-important, she tender, indulgent, anxious. She no longer believed in his deal, it would bring trouble to the house, but was afraid of his returning to his mother.

Paul's manner is becoming lighter, his tone of voice more singsong. This tall strong man runs in and out of the house at all hours, sings to himself, speaks in a childish pouting voice. When Fifi begins to speak to him he runs into his room, turns on the gramophone, plays a trifle on the piano, leaves his door open, humming and tapping with his heel. Because of the increasing protests of the alarmed landlady he sleeps with her three nights out of four; and when this is not enough to bring her into line, to punish her he invites his enduring girl-friend. She is a young creature of a lower class, an office worker he has been going out with for years. He tells her that he cannot marry until his two sisters marry or his mother dies.

La Grande Fifi is curt with the young girl, who comes at lunch-time and goes to Paul's room. He leaves the door open, shows her his sacks of astrakhan, tells her about his business transactions and plays the gramophone. On the day of her second visit they lie on an old horsehair sofa which stands in the hall under the cloak-pegs; they lie there obstinately with the coat-tails and scarves tickling their faces until the other boarders, returning to class or office, come to get their coats and hats, making rude but not insulting remarks about the progress of their love-affair.

The landlady with dignity tells them to get up off the sofa. 'I shall lose my licence. Is that what you want? They will say I am running a disorderly house.' The other lodgers joke and soothe her. But she is outraged and Paul is satisfied. In the evening, when the dining-room is cleared, he goes in to talk to her; she protests, cries, he cries too; and again they are friends.

The second month comes when he cannot pay for his room and board. 'You cannot turn me out,' he says, weeping. 'We have been together for nearly nine years now, ever since I left home, almost.' After a while she says, 'Paul, you must do something. I am very short of funds. You know my son does not always pay for his room. Now I have two boys with me, two sons, you and Michel, who don't pay for their rooms, nor for food. I am only a poor woman. I might seem rich to you, but if they turned me out I haven't a home to go to. If he is forced to, Michel can marry the girl in Geneva, so that he can have a bed from which to start out for the mountain. He would marry for that. My old friend on the farm has just died. I always thought I could, if necessary, go there as house-keeper. But not now.'

'Do not bother with such fantasies,' he cries. 'It won't happen. Think about me. My poor sister has no money. She lent it all to me. She hasn't managed to find a husband. She has got to go on working as a shop-assistant. She is doing it for me. She believes in me. Besides, if you are so insistent, I can give you twenty francs.'

'But that isn't enough, my dear little one.'

'No, but it will help you get through the month and next payday I can give you something. My position is very difficult. The man who lent me 1,000 francs is taking back 1,500 francs' worth of furs on the fourth of next month. I can't escape. I've been dodging him for days; but they know I'm here at lunchtime. Where else can I eat? I can't afford to buy a sausage. Is that a way for a man of my age and position to be?'

The students are moderately entertained. 'Will you take the four sacks of astrakhan into eternity with you?' one asks with concern. 'We are really quite worried about it, for they say St Peter will never allow the skins of dead animals inside the pearly gates.' 'Nonsense, he is a far-seeing man,' says another. 'They are for his grandchil-dren. He is provident.' Paul listens, muses, laughs; and in a few days he explains to them at table, 'In business we say converted, not exchanged.'

The next month his salary is gone; he owes several thousand francs, his sister and his friend have no savings and La Grande Fifi is behind with her bills. She now talks about the couple in the next room where the professor once lived. 'I should never have allowed it. They live high, spend money like water, they eat large meals in there. That money should be coming into my pocket. It is my house. They don't sleep well at night because they have eaten too much. I should never allow myself to be taken in by foreigners. But then I have a soft nature.' And in a moment she is telling them a wellworn tale about the officer who loved her. She dreamed of him on a white horse, in a blue coat and a gold képi; and within three days of the dream she had a letter from him from Le Havre where he had been on manoeuvres, on a white horse in a blue cloak with a gold képi. He said he had dreamed of her. 'How I miss you, Fifi. I am coming back to get you.' All this happened ten years earlier – twelve, perhaps. But she would not be surprised at any time to see that French officer return to fetch her. Her good humour is restored. She is affectionate towards the lodgers in the big room; and she goes out in the evening to a show with *le petit.* They come home, they have a little drink of cordial, and sit for a long time talking. They are happy making each other promises for the future, when he will have money and free her from worry. Both believers in white horses and képis of gold, they have their moments of joy.

One of the jokes at table – for all are interested in the Italian ceramics – is that they will be able to buy some cheap Christmas presents for their sweethearts and families; or even for themselves, since some of them will eventually set up house.

One day Paul receives advice that a large consignment of Italian chinaware is awaiting him. He must present his papers, pay Customs duty, and remove the goods. He returns home depressed. He cannot dispose of the goods and he has nowhere to store them. His sister and brother live at home; so he must press Fifi to take them into her house. The ceramics are, of course, much bulkier than the skins.

'I could do with some new china here,' says Fifi. 'Some of my plates are burned, others are chipped. You really ought to make me a present because of what I have done for you.'

Paul is silent. One of the students says suddenly 'They're bedroom services, jugs and basins and – chamberpots!' Silence.

In the evening: 'I *must* bring them here, Fifi.' 'No, you will not.' 'I must – I have no money for a warehouse.' 'What things are they?' 'Chamberpots.' 'You might as well chop them up into little pieces.'

But he comes back the next day. 'Fifi, my friend in the café tells me something really interesting. You never know, do you? One must keep one's ears open. I have found out that you can export them to America. The Americans are buying all kinds of antiques.' 'Antiques?' 'Yes, they are using nineteenth century wash-basins for saladbowls and chamberpots for ferns. They stand them on a pedestal in the living-room; and they serve sweets in them. I'll go to the Consul and get the addresses of some American buyers.'

He tossed at night, feverish. 'Paul, accept it as a dead loss. You'll be ill. You won't be able to go to the office and I'll have an invalid on my hands.' She tells him to go to the polyclinic for an X-ray; no, he must have a private doctor. 'We mustn't live on the level of people who go to the public hospital, Fifi.' The doctor comes. Paul must stay in bed.

She tells her troubles to the lodgers at table. 'Send him home,' one of them says. 'He has a good home, sister and mother and brother to look after him. Why should you do it?' 'Ah, my dear, you don't understand. His mother is impossible, a medusa, a gorgon. She is as hard as rocks and doesn't understand him. What would he do up there among all those hard hearts? He would die of loneliness.'

His sweetheart visits him. She is admitted unwillingly; and when she leaves Fifi says to her, 'Now you have seen him, you may stay away. This excitement is not good for him. Why do you come? He will never marry. He is an honourable man. He wants to make money first, and that is going to take years. That is what has laid him on his back. I don't want to see you here again.'

When Miss Corelli leaves, Fifi talks to Paul a long time, soothing and insinuating. 'This is very bad for you, don't you see? She has only marriage in mind. These sentimental situations are very unhealthy. Now with me you have a home, a tender heart that loves you and asks nothing.'

And so it is. He stays with Fifi.

Trains

Most international travellers not flying on their way to
Switzerland or Germany go through Basle in the train.
It's a big stop where you may stay overnight or change, or
eat; or go on. The Swiss city of Basle is situated on both
sides of the Rhine and in a narrow loop of frontier
between Swabia in Germany and Alsace in France. Like
some other frontier cities, it is rich, independent and
brave; brisk and local. It numbered about two hundred
thousand then and is about six hundred miles from the
sea, the port of Rotterdam. The Rhine is a great river
highway. Here it is swift and deep as it rushes through the
Basle gorge; and numerous bridges cross it, some of
which open; the motor and towed barges have masts,
which, worked by a hand or motor winch, crack before
the bridges and rise again. Flags of all nations pass,
principally Dutch, German, French and Swiss. There are
river-boats and launches and they have a water game,
which is played in long clumsy canoes which the youths
pilot quickly zig-zagging across the twisting rushing

waters from one bank to the other.

We lived in various parts of Europe where Americans with money send their children to school. I was naturally delighted when some parent-friend wrote to me to say:

'Oh, we're so ashamed to burden you, asking you another favour after all the favours we've asked you; and this is the worst' (etc.) 'but if you could and *would* meet Joe at Basle Station and see he has a room and eats something not only coca-cola and icecream sodas and see him on the train again. I am sure that damfool school has got all the arrangements mixed, in spite of telegrams and letters and the rest, well, we would be eternally grateful though eternally ashamed for this BURDEN we are placing on your only too willing shoulders. Oh, why do we have such good kind patient enduring friends? and why are we so shameless? Joe arrives at Basle railroad central station at 5.10 p.m. and is leaving next morning on the 7.15 a.m. Will you see that he has got his luggage, passports, ticket, something to eat on the way, enough money to buy at least fourteen separate meals in the dining car and to take the taxi when he gets to Paris – if you wouldn't mind? And see he gets something to eat at night, find out if that cold of his is really whooping cough and see if you can worm out of him in your well known way whether the gold wristwatch he lost was ever returned. He's so loyal to his comrades and there was some sort of scandal at the school. The janitor was accused, then the waiters and at last a little comrade of Joe's, some Greek or Turkish aristocrat. I don't know, probably race prejudice is dictating this! *But has he got back his wristwatch?* That fool school ($3,000 and extras) did not tell us after frenzied telephone calls and discreet letters to Joe who won't give away his comrades, very loyal but slightly nerve-wracking to parents. And would you manage to find out whether he has changed his politics; there are very strange contacts at that school, but of course don't put him on the rack – leave that to us, we're good at it; and another thing, will you see he cleans his teeth? I know it's a shame but he must and write us darlings saying what you think of him. Is he too awful? Do you think he has improved? Can he speak any French after only one year and three months in a private sanitarium for American boys brought up at great expense in New York City to begin with and so knowing no word of any other tongue but basic Brooklyn? . . . And, oh, dear, this is embarrassing, but Joe must get up every night at two or else – so could you see to that? Oh dear what parents must do! Lost to all shame!'

Getting such a letter, I concealed my extreme animation from my husband; for husbands may not like wives to become excited about other people's children; and then there is the expense, which wives do not think of. When I see a strange child, I become lavish. I become a heady greedy giddy six-year-old, the sort I never was. I have fantasies about buying icecream, orangeade, comics, magic tricks, cake and circuses.

'Oh, well, it's only one night,' I said.

Other letters came from the parents. They were anxious because he had spent over a year in this fashionable boys' school tenanted by as well as the polyglot staff, some Greek, Armenian, Turkish, Egyptian, Italian and other refugees, by which I mean rich lads whose fathers, richer still, were in countries in social turmoil, their own class stability relying for the moment on American aid, but the future uncertain. These parents, our friends, worried about the possible aristocratic savagery of the Turks, Greeks, Armenians, Italians of that class. They sent on some of Joe's letters to get us acquainted with the boy. They contained no hint of such troubles. They were invariably of this nature:

'Thanks for your letter, hope you are well. I am well. I am doing OK I think. Well, write you soon. Love, Joe.'

When Joe received one of their usual heavy packages of food, sweets, socks and writing materials, say, he would write:

'Thanks for your package, hope you are well, I am well. We beat St Sulpice today 4 to 0. Well, write you soon. Love, Joe. PS. The pocket-lens was OK.'

The boy with this verbal gift had learned some French and forgotten an equal amount of English, which left him rather short. His French exercises (which we received also) now ran: '*Je lui écrit une lettre.* I rote him a letter.'

He described his own conduct as irreproachable. The classes were not the extremely well drilled classes of the French *lycée,* and the boys went off for swimming, skating, ski-ing, horseback riding. Joe was a great success it seemed; he had charm and he instantly adopted the boys' code. In fact, his parents, in a letter, had already decided to get him into the diplomatic service. Joe was between ten and eleven years old.

Three letters later the parents brought themselves to reveal Joe's small defect. After a good deal of explanation and talk of psychoanalysis, schools for speech and other defects, the rights of childhood to grow at its own pace, troubles brought on by nightmares, neglect by grandparents at a certain time, misunderstanding by teachers, a soft heart easily wounded, they came down to tintacks; we must buy a ground sheet for Joe. Perhaps Joe would forget his. We took care of this too. We bought some fruit and chocolate in case Joe was hungry at night. We said he would have some comics with him and perhaps the Greeks and Turks had got him out of that American habit of comics. We rented a room in the pension in which we were staying. Frau Wendel, the pension-keeper, told Maria the Italian maid to tell Elise the German maid to be sure that a handsome corner room was ready for the famed boy. We ordered wine for the dinner. When the day came, a Saturday, we went to the station several times to ask about trains. There were a lot coming in and school children of all ages travelling on that day for their vacations. Some of the trains did not carry luggage. Some of them went right through to Paris. There was a big switch station some miles back where trains changed and went on to Geneva. One could also change and go on to Brussels. Supposing Joe – yes! What a number of people sprang up around us who knew of people who had been carried on and got to Geneva or Brussels. We went to the information desk and asked what would happen to a boy of ten knowing little French who got carried on to any of those places without the right ticket? Then we knew Joe. Perhaps as a prank he might have gone on to Paris anyhow, knowing that his parents would rescue him? Or to Geneva with some of his mates? Or got lost? Or even have gone by plane after all? Or perhaps (there was a mild epidemic at the school) they had kept him on for a few days? Or perhaps they were keeping him to see his grandmother, who was on her way from Italy especially to see him? She might have picked him up. 'Nana' and the parents did not see eye to eye; in fact Joe was disputed territory. We got to the station three-quarters of an hour before train-time. Four or five trains later back to the information desk; not distracted but certainly anxious. 'You need not worry,' said the man. I had not liked his looks; but at once he became a grandpa; he was soothing. 'The station master at Geneva will certainly telegraph me.' We went off home at last.

There was Joe waiting in our attic room in the pension. He said, 'I just took an earlier train, why wait around? So when you weren't on the platform I just came on here. I bet you're glad to see me.'

'We are.'

'Yes, I thought you'd be relieved,' he said.

Though not yet eleven, Joe was already five feet tall. We felt a bit foolish as we marched into the dining room with Joe because we had given out that he was a little boy of ten. However he was smooth-looking, handsome; and bursting with pride we sat round the little table and read his offered school report. Joe's report disturbed him because of the marking, 'Conduct: 2 out of 10.' 'I don't understand it,' he said. 'Well, what did you do?' 'I behaved all that term. I was just perfect this term,' he said. So we at once got the feeling that the school must have been wrong, or prejudiced against the American (not an aristocrat) or that Joe's real marks got somehow allocated in a shuffle to someone else, some wild Algerian or Armenian aristocrat. For American boys are not wild – well, not that way. What way?

Joe had changed a great deal. He looked us over with considerable reserve. We could see we were not up to scratch; he eyed our clothes. However he was polite about the food and drank the wine with enjoyment. They had it at school. After dinner we took him to a bizarre café we had been to. In a tall dark smallish room with a big window and a bar counter in a grotto, were round tables of solid metal with plate glass tops. We sat down at one. Under the plate glass was a deep basin roughly carved to imitate a creviced rock pool and painted green and blue and in this rock basin was a living baby python. Other tables had living lizards, frogs, other snakes. Joe was enchanted. When we got back, we found the real owner of the fine corner room had returned unexpectedly (they rented it temporarily in his absence) so that I made up my bed for Joe in our room and I slept on the floor between them and put the alarm clock set for 2 a.m. at my pillow. It did not ring.

Joe got to Paris safely. Already I knew the moderated gratitude, comic spirit of the parents. These offstage voices soon uttered 'Ha-ha-ha, well perhaps Joe did drop the alarm clock into the guttering, but it will stir up George and Helen to have a child around.' And they did indeed write, 'Joe was crazy about that café with the snake in the table. And we laughed and laughed at his description of you sleeping on the floor between the two males. Why did you do that?' Did it cure us? No.

6   *England*

Street Idyll

Jenny was going to the hairdresser down the hill. Everything was in order, gloves, bag, key in purse, milk bottles to take down, fires out, time to go.

At the last, she held up the magnifying mirror to her face, checked in the bathroom mirror, wardrobe mirror for skirt, shoes. She knew she would see him somewhere on the hill.

She came neatly downstairs, not to fall on the old ragged matting in the smeary brown hall. Up the street, fresh and bright: rosebush, white patch on stone fence, don't stare at it, it resembles a face; curtains in basement opposite, sort of crochet grid; flagged yard, hello to red-haired cleaner, garage to let: and so to the corner where the big church is and the red pillarbox where she posted so many letters.

Beside it, a seat for old people for sunny days. Once, even she and Gill had sat there. A wedding for a neighbor's daughter; her tears dried, her throes past, the future assured. They were not invited, but they were glad; women, men, girls, craning like pigeons at the church gate, confetti like pigeon food.

Jenny and Gill liked to look at weddings; marriage was in their minds. They had nothing but good to say of marriage. It was the best state for men and women; there was a calm and thrilling joy, there was forgiveness, solace, peace, certain home and country, without passport, rent book, marching, petitions.

Otherwise, Jenny would not have sat on a bench; she had a horror of it, as a proof of old age, impotence, neglect.

True, she thought, if some old person actually was sitting there, it is sad to have to creep out of a back room, unloved by relatives, or a sole chamber, a bedsitter in one of the old buildings down this street.

It was, in a way, a very good place, in the air at the top of the hill, with traffic going ten ways, the schoolchildren from the council high school and three private schools up and down, the respectable girls two by two for church, from that school; what? The Rasputin? The Razumovsky? Voronoff? Impossible. Some Russian name.

Name of Royal family?

The people saw children in the lunch hour heading for the wine shop at the corner, which also served as a tuckshop, ice-cream, peanuts, chocbars; the women toiling home with shopping trolleys, dog people walking dogs, the greyhound, hairless dachs, longhair fox, ancient alsatian, small white peke, cherished mongrels.

Yes, old lonely people liked the noise, dust, oil; they liked the hundred children, fifteen dogs – it reminded them of another earlier life perhaps. Loquacious, silent, self-muttering, frozen in bitterness, terribly ridged, valleyed with age; what were their relatives – loving, rude, sullen, venomous?

They were people who knew they did not count except when they showed up at the post office for their pensions or at the polling station.

Jenny softened her heart. Gill liked to sit on park benches and talk to people. He liked everyone. Once or twice she had met him there, in the park and he told what people said, or what the children had done, dangerous things or naughty things. 'The woman did not answer, she seemed offended; we had not been introduced, this is England.' Gill believed everyone was his equal and had a soul as sunny as his; he hoped others were like that.

Such ideas would flit through her head in an instant as she passed the bench by the letterbox. Now, she was round the horseshoe bend of the churchyard and she started downhill, searching in the far distance for Gill who might now be visible among the shopping crowds.

She stared carefully, not only to see him at the first moment possible, but to see him make the crossing, for it was a death spot, a traffic black spot down there, where three streets met, not to mention the station yard, hotel parking lot and parade. Gill was shortsighted.

Gill had beautiful eyes, hazel with a bluish rim, and, in fact, his father had dark blue eyes. Gill said blue in a peculiar manner, 'blew' to rhyme with dew, and she teased him, saying: 'And twitched his mantle blew.' He laughed and was hurt. Though perhaps, who knows, that was the way Milton said it?

When they played *Cymbelline* at Newcastle-upon-Tyne in 'the Doric,' as they say up there, in Northumbrian; Cymbelline, Cloten, Guiderius, Arviragus, even Philario and Iachimo spoke Northumbrian – the program notes said that this was closer to the language in Shakespeare's ear than anything you will hear at the Old Vic or on the BBC.

Iachimo, Lachimo, yes. Was that where she got the

name for one of the two large glossy photos of Gill she had, one sober, one glad, and which she called *Tristan Lachrimo* and *Baron Lachlaches,* which pleased Gill?

There was Gill, a short square peg in a quadrilateral situation, streets, footpaths, flagged courtyards, low block buildings, trudging along.

She could see him and knew that soon he would mark her out, coming down the hill with no one about. What is more, he knew her height and lope, which he called a stride. 'You think I stride?' 'You do stride.' She reined in her steps, but on the hill you had to take long steps, go fast. He was looking about now, crossing; he could not see her yet – five hundred yards and more.

Just where would they meet? It was always exciting; her heart beat a little faster. Not too soon – spin it out! Now he was across, looking left and right and over.

He began to pass the real estate agent's, the little alley, the dress-shop, the bingo parlor, once a cinema where they had seen foreign films; now he was at the auctioneer's.

Now they were close, they did not look any more. She glanced to one side – the house converted to business premises, with neglected lawn and low bushes where someone threw away his or her gin bottles.

Now his big dark eyes were on her; she looked away. They met, their faces lighting up. Why were their eyes for a moment on the ground? So that passersby would not see the rapturous, intimate smiles which they felt irrepressibly forming behind their cheeks right up to their ears. They halted, fastened their eyes on each other.

This had all happened before. Sometimes, a passerby, a pillowy, hatless woman, in a print dress with parcels, a nice thinning elderly man in a hat, climbing the hill with his washing, had hesitated in surprise, almost as if they feared an incident.

This square-cut, dark man, and this tall fair woman who came to a stop suddenly, and, without greeting began, to murmur – they were not alike, they looked like strangers to each other; and they had never lost this look; reared in different countries, different traditions.

They stood there, not knowing what to say, for there is nothing to express the emotion that brought them together the first time and now brought them together.

She described arcs with the toes of her shoes – her best shoes, for she had known she was going to meet him; he looked around, filling in time, as a cat or bird does.

Then they looked at each other flatface, smiled and she said: 'I saw you when you were passing Sainsbury's.' 'I saw you too, way up the hill.' 'You know my look.' He corrected her: 'It was your walk, your Australian walk.' 'It's true, I saw an Australian in Tottenham Court Road the other day; it was his walk.'

There was a pause, because the last words were only to fill a pause. There was nothing to say, but they could not break the web which had already grown between them, a quick-weaving, thick-netting web, which occurred always, in speech, in silence; but was more embarrassing in silence, because so felt.

It tugged like the moon at waters, sucked like a drain, had already grown part of them like barnacles on rocks, difficult to get away from; nothing fatal in it. They stood quiet, embarrassed, unable to move away; their thoughts going 'Er-er-er-.'

'Well,' then a slight smile, a grin, too, 'All right –' 'I won't be long.' 'OK.' Each takes a step to pass, hesitates. The tissue is dissolving, but strands hang on; they take another step and turn, 'Goodbye.' 'Goodbye.'

They wave. They really hesitate to quit each other. It would be better to turn and go up the hill with him, than to go on to the hairdresser; it seems a pointless, vapid business; but to go up with Gill at this moment when he knows she is expected elsewhere would be impossible, an extraordinary weakness, and inconceivable swoon of personality. There is danger in such disorder.

Elle garde son secret, elle le garde.

'I'll be home by twelve,' says Jenny. 'I'll be waiting for you,' says Gill.

For the fact is, though this took place every time they met, this leaning forward to meet, this painless suffering of separation, Jenny and Gill were husband and wife and had spent nearly forty years together.

Jenny and Gill are no longer there; someone has hacked to pieces the bench for the old people; there are small changes; but very often I now meet on the hill another couple, he short, handsome, with his fair hair bleached by age, she bleached too, but once very pretty; and they have one motion, in harmony, and predetermined, like figures on a town clock famous for its coloring and carving; and by the air they carry with them, and the look of gold, I know that is how they feel, also.

1954: Days of the Roomers

Fairlawn Gardens, a short wide street ran between Swiss Cottage and West Hampstead, bordered on one side only, at that time, 1954, with well-built brown or red villas, all belonging to an old estate; and there was number 33 a students' boarding-house registered with the University of London. The immense City of London has a thousand names for green, Wood Lane, Forest Gate, Oak Park, Hollybush Hill, Wimbledon Common, Fortune Green, and countless Greens, Commons, Hursts, Heaths, Beeches, Laurels. In spite of dirty streets stiffly armoured with terraced houses and giant multiple dwellings rising every month, a view of London from Primrose Hill or Hampstead Heath shows many patches of green and blowing trees, over a wide landscape; a local Forest of Arden not yet eaten up by toad and snail. Fairlawn Gardens, too, was not a lie. Hidden inside the big square of villas, and reached only from their backyards, was a common or green, lined with old trees in which tenants might cautiously stroll and children quietly play.

The Watson couple, literary hacks, had the large front room on the first floor, with two windows on the fire escape and with a locked door to an adjoining closet, once a dressing-room, now rented as a bedroom to a Swiss student from Basle. Each morning, his friend, another student, would come in, 'Steh' auf, Mensch!' cried he. The Watsons had already long been up. Bob Watson knew German, and on hearing this, would sometimes break into German, a mellow rich Rhineland German which made the Swiss students laugh.

These rooms had never had the sun since the roof went on. The front room underneath, never heated, even in midwinter, sent up the cold. The landlords were saving money to have their three children educated in private schools and the two elder at least were to go to Oxford. Mr Warren, a deep-eyed, tall dark man, with a narrow boyish head, was the son of a French mother and an English father, and Mrs Warren, born in the City of Lodz, Poland, had gone to Paris, to the Sorbonne, as a young girl, after much argument with her parents. Mr Warren was ashamed that his children had foreign parents. Mrs Warren did not mind. 'You are educating your children to be ashamed of their father and mother,' she said gaily to him; 'you know I will never lose my foreign accent and you have a foreign accent too, except in French!' She said it only to chaff and stir him; for he was sober and stiffnecked, fierce with his struggle. 'I speak perfect English!' he declared. 'They will be ashamed to say their mother runs a boarding-house!' 'At least, they will not have to run a boarding-house!'

The entire house, four floors, an attic and a cellar, all the tenants' rooms, were cleaned by a robust redheaded woman who came in once a week; and had, for cleaning, one dustpan, one mop, a stairbroom and a rag; that is to say, the house, painted in brown and furnished with secondhand brown rugs and chairs and beds, looked rather dirty. There had been a vacuum-cleaner, but this was now located at a house some distance down the same road, where the Warrens had taken on another lodging-house for students. They did not have to advertise, for they took in Indian and Pakistani students; though the 'Estate' would not allow them to take in Jamaican and African students.

The Watson couple, middle-aged, were grateful; because their room was better and cheaper than others they had seen and the foreign landlady, tolerant, friendly, was neither inquisitive, smug nor ignorant. She tried to make up for the shabbiness by little gifts to the Watsons, of canned fruit, tomato juice and soup, which her husband bought in bulk (he was in that business) and once gave them a quart of pure olive oil, which he had received and did not like. What is more, she did not complain, though they both worked most of the day on their typewriters. The rug was small and the rickety little table thumped on the bare floor when the typewriters ran. The landlady, who was sometimes sick in winter, slept in the freezing front room underneath, lay there all day when sick, but she did not complain; and they were ashamed, but they could not stop working.

When the redhead came in to clean, the Watsons would take a walk, always on the lookout for a better place. Tens of thousands of people, even families with one or two children, live just so, in one room, in the great city. In all the houses of London, it seemed, behind white facades with pillared porches and lofty railed steps, with high walls and handsome windows that promised significant space, were thin partitions making cubicles for roomers. Walking about to get the sun, they looked everywhere, noticed the partitions dividing the light and space; but they watched and hoped. In one place, up two flights of stairs, there was no water, but water could be brought up by the landlady's son, at sixpence a jug. In another place, in 'Hyacinth Gardens', the old German landlady let them in with four keys for four doors; but they had to be in early to be so let in; for she gave no keys. But at a writers' meeting, they heard of an old mother and daughter who were looking for tenants 'of their sort, likeminded people' and following a long ecstasy of hope and despair, they left the front room of Fairlawn Gardens to others.

We were there too. What I remember most, of that place, are a few strange scenes. We went for Christmas to a friend, were away for four days and when we returned the kind landlady reproached me, for the sparrows always fed by me had been dashing themselves at the closed front windows looking for bread. One moonlit night, an owl tried to pick up a black cat sleeping on the gatepost. The clawed owl hooted and the clawed cat ran screeching up the street. Another night scene – I heard crying in the street; a small young woman was running up the unbuilt side of the street, stumbling and sobbing; with a tall soldier grimly striding after her. Last, a beautiful morning scene. I was working in the office of a hospital over the other side of Hampstead Heath and caught a bus every morning. It was February, very cold; there had been rain and a sudden freeze which caused an ice-storm. Every trunk, branch, twig and fibril was coated in thin glass and shining in the sun – a woodland in glass.

I might add that a miracle occurred in that hospital in my time and I was responsible. A young timid nurse came to me to ask very diffidently about a patient; Mary Smith, let us say. We looked at the filing-cards (filled in in the last few months by me) and there she was – 84 years old and she had just had a child. But there, a few cards away, was another Mary Smith, aged 22. I transferred the baby.

That year we translated several books; my husband went to Grosvenor Square to work with an American TV company. How do I remember it? Yes, 1954, when the French lost Indo-China, the *Nautilus,* the first atom-powered submarine was launched, and SEATO was formed and West Germany joined NATO, all of which mattered to us and the TV writers and the students and the landlords, from the American, British, Polish, French and Swiss POV, as they said in the TV company (point of view). That year the United States began to get rid of the unconscionable egocentric, Senator McCarthy, who had rashly started to investigate the US Army as well; and yes, *Overland* was born, though through all that rattle and clang, we did not hear its infant joy.

A Routine

When, with a high flush, Caroline flounced out of the government building, she found the pubs were open. The Bear suited her. She had a quick one and telephoned her brother-in-law Alf, a dance-band leader and music-teacher, who had a couple of rooms in a building ready for demolition, near Hammersmith.

'Hello, Alf, how's Daph? Nervous? Mm,mm. I'm all right, Alf. I thought I'd call you about that job. Well, Monday, Alf, I had to go in for the Civil and today you know that I had to come down for the test. Well, Alf, you'll die, I f-f-failed! Yes! Awful mathematical problems and all that. I thought the calculating machines did that. Yes, well, Alf, ten really difficult problems. Yes, it would have been better if I'd gone out with a man or something; but I really went there. You think you're so clever and you find out you can't do a simple mathematical problem. Yes, but they weren't, Alf; awful. Percentages! Five-sixteenths and catch questions, you know; like a woman has so many oranges, ho-ho. Oranges, Alf: divide oranges! And decimals! Haven't you forgotten all that, Alf? I have. Well, isn't that nice? Listen, Alf. I went in and the girl was very charming. I nearly started giggling right away. I suppose I was sort of pensive, Alf; and she said, "Are you bothered by the problems, Mrs Warren?" I said, "I'm afraid I'm rather slow." She said, "I think the worst part about these tests is that we get so nervous. I'm sure I don't know who is more nervous, you or me watching you." I said, "Oh, don't get nervous for me," I said, "I won't lose any sleep over it." All the girls in the place started to titter. Oh, that's nice, Alf, but I don't know if I can come down now. I promised to go in to see Pop Bailey: he wants to show me some office routine. He said to me, "You won't get that job; I'll give you a job." Yes, perhaps I'm better off, Alf. Well, just time for a quick one, Alf, for Noel wants his dinner; and I really must go down to Pop Bailey, he expects me. I'll take a taxi.'

Alf had a drink in his desk. He could not leave till five or five-thirty and he had an engagement from seven onwards. Caroline had to get home to make a meal for Noel: she never let him go without his evening meal; and she was a fair cook. She sat close to Alf with her blue skirt raised on her fine plump legs; and she apologised for not having time. 'But I get as much kick out of just coming down to your place, Alf and having a chat and a couple of doubles out of the bottle in your desk, as I do out of drink, dine and dance. May I use your phone to have a word with Joan, Alf?'

'Joan? Hello! You'll kill yourself, you'll die. I'm down at Alf's. I'm using his phone. He's going to show me office-routines. Don't die! No, that's just it, Joan. I went there, Joan and it's not what they said. That about the machines is just a come-on. I went there and the girl said to me, "This machine can do practically everything; there's really nothing it can't do;" and I nearly killed myself the way she raved on; and then, "It's just the manipulation, but I'm sure you can do that because you've done all that, I see by your form." She encouraged me and I nearly died then and there; but she went on, "This is just a little test," and she put a card in front of me, and you'll die, Joan, but I said "Don't get nervous about me, don't lose sleep on my account." And well, millions, Joan, nine millions, eight hundred and seventy three thousand and three and subtract something from it. And of course that was all right. But percentages! Take sixteen percent of oranges and give it to someone. Oh! I know Joan but you went to that school. Well, I felt like bursting out then; and something I said, well, the whole room was simply giggling. And then one was tons and hundredweights and quarters – well I got that one right. But then, if the machines can do it, why ask me? Oh! of course I am quick at figures; but decimals, do you remember decimals? Yes? Mm, but who does really? I felt quite sorry for the poor girl. Well if they want mathematics. If I am going to spend my time poring over figures, I can just go up and see a man I know in the Food Department at Warpedges and get six pounds a week, too. Well, I could do with one, Joan but I must get home and tell Noel. With his background, he will laugh at me and he will say it is child's play.'

Caroline felt a little braver. She dropped into the Bird in Hand for a quick one, had a laugh with a sound big type she met there, bought a bottle of good sherry for Noel and went home.

Noel was quarrelsome when she got home because he was hungry; but he soon began on the sherry and had drunk half the bottle by the time she had heated the dinner.

As he cheered, she sized him up. She liked his looks. He was a London-born man, but being a salesman, spent much time in the country: he was rosy, lank, with a prowling walk; very black hair. His handsome well-kept little van standing in the rough grass of the backyard, newly polished, could be seen from the windows of their second-floor back. Under these two windows was a fixed bench he used for a drawing-board and work-table. He sold every kind of tackle, rods, flies, sinkers, lines, baits and also aquaria, tropical fish and their food. He produced scholarly and elegant books on tropical fish, both the text and illustrations. He was an expert and an artist. He was the youngest of three sons and had not married till he was forty, just after his mother's death, ten years before. One of his brothers was the captain of a modern trawler that used radar. This brother was making money and expected to retire from the sea and buy a farm. The eldest brother now ran the business in the City his father left, a business in woollen goods.

Caroline was from the country, a husky yellow haired woman.

It was nearly seven o'clock, a grey dry dispiriting London spring evening. Noel when he had drunk his sherry was in a good mood, very hungry and quite without his usual dyspepsia. He began to laugh and talk about how, when he sold his next book and they had her safe government job, they would live better. He would of course still run out to the country, but he would have an assistant.

'You can rent a shop for this sort of business anywhere. All the aquarium shops are in side streets and it doesn't matter how small they are, if it runs back to a yard. We could live upstairs; and I would build an annexe for the fish tanks. I'm writing about them, drawing them, I've got a reputation and I haven't any tanks. I'd always like to do the trips myself, keep up the contacts, but I'd get a boy. For you, Caroline, it isn't the money they'll pay you; six pounds isn't much, you've had twelve, but it's the regularity; and then these other places, they take you today and tell you to go tomorrow. They don't know who you are. That's the trouble nowadays. We can get out of here and begin again in a decent neighbourhood where you can run up bills; I'll get this load off my back. I was sure you'd get it Caroline; I know you're good at figures.'

Caroline was brave enough. She began to lay the cloth, and facing him, said.

'Well, Noel, you're going to laugh, but I failed in the business test. You'll never believe what they asked me, Noel: sixteen percent and two and three-fifths, add them. Could you do that? Well, I suppose you could.'

'I should hope so, yes.'

'And then a pound of feathers, a pound of tobacco and a pound of gold; how much do they weigh? Trick questions. You're supposed to know so much.'

'Well, now I hope you appreciate what it is, bloody porters shouting at you and bloody waiters talking back to you and wanting six pounds a week and they want bloody mathematicians for six pounds a week and there you have people who can't damn well sign their names, porters and such. A little more of this and you'll change your politics, instead of running round with bloody communists.'

'My friends are not bloody communists, Noel: and besides there are good communists and bad communists, just like everyone else.'

'I did not say your friends were members of the Communist Party. I said you must be careful in times like these, always going into things with left-wingers and listening to bloody impudent irrelevant remarks on the TV about Conservative MPs. Now you see where it comes from.'

'You do not understand the left wing Noel, on account of your social background; but that does not mean they are wrong. It is a question of viewpoint. They are very good businessmen and it is better to do as Rome does; what is the good of last stand psychology? You said you would sink in blood if they introduced the decimal system and now they have done it. You do not mix, it is like oil and water saying the other is no good.'

'What is that?' said Noel.

'That is lamb stew.'

'I don't want lamb stew.'

'You are cranky, Noel; you are a stickler.'

'I can't fit my appetite to what comes into your head.'

'What are you doing, Noel?'

'I am going out; I want my shoes.'

'Wear your sandals.'

'I won't wear my dirty old sandals.'

'Well, keep on your blue suit, Noel.'

'I won't go down there in my working clothes. The blue suit is my working suit. I have to look like a decent middleclass man.'

'Why do you say middleclass all the time!'

'I'm middleclass and proud of it,' said Noel.

'I know you are, Noel; and I respect what you are. But why are you so querulous?'

'I'm not used to these conditions.'

'I know you are not, Noel; but it is not the first time you have seen them.'

He grumbled, 'I can't find anything in this blanky mess. The laundry is in a mess. And all in two rooms. All your dirt and untidiness!'

'Dirt? I want you to qualify that word.'

'I will not qualify that word. That is dirt – and what about the mice in the cupboard?'

'As if we hadn't seen mice before! Noel, I respect your background; but we have seen mice before. And we were glad to see them.'

'I want to go down the street; and I can't find what I want. I'm not paying rent for this: two rotten blanky rooms and no cleaning. I'm not used to it: I'm not paying.'

'Oh, Moses! Can't you leave it alone? That's all settled. Pipe down, now. Nuts!'

'All right, all right, I'll be back in a while.'

'It's all right now!'

He said, 'I see you're mad with me; you want to knock me down.'

'Did I say anything, did I say anything? I think I'll come with you. Are you getting a beer? We'll get a beer. Let's have a beer. Be a sport.'

'I wouldn't mind,' he said, relenting grumpily, 'if a beer meant a beer: but it means a couple of doubles.'

'Be a sport,' she laughed; 'you don't know how to mix, Noel.'

'I don't want to mix with bloody wasters in a bloody pub.'

'Come along darling; don't be stingy; come out and mix with people. That's what's lacking in your make-up.'

'No, I don't want you, Caroline: I don't want to go to a pub. I want to walk about. I don't want to be a bloody sport. I don't like your sporting crowd. They're all laughs.'

'They are not laughs, Noel; they are citizens. You are not a citizen. That is not your forte. You are a tory by birth; that is your trouble. You do not know that others exist.'

Noel was softened, agreed to take her. They went out together and returned together some hours later, Caroline grand in manner, Noel depressed.

'It is your own fault,' Caroline argued; 'it is because you are not popular.'

'And how can I be popular with those bloody outsiders?' he enquired in a weeping tone.

'Make general conversation, Noel; everyone else does. I was talking about the theatre and so forth to make general conversation; but because you were drunk, you must get into a lather about the Labour Party. You talked across me and across others. I don't mind across me, for I am a woman and used to that,' she said in a very reasonable tone; 'and so I turned to you two or three times to bring you in; but when you came in, I had cause for regret, because you went on and on about fish and tackle and the season. How you could have done seven hundred but you only did one hundred; and on about the tides and what the season was like; and you see I know it all by heart. But I turned to you to bring you in and I quipped with you; and you did not understand it was a quip.'

'You said I must make conversation and I made conversation.'

'Yes, Noel but why must your conversation be so fishified? You, Noel, talk always on one subject. You are interested in fish and tackle and aquaria and you think everyone is. That, Noel, is the hallmark of the boring companion.'

'Yes. I noticed you did not mind that dumb bore who was blowing and spouting, that waste of time who was buying you drinks. I don't like him.'

'He is not dumb, Noel: he is not a bore. You don't like

him: but, Noel, you don't like anyone who can talk you down. He is a business man. He is not dumb, Noel. But he does not talk about it all the time, good season and bad season. He could. Anyone could. That is something you don't understand, Noel. You are a semi-educated man, you have your background, your career: you are middleclass and you could make conversation, but you don't.'

'What do you say I was doing if I wasn't making conversation? I am not afraid to talk.'

'When you are drunk you wax eloquent. All right, if you must, wax eloquent: why wax about tackle? No one is interested but you.'

'Then why do they ask me? And I talked about other things.'

'Yes, you were talking about the theatre and ballet and such things to the woman next to you: and I was quite sorry for you, talking about things where you are unconversant.'

'I was telling her I met you in a concert party and you had been to Egypt and Algeria, if it would interest you to know. But I noticed you talking to that noisy knight, that cavalier with the big mouth. What is he, her fancyman, that woman next to him? He's a laugh: and you see a lot of him.'

'He is not a knight and a laugh; he's a married man, like all the other men at the pub.'

'Well, I should hope he's married to that woman next to him.'

'I'd like to know what you are coming at. She only met him, and she didn't know his name. That is what they were laughing at.'

'Well, I don't know,' said Noel, himself laughing.

'No, you didn't know, because you weren't paying attention. You never pay attention, Noel and that is why you are always misled, misinformed and behind the times: always woolgathering in the moon. Pay attention to others and you will be popular. Now, I am popular.'

'Here I am thinking about my work and you go on bloody nagging, bloody insisting, bloody insults. It is only to annoy me; you know it is. You don't care as you pretend to,' he said with the long, dry, weary note of much said things. He continued quietly, 'You think you are good company; you bore everyone; you don't know you do; everyone is bored with you. You bore me, Caroline.'

She said, very reasonable, gentle, 'You bore me, Noel. You do, Noel. You bore me, I assure you, you bore me.'

'You bore me,' said Noel; 'always talking on and on. You ramble. You ramble for hours and hours – and – hours,' he continued in a low slow way, as if dropping off: 'about – Don said and Alf said – Pop Bailey said – your friends in the Labour Party, spivs I call them – and – so and so and such and such – and – people – I don't even know. No, you don't think so: but you don't know. You are – unselfconscious, Caroline,' he finished very slow and gentle.

'I'm bored all the time with you, Noel,' she said, also gently: 'I can't tell you how bored I am.'

'You are twenty years younger than me, Caroline: it is only to be expected.'

'Yes, but granted that, you are unnecessarily boring. Look at you now: you are drawing a fish.'

'When I was at home with my mother I was allowed to draw fish without nagging and boring.'

'Granted you have a fine background, you should come

out and show it. Talking about World War One is of no interest: and neither is World War Two. All this is very boring.'

'What is that, Caroline? I can't eat now. I don't like lamb stew I said.'

'It's been cooking three or four hours now: you don't doubt that.'

'I like what I like.'

'Why are you so dogged and mulish?'

'I am only wanting to get on with my work and I could eat but you upset me.'

'And then next time it suits you, you will say I am not a good wife.'

'You are a good wife! I never said that. I am quite satisfied. I asked you to be my wife and I would ask you again. I don't know whether you would say yes, again.'

'Of course, I would say yes again, Noel. Do not split hairs: you love a wild goose chase. It is because you have qualms, Noel: you are nervous. You are of a higher class and you are used to better things and so you are neurotic. I am proud of you, but you are an inverted snob. But there are members of the Labour Party who are knights and even lords and who do not drop their aitches. I know them. They are making a lot of money, some of them. I mean members of the Labour Party. I could introduce you to some who would get you into some business relations with quick results. But you sit here and think yourself superior. Noel, that is at the root of your boring quality: it is snobbishness. It is boring and snobbish, Noel to be always thinking of your work and not your fellowman.'

'By my fellowman, you mean someone in a pub,' said Noel dolefully.

'Now I resent your tone; that is an example.'

'I am doing my work and you interrupt me all the time.

Let me tell you something. Your talk is boring because I am a student and a man who works in the daytime and does his own work at night.'

'But Noel what can you hope to make up at fifty?'

'When I get this finished I will sell it. I have people who collect my books, in other countries of the world. I have regular correspondents everywhere.'

'Yes, I know: and I am proud of that fact, Noel.'

'I am glad Joan came down in the car to take me out,' said Caroline the next evening. 'You don't know what it is. I was watching for you in the van and I was watching for the Cobbs to go out. The only advantage of having the landlords opposite is that you do know when they go out. But it is terrible standing there behind the curtain in the hall. Perhaps they are watching behind their curtains, too, for when you come home, to come and ask for the rent. It is just the trick they would play; and there are six of them to two of us. And how do we know the downstairs tenants, the Walkers, don't talk about us? Do you know that Mrs Cobb had the Walkers to tea this afternoon? Did you ever hear of landlords having tenants to tea? What can it mean? I was watching there and I saw them cross the road and I felt so nervous. The Walkers were there nearly two hours and while they were away a man came to the door. And meanwhile I thought I heard someone breathing inside next door to us. You know how you can tell them, the plain clothes. It was awful, Noel; but I was quite bright and normal. He said he belonged to the railway police and asked for Mr Clumber: and I said, there was no such person here. He said, "It has to do with a Mr Clumber, a young man who moved in here and who has lost a watch on the railway." Well, that does not sound right, does it? I should have said, "I am not the hall porter"; but you know how the Walkers go out of their way, obsequious and hail well met with all: and I thought someone was looking at me through the curtain over the way. So I said I would go and knock. I knocked several times; and I heard this sound of breathing, but I did not say that, of course.

'But I thought I would go and say to the Cobbs, "This is no place for us, with people rolling under the bed to hide from the police." But I could not, Noel; he is our fellowman. If he is on the run, who knows why? Others have been on the run. I told Joan there was some trouble here, and strangers calling and I just said, "Joan, how soon can you get here?"

'When she heard the story, she said, "What you need is a couple of bracers to begin with, you're strung up with your father so ill." And I said, "Yes, I can't hold down any jobs under these conditions. Noel can get away from it all." And I told her the living conditions. She said we ought to withhold rent. They are doing so in St Pancras. I told her about the place in Streatham; that we simply walked out, it was so bad: and she said that we must be unlucky. I said, "Let Mrs Cobb try to collect." But of course, she wouldn't dare to get us into court. And now this. They must take us for April fools, mice and railway police and a violinist with his scales. "It's the way we live," I said: "pin your hopes to a straw and hope for a bed of roses." I tell you I felt like making a night of it; but I brought you back some chops, Noel.'

'I hope you're satisfied, now,' said Noel. 'Those Walkers went to tea with the landlords.'

'What do you mean?' she asked, from the stove.

'The Walkers are Jews: they're just spies for the landlords.'

'I don't think that's proved, Noel.'

'The landlords are Jews; and you know how they stick together.'

'Yes, but Walker is not a Jewish name.'

'Names can be changed. You say they're out now, the Cobbs?'

'Yes, they're all out.'

'Perhaps they're waiting at the corner of the street.'

'I can take a walk and see,' she said. 'I can get some milk.'

'Where are the others, the Walkers?'

'What does it matter? We've a right to take out our lamps and mats to be fixed. Clumber pretty soon left; he went the other way. The violin teacher went out with his pupil, that big blonde who's pregnant: they went out holding hands as usual. And that's funny, too. She rang and I let her in and she said, "I'm Mr Jules's cousin," and I was so surprised I said, "How do you do?" and then we all looked blank. And the Walkers are out the back fixing the trellis. They don't care. I assure you, Noel, that is an *idée fixe* of yours; it is fallacious; no one here is keeping tabs on us.'

'That violin student in the attic, Mr Robinson is a Jew,' said Noel: 'and Robinson is not a Jewish name.'

'Granted that he is Robinson, Noel, why does it gnaw at you? He is a nice boy. Now I will go and get the milk and have a looksee: and you do a bit on the bathroom and I will come and pack a few things and we'll take a ride.'

While she was away, Noel took a chisel wrapped in a rag, and a mallet, and attacked the bathroom ceiling and walls, and dropped bits of plaster down the drain.

Caroline returned, grandiloquent and stagey, and they began to run up and down stairs with things in their hands.

'Have you done the bathroom, Noel?'

'Yes. Mr Robinson came down and asked could he help me repair it. I used him for a witness that the pipe is clogged.'

They returned at midnight and ran a bath. They had stopped up the overflow pipe and ran it till it overflowed, soaked through the damaged floor and began to drip through into the locked lumber room underneath. Then they went to bed. The next morning they sent themselves a telegram: 'Warren, Hindmost Lane, Vinculum, London. Father moved to hospital, please come, Mother.'

They took this telegram to the Cobbs, apologised for being eight weeks in arrears and said times had been very hard: Caroline could not work regularly, with having to visit her sick father in Bury St Edmonds. Her father was dying. They begged the Cobbs to keep the flat for them. 'Being Jews,' said Noel, 'they won't like to put us out when your father is dying, when we say we have nowhere to go.'

The Cobbs consented to wait one week. Noel then went out on his business. That evening they took out more packages, deposited them with Joan as before, and then went down to Bury where Caroline's father was, in fact, very ill: and so they came and went each day, as they were used to. But it was a hard life.

Caroline could not help buying new clothes. She loved to amble out the front door each day, blessing the spring, well made up, healthy, pink or blue and gold, in new clothes that fitted her big curves tightly. She wore underclothes of silk, satin, lace, specially made for her at private addresses in streets off Baker Street, Marylebone High Street, Oxford Street: one here, one there, not to be tied, too cosy with any. She used the upstage married woman manner and preferred to be thought respectable. Her needs drove her to do business with these establishments, but she followed a regular routine and always came home to cook dinner for Noel. She prided herself on it and on her marriage to a man educated in a gentlemen's school. She might explain his curious attitudes to other men: she never depreciated him.

The flat was now half empty. They had their ways. Sometimes a half bottle of milk, a pair of white shoes newly cleaned, or a lamp with a little shade, stood inside the transparent net curtains to be seen from the yard; but they had had to take away the shower curtain, the mirror and the medical cabinet from the place in the kitchenette where they usually washed: and if the landlord or nosey tenants cared to look, it was pretty clear from the backyard that the place was being emptied.

And now it became indispensable to quarrel with the landlord. Noel, a man who was quiet, when sitting alone over his work, would turn up the portable radio so loud that the walls seemed to tremble; and he trembled with anxiety and exhaustion, as he waited for someone to knock on the door, ceiling or wall. No knocking came: either the other lodgers were out, or did not care. The Walkers had the entire floor downstairs and could always retreat to some other room. At last, Mrs Walker did come, a pale tired blonde whom Noel rather liked. 'Would you mind,' she said politely and softly, 'it is a little loud?'

'Certainly, I am sorry,' and he turned it down: but presently he thought that Caroline would soon be back and ask about it, so he turned it up again. There were no more complaints. It was a very strange house, full of students, some from Israel and India. He once thought he heard a consultation in the hall below and he quickly looked out hoping for some unpleasant remark; but the talkers had scattered and no one had crossed the street, to Gad's Hill, the landlord's house.

The Warrens were desperate now.

'Noel, something has got to be done. Listen, Noel, you know what we did at Guildford?'

'I don't feel like it. I haven't had my dinner yet.'

'All the better. It'll start you off. Do you know, Noel,' she said loudly, for all to hear, opening the door to the landing, 'where I was just now? I was out with Alf! I went along with Alf to the Palais and we had a few quick ones on the way. When we got there, I said to Alf, "Oh, Moses, Alf, for God's sake, let's step out, let's have a fling. I am smothered down at home with Mother and Grandma and watching at the hospital: and Noel does not see the necessity for a little fling. He has always worn white shirts and starched collars and he is afraid the sweat will come in his armpits, he is afraid of a bit of my lipstick on his collar: let's dance," I said to Alf. And Alf, said, "Attaboy, I'm game, I've been waiting a long time for this." He can dance, Noel. Noel, he's a warm boy that Alf! My sister Daph's very lucky and she doesn't know her luck. He's got style; he's sharp: no wonder I like him.'

'Don't you say that to my face, you bloody twotimer; how dare you say that to my face, even for a joke.'

'But Noel do you want me to lie to you? I don't want to do that. One thing you can say of me Noel is that I'm honest. I don't mince. Do you want marked cards or do you want a fair deal?'

'It's not the truth that matters; why do it at all? What harm have I ever done you? Why do you wipe your boots on me?'

'Listen, Noel, it's because you always bite at the olive branch. You take everything lying down; you do, Noel. A woman can't respect it. I try to get a rise out of you, Noel, but you sulk, you just scowl and look down your nose. It isn't a man; it isn't a husband. As a man, Noel, you're an understatement. I've never forgotten the time we were sitting in a pub in Old Compton Street, Noel; and those men were sitting there, having round after round. They noticed you and the young man got up, he must have been easily six feet two in his stocking feet and he came over and started to insult you. He said you were a counter jumper and I was the counter jumper's mate. And what did you do, Noel? Noel, I know it is not in your social background to fight in pubs, but you should have given him to understand thus far and no farther. But what did you do, Noel? You got up and went away, you left him standing over me, insulting me and you went and got the bouncer. How do you think I felt? I had to give him as good myself; and I did. I said, "Go home, you're drunk!" and he began to weep and say, "I'm not drunk, I've only had four longshoremans." And I said, "Go home to mother, ask her to rock you to sleep." And he went off and began to cry and explain to the other men. But how did I feel? Supposing because of conditions you were a sock salesman at one time, in a small shop, no one had a right to hold it against you, we are all human-too-human; and you should have come back at him. But did you, Noel? You come from a sheltered home and you are ill at ease, not used to the rough and tumble. But what does that make me when I am out with you, Noel? Anybody's game? So how can you blame me for stepping out once in a blue moon with Alf? Now Alf takes a man by the neck and shakes him and says, "Say that again, mate, don't let me stop you, say that again, because I'm dying to pick you to pieces and see what makes you tick." A woman doesn't want a fight, but if a fight comes, she doesn't want a man running to the bouncer.'

'For God's sake, shut up,' shrieked Noel, 'have you been harbouring that against me all this time?'

'I have not been harbouring, Noel; but the scene has remained with me. And I often say to myself, supposing I am out on the street and a fight starts, who will protect me? I am a woman; I expect protection; and you, Noel, owing to your sheltered life and your personal pacificism, your ironical nature, are a hazard to a woman.'

'Stop it,' said Noel, rising and rushing towards her with his hand out to close her mouth, for she was shouting now. She at once gladly rushed out on to the landing shouting, 'Don't hit me, Noel, don't hit me. Help! Help!'

They both listened. The student on the top floor had friends in. There was a slight silence and then young men and women began laughing. A minute later, a door opened on the top landing. Caroline made a sign to Noel who cried, 'Get out of here, you drunken bitch, you slut, you lousy –'

'Don't hit me, Noel, don't hit me! Oh!'

'Get out and stay out.'

'I won't let you knock me down, Noel!'

'Go on, go back to your Alfs, your Pop Baileys and your spivs and yours MPs.'

'Noel, don't touch me, I'll scream for help,' and running to the hall window which faced Gad's Hill she struggled with the stuck window.

'I'll give you a hiding to remember –'

'Help! Help!'

Down from the attic came the Israeli student, Mr Robinson, a charming polite young man, in grey, holding a tea-kettle and smiling. 'Oh, Mrs Warren, could you lend me your kettle? I am going to make tea and the one that was left in the flat has a hole in it as large as a walnut.'

'Oh, these landlords,' said Caroline, in true good humour, 'they do nothing for the tenants. Think of leaving you a kettle like that! You should see our bathroom. It has no pipe in it at all; the water runs out the window! I'll lend you a saucepan and you can keep it.'

When Mr Robinson had gone back, Noel said 'Why did you do that? What was the use of my nearly killing myself; and you got me angry too. You oughtn't to say the things you said.'

'Noel, I had to get you started: you are slow off the mark.'

'I'm not a ham actor.'

'No, well I'm going to get a porkpie; or would you like cod roe, Noel?'

'You said you'd make me a steak and kidney pie.'

'The butcher wouldn't give me any more on credit.'

'Bloody fellow! It shows the kind of neighbourhood.'

'I'll get you a sherry, Noel.'

'If you can buy sherry, you can buy steak and kidney.'

'Oh, I'll get it at the pub. They know me there.'

'I ought to take care of you, not have you running out to beg strangers for sherry. It makes me want to – it makes me feel – I can't tell you how it makes me feel. I'll cut my throat, that's what I'll do; that's what I'll do, I'll cut my throat.'

'That is your sensitive nature, Noel. There is nothing wrong in it. Well, goodbye, Noel; do your work.'

'I'll do my work without being nagged. I like my work.'

But he thought she might have meant something else. So he took a knife and the chisel and worked at the bathroom floor for a bit. When Caroline returned, she said loudly, 'Noel, I see that the ceiling is falling down in that little room downstairs. I looked through the keyhole because I thought I heard a crash. The upstairs bathroom floor is hanging by a thread; it is a deathtrap. We must complain to the Council.'

'Oh, I can't get used to this,' cried Noel, suddenly; 'I want something to eat and somewhere decent to live.'

'Well, Noel, we had the war and then the cost of living and then the pressure of population and they can rent any old building at all. We are not better than others.'

'Why not? I'm not satisfied with my lot. There's a whole row of villas down there full of bloody spivs and their women, with two cars apiece. They were burgled last week and the burglars got away with furs and diamonds and all kinds of loot. And I live worse than a bloody policeman. It's like trying to crawl through treacle.'

'We are not better than others, Noel; and you did not learn to face the stern realities; you are not a democrat. You were a confirmed bachelor, Noel; and you know they are selfish and unrealistic, worrying about their mothers.'

At this moment the doorbell rang and the Walkers let in the beautiful buxom girl who was the violinist's friend. She was tall with a strong neck, yellow curls piled up. She was about seven months pregnant. The violinist was forty, going bald with a dry fringe of black and grey; he had a long thin pasty face and lively dark grey eyes. 'Do the neighbours still play that tin symphony on the rubbish tins when you practise?' the girl was asking.

'Yes; and they got up a petition to the landlord. I went to see the leader,' said the violinist, laughing; 'but he won't see things my way; and so every Saturday, when he is home –'

They were upstairs.

'Is that his cousin or his fancy woman?' said Noel.

'They are in love, Noel; I suppose that is his child, too.'

'And then,' continued Noel, 'we should have known better than to take a flat with the landlord living opposite.

You'd think we were kids in a reformatory. Please, Sir, may I go to see my father-in-law? And that is his cat you find everywhere; he doesn't feed it. She had kittens in the fiddler's place last year and this time it is in the Walkers' cupboard. And the Walkers actually buy fish for the landlord's cat. There you are.'

'Perhaps they like cats.'

'Listen,' he said in a low voice, 'you know what I think? I think they're communists. I want you to go down and ask for a book. If they are communists they will give you some propaganda.'

'So what? I don't want to read that.'

'Then we can say something about that to the landlord.'

'All right.'

'And have a look at all their books; see if you can see Karl Marx, anything like that.'

'All right.'

When she returned with two books, he asked eagerly, 'Well then?'

'They have a lot of foreign language books: she gave me these,' and she showed a story magazine and a book by Evelyn Waugh.

'You see how crafty they are? But why are they so interested in everyone's affairs, answering the telephone and opening the front door. And so helpful. Trust me, it's communists, help the neighbours. Then get them to sign something, organise them; be friendly, get them to like you. Taking in telegrams; opening the door to the landlord.'

'Well, we haven't a doorman here.'

'But no matter what happens, with the damp walls, they pay the rent week after week. They are satisfied with these conditions. No decent people would just meekly pay the rent in a house like this, in a neighbourhood like this. There must be something wrong. What is it? It's because they're Jews; and Jews are afraid of troubles. They don't stand up like Englishmen. I stand up for my rights. I don't pay for roguery.'

'All right, Noel: we know all that.'

'This is my country and I'm used to the best. Englishmen don't swallow mice and plaster in the tub. You can see they're foreigners.'

'But the Walkers aren't foreigners: be reasonable.'

'I won't be reasonable. I've got my point of view. Be reasonable means be trod on: it means pay the landlord every bloody cent. What counts is the principle of the thing. The principle is they're all kowtowing and paying, so we look in the wrong. If they aren't put up to it by him. I don't say they are: but there's a tacit agreement. Oh, yes, they understand each other. Our plan worked before: and why is it not working now? It's because they're all Jews.'

'It's all settled, Noel. Don't go over it. It's very boring.'

'I'm sorry,' he said. 'I'm sorry. I'm always boring. No one bores you but me, as it happens.'

'Oh, it's so boring,' she said yawning.

'Listen,' he said suddenly, 'I'm not going to use any more subterfuges: it's not my nature. I'm sick of it and they don't work. We'll just go away because of sickness in the family and we won't come back. And I'll jab a hole in the waste-pipe to show how rotten it is. I'll prove it's a place only foreigners would take. It's a place to squeeze foreigners who have nowhere to go. The place is overrun by foreigners. Next door, that's his, too, isn't it? Next door, black skins, Indians and –'

'Now Noel, you know I won't hear any race prejudice.'

'You're so bloody fairminded. I don't like it: it makes me sick. I'm half dead with worry and the vexation. Whenever did you know me that I didn't have enough sales? I make good money and I can't make a go of it. I feel I'm going to sink. If we had to pay the rent here, too, we just couldn't live, Caroline, we'd go down, I give you my sacred word.'

'Who says anything about paying the rent? Oh, do hush.'

'I'll put my fist through the plaster to show them what condition it's in.'

'That's by law illegal, Noel; be careful. You're naive, you're unworldly: that's by law illegal. That's damaging property: you would put your foot in it. It's by law illegal.'

'I don't know why I am always wrong and illegal.'

'I'm all packed now. Let us go.'

She halted in the passage and said in a low tone, 'There is someone looking out behind the curtain at the Cobb's. I can see the light behind her. It is the woman. Why is she always looking over here?'

'She can't stop us taking away the van.'

'Hello, Joan. Just to let you know I'm in Bury, not in London: that is why I did not get in touch. Of course, Dad, Joan, it's awful. He hangs on. It's willpower and he won't take anything, afraid he'll die in his sleep. He's so cute, they can't slip anything over on him; never could either. They told us he would sink into a coma and that would be the end; but he doesn't sink. He's fighting, fighting. And it's awful for me. Every time a car comes down the street at night, I think it's for us. And the doorbell. With Dad it isn't life and it isn't death. And we all have to hide our feelings. Auntie Belle is quite a trial and Granny never lets anyone be. We all have to go and sit round the bed keeping our faces straight. Because there are the games, Joan, the games. The games. It's awful at a deathbed. I suppose they think it natural: they don't think it's games. I suppose he sees everything. He was always cute and knowing, giving you that salty quizzing look. But Granny never gives up, trying to play on feelings.

'I don't know what death means to some people, Joan: it seems to mean a free-for-all. Auntie Belle said to Mother, "Ada, I'd like that Indian blanket for a keepsake when Jack goes and I've got rheumatics so bad now," and she held it up to the light looking for moth-holes. And at the house, the others, going through his things. Granny found some long underwear, you know that stuff that's such a scream now and she said, "Well, this will do for Grandpa; they're of a size," and other things, tucking them under her arm. And the way it is at the hospital. Granny there, "I was always strong as a horse, heading for a hundred the doctor said," and keeping it up as if we were all still seventeen. "Mm, mm," says Granny, "three estranged children, mm, mm, well, it couldn't turn out well, could it?" She means my half-brothers Bert and Willy and me. And meaning, she never thought Dad was much, just a carpenter. "Mm, mm, I kept my home together, you see," she says to Mother with Dad lying there between. That means, you ran off, married a motorcar salesman, with fat commissions and he died on you, then you married a carpenter. "Mm, mm," she says, "Unlucky with men: some are and some aren't." That means, her daughter, my aunt Nancy, is in the States, the goose hangs high you see, and then she says, "Where would we all be, I wonder, if I had been the flyabout sort," meaning Mother went to work, Granny insisted on taking my brothers Bert and Willy. Where would they have been if Granny hadn't taken them in? And do you know what happened? She sent them to work as soon as they were allowed. They went to work on ditches, on roads, Joan. She took them in to keep her. The tears come into my eyes, even now, Joan. Though why, I don't know. We're estranged. Yes, but whose fault? Joan, I must say goodbye now. Keep the things that came for me. They'll be paid for. And it's just a little secret between you and me.'

'Hello, Dad,' said Caroline, bending over the bloated yellow man. He had been a spare man. His loose yellow hair was greying, he had a long loose moustache.

'Watch the shrubbery,' he said weakly; 'I couldn't use my shaving tackle. But I think I've taken the turn now, I think there's a chance. You tell Mother to ask Sister on the quiet, Caroline.'

'That's right, Dad. We'll cross the ditch on a rainbow. Look, I brought you a half of champagne, Dad.'

'Press the bell for the Sister,' he said, smiling, 'I have been so dry here, longing for something tonic. It would set me up.'

When the glass had come, he sat up a little and drank the fizz with pleasure.

'You're the life of the party, Dad,' said Caroline: 'next week you and I will make a night of it.'

'Life of the party,' he said smiling.

Aunt Morrie sat on the other side of the bed on a long stool that could be pushed under the bed. Aunt Morrie, unmarried, was a flatfaced, darkhaired woman with good colour, pink lips, no makeup. 'Oh, Caroline,' she said, breaking down.

'Why, he's looking better,' exclaimed Caroline: 'cheer up, Aunt Morrie.'

'Oh, Caroline, a while ago, about two hours ago, he

nearly died, he was so bad. Oh, Noel, he nearly died and I was here all alone. I didn't know what to do.'

'Where was Granny?'

Aunt Morrie whispered, 'Gone to the dressmaker to get her new mourning things.'

Aunt Morrie broke down.

'Aunt Morrie, you are upsetting Dad. There you are, Dad. Fine and dandy!'

'Hitch your wagon to a star and life will be a bed of roses,' he cackled.

'Keep a stiff upper lip; a merry smile goes all the way; cross the ditch on a rainbow. Oh, Dad I can't help laughing.'

'Well, laugh then,' he said. 'I was laughing myself, a while back when Morrie was here. I told her I could just see myself getting along in a wagon full of roses hitched to a star.'

The daughter laughed; Morrie burst into tears.

At this moment, Caroline's grandmother came in, a high-coloured woman with a new hairset and new black clothes.

'Who had the champagne?' she said. 'You did, Jack? Where's Ada? In your condition Jack, soft foods, non-alcoholic liquids.'

He began to speak, but she went on, 'I'm not surprised, Jack. You loved your food. You were thin but your waist was a yard round. And as a boy you had a weak stomach, stomach and liver. As a boy you didn't drink, teetotaller remember. You were always warned against habits. Break any habit I say, just to show you can, even if it's a good one. Keeps you young. My side of the family was always noted for its healthy looks, good hair, good skin, good teeth, good stomach. Ada, look! Another letter from your sister Nancy! Isn't that a joke? She never gave a thought for twelve years, then she started writing and now every

week. Come over, she says now. I'm to take the jet, fly the
Atlantic, then take another plane, get to this place called
Uttah –'

'Utah.'

'Uttah! And live there with them and the Mormons.
She says, "You've kept the family together long enough,
Mother. Now let them mind themselves and come out to
us!" And Ben, her husband, you know Jacky, he says,
"We'll have a brass band and get out the flags!" And
Nancy says she's like me a very good cook and I'm to
have a complete holiday and she sent me an American
recipe, potroast –'

'Granny don't tell us about cooking now. Aunt Morrie,
tell us about your holiday.'

'How can I, Caroline, with your father lying there and
never to take another holiday.'

'No, tell me about your holiday, did you enjoy it
Morrie?' said the patient.

'Oh, tell Dad how you fell over the mountain pony in
the mists –' said Caroline.

'It's heartless,' said Aunt Morrie, crying openly, 'talking about holidays and ponies and recipes and Jacky
there.'

'This'll break Morrie up more than anyone else,' said
Granny: 'Why Jacky, Morrie was always a great fan of
yours. Look, Ada, Nancy has kept herself up, look here in
the bikini on the swimming pool, isn't that cute; and that
hairdo. She's five years older than you, Ada. And look at
Connie called after me, eight years old, that's her English
governess and look at the kid, with the cocktail shaker.
And do you know she has a hope chest already. All the
little girls do in Salt Lake City. And they get mash notes.
Eight. Oh, ho, ho! Like Granny. Look, "Kisses from your
granddaughter, Connie." '

'Granny, Dad looks tired.'

'Take his mind off,' said Granny quickly, opening her big black purse and taking out a bundle of photographs and papers; and she went on showing and explaining them.

'Oh, my God,' said Caroline, 'let's get out of here and give the patient a little rest. All right, Nancy did a little better than the rest. What of it, Granny? Dad doesn't care. He never was that sort.'

'Those who fell by the wayside pretend they never wanted to get there,' said Granny, with good cheer. 'I'm a grandmother. I like to be liked. Those who like me will hear from me. But I do my duty. I come to see your Dad. Your Grandpa wouldn't hear of it. He said, "I never liked that man and I'm glad Ada's getting rid of him, better late than never," but I said, "I want to show Ada I'm on her side. No preferences among my children."'

'Oh, Moses. Well, Dad, remember you're the life of the party,' said Caroline, 'be good till I get back.'

'Come back soon. Give me a kiss,' and then in a low voice he said, 'Caroline, get the Sister by herself and ask her, is there any chance?'

'Yes, but Dad, you're going to be a big surprise even to yourself, you know.'

Caroline hurried after the others, who had been turned out by the Sister. She had tears in her eyes.

'Oh, my God, Noel, let's get out as quickly as we can. Granny only goes there, not out of duty, but to chew over, believe me. Every time she sails in with her Nancy to let mother know she can't rely on Granny if she ever needed a roof. It's her Roman holiday raking up what is, what was and what isn't and after all those years when we couldn't mention Nancy's name. Look at the bikini and look at little Connie shaking a cocktail. Well, poor Auntie Morrie. Dad was her dream man. She'll crack,

you'll see: she'll get old. And Granny with her cracks.
Nancy kept her looks like me; kept her men like me.
Look, there's Don. Don! Don, we're going for a quick
one, we're all to pieces. All right, Noel. You go back with
Mother and I'll go along with Don. We'll pick you up at
seven o'clock.'

'Well, all right then, Don, another double: but I expect
we ought to cut the session short this time. Poor Noel
sitting there, his hands between his knees, wishing he
was at his drawing board or somewhere in England with
his customers and all the time thinking about conditions,
not telling anyone but me. I hand it to him, Don, I do.
He's got his kind of guts. "You have to go on your bally
parties," he says, poor soul, "and all the glad rags." What
I wear and what I drink is my business. I earn. But he
doesn't see it. I blame myself, I don't earn enough, he
says. A man blames himself but what he does not realise,
Don, is the tedium. He likes tedium. But for me! Every
day, every night, the petty arguments and the covering
up, Don, the covering up. There are too many people in
the house. And then it's dull. Why shouldn't they listen
on the staircase? And then the Walkers carrying phone
messages and telegrams to everyone. It's nice. But Noel
thinks it's too nice. It makes him nervous. He's used to a
starched respectable life, where people don't co-operate.
He thinks it lacks dignity, it's officious. You see he isn't
used to conditions, Don. And then – borrowing. I don't
mind. Mr Robinson is a nice boy and only a kettle: but
Noel feels they're just outside the door and he's gagged.
He tosses, he doesn't sleep.'

'Well, all right, a double, Don: but then I must get
back. When Noel's angry with me, I get the jitters. And
then tomorrow I have to go back to the Cobbs's flop-

house, we call it. Yes, telephone to Bury from there, so that they'll all know what we're doing, in the hall: and then they can tell the landlord. Well, it's that kind of place. It's rotten, yes. But they're halfway decent; and you see they'll give us a breathing-space and we can get out. Because no one would, would they, dun you, beset you, well, when there's a death on the way? So I have to be there when they're all in for supper to get a batch of news in for the Walkers and it goes straight to the landlord and all meant well, probably.

'Well, you get just another, Don, while I'll telephone this Mr Harris, who is going to get me a job. I have just to go in to get the office routine.'

When she had telephoned, she was flushed, pleased, 'How do you like that? How's that for luck? He thinks I'll suit and he hasn't taken anyone. It's a front job. I'm a sort of supervisor, but have to turn my hand to anything. And maybe extra hours. But good pay, Don. And now Don, let's go. And thanks for the drinks, Don,' she said, after they had exchanged kisses, 'a present help in time of need, as Dad says. I'll see you tomorrow evening, DV.'

Noel took her up to London the next day, she got her job and called on her friend Rose, who made expensive underwear and had a small shop in a quiet street, off Baker Street; she kept some of her clothes there. She inspected the underwear Rose had made for her and made some further arrangements.

But this afternoon she had free. She did not feel like the movies or a teashop and the pubs were not yet open. She found herself near Hindmost Lane and after walking busily up and down the shops on Heathcote Street, she suddenly made up her mind and went to Gad's Hill, to call on her landlords, Mr and Mrs Cobb.

She was handsomely dressed in pink bouclé, with a

five-string bead necklace in peacock and flower blues and she had new shoes on. She felt excited, hotheaded, almost intoxicated by the clothes and the warm empty afternoon hours. She enquired for Mrs Cobb and heard that she was out.

'May I have a few words with you?' she said quietly.

The landlord, a short lively man with brilliant blue eyes, darkfringed, and white teeth, spoke like a business-man. 'Come in, please, I've been expecting to get the rent from your husband.'

Caroline said she liked things to be on a business footing. She was used to business herself, she was much more businesslike than her husband; and she wanted to talk things over.

The double front room had an archway, windows front and back, carpet, sideboards, tables, a good many things, awkward in size, but clean and bright. There were waxed surfaces, lace mats everywhere. On the sideboard were some decanters and bottles. She looked at them but was offered nothing. There was a pair of chairs of Georgian design. She was offered one. She expected the landlord to take the other which stood beside it; but Mr Cobb sat at the polished dining table, facing her.

'Since you have come to talk business, I suppose you are going to pay me some of my rent.'

She had come up to London to get a change of clothes. Noel was out on a selling trip trying to dig up the money. Conditions were bad; her husband's nerves were frayed. 'It is a chapter of hardship, Mr Cobb, but we are both doing our best to dig a way out of the ditch. We pay our way. We want to pay. Believe me, we would do anything not to let you down.'

Mr Cobb was looking at her in a peculiar way, as if he understood her and wanted her to know it.

She was heavily built. She eased her legs by crossing them.

'That is a nice style of couch, Mr Cobb. I like the blue silk. I've seen it somewhere else. What is it called? May I try it? I've seen it somewhere.'

'Where have you seen it?' he asked, surprising her.

'Oh, I think, let me see – I believe my dressmaker has one.'

'She must be an expensive dressmaker.'

She laughed her triumphant throaty laugh. 'For me she is quite cheap. I never have any troubles in that direction. No unpaid bills. I don't like it.'

'I see! Well, in that case, I shall expect to see you on Saturday with the money in your hand. Don't come again, please, without having the money in your hand. And now, if you please, Mrs Cobb will be home soon and she will be very busy getting supper; and I have some work to do.'

Caroline was shown out and found herself in the street. Her head buzzed with this suddenness. She was puzzled. 'Sent away with a flea in my ear,' she muttered to herself. 'He just doesn't know the ropes.'

By the time she met Noel at the house, she was almost drunk and was so unwary as to tell him that she had called upon Mr Cobb to work on his sympathy about the rent. 'Hold him off a while; but the time wasn't wasted. I met the Israeli violin teacher. He told me the Cobbs are going away for two weeks to their Eastbourne cottage, on Saturday, so that gives us our timetable.'

'Why did you go there?' complained Noel. 'The rent is my business. Everything to do with the house is my business. I don't want my wife bothering about the rent. And another thing, did you have a drink with him? I don't want that. I didn't know he was such a knight. I'm going over to tell him what I think of him.'

'I had my drinks with Joan. I was in an awful state and sort of worn out with everything. I phoned her and she said, "What you need is a bracer and tell me everything." So I took a taxi and went over.

'Oh, it's the ruck and tumble, I told her. Of course, it's an awful blow, hard to look on the bright side, I told her. Hitch your wagon to a star, Dad always says and he laughs. See me up there in the starry world, he says. Then he laughs and I laugh. Soon he will be, in a way. I'll soon be a cosmonaut, he said. And Granny sitting there, all ears. What does he mean? she says. Well, wagon and stars. But it comes to me, Joan, I'm unlucky. So I said. And I feel it, Noel, deep down. It's because of Bert and Willy perhaps.'

'I'm hungry, what have you got?' said Noel. 'And I'm sick of all that.'

'Well, I've got liver and onions, if you want that.'

'I like that. You're good to me,' he said, looking up at her; 'You've always got what I want.'

'I think of you, Noel, I do assure you.'

Her father had little time to live. Noel came to Bury from a trip to East Anglia when it was long past meal time; but Caroline had steak and sherry for him, saw him eat it and then, because he was tired, saw him settled down beside her mother, who was making a white blouse out of some unused nylon curtain material. Noel was very much interested in the simple pattern she had devised and made a suggestion for slipping through the tie-belt.

Caroline went out, telephoned Don, and was met by him in his car.

'I can't stay long, Don: just time for a double and a little chat. It's so awful there; though Noel, thank goodness, is always happy with Mother. It is so surprising, he so tidy and Mother living in a junkyard. But they fix things up together.'

'My brother Bert is here, Don, my half brother. Yesterday, after you left, we telephoned Bert and of course wired Willy. Willy is on a construction job and can't get down. Bert said, "Would Mother like him to be at the funeral?" And he said if Mother would like it, then she must send him the money. He hadn't any. We wired him the fare. You have no idea how he looked. He looked so awful, Don, so down at heel. Frayed trousers and a frayed dirty shirt, a yellow shirt. And in all that we had to start washing shirts; and it was in that downpour. So Mother lent him one of Dad's to go to the hospital, a bit frayed too, but it fitted. The suit was so bad, we were ashamed, so Mother lent him a suit of Dad's too, and it fitted him, though they're no relation. And he went over in Dad's things. Dad looked him over solemnly and said not a word about the clothes. Then he shook hands, "How are you doing, Bert?" "I'm down, never will be up," Bert said. And he couldn't stay, had to get back to work. When he was ready to go, he said, "I suppose you know I have no money to go back. I haven't a penny and I'm hungry, also." So we had to take up a collection for him to pay for the favour. Yes, Don, he did us a favour, as he saw it, coming to see a man who wasn't his father; and we had to cover the cost. If only you had seen him!'

'I'm glad I didn't. Come on, drink up.'

'With Granny's big ideas, you wouldn't think she'd make him a roadmender. As I understand it, Don, he's living, Don, four or five to a room, some awful sort of room over a teashop, the worst kind, near the railway bridge. They have to keep the windows shut for cinders and dirt. It's hot and there are insects. It's almost under the bridge. And the noise. And they fight, Don, he said; they fight to get the bed near the door. Someone's always moving out, and they shift around, musical chairs, you see. They come in, the color of the road they're working on, they go into the canteen for a cup of tea and a crust, and some go right upstairs if they haven't got it, straight up the wooden stairs, no wash-basin. Oh, he made it so clear and without complaining, just laughing sidelips, like a dog. And they say they'll look out for a landlady, I mean star boarder sort of: but the way they look, they aren't the kind.'

'Well, he never liked books,' said Don.

'Mm, he never liked books, a lost sheep you might say. Tunnels, building, casual, no home. Mm, mm, and Granny going to Uttah, as she says. It's funny, isn't it?'

'Maybe you'll stay here a bit, love,' said Don, ordering another couple of doubles.

'Oh, thanks, Don. I needed this. Well, Don, Granny's in and out, bossing the show and I don't know if we could, it's a sort of trap. But Mother is so funny too sitting there mending things surrounded by junk; "It might come in handy" – and the attic full. And of course, people gibe. It's such a clutter and she sits there and says, "Do not tidy up or disturb anything. If you put it away I can't find it." But funnily enough, Noel does not mind. He laughs, and he says, "And where is the coil of picture-wire?" And when she can lay her hand on it, he is delighted. He calls it, The Ada Unique System. He makes such a fuss about conditions; but he is quite another man with Mother.'

'Then you can be happy down here,' insisted Don, holding her hand. 'That would be nice for someone.'

'Mm, mm. But it is Granny, popping in, and a regular inquest, a cross-examination about your experiences.

"What did you do after the hairdresser?" Just like gossip and keeping tab. "I can't remember," I say. She says, "Oh, you have a very good memory." Now, what does that mean? Won't leave a clod unturned. It's vapidity, just idle curiosity.'

'Just likes to be the boss.'

'And another awful thing, Don. Granny insisted upon an autopsy as if – and there will be all that mess. Of course people are pricking up their ears, wondering if there is a rat in the woodpile. And they look at Mother. But what has he to leave? Has she got someone else? And Noel was furious about it; it's irrelevant, so bloody irrelevant, he said. He is very fond of Dad. Cutting him up like a frog, he said. And why is it? Granny just wants to prove the doctor and nurses were careless. Mm, mm, dereliction, or something. And someone she knows had one, so she wants one.'

'Had one what?'

'Had an autopsy. She wants to talk about hers; and how Mother didn't feed him properly. And then she's afraid.'

'What do you mean?'

'Well, Don, she's uneasy about death, how it might come to you. She wants them to look in and find out. And then throw mud on the hospital and me because I brought Dad some champagne, when he asked for it. "I'm so thirsty," he said, "just a little drink; just slip me one, in case I'm going where it's dry." I had to. Dying wishes. And how did Dad feel with his wife sitting there being overruled and the talking about neglect and bad strains and postmortems?'

'Sitting there! Holy smoke! While he was alive?'

'Granny said, "Ada, if he goes I'll insist on a postmortem," and Dad opened his eyes and said, "Over my dead body!" Nothing could have been worse; a man on a deathbed saving our faces with cracks. And at home, Granny queening it, because Mother doesn't care, mending things, painting the sittingroom and Granny, "I'll insist on an autopsy." "But why, Granny?" Noel says. "You never know; I owe it to Ada," Granny says. "What is it you never know?" says Mother. "Never mind, I'm within my rights," says Granny. And Daddy turns the tables on her, leaving his body to the medical students. Granny runs to a lawyer and proves you can't do it, you don't own your own dead body, it belongs to your heirs. Noel was furious. He had tears in his eyes: it's sacrilege, he says. Well, Mother didn't argue about it. She had started to mend a china service that was in bits and that she hadn't touched for years. And Granny had Aunt Morrie and Auntie Belle crushed under her wings: and Bert going off in one of Dad's suits. So they'll have it. What a story, Don!

'Well, I must go. We have to go to the flophouse, to pack our last bits. I hate it and I'm afraid to go. I may lose my temper if I see the landlord. I ought to take him to court, but it's better to let sleeping dogs lie, I suppose.'

Before she left Don at the pub, she telephoned a certain Tommy, arranging to meet him for a quick one at the Tartan Club near the flophouse in town. Noel had to go down to his suppliers. They met, went to the flophouse for a snack and then to the station. Tommy showed his fondness for her, and promised to look for two rooms for them in his neighbourhood.

'I know it's hard,' said Tommy. 'I looked for months before I landed the one I have; and what I saw on my trip! The best was a room that had never seen the sun since the roof went on; with an enamel jug to fetch the water up two pair of stairs. The room was built out over the little brick and plaster porch, which was so ready to fall down that you didn't knock your pipe out on it. Why, anywhere around here, you'll look in the bow-windows of the old nabob houses, and see a thin partition running from the bow-window to the back. There's a family on either side of that partition, with half a room and a window-and-a-half each. Well, I'll fix it. Maybe in your house. That would be sort of cosy, Caroline, wouldn't it?'

'Now I want you to realise you have to be serious, Tommy. I respect Noel and I want him to be respected where he lives.'

'OK, leave it to me. A word is as good as a picket line. I'll ring you.'

'No. I'll ring you. We've a few minutes. Let's go and have a little one. When I think what I still have to face, here and down at Bury. That's the very word.'

'The trouble with you, Caroline, is that you're a gypsy; you're both gypsies. You ought to get a caravan.'

'We're not gypsies, Tommy: it's conditions. And at least gypsies are free –' she sighed. 'When Bert left, he said, "This is the last you'll see of me, till next time: it may be my time." Wasn't that an awful crack? But he didn't say it in a smart way: but in a terrible way, so depressed and spineless. Oh, Tommy.'

In a few days Tommy had found them a room which he said was quite good, a bow-windowed front room, divided, it is true, but only by a small boxlike partition, which gave them a kitchenette.

He said, 'The landlord is proud of it and there is also a basement coming free with a separate kitchen. The latter is paved with flags and cold as death and streaming with damp, but it's a real separate room. It's half below ground and it's free because the last tenant has died in hospital with multiple arthritis which she got here: and the daughter is moving.' For some reason they all laughed.

He laughed, 'It's not funny, is it? You had better try the upstairs. It is right on the front hall, next to the front door: so it's a sort of privacy. And there is someone to clean. The only thing is that it's on a thoroughfare with all-night trucks and they're tearing up the street to lay mains. But take a couple of doubles and a couple of aspirins before you go to bed. And there's a real good light for Noel's work.'

Not quite trusting her daughter's stories, Caroline's mother gave Noel thirty pounds to help out. They went to see the new landlord to pay the requisite week in advance. Her name was Mrs Hope. She was a blackhaired handsome woman. 'Where were you last? And why did you leave?' asked Mrs Hope.

They stood in a large room in her Highgate villa. There were well spaced pictures, rugs, a polished floor, some impressive furniture; and just outside, in the roomy hall, a woman's writing desk, exquisite.

They said, they had been living in Bury with Caroline's family. Mrs Hope brought in her husband to do the business, 'It is better so, no?' He signed their rent book in exchange for their first week's rent of three pounds. Mrs Hope had already telephoned their two references, Noel's bank and Noel's publisher. The Hopes, exceedingly polite, said they were glad to know Noel and Caroline. They called the front room they had rented to them a flatlet.

'The flatlet has just been painted and renovated. We put in a partition and new gas cooker. We think you will get on with our other tenants. We don't have tenants we don't feel we can get on with.'

Noel was polite, but in the van he said, 'Foreigners

who can pick and choose among Englishmen, saying who will get a room and who not – we should be able to say yes and no to them. It's our country. It shouldn't be legal.'

'Well, Noel, you will have to admit sooner or later, that property is king. If they own English houses, they can pick and choose English people.'

'That's an irrelevant remark, property is king: I don't like it.'

'I know your sensitive touchy nature, Noel. If you had a house, you would pick and choose. Why did you dislike the flophouses? You said that the Cobbs just let in anyone at all and you felt in the ruck.'

They drove the van down the alley alongside their new dwelling to a patch of grass at the back. The Hopes had promised to fix up a shed at the back for a garage. The Hopes had seemed very pleased with the good condition and fresh paint of the van. It was gracefully inscribed with Noel's name and business and the place of registry.

'They always do like it,' cackled Noel: 'it is something to seize; and it is something to get away in. It works two ways.'

'Yes,' said Caroline: 'I am thinking about that telephone in the hall. It is a pity. It will disturb you in your work. You, Noel, must never answer it. Not for the other tenants.'

'Don't make me laugh,' said Noel. 'Am I going to answer the telephone for the sort of person living in a place like this? I would sink in blood before touching their telephone.'

'Well, that is all right. Don't take on. I just want you to have quiet for your work.'

'Don't you worry about my work. You know, I can't bear to be egged on and badgered.'

'Noel, that work to you is like a sick child; you are broody about it.'

'Did you notice the shops?' said Noel. 'You can't get more than a week's credit in this kind of street; you pay on wages night. It is no good.'

'Well, Noel, we have our plan, our routine. If we don't like it, we bring it into action; and we don't pay.'

They had called at Joan's on the way, for some of their goods. When they got into their new room, into the clean and cheerful room, they ran in and out happily, moving in their things, lamps and knick-knacks. Caroline threw a fresh blue bedspread over the bed and unrolled a white wool mat. This made the bed, which stood in the centre of the hall-side wall, very conspicuous.

'The room's all bed. I've had enough of skirting round beds to get to the table. I have to do my kind of work wedged between a bed and a wash-basin.'

They moved the bed to another wall, though now it made it the first thing seen on entering. Anyone at the door could see it.

'Noel, we have that screen we left in the flophouse.'

'I won't touch that filthy old screen again, someone's throwout.'

'I'll paste things over it. I'll get a length of something.'

'You say you will, but you're always out. Besides, I don't want to go back there. It's unlucky.'

'I told you, Noel. That Jules Robinson, that music-teacher, told me that the Cobbs have gone away for two weeks to Eastbourne. They went last Saturday.'

'I don't see why you hobnob with Jews in a place like that.'

'Noel, you have too many ideals. Life is a compromise. Now let us go and get it. And I left a few things we can use. What a pity there's nothing there worth taking. Don't dawdle. I'm just a bundle of nerves. We'll pick up a quick one.'

Going out, he laughed grudgingly, 'You and your nerves. You're like your Granny.'

'I have nerves, like other people.'

'I didn't say you had no feelings. What I object to is your taking the word of every Tom, Dick and Harry. How do you know it wasn't a trick?'

'Now Noel, I will not hear that. He is a very obliging friendly young man. He is not hand in league with the landlord.'

'Oh, yes, I know that. Obliging friendly young man.'

When they got to the 'flophouse', they decided to use up some bacon and eggs Caroline had left there. Noel hoped that if she ate, she would not want a quick one. While they were eating, the doorbell rang, someone came upstairs; and next, the landlord stood in their open doorway, looking at them eating from the frying pan on the cooker. He said firmly, 'You are going without notice, I see; but you cannot go until you pay me the ten weeks' rent you owe me. I know you can pay me.'

'I can't pay you,' cried Noel, starting away from the cooker; thin, raffish, despairing. He came and stood near, head and shoulders over the bright stout man. 'I'm broke, I haven't a penny, I haven't had an order in weeks, because of my wife's father's illness. My wife lost her job. We have nothing in the bank. I have to go down to Reading and live with my aunt; and I can't pay you even for one week's rent. I haven't two pounds in my pockets. Look at the way we're eating. Would you live like that? Not you. Rather not. There's nothing here you can take. I need my car for my business. Without that, I'll be walking the streets. Do you want me to get a job as a shop assistant?' he said, with dreadful wildness in his thin face and deep dark eyes. 'I can't carry on this way. You'll have to wait. If you can wait till I get to Reading, my aunt will advance some money; I am sure I hope so. And my wife's family will see you are paid. They have money.'

All this and more he emptied out in a cantankerous, whining and sometimes tragic tone, an experienced beggar and a suffering man.

Behind the landlord appeared his son, a tall, young man with a serious bitter face.

Mr Cobb said, 'If you were really poor, I wouldn't trouble you; I'd wait. I'd give you a chance. But I know you. I have found out. I have been making enquiries. I know about the rooms you left, about Madam —'

Caroline turned towards him. Her bold, fat, colourful face had turned crimson. She opened her mouth, but said nothing. She tossed her head, went over to the sink and threw the rest of their meal into a piece of paper. The crimson slowly flowed away.

'I'm not used to these sordid fights,' said Noel, 'I can't take it. I'm not used to conditions of squabbling and name-calling. I don't know how a decent man can rent a place like this with holes in the floor.'

With tears in his eyes, he pulled out his wallet and handed over twenty pounds. The landlord gave him a receipt and said, 'I will let you go without the week's notice or week's rent. I am glad to have the money owing, but I would not have let you go without it. So do not start regretting that you didn't bluff me, after I have gone. I know people like you; and I don't intend to be cheated.'

When the Cobbs had gone, the pair stood dully against the wall and the sink: surprised, taken.

'Well, that is a nice thing,' said Noel; 'I should have let him write to your Mother.'

'I'll never bring the family into things like this. They

don't understand such things. Granny for one, would make such a tale out of it. As it is, you are the one thing Granny thinks I have done right.'

'I know what he meant,' said Noel, after a while, 'when he said he had had you followed.'

'That was bluff. He found out I lost a couple of jobs; and he made up this story.'

'I know what he meant,' said Noel.

'That was bluff. Forget it. That's over. I'll just do the pan and we'll get out. Nothing went right here. It was one long streak of bad luck. And if the other place doesn't work out, we'll go back to Bury for a while. But I'm not quitting. Only for a while. I know you like Granny and Mother; but I'm not staying there under the hegemony. It's too boring.'

'I know what he meant when he said he had you followed. He did have you followed. Otherwise, why would he say it?'

'I don't believe it. That's all.'

Noel began to weep. 'You ought to be ashamed of yourself. Aren't you ever going to go straight?'

'I don't know what you mean,' she said calmly. 'Now stop lounging against the wall, Noel: and let me get the curtain down. I'm not leaving it after that.'

'I know you're much younger than me. I know that. But I thought when you were thirty you'd reached the age of reason. I thought you'd settle down.'

She bustled about, tugging and banging.

Noel weeping, said 'Everyone knows. It's always the same. I ought to knock you about. I ought to hit you. I ought to say, get out. But I don't say it.'

'Oh, Moses! We've been over all that. Oh, Noel, don't bore me; don't please, darling, please don't. Oh, it's so awful.'

'I can't help being boring. I know all those people are rotten: but they're good company for you. Who would have thought I'd ever find myself in a place like this? It gets me down. It's my nerves. And the new place. It's only one room in a slum. And they're foreigners, too. And look how they live!'

'Noel, don't be so cranky. People live like this. Bert lives worse. If you understood conditions, you wouldn't feel so low: you'd take heart.'

'Conditions,' he said, weeping. 'Understanding those things won't make the mice and dirt and the awful life any better. I stand it for you. That's the only reason I live, for you, Caroline. You must understand that. I have nothing else to live for.'

'Don't say that, Noel; you mustn't. You must stand on your own feet.'

'I don't want feet: leave feet out of it. I want you and if I don't have you, I don't want anything. Nothing. Certainly not life.'

'I can't stand it,' she said nervously. 'It's horrible. It frightens me. It's like living in a black awful smothering room.'

'I live for you,' he said boldly. 'I don't want anything else. I live for you and in you, and you know it. Your life is my life. What else have I got?'

'My God,' she said, in a suffering tone, 'My God! This kills me, Noel. I can't tell you how awful it is. I feel as if I want to die. I don't want people to live for me. Don't smother me. I don't want you around living for me.'

'But I do,' he said firmly.

'Let us get out of here,' she said, 'and if we don't like it, well, we'll go down to Bury. You like Mother.'

'Wherever you're going, I'm going. If you leave me, I'll follow you. You can't take a train away from me. I'll be on it. If you take another man, I'll go and see him. I'll tell him I want you. He'll let you go; I'll make him. You can't get away from me,' he said boldly: and he began to laugh.

She began to laugh, too. 'Oh, Noel, you're a card, you're original. No one knows you but me, oh! Well, come along.'

Humbly, without their usual flash and high talk, they went downstairs and into the van. They drove off.

The landlord, in a blue suit, stood in the door of his house, Gad's Hill, to see the last of them. His wife, a fairhaired plump woman dressed in light colours, wore an apron and held a chamois polishing cloth in her gloved hands.

'We should pick the tenants more carefully,' she said.

'Oh, my dear Dora, there is no way of being careful with tenants. I don't like going over them like a basket of apples. I say to myself, tenants are people: they have troubles and their troubles are tenant troubles: and what I have are landlord troubles.'

'No, I mean children,' she said. She added sadly, 'But isn't it strange that we have no one with children in the house? You know, Harry, when we bought these five houses, three here and two facing, I said to myself, "One day I will have my four children grown up and married and living all around me. I will be able to look out of my windows and see all my children and grandchildren." But now two of them are going overseas: and for the other two, we have years to wait. I sit in the window every day and look over there and think, it seems so unnatural. If only I could look over there and see children running in and out. Two whole houses without a single child. How can people be so selfish? Tears come into my eyes every day, Harry.'

'I must give it to the first person who needs it.'

'I sometimes want to go over and knock and say, "Oh, don't you understand? Are you really selfish? Let the children come, let the children run." '

Mr Cobb turned inside.

'Nothing else counts,' she said vehemently, 'nothing else on earth is worth having.'

Mr Cobb shut the door.

Accents

Early winter, a sunny day: the villas along this part of
Broadfield Avenue back on to a large grassy square,
surrounded by old trees. Owners and tenants around this
green may use it for walking, and the children use it as a
playing field. The houses have balconies extended into
terraces overlooking the green; the three corner houses
are lodging houses, or boarding houses. At the corner
where Mrs Turtell (pronounced Tur*tell*) and Mrs Jones
are neighbours it has become gossip corner.

Mrs Rose Turtell, fair haired, bent, weary, looks as if
she has begun her old age, yet she is forty-five. She is
stocky, thin faced, dressed like a poor housewife, and has
no sense of colour of dress. She has no make-up, wears
mud coloured rayon stockings, worn fur-lined
houseboots, a brown dress with the hem down, and over
that, a brown knitted jacket, a green knitted sweater and
over these a coarsely knitted red waistcoat, too small and
too tight; with these, a soiled apron. She speaks English
perfectly but has traces of a foreign accent. Mrs Jones is

nearly sixty, a thickset energetic woman, without waist-line, her grey hair back in a tiny bun, blowing loose however in the wind that harps down the side-passages: she wears a dirty thin grey dress and a dirty white apron: she has a very marked Welsh sing-song.

Mrs Turtell is at present listening to the radio serial *Mrs Dale's Diary,* sitting in her living room which is spacious and gaily furnished in colours at variance but so worn by family living that they seem to fit in.

Mrs May the charwoman doing the housework mean-while goes out on to Mrs Turtell's terrace from which she can see Mrs Jones standing on her terrace in the sun. On Mrs Jones's terrace there is a motor-boat under a tarpau-lin. Mrs May is about forty-five, fresh colour, red hair, too plump, fresh print dress and green cardigan; she has taste. She has a working woman's voice but does not drop her aitches. She has an apron, a mop with an old cloth pinned round, a dirty dustpan and a few rags in her hand. She dusts the dustpan and shakes the rags and the mop.

Mrs Jones said, 'Hello dear.'

'Hello, Mrs Jones.'

'Everyone calls me Gwen, dear. You know that.'

'Look at that, Gwen. An old mop and dirty rags and a dustpan to turn out a house of seventeen rooms and the rest. The staircases are that dirty, with the children running on them, the staircases are that dusty – can I get the dust and dirt out with these?' Her voice is wrathful and more than plaintive, almost crying.

Mrs Jones said, 'Well, the children have gone back to school now.'

'I'm glad of it. I couldn't stand their noise and their running on the stairs. Three of them all day. It was too much for me.'

'How's your husband, May dear?'

'He's at home today, Gwen. But he'll sit there without eating till six o'clock if I don't get home till six o'clock.'

Mrs Jones said 'Would you like a cup of tea, dear? It's boiling.'

'She'll think I'm wasting time. But I'd rather have your tea. Her tea's so weak. And I feel so dizzy – what is it, do you think? I feel I can't stand.'

Mrs Jones said, 'You're hungry, that's all. You're a big woman, you work hard and you're hungry. You need lunch. You know her, May: tell her you need lunch.'

'She used to give me lunch,' said Mrs May, 'but she said she didn't take lunch and so she gave up giving me lunch.'

'Well, I'll make you both a cup of tea and bring it in. You go inside and I'll call her.'

Mrs May said, 'It'd pay her to rent a hoover or get one on easy terms and do it herself. I wouldn't mind. A whole house and the stairs – I've never seen such a dirty house.'

'Well,' said Mrs Jones drily, 'you get in, May.'

Mrs May continued, 'They had a hoover here but they sent it to their first house, which they've rented furnished. It was their house at first. They send their children to the best private schools. It costs them all told more than a thousand pounds a year for two children: a boy of fourteen and a girl of ten. I don't know. (Undertone) She looks poor and so does he.'

At this point Caroline, an actress aged eighteen, a tenant in Mrs Turtell's house, in a nightgown and dressing gown came out on to the terrace.

Mrs May continued, 'The children were measured for jodhpurs these holidays. A thousand pounds basic for two children!'

Caroline made as if to go.

Mrs Jones called, 'Rose! Rose dear!'

Mrs Turtell came out dressed as mentioned, but she was fingering her tight red vest in a proud self-conscious way, her finger on the lowest button. In every way, except for her bright fair hair, she looked like an old woman. She said to Mrs May, 'I heard you upstairs in Mr Arkwright's room. You know he is a hardworking man, but he's very dirty.'

Mrs Jones said, 'You know he has no time to wash, day job and night job.'

Mrs Turtell said, 'You should see his sheets; I think he goes to bed without undressing. There is Sunday. On Sunday he goes boating. He has a boat tied to a jetty.'

Mrs Jones said, 'More likely he looks after it for someone else. Do you know in a boom more workers collapse from overwork than in a depression? It's because they think there's a chance for them.'

Meanwhile Gwen Jones kept eyeing the new red vest.

Mrs Turtell said, 'Is that a way to live? Nothing in his room. Nothing on the table. He owns nothing. He's mean. Everyone in my house is so mean. That's no way to live.'

She noticed Mrs Jones's glances and continued, 'Yes, I finished it. Does it suit me? It looks tight because I have it on over the other things. I can't stand the cold in this country. It's worse than Russia, worse than New York.'

She said with false modesty, 'I couldn't get the right buttons so I put on anything. The buttons spoil it.'

Mrs Jones said briefly, 'It's very nice, Rose. You need colour.'

Mrs Turtell laughed modestly, 'I'm not sure it isn't better for my girl Boadicea, though, who's ten years old. Looks more her size.' She laughed. 'I think I look funny in it.'

'Come in and have some tea,' said Mrs Jones. 'I made a

cup for Mrs May too. She's worrying about her husband.'

'She does nothing but complain,' said Mrs Turtell. 'I asked her to wash down the stairs and put up new curtains in Mr Hasma's room – this one.' She pointed upstairs to a room in the back. 'He's got this one now. She complained about everything. I need a younger woman. I won't come in, Gwen.'

Mrs Jones went in and came back handing two cups of tea over the fence. Mrs Turtell called, 'May! Come and get some tea.'

At that moment the wooden gate to the green opened and there strolled in Mrs Javert, thirty years old, once beautiful but pale and very much neglected in appearance. She was wearing a dirty dressing gown and slippers.

Mrs Turtell said, 'Hello, Mrs Javert. How is your husband? Is he working yet?' Taking the tea in both hands, she said to Mrs Jones, 'Mrs May doesn't get through her work. I used to give her lunch. It wasn't the food I objected to, it was the time she took. She wanted to sit and rest there. She lost half an hour, three quarters of an hour – I lost the food and I had to pay her for the time.'

Mrs Jones said, 'You see houseworkers here are used to getting a bite as well. They count on it.'

Mrs Turtell said, 'Oh, I'm mean. I'm grasping. I'm hard. I know it. But I don't take lunch myself.'

'You need it,' said Mrs Jones. 'Everyone needs it.'

Mrs Turtell said, 'I was told I looked better since the children left. It's the only consolation I have.' She turned to Mrs Javert, who was having a cup of tea handed over the fence by Mrs Jones. She said to Mrs Javert, 'My husband is a romantic. He wants his children to be the perfection of the English lady and gentleman. It's ridiculous. He's old-style. I told him, "You're a stuck-in-the-mud." He's in love with something that doesn't exist.

What will my girl and boy be? He won a prize in Latin: she's like me, good natured and not interested in studies, not enough. They'll be school teachers. That's what he should have been. I'm in the wrong country and I married the wrong man. This country is full of stuck-in-the-muds. They'll just be through their schooling in ten years and I'll be fifty-two. When he married me I was studying medicine. I would have been a doctor long ago. But,' she said with a sudden change of mood 'he wanted me to be his wife, "my wife doesn't work," he said.' For a moment she glowed, then with a sudden change, she laughed 'Now, I clean out rooms for other students. If my daughter ever falls for any of these students –' and she became fierce, 'I'll show her the door. They're mean, lazy, no-good. No good. Mud-stickers. Mr Arkwright works, two jobs, but he's a mud-sticker; no ambition. Get some savings, buy a van, get a van business. What sort of a life is that? Grub, grind! His mean old mother made him like that. They aren't men! If she starts to get starry-eyed about any such man, I'll say "This way out Boadicea." Go and learn about life. Forget about Mrs Fairley-Wallows school.'

'What's that?' said Mrs Jones.

'That's a school on the radio. They teach them an accent as if they were chewing soap and liking it and to be snobs. "The Archdeacon's niece." ' She laughed gaily. 'I'm in the wrong position, Gwen, everything is wrong.' She kept laughing. 'You really like this vest? I just cobbled it up. It's not good knitting. It doesn't look smart. I'm an old frump now. I was the first girl ever to leave my town. It was on a river too, we lived near an old bridge. My father sold cattle. I said I was going to Paris to study medicine. It took two days and two nights to get there. When I got there, a boyfriend of mine I had at school, wrote me a letter saying, "Is it true that the prostitutes have tents on the pavements in Paris? How I long to go there." That's the kind of little town I come from. My mother's neighbours were all sure I was leading the life of a prostitute. What old fashioned people! When I first went there, I used to go round collecting for the miners on strike. You could have enlisted me, then, Mrs Jones.'

'Gwen!'

'Gwen.'

Mrs Jones said, 'Now you believe everything your husband repeats. You have no principles. You won't sign a peace petition. You throw my leaflet against the H-bomb in the rubbish tin.'

Mrs Turtell said, 'Everyone for peace is a stooge for Russia.'

Mrs Jones said, 'Yes, your whole family was burned to death by the Nazis and Russia wants to stop that forever; but you prefer the burners. That's the kind of person you prefer now.'

Mrs Turtell said 'I'm selfish. All this activity, everything I do is selfish. It's for two children, not even for my husband and myself. To make two children into little snobs without any sense, living in a past age. I don't care if mankind is burned to death by the H-bomb, because Aelfred and Boadicea have to talk as if they were chewing fancy soap. That's why I went to medical school, that's why I married a foreigner. And that's why John married a foreigner.'

Mrs Jones said, 'Well, Gwen that's something in your husband's favour: if he married a foreigner, he can't be so stuck in the mud as he seems.'

Mrs Turtell burst into violent but not bitter laughter. 'He's a foreigner himself. Half Spanish and half German.

His father's a foreigner. He's a Spaniard or a German. I'm Slav. That's why we're more Catholic than the Pope. More English than the English. That's why our children have such ridiculous names that I can't pronounce them. I said to him "John, you purposely gave my children names I can't pronounce. And now you are sending them to schools where they will learn to speak in a way I'll never learn." '

She laughed sturdily. 'He's crazy. I married the wrong man. When I first went to France I met a student in a hostel who wanted me to go to the movies the first Saturday. I didn't understand a word he said. He made signs and I went with him. We sat there in the movie not saying a word, but he kissed me. Then the next Saturday the same. But I got hold of a compatriot who spoke my language and French too and I said, "Tell him, I'm studying, I can't." I felt foolish and I didn't know what he wanted. I suppose he just liked me. I was naive. I'm still naive. When I met John I didn't know what he wanted and I went away. That made him follow me. I was surprised when he proposed to me. I accepted though. He seemed to know so much. Now I know he doesn't know much. He just likes to lecture. I knew more.' She laughed.

Mrs Jones said, 'Your tea is cold. I'll give you more.'

'Oh, I'll drink mine cold,' said Mrs Turtell. 'She doesn't want hers. Take it back. If you wheedle her she thinks about her troubles.'

Mrs Jones said, 'No, I promised it to her; give it to me; I'll get fresh.' She took it back.

Mrs Turtell said, 'Oh, well, I'll call her then. Then she won't feel she's so oppressed. She thinks I'm a slave-driver. May, dear.'

Mrs May answered from Mr Hasma's room on the second floor.

Mrs Turtell said, 'Now she's loitering round the student's room. Mr Hassam or whatever his name is; John says Hasma. He's a nice boy but too still. Everything is done according to a table of work. He has it on his wall – Table of Work. On Tuesdays and Saturdays he goes to the theatre. On Wednesdays he goes to an oriental restaurant to meet friends. He never sees a girl. He asks me to do his repairs and clean his suits. He came to me when I was listening this morning with a pair of trousers held out in front of him and said, "Please fix up the zip"; and he tried them on, dropping the others in front of me. Penny-pinching like the rest. He sits in the lavatory a whole hour and meanwhile reads *The Times* and *The Observer*. I walked in on him, he hadn't shut the door and there he was – slim small brown legs, very smooth and young really. Of course, no harm in that. It's a good way to while away the time. My husband loves to read *The Observer* in the toilet a whole hour on Sundays. It's characteristic. Waste not, want not. I'm a nasty gossip. Poor man. He says he likes to talk to me because the English are so cold and rude to foreigners. Especially orientals. He holds a door for a lady. She sails through and doesn't notice him. "Even if I were the door-keeper she ought to say thank you," he says.'

Mrs Jones said, 'He's very rude himself. I say hello to him: he never replies. He's just the son of rich people used to oriental servants. He thought I was a servant, because I had an apron on, you see. People always complain about their own faults in others.'

Mrs Turtell smiled, 'Oh, to me he's always very polite. He says I'm a real friend. His mother asked for my photograph and he took it here in the backyard, with the children. I'm not cold as a fish. My own husband aping the English treats me like a foreigner. "Don't deal with foreigners," he told me. "I'm a foreigner," I told him; "and you are more Catholic than the Pope." You can't move him. I'm very unhappy. He's teaching my children to despise me. He may not know it.'

Mrs Jones went in and came out, 'Here's May's tea.'

'Yes, I'll take it to her. May dear! Thanks, you're a good neighbour, Gwen. Yet you're a red and I'm a tory. I vote for the tory watchdogs.'

Mrs Jones said, 'Yes, but we're neighbours on the green. We have the same interests.'

Mrs Turtell laughed, 'Yes and we let rooms, we have tenants; we're landlords.' She laughed good naturedly at this comment on Mrs Jones.

Mrs Jones said, 'Yes, dear, that is so.' She came to the fence and began to gossip.

'Mrs Javert has just gone out the front to the grocer's. She's afraid her husband will think she's been having a cup of tea with me. "Let him get his own coffee," I told her. "He'll manage all right." "You don't know him," she said: "part of his enjoyment is that I get it for him." She's the man's slave. Do you know what she told me about – them?' She nodded towards Mrs Javert's house next door. 'Mrs Javert told me that she left her husband because he said she did not clean his shoes. She told him off and left him, taking her little girl and now she paints all day up there.'

Mrs Turtell said, 'I saw her painting the nightwatchman. Sometimes, she says hello, sometimes not. Do you like her hair streaming down – so white – old grey hair streaming?'

Mrs Jones said, 'Mrs Javert's other two are a mannish couple: always wear leather breeches; handy for painting the house.'

Mrs Turtell said eagerly and looking younger, 'Do you

know the couple who used to be in the attic? She is having a baby; I had a letter from her.'

Mrs Jones said, 'A couple in your backroom, where the young man is now, left because they were having a baby; just before you came in.'

Mrs Turtell said, 'Gossip corner. Here we are. I'd better go in or she'll say I spend my time gossiping and never help her. She thinks a lot of you. She told me you always go down on your knees and help her, and she said she knows you're a communist but she respects you. She says you talk to her a lot.'

Mrs Jones said, 'I talk to everyone. It's the only thing to do. I talk to you, Rose, you're a good neighbour.'

Mrs Turtell said, 'You're a good neighbour too. But we're on different sides of the fence. Oh, it makes no difference. I'd trust you in hard times and my tenants would trust me in hard times. Politics are on top: they tell you nothing about people. Look at you and me. Both old landladies.' She laughed. 'And the women in leather pants, next door – landladies. And everyone in the row – landladies. That's what we are! Property interests. Meat markets! We look at all human flesh as what sort of tenants would they make.'

Mrs Jones said, 'I look at them and think, "What sort of comrades would they make? Do they care enough to work for people?" '

Mrs Turtell said, 'Yet you got into trouble with the district: you made enemies. That's what I hate about politics,' she bared her teeth, fine strong white teeth, '– politics justifies hatred and nose-poking. Organisers are private tax collectors and spies and censors and nose-pokers. Paid or unpaid – unpaid are worse.'

Mrs Jones said, 'There you are, sacrificing your whole lives to educate your children to a class system and class ideal which are dead and won't last their lifetimes. If they believe in it, they'll be trodden on, because they're lower middle class, the children of a boarding house keeper and a foreigner – or two foreigners if you like; and if they don't believe in it, they'll have to fight their way back through the same roadblocks and they'll throw it in your teeth. You don't believe in it. You're educating them against yourself. And you're not sincere. You take advantage of the medical services for you and your husband and your children.'

Mrs Turtell said fiercely, 'We pay for them: we can use them. Bad enough too they are.'

Mrs Jones said, 'Look at you, a woman washing floors and changing sheets for idle young men who have never done a stroke of work and perhaps never will. What are you to the others? A poor and despised woman, a boarding house keeper. Your own son won't bring his friends here. Did he have one friend here last holidays? His whole holidays?' Mrs Turtell said, 'He moped the holidays away. His father won't let him play with the other boys round here, he may not even go out on that green, because they're middle class and he goes to Beowulf School. They'll ruin his accent. He's underfoot the whole time. I pity the boy, I don't blame him. I'm in a dilemma, Gwen. I don't know how to get out of it. I'm shut in, padlocked. He's a good boy, too. He sent me a letter thanking me for everything I do for him. "I had smashing holidays Mother"; and I only took him out twice. He spent the whole time here in quarantine because his father won't allow his school friend to come and he's not allowed to play with the neighbours. He has got to speak and think Beowulf School. He's a prisoner of an accent; we are living for accent. Did you ever listen to the plays on BBC? I was getting bored with them and then I noticed some of them are all about accent. A railway porter, he has a certain accent, a schoolboy on the train has a better accent than his mother, who has a tea shop accent because she used to work in a tea shop; and better than his father, who has an accountant accent because he still works as an accountant; and there's the office head – fine middle class Embassy accent, you might say; and the railway clerk, better accent than the railway porter, and the char worst accent of all. Then the public house owner doesn't drop his aitches at least because he owns a business and the headmaster of course a very fine accent, because he is related to a bishop and the Latin master a good accent but not as good as the head; the science master, sort of Croydon accent and so on. And I said to myself, "It's necessary here because they wouldn't recognize the characters if they had the wrong accent. And who but the middle class English would be able to understand it all?" I listen with astonishment and I say, "That's Aelfred my schoolboy, but when he grows up, what accent will he have – railway porter, head or science master?" For you never can tell. It alters when you get a job; they don't care for an assistant accountant to have the accent of a headmaster. At the BBC casting directors must have ears like blackbirds, they must have sound-files. And it is so delicate, so difficult and so clever.

'But my husband is a blackbird. He is mad about pulling one of those better accents off the tree because he sees Aelfred automatically a head, a classics master – do you know, I saw a job advertised for classics master in a county town at four hundred and fifty pounds a year? I wanted John to get a school job – he loves lecturing to people; but we need four times that to scrape through. I must run in. Oh, there's May's tea – it's cold again. Well, she doesn't need it. If she needs any there's the teapot from their breakfasts.'

Mrs Jones said, 'But you'll lose her, Rose. You're used to servants who were glad of an old dress at the end of the year – though I'm sure they weren't glad.'

Mrs Turtell said, 'I don't treat her as a servant, I treat her as a friend. I wear old dresses at the year's end and I go without lunch. I feel no difference. There's no difference between us. I have no class feeling. You have to be an Englishman to feel that. She'll think I'm wasting my time gossiping. I must go in. Probably she is telling her troubles and finding fault in Caroline's room. Caroline's a nice girl but all girls are dirty. I prefer men. I'm going to give up girls and have all men. Caroline has fifteen pieces of unwashed crockery in her room. And Miss Wacker too, on the stairs, going to the wash closet, trying to talk to Mr Hasma – he won't look at an English girl; and stretching her legs and her bottom in that way she learns at ballet class.

'Now, there isn't a dirty man in the place but Mr Arkwright – and of course, Mr Bellamy, whose girlfriend dropped hair stuff on the dressing table where it took the paint off. "I suppose I have to pay for that or clean it up," he said, the poor young man, innocently. "What do you think it'll cost me?" He's a nice young man; but Ski-Pants, that's his girl, that's what my husband calls her, Ski-Pants is not his type, he's making a mistake. But of course, it's not serious. She may be serious but he isn't. He told me – I teased him about getting married, leaving me and getting married, and he said, "I'm not getting married." "But you have a girl," I said. He said, "Yes, but I'm not marrying her. She may think so and she acts so, she stays here and she gave you the impression, but I'm not ready to get married yet. I'll stay and let you look after me." '

Mrs Jones said, 'They are right not to marry young.'

Mrs Turtell pursued, 'She's always in and out: some of

the boys call her Mrs Bellamy. I told them, at breakfast, "They're not getting married" and at least, he's not; perhaps she is – but to someone else. "She's after him," I told them, "with those thin long legs in ski-pants. But he's too fine for her." I asked the boys at breakfast, "What do you think of her?" "She doesn't appeal to me," Mr van Leeuwen said. They don't think she's worthy of him. She's all right in her way but he's too good for her. And Caroline, you know – Mr van Leeuwen is nice to her, he likes her, he takes her to the theatre, but he's not wild about her: he sees through her. She has no brain, she never reads a book. I told him, "Do you know there is not a book in her room?" And I asked her, "What do you read?" She said, "I have no time to read: and of course, the theatre leaves you no time for ordinary life." I said to him, "You're an intelligent man with a career, you're widely read, you're not the kind of man to go seriously for a girl with nothing in her head, just theatre and taking different parts." I read that an actress has no personality at all. She just takes on the personality.'

While she was telling these tales about the girls in her house, Mrs Turtell did not look bitter, but despondent and rather younger, as if partaking in her way in the life of the student girls.

'Gwen,' she said, 'if only our lives ran in reverse. If we did not want anything while we were young, but to study and get on – how far we'd get! And then when we got there, we could do as we liked. Supposing a woman could get married at my age, when she knew what she wanted! I said that to Mr Binzli the other day, the Swiss boy, that tall fair boy. He is going to get married next summer. I don't know what she's like and I'm sure he doesn't know. "Why are you so anxious to get married? You are too young." He is a very nice boy, but not like Mr Hassam or rather Hasma. Hasma – he is too serious, nothing but study – no girls, no waste of time. "When the summer comes," I said to him, "you'll be running round Europe looking for girls." "I'll never take up with a European girl," he said, "only my own kind. I can't get on with European girls. They seem coarse to me." And Mr Nirogi said the same. You know that girl who was here in the side room?' she pointed, 'She used to call out to him on the street when they were passing each other, "Hello, are you alone?" It was a way of getting to talk to him; for she could see he was alone. "She could see I was alone," he said to me; "she was trying to make friends." "Well, perhaps you may take to some girl one day," I said; but he said "No, never an English girl." Never an English girl – that is what they all say: they don't like the English girls. There is something that doesn't attract them.'

As she talked and mused over this, she bent forward more and more as if oppressed.

Mrs May appearing at the window to shake her mop and rags, called, 'Mrs Turtell – Mr Turtell is just coming in: the van is letting him out just now.'

Mrs Turtell exclaimed, 'Oh, what has happened? Why didn't he telephone me?' She started to run in, as John Turtell came out of the breakfast room. His appearance shocked people at first. He looked ten or fifteen years younger than his wife, though he was not, handsome as a musical comedy star and in general like a man eternally young, the eternal undergraduate. When he turned his head, or walked down the street, upright and stiff, again there was a shock, with his flat-backed head he looked like a ten-year-old schoolboy grown too tall. There was something odd about him. He walked stiffly, wore a strange costume, a carefully devised variation on a city man's clothes with a resemblance to Anthony Eden, his ideal: yet there was a clerical touch to it, too. He carried a satchel that might have been a despatch case, with his initials and a key. Once an assistant in a trade mission in South America, he had lost his position through stiff necked pride and was now a salesman, in South American imports. His voice was beautiful and his accent not affected, but musical, impeccable.

John said, 'I was going past in the van, Rose and I thought as the van was empty, I could –'

Mrs Jones who had not been greeted, looked at him meaningly, folded her arms over her barrel abdomen and went with dignity into her kitchen.

'– take along the oil heater to be fixed. There is an Englishman along the street.'

Mrs Turtell spat fire, 'In other countries there is no heating because there are no Englishmen.'

Mr Turtell said severely, 'In this house, we will employ only Englishmen. They do better work than foreigners. We will not encourage foreigners in this district.' He said this in an inconceivably prosy way; it was hard to believe he was not joking.

Mrs Turtell cried, 'John! Your mother is a foreigner, your father too. I am a foreigner. Aelfred and Boadicea were born in Buenos Aires.'

Mr Turtell in the same strange way said, 'British labour is the best in the world and if we live in England we have the chance to get the finest workmanship. Therefore it would be unreasonable to employ foreigners who are always inferior and who cheat. You cannot depend on their word, their materials or their workmanship. Whereas with British workmen you are sure of not being cheated and getting the work done on time. If you had not bought the oil stove from a foreigner in the first place, we should have avoided this trouble.'

Mrs Turtell said, 'I don't see. It's a British oil stove. He just sold it. You're more Catholic than the Pope.'

Mr Turtell replied, 'The mere fact of his being a foreigner and not born here makes him inferior and induces him to pick inferior goods to sell. If you deal with foreigners you will get inferior goods and I have asked you time and again, Rose, to be advised by me in this matter. When it comes to British workmanship, it is a matter of common knowledge and experience that the British are first and the rest nowhere, not only here but in any market in the world. Why did the British develop their empire? Because their goods were so unquestionably and demonstrably superior that all others had to leave them the field. Now when you have a British oil stove and you go out of your way to buy it from a foreigner, you are certain to get inferior materials and service because he must have bought inferior goods.'

Suddenly he cried, 'Hurry up, the van is waiting.'

Mrs Turtell said gently, 'I will give you the oil stove. Take it to an Englishman.'

Very gently Mr Turtell continued to remonstrate, 'A person who has an opportunity of getting British workmanship and who –'

At this moment a key was put into the front door and a boarder, Mr Wright, came in and as soon as he saw them, began a merry fearful ringing laugh, 'like Raskolnikoff' said Mrs Turtell, pealing laughter, a braying voice, ludicrous but terrible. He was overdressed in black and white with a bow tie, a bowler and fine shoes and he carried a stick and a satchel. He had been looking dispirited as he walked in, but as soon as he saw the couple he gave his extraordinary laugh and called out, 'You'll think I'm early. You're right but I'm really always Wright, I am all right. And what were you doing Mr and Mrs Turtell? Billing and cooing, killing and booing? Ha ha. I have a friend, my friend called James Bigger. He has a baby in the family this week and I said to him, "Now who is Bigger?" And he said, "Well, my son is a little bigger." ' He rocked and laughed himself through the hall and upstairs, when he ceased and with lowered temperature and a sad face passed along the hall. He was a salesman, selling silverware, he dressed like a bridegroom, lived alone and in the weekends would go and visit his mother in Leamington Spa.

When Mr Turtell left with the oil stove, Mrs Turtell went out back to the fence and called her neighbour.

'Gwen, how can I make money? What can I do? Lampshades – I had a friend who sent her son through high school making lampshades. Or cooking – I mean extra cooking for a bakery? Or get private customers? Or make little dishes – if only I had a van like Mr Arkwright – perhaps he would go in with me?'

Mrs Jones said, 'But you are making money now.'

'Yes, but it isn't mine. There always has to be more and more. We rent that house we used to live in; and with that rent we're paying off this house; and the money from this house has to pay for the children and then put aside to buy the house next door, where Mrs Javert is – he's going to die, anyone can see that. But I have no money for myself. And if I had money – I'd run away. Why can't I go back to when I was a girl – and start out again, learn medicine and be a doctor, and do something for people? I'm not doing anything for people now – who wants to look after these lazy boys who always had mothers and sisters and nurses and will soon have wives and cooks? My life is wasted – and I'm tired and I have nothing to look forward to. Aelfred and Boadicea won't want me when they grow up and sometimes I think I cannot stand another day of John – he talks of going on holiday and oh, the boredom and disgust, it is as if I had mud in my throat. If only I could go away by myself.'

At this point Mr Hasma came out onto the terrace with a letter in his hand. 'I have a letter from my mother,' he said stuffy with pride and gleaming with pleasure, 'and my cousin is coming to London. Do you think she could stay here? I told my mother you could be her chaperone. I told my mother you are a most honourable respectable married woman, of middle years, and it would be quite suitable for my cousin to stay here.'

'Then your cousin is a girl?'

'Oh, yes,' he said. 'A very beautiful Bengali girl, very rich and I am affianced to her. When I finish at the London School I am going home to marry her. But mother is afraid I am here too long and so she has arranged this trip.'

'I don't know if it will be convenient for your cousin to stay here,' said Mrs Turtell. 'I cannot be a chaperone to young girls and men. Perhaps I am not respectable enough, for such a beautiful rich young Bengali girl.'

'Oh, but you are – I told my mother you were the age of my aunts and that you were a sort of aunt, a nanny and a good old servant all in one, to many respectable young men – and girls.'

'Your cousin must be quite advanced for an Indian girl,' said Mrs Jones, staring at him.

'Oh, there are many modern Indian girls: they are more modern than English girls or than Russian girls,' said Mr Hasma.

'Well, I'll see, I'll talk to my husband,' said Mrs Turtell.

'Thank you,' he said politely.

Mrs Turtell flew into a temper, 'You see what it is? I mend his zips, I clean his room, I cook for him, I lend him my *Observer* on Sunday and now I am a faithful old family servant. Gwen, I am sick of this life.'

'What can you do?' said Gwen.

'And I loved that boy, I loved him like a son, he knows I love him and he is taking advantage like the others. I idealized Mr Hasma, Gwen; because of his quietness and decency; and now he wants me to incubate his fiancée.'

Mrs Jones laughed; but Mrs Turtell, in great sadness went inside, and settled down to have a long chat with her favourite, Mr Hasma, who had established himself in the morning room where he had so often sat with her. She forced herself to talk to him about his family, his fiancée, his sister, his career. She had never hoped to have him as a lover, she had always recognised his cool conceit, his spoiling; but her heart was in her boots.

Presently Mr Turtell came in. 'Good evening Mr Hasma,' he said.

'It is Hassima,' said the boy.

'It is not Hassima, it cannot be, there is no such name in India,' said Mr Turtell.

'John, I suppose Mr Hasma Hassima knows his own name.'

'He does not,' said John Turtell, 'such a name is impossible.'

Mr Hassima was silent looking with curiosity at Mr Turtell. Then he quietly went away. Mrs Turtell sat down and cried.

'You are so wrong,' she said, 'and making us call ourselves Turtell, when it is Turtle. You did not want me, Rose Dubrovsky, you wanted a woman to clean your boots, to dominate and probably all along you had the idea of a boarding house where I could cook and clean.'

Mr Turtell looked at her crying, went to her and patted her on the shoulder. He kissed her fair hair.

'I am an old woman now,' said Rose; 'it's all over for me. And I live in a house with nobodies and I wait on freaks.'

He went to hang up his coat and hat and got out his papers.

'I got the idea from Mr Wright,' he said; 'I am taking on a line of jewellery; costume jewellery. I might make a bit more that way.'

7 Biographical and Autobiographical

A Waker and Dreamer

Samuel, the father, was born in 1846 in Maidstone, 'a man of Kent'. He spent his childhood round and about, his holidays at the sea, at Margate and Ramsgate. How he used to say those two words! Ramsgate, the harbour, shipping, lifeboat, beach; Margate –! He went to work at twelve with paintpot and brush, up a ladder, thick hair upstanding, lively Sam, cracking jokes and singing songs he handed on:

> Slap dash slap with a whitewash brush,
> Talk about a County Ball!

He loved Charles Dickens, lived in a Dickensian world. The family talk after him was full of Dickens words; 'Only Brooks of Sheffield, when found made a note of, cowcumber, a lone lorn creetur, Mrs Harris, Codlin's the friend, not Short.' Dickens in 1861 brought out *Great Expectations,* in which the transported convict Magwitch makes a fortune in sheep in Australia and secretly supports a boy in England. In 1864, Samuel, aged eighteen, made himself a small box like a toolbox, of wood bound with iron, with a light padlock; and with it under his arm stepped aboard a sailing ship for Sydney, leaving behind him parents and numerous brothers and sisters. He was one of the youngest.

Samuel got a job in North Sydney at his trade, carpenter, painter, builder, married, had children, became his own man, built weatherboard houses for themselves to live in. The second house was called Minstead, after his second wife; the last, at Mortdale, was called Gad's Hill. He was a freethinker, an Oddfellow, (of which he became Grandmaster), belonged to the Dickens Lodge and, at its annual meetings, recited and acted from *Nicholas Nickleby, Pickwick Papers, David Copperfield, Oliver Twist.*

In the nineteenth century little in England was Merrie. To begin with they feared French invasion. The agricultural workers in the south hoped for it, believing the French would bring down their oppressors the landlords. There was 'Captain Swing' (rick-burning, machine-breaking with the anonymous threats to 'swing' the landlords); the Chartists; and 1848; major epidemics of typhus and cholera (1847 and 1865); and they were still transporting for a sheep or a lamb, a loaf of bread and a meeting.

The government, finding this did not deal with the ferment, was encouraging emigration. A copy of *Punch,* 1848, shows two pictures, 'HERE' and 'THERE': 'Here – Poverty; There – Paradise', the legend runs. HERE (England) is a homeless couple, in torn clothes, with five dejected children sheltering by a wall bearing the notices: 'Whereas all such meetings . . . ILLEGAL. Meeting – CHARTER . . . LECTURE ON SOCIALISM . . .' While in picture two, THERE (overseas), the same couple, contented, robust, their children bonny (not bony), are eating in a roughhewn highroofed cabin with hams hanging from the rafters, a whole slaughtered sheep of their own hooked to the wall, an open halfdoor showing a palmtree; and leaning on the halfdoor, an attractive darkskinned man, to whom the pretty daughter is bringing food. The tables are turned; it is now they who can make handouts to the natives. An engaging travel fiction.

There was the American Civil War (1861-1865) with the promise of freeing slaves; the foundation in London of the First Workingmen's International, 1864, and the Communist Manifesto – 'you have nothing to lose but your chains.' The Government, anxious to lose the discontent, had luck too. Six hundred thousand British people went to Australia between 1851 and 1858 (the gold rush), and others to California, Canada and the Argentine. The Government also was looking abroad, sending big money to India, the Argentine, Australia and elsewhere. The Empire was on the move.

So that Samuel, though enterprising, was not a pioneer nor a soldier of fortune; just a young optimistic artisan, among many. The old country and its troubles did not weigh on him; and if his older children had some sentimental and quite uninformed views of England, which his gallant daughter Jess called 'home', the younger ones, and especially David, youngest boy, were a little like the dream children in *Punch*, all bad times forgotten. David was an Adam; Australia was his prolific and innocent garden. This was his nature. He came to his young manhood and prime in the time of 'the optimists' (Manning Clark); and he was a naturalist with a new (old) country and its wildlife to explore; his imagination and ardent love for his country called forth marvels. He was a kind boy. He loved his parents, and his brothers and sisters, who had a great love for him.

The boys all went to work at twelve; the two older

boys as painters (ships' painter and signpainter); and David, at twelve, was apprenticed to a rubber-stamp maker, where he learned the careful lettering which was his pride; which was of use to him when he entered the Fisheries Department as a junior. He lettered the labels for the specimen cases in the department. He went to Sydney Technical College for zoology; and during the course, boiled down and mounted a cat and a dog, the only cat and dog in our home life; we always carried these two glass cases with us. David had a horror of cats and dogs, for carrying disease communicable to man; hydatids (encysted larval tapeworms), rabies, tetanus, for example. Hydatids, in fact became with us a comic danger cry; 'Watch out, hydatids!' Our pets were wild animals.

The mother, Christina, was of Scots extraction. Her views were not those of her husband. She was nonconformist in religion and strict, with many tabus; no dancing, smoking, cardplaying, alcoholic drinks, theatre and so on; yet between them they represented the two forms revolt had taken among the working classes in England. The nonconformist churches, after the 'Swing' and allied troubles, gathered in people dissatisfied with landlords and their hired men in the vicarage; while in the towns especially, the lodges (to begin with, Manchester Unity) attracted the more go-ahead and liberal type of workmen. The parents' background was much the same; and family life was quite cheerful. They were a musical family; gathered round the piano, sang the old favorites, the men whistled like blackbirds, all had clear light voices, soprano, baritone, tenor.

This bright picture was fogged in one corner. Samuel, the father, had 'habits', about which the women spoke in lowered voices (which failed not to get the attention of every child within earshot). Samuel took snuff (and always sported a handsome clean dark red handkerchief, sailor style) and he liked a glass of port.

This is what comes of freethinking and acting Quilp and Sam Weller in Lodges!

On her deathbed, when David was fifteen, his mother, as he told it later, made him promise to keep her rules of life; and he was proud of doing so. He never went to the theatre or to concerts; he abhorred dancing, because of the contact of bodies; he did not allow kissing or embracing in the home, nor endearments, nor cajoling, which he thought led to degrading habits of mind. The home was however, because of his own gaiety and talent for entertainment, and endless invention, gay and lively. He liked to lecture, he liked meetings and he did not miss the arts; he had the outdoors, the sea, the shore, the bush. He whistled very tunefully, and usually tunes from operas, but only moral operas – *Martha, William Tell, Maritana,* and a *motif* from the overture to *Semiramide.* He was shocked that the arts so often dealt with what seemed to a pure man, unsavory subjects; and then, the wrongdoers were not usually admonished, punished, made to repent; or not chastened in such a way to discourage others. Vice was made attractive. Yet he never censured his brothers and sisters for their good times; he always excused them.

He extended his sobriety to the intellectual world; he added prohibitions of his own; for instance, no French or no history. He hated us learning history at school, because it was a record of old European villainy and bloodshed; he gave the French no credit for their enlightenment or struggles for liberty; and he disliked Pasteur, perhaps because Pasteur thought wine good. He did not speak French; perhaps he had an intimation of their intense rationality, subtlety and wit; feared them in argument; and the shy boy fears the bogey and tourist tales of French licence.

David was 'floodlit' (Claud Cockburn), remarkably

fair, with noticeable thick yellow hair, tender blue eyes and a speaker's mobile mouth. For a long time the cameras caught this pale blaze. It was not merely his fairness, but a sign of his vitality, his self-trust and restless inner and outward life; and a sign, I think, of the tribe of Abou ben Adhem (may his tribe increase!) who love their fellowmen. I have seen it in one or two others such. Among humane people, some are quiet, almost taciturn; but others rejoice openly in the mass of humanity, in teaching, bringing the light, and when they are in the midst of people and their own good work, they actually shine. This accounts for some of the mysteries of mass illusion; as when the congregation of Latterday Saints (the Mormons) saw Brigham Young turn into Joseph Smith (to justify his election), on the platform, before their eyes, as he spoke.

David's appearance, of whiteness, fairness and all that goes with it, dazzled himself. He believed in himself so strongly that, sure of his innocence, pure intentions, he felt he was a favored son of Fate (which to him was progress and therefore good), that he was Good, and he could not do anything but good. Those who opposed him, a simple reasoning, were evil. This was not his mother's work but his own nature. He would sing certain songs, especially when something went wrong in the Department or his work in the naturalist societies, some defeat, jibe, unkind joke; he would sing, 'Dare to be a Daniel, Dare to stand alone, Dare to have a purpose true and Dare to make it known.'

A friend in his early years took him to a séance at which the medium said, 'There is a young man with fair hair standing at the back of the room with a friend; and by his side I see Charles Darwin who is saying to him, "Go on, persevere, you will succeed." ' David was encouraged by this, believed in the message; it never occurred to him that the friend might have prompted the medium.

I turned this peculiar incident over in my mind for some time, as a child, because I could not believe it; it was too apt; but I was not the sort to express doubts; and it did not pay with David; he was capable of turning the incident into a three-ring circus.

The youngest of David's family was his sister Florence, a very lively, pretty girl who went to work at fourteen in David Jones's workrooms, where she made a friend, Ellen, another slender dark girl. Florence introduced Ellen to her brother and eventually they began to go on nature excursions together. They married, a child was born, and Ellen died. For two years or so, we had a very merry household at Oakleigh Villa, a white cottage near Rockdale station, where Florence kept house, looked after her own infant girl and her brother and me.

In the front was a picket fence. In the backyard were echidna who helped us with the numerous anthills, a tortoise large enough to bear two small bare feet (and so it is true about the tortoise who holds up the world), a duck who dabbled madly at the iron porridge saucepan; and a darkroom, for David was a fond photographer. The duck dabbled desperately for the porridge was often burned and stuck to the saucepan. The reason was, that while David shaved before breakfast, whistled, sang, and expatiated, Florence would have to make many little sorties from the kitchen to relate breathlessly to her brother the latest gossip from the *Green Room* – a theatre magazine she took in. She was stagestruck and had once belonged to an amateur repertory company in North Sydney, which did the Savoy operas and others.

The two baby girls were full of stage lore, knew all about divas, prima donnas, jeune premiers, entrances, exits and all the rest. But the porridge, left to itself, boiled and bubbled and blew its top (so that it was always true about the Sorcerer's Apprentice).

Before sitting up in my high chair to breakfast, there was another ritual. I was lifted up by David and we did the rounds of the dining-room, while I had to name the fish, bream, trout, gurnard, john dory, their fins pectoral, dorsal, ventral, caudal; the photographs of men, Cuvier, Buffon, Darwin, Huxley, and Captain Cook. These were the first words I learned; or rather the first word was 'itties' (fishes).

David never objected to Florrie's stage talk. She, poor girl, would have loved to spend her life in one of the suburban repertories that go on for ever, growing older with the same leading man, leading lady, understudies – but Fate, which she always called Kismet, was not good to her. She led a life of drudgery; without the slightest complaint, cheerfully, happily, in fact. In trouble, she was not woebegone, or only for a moment and then would say, 'Well, it is Kismet, isn't it?' and 'A merry heart goes all the way'. These were very gay years with the brother and sister in the house together; but David was very young, he had to remarry.

He would be out in the weekends, on naturalist excursions; and in the week very often, either on day visits to a near place like the trout hatchery at Prospect Dam; or on long trips to inspect the rivers which were being stocked with rainbow trout; or to the oyster leases. At oyster leases at Camden Haven he met his future father-in-law Frederick Gibbons, a pleasant Edwardian, dressy, well-to-do, who owned considerable property in the then undeveloped district along the Wollongong Road (Arncliffe and Bexley); and had a Victorian villa in five acres of ground on the road. He and his wife, Kate, from a South

Coast dairying family, had had ten or eleven children. There were only two now at home, a middle-aged bachelor brother and the youngest daughter, Ada, a very pretty dark slender girl, who became David's second wife. They had six children and lived at Lydham Hill (the original name of the place, not Lydham Hall) in a cottage built of large sandstone blocks cut in the quarry at the foot of the hill, by convicts in the old days. The house stood on top of the rise, facing the Pacific Ocean directly through the headlands of Botany Bay; Cape Banks and Cape Solander. The monument to Captain Cook at his landing place at Kurnell was visible from the attic windows. David was very pleased at this; he never failed a Kurnell anniversary.

The house was surrounded by two paddocks, an old orchard, grassy places and a belt of trees, pines, camphor laurels and others, some seventy years old. It was a splendid place for children. One of the paddocks was occupied by two emus, which came to us as striped chicks (about the size of fowls). There was a paved courtyard surrounded by the stonebuilt kitchen, washhouse and servants' rooms; in the middle, an old well. David and his boys filled it in and made a tall aviary there, with many birds, budgerigars, a cockatiel, finches. In the other old well outside the kitchen were two large turtles. One of the servants' rooms was used by David for his Museum, to which the children had access every Saturday; a miscellany, Aboriginal weapons, a humming bird, crabs, a crocodile, a whale's tooth, a painted dried head ... Sometimes in the other room we had a servant; not often.

Round the courtyard stood the cages containing snakes, a boobook owl, a kookaburra, two kinds of possum, black and honey colored, and in various corners of the house were aquaria and various small beings, such as fire-bellied newts and pygmy opossums. It was a colorful house, a good life for children.

In 1915 David became general manager of the State trawling industry, and felt part of his dream of state socialism, the state for the people, was coming true. He was supported throughout by the Labor premier W.A. Holman; and went to England in 1915 to buy three modern trawlers in Hull. The trawlers sailed out across the world and for five lively years we had nothing but trawling and fishing talk. In the meantime, we had moved to Watson's Bay, to a harborside house with a good natural swimming bath on smooth soft red kerosene shale and surrounded by fallen sandstone boulders. The water was clear, we caught octopodes, and fish and even a shark there (which we boiled down in the copper, a reminiscence of his student days when he boiled down the dog and cat in his family's washboiler). We swam there and the boys made friends of the fishermen and the watchman on the dredge in the bay. It was a fine place for children.

In the course of his long career in the Department, David ran into bitter opposition, which he ignored when he could, laughed off when he could; but which he allowed to grow out of containment, because he could not consider compromise, nor any view but his own. The state industries did not make money; but he always cried out that a young socialist industry is not supposed to make money, it is for the people. Nevertheless this failing was made the excuse for many shocking crass attacks, both on the government, its ministers and on him personally.

Private fishing interests also injected their disingenuous arguments into the debate. It was stated, for instance that the waters were 'fished out' – of the Southern Ocean and the Australian coastline, in five years! This didn't prevent private fishing interests from buying the trawlers when the State industry was smashed and the trawlers sold.

David was a state socialist, but he knew little about socialism. He believed in 'evolution not revolution', in men of goodwill getting together and producing happiness for all. He accepted the Labor Party's platform in those early days, even Article One, the White Australia policy; but this was not his view. He fought for the rights of the Aboriginals; when in Singapore and invited to sit on the platform by the Governor of the F.M.S. he refused because there were to be there no native representatives, only British people. He was there as Acting Director of Food Supplies to the British government in Malaya in 1921-23.

When he returned he never tired of talking of his secretary Tan Guan Hoe, a very able Chinese who knew five languages. 'Guan Hoe' (as David always said) had to abscond, because he was ruined by his father's funeral, given lavishly in the Chinese manner. Then there was Abishegenadan, a Tamil, the engineer. Abishegenadan's wife had just had a baby and David visited the family in Singapore in an area said never to be visited by white men. He pictured himself to us, a tall fair man, all in white, treading cheerily down the dark streets in the evening, a smile for all along the crowded noisy pavement and littered road, in what was called in Kipling and Maugham days 'the native quarter' (where the native-born citizens lived).

He believed he was safe because he was Good; and from the word Good we get the word God, he said and from the word Evil, we invented the Devil. He was ousted from the department, from the industry unfairly, because they were able to bring against him a serious charge, an error of judgment, made in a fit of righteous anger. It sprang entirely from this firm belief he had in his own purpose: opponents, particularly political opponents, were really Evil in the flesh.

He could speak of this to no one (but to me); but he knew now that his career in the department was ended. Not only that, they robbed him of his pension, though he had spent his life there. Whatever the weather changes in a family's atmosphere, I can never forget his expression, in misery, at the numerous unfair and even rascally charges voiced in Parliament and carried in the newspapers. 'Dare to be a Daniel' – but the time had come when it was enough; it was no use at all.

That he recovered sufficiently to go into other enterprises and that he always worked for the natural history societies, until his health failed in his seventies, showed his great courage.

He had done much writing on fish, crustaceans, deep sea mammals, written weekly fishing columns and sent many public-spirited letters to men in place; his pen was a brave one. The fish on the wall in those early days were beautifully tinted drawings done to illustrate his first book, *Fishes of Australia* (1908). After his death, his widow Thistle Harris produced from his MSS. another book, *Sharks and Rays of Australian Seas*. When I dip into this book, I am at home again and hear the old sea names I knew well. For he told us everything he could; he 'expatiated', as he said. Now, I read a bit about the Wobbegong and I see suddenly a real wobbegong I saw somewhere, at Bateman's Bay perhaps, when a child; I hear the eucalypts rustling at old Lydham, the cockchafer beetles, burnished gold, falling from the boughs, smell their peculiar smell; and the whole landscape of childhood rises up, a marvellous real world, not bounded by our time, fragrant, colored by the books he liked, *Typee, The Voyage of the Beagle, Extinct Monsters,* a book I loved as well as Grimm, *The Sleeper Awakes.* That landscape stretched far and wide, with his talk of foreshores and rising and depressing coasts, the deeps, the desert; the landscape had no time limits – it had 'giants and pygmies of the deep' (one of his lectures), extinct monsters roaming among extinct cycads and mud swamps, it had Triceratops, Mastodon, Diprotodon, Labyrinthodon, Palorchestes, the extinct giant kangaroo, all brought near by the living fossils, and in the wonderful talk there were volcanoes, Krakatoa and Mauna Loa – how is it possible to reconstruct in a few pages the life of a man and his children when the man has a genius for verbiage, a tireless 'interest in every aspect of nature' (his words) which he brought always to his friends, his writings and his family?

But I know, I can remember, how my life was filled with story from the first days, and this book of Rays and Sharks is to me the life poem of an unusually gifted man and of our long morning.

A Writer's Friends

Such a poor fist! But as soon as I fisted cat before mat, they recognised at school that I was a word-stringer (as my medical friend says, he a pill-doler). The teachers were friendly to me. At home, in a mass of children and potage there was no time for vanity. So although I was not good at lessons, I was quite happy in the classroom – except in that hour from two to three, the siesta hour, when we could not keep our eyes open in the pollen-yellow dust-cloud of sun that poured over our heads from the high windows, built in brick walls, in courtroom and penitentiary style, and good for discipline; so that we could not turn our eyes to the interesting yellow dust playground divided by pepper-trees and coprosma and privet from the enthralling yellow dust street, on which were steel rails blinding in the light; and sometimes dusty men working at them. Then, in the heat, my leaden head!

But in the mornings, fresh and blue (the mornings), I was all right. I first made my mark with a poem written suddenly in arithmetic class, at the age of eight, of which all is now forgotten but the line 'And elephants develop must'. Mr Roberts, a fatherly and serious teacher, confiscated whatever it was, was making the second backbench giggle and asked suspiciously, 'Who wrote this?' and 'What is must?' I explained, but he did not return the paper. This animal learning, though shallow, has been a pleasant solace.

My next achievement, my first novel, was an essay, at the age of ten, on the life-cycle of the frog. I was content with it, it could not have been better; the style was good, I defended some irregularities and the teacher stood by me. I remember the feeling of certainty accompanying both these productions. You are lucky to feel it: it is rare.

Later than that, at the age of fourteen, I found ideas in my rather addled head, wrote a malicious poem called 'Green Apricots' about a teacher who had never done me any harm. (She was almost driven from the school by the dislike of the pupils and no one knew why – she simply told the first year girls not to eat the apricots.) This school was an old house just turned into a school and with garden beds, fields and part of an orchard still growing. After that, a mnemonic poem intended for examination girls, incorporating the rules for the bodice basic draft. (No doubt it was easier to remember the rules than my verse.) About this time began the first great project of my career, celebrating a teacher of English I had fallen in love with (in schoolgirl innocence) and called the 'Heaven Cycle' – I am mildly concealing her name. It was supposed to be hundreds of poems; it reached thirty-four. She was grateful I think. The other teachers were accustomed to adolescent eccentricity, all except one, a teacher of French, who was heard to say that she thought it disgraceful to take the name of a teacher in vain. This view of literature astonished me and did not move me. (It is common enough – 'How can you write about real people?')

It was accepted by this time at school that I was a writer; and I accepted it simply, too, without thinking about it. I had never considered what a writer could do. I had no ambitions of that sort. Later on, at Sydney Girls' High School, I had my first serious project, based on a footnote in the textbook of European history we used. The footnote referred to the *Lives of Obscure Men* and this appealed to me markedly. I planned to do that. (But I still did not think of being a writer.) It came back to me later, when I returned to England, after the war and felt I did not understand the people. I began to collect notes for an Encyclopedia (of Obscure People), to have another title; a sort of counter Who's Who. By this time I knew something about official reference books and I knew some very able people who would never appear there, because of their beliefs. Anyone I approached was willing to help with his life-story; but I had to do other things; and the Encyclopedia was a time-taking idea.

At teacher's college in my second year, there was a young art teacher, engaged to be married, who was sensitive to the charm of girlhood, young womanhood and all that was interesting in her own position. She had soft brown hair, brown eyes; she was lively, romantic and severe to her fiancé, la Belle Dame Sans Merci, she thought perhaps. He was in the navy and had to pass such and such examinations before she would marry; in fact, another two years. I thought it cruel and wondered at her. She took us out on a sketching expedition and we stayed the night in some country boarding-house in a pretty place. It was full moon, fair weather. She called the girls to come out in the moonlight, take off their shoes, loose their hair and dance in the moonlight, on the grass. She did grass-dancing nicely and some danced with her. Others felt embarrassed or amused. She said she could read destiny in our hands. She took mine, thrust it back at me with a hard look – thinking it over, I supposed it was my calloused hands. Before that, I had had to carry a heavy valise full of schoolbooks several miles each day, up and down dry and streeted gullies; and this had caused the callouses.

I was surprised, then, when she said that if I did a book of short stories she would do the illustrations. I did the stories, she did the illustrations, four or six; and offered it to a well known publishing house in Sydney, which in the spirit of colonial enterprise said they would take some if a British firm did it first. (It is now quite common here for a British firm to say they will 'take some' if an American firm takes it first.)

I made no attempt beyond that. I never had any idea of publishing and in a way I do not care about publishing now; I only do it because it is something that is done and if you do not, others think that you are writing for yourself. That is thought to be shameful. (I don't think so. If I were on a desert island, say like Australia or even smaller, what would I do? Classify the birds and fish, write poems and ideas in the sand: just as good as anywhere else.)

With regard to the 'obscure men', I did eventually do something of that sort. My first novel was called *Seven Poor Men of Sydney* (title taken from Dickens's *Seven Poor Travellers*) and one of my most recent, *Cotters' England* (the workingclass north of England) has this subject.

The MS. of the first book of stories (offered in Sydney) was lost in a Paris hotel. I paid the rent all right but had not the space in the small room I then took for two large valises, which I left at the hotel. When I went back for them two months later, the voracious Swiss hotel-keeper asked for 400 francs for keeping the two cases; so he said. I had not 400 francs. My belief is that he had already opened them and sold the contents, some of which (my presents from Australia and some beautiful art-books I had been given later) were valuable enough. The MSS. – I often wondered where they were – nowhere no doubt. However, I remembered three of the stories and put them into *The Salzburg Tales* (*On the Road, Morpeth Tower* and *The Triskelion*).

I wrote my first novel, *Seven Poor Men,* in a London winter, when I got home from work and was in poor health: something I had to do 'before I died', but this was only an instinct. I must have mentioned it to William J. Blake for whom I was working (in the City of London in St Mary Axe, opposite the Produce Exchange in a new white-tile building which was famous then as a novelty). He read it over a weekend and returned it, rather surprised. 'It has mountain peaks,' he said. When I went to Paris to work in the bank in the rue de la Paix, I took it along.

As a hobby I took up bookbinding, popular then with foreign girls in Paris as it always has been with French people. There was an atelier in the rue des Grands-Augustins, near the Pont Neuf, an old quarter. This atelier was run by Fru Ingeborg, a lively goodhearted yellow-haired Danish woman, who used to call out when she saw me come in, 'Oh, Mrs Stead' (as she said), 'tell us some more about Eric's wonderful stories!' and turning to the young girls, mostly handsome Scandinavians, in the workshop, she would say enthusiastically in a loud lilting voice, 'Oh Mrs Stead has a wonderful friend, he sits all day at the *Deux Magots* and tells the most marvellous stories,' when she would proceed to tell some of the stories herself, saying, 'Oh, tell us the one about the thunderstorm' and tell it herself. This true story related that Eric and a friend were out in a car somewhere around Baltimore (Eric's hometown) when they saw a thunderstorm coming up behind. They raced it, beating it home; but the dog which followed them, reached its kennel wet to the bone. There was also the story (which she told) about the frightful wind which blew all the water out of the river, leaving the fish gasping in the mud. (Which river? The Susquehanna?)

Eric did tell me stories, but not these. He was the eldest son of a thriving Baltimore business family which sent him an allowance. He was tall, quite deaf, something like Robert Louis Stevenson, if R.L.S. could have lain under leaf-mould all the winter, that is pale as fungus, tall, graceful when not toppling, with long moustaches hanging over his long teeth, which he bathed all day in Pernod, drinking his Pernod at ease, consummately (to get your notice) balancing the pretty perforated spoon with the sugar lump, over the delicately coloured drink until, with the addition of water, it turned blue opal. Meanwhile, if you listened (and I am a listener), in his low deafman's voice, he told tales!

He had studied chemistry in Munich, retired to run a press for rare and obscene books, run a press in Paris with a few choice nonchalant friends; and did not work at all, not even to the extent of opening his family letters. Some friend or other would slit open the envelopes with the monthly remittances, make him sign, take them to the bank. He told tales of Corsica, Italy, Sicily, North Africa, where he had been – all his tales had an improper idea to them; I often missed the point. He retold Terence, Ovid, Petronius, shortly and to suit himself. He was never amorous, though he had a son (so he said) in Denmark (not Ingeborg's, no connection here); and he had left a pretty little wife, whose picture he had, at home. 'I don't know whether I am divorced or not.' He remained there till the Germans walked into Paris, then employed a Jewish scientist in hiding to write articles for him for the occupant and this was how he got his Pernod. (I found this out later, when he came to New York on a Red Cross boat. He had meantime married two women and deserted them.) He was a friend to me. He named all kinds of books, novels, I had not read, every one of them a masterpiece. When I was sick and alone in a small hotel room, he came and nursed me, brought me food and talked to me, not now his erotica; and he knew, from chemistry, a great many household hints: 'a glass of milk will kill garlic'. (I still do carrots à la Eric.)

At this workshop where he was the unseen hero, I bound the manuscript of *Seven Poor Men,* and once it was bound, William J. Blake took it, unknown to me, to Sylvia Beach, of Shakespeare & Co., 12, rue de L'Odéon, a very famous person and address to all literary Paris, an American woman who had lived all her life in Paris. She had helped many writers by finding them. With her commendation, we had the courage to send the MS. to England and after a roundabout run (which brought in another friend always devoted not only to me but to any wanderer and to letters), I had a letter at the Bank from Peter Davies of London who said he would meet me at *Philippe,* a famous restaurant in the rue des Petits-Champs. (That part of the street is now called rue Danielle Casanova, after the resistance heroine.) This restaurant I knew because it was just around the corner from the Bank where I worked (I lived in a little hotel in St Germain des Prés and took a bus to the Opera to work in the rue de la Paix).

When we went into Philippe's, we saw at the back on a little table, my MS. bound in one of Ingeborg's home-made dazzle papers. This was the beginning of a friend-ship. Peter Davies (a famous man, godson of Sir James Barrie and the original Peter Pan), was a friend to many writers; he admired Australian writers. He said he would publish *Seven Poor Men*, but for me first to give him another book. I went home and began the *Salzburg Tales*. I had been to Salzburg in the meantime. I wrote a story every first day of a pair, finishing it and putting in the connective tissue the second day; the third day starting another story. They let me do this at the Bank, where really they only wanted me to write private letters at times, for private clients. (Sometimes I filled in at the cable switchboard, telegraphing from the code book to New York, spelling out the code; and I still tend to spell A, B, F – Alice, Berthe, Fernand, etc. in French.) I wrote the *S.T.* very fast and it gave me the same satisfaction I had with the History of the Frog; simple, complete, no questions asked. It doesn't often happen.

This book was well received in London and I was out of it all in Paris, and so I have remained. It was good for me. I think I have remained out of it to have a quiet life. I know the literary life is just what some people need, it helps many; but my life has been spent in different places, in touch with businessmen and people interested in economics – and even medicine.

How many other people have helped me! In the first place, those businessmen – they are good raconteurs; for some reason they will tell a writer anything, even busi-ness secrets. I have some close friends: one, the American poet, Stanley Burnshaw, who when able to, saw to the revival of several works he had admired, one was Henry Roth's *Call It Sleep* and one was *The Man Who Loved*

Children, which became a success commercially. There was, in the beginning my father, who told me endless tales, night after night, when I was a little child; and gave me a strong feeling of affection for Australia and an understanding of the country. Then, of course, a great friend, devoted and true, my husband William J. Blake. But there is too much to say about that: not here; and indeed, a whole book, the others, the writer's friends. Who are they? And wonderful this devotion to a writer.

Les Amoureux
(Life of Two Writers)

A friend once asked me how it worked out, two writers living together. We lived all over Europe in little hotels, pensions, rented rooms and not often did we run into anything out of the way. The Hotel Athene in Brussels was a little different.

We lived in Belgium before the war and the occupation. Bill was working for our old friend Alfred, a grain merchant in the Grain-Union, offices in a house he owned near the Bourse in Antwerp. Many Antwerp businessmen lived in Brussels; it takes about half an hour by train, just a subway ride. At first we lived in a large hotel near the Antwerp station. Alfred had several rooms; we had one room. When the men went to work I typed and went out to lunch at a little eating-place opposite where every day they had roast squab and peas. When the men came home we went to a wine café (port, malaga, sherry) and Alfred had his brief love affairs. Later we moved to the Hotel Scheers, near the station in Brussels. There I wrote a novella called *The Blondine,* which later grew into my book, *A Little Tea, A Little Chat,* about wartime New York. I worked well in the Hotel Scheers, a large hotel with a roomy café and restaurant downstairs. We breakfasted there, sat about till nine-thirty. I drank one porto and one Luxemburg beer, which I found both calming and exhilarating, and then went upstairs to work while Bill went out.

A woman who washed the floors and the halls did not like my typing. She talked to herself as she washed, quite loudly, so that I could hear, saying such things as *'Est-ce une vie, çà – toute la journée à taper?'* and so on. I felt worried about annoying her, but it was my work, that was why I was there. The only other person who thought about me so, was a mad woman in a side street in London. She had lost her husband in the first world war and lived with a small elderly bachelor her son, who went out to work. She treated him badly. When discontented, she threw him out, and the dishes and tableware after him into the street. After a while, he gathered up the things and pieces and let himself into the house again. Everyone knew him: no one, for his sake, dared to speak to him. Twice, in the daytime, when he was away, she stood on the kerb opposite my kitchen, where I typed, and shouted, 'Poor girl, poor child, they have locked her up and she must work there all day.' I was touched; but apart from the irritable sympathy of these two ladies, I have rarely noticed the sort of life I lead. It must be.

We returned to Antwerp from New York by the first boats we could catch, after the war, two Victory ships, cargo boats, taking a few passengers. Bill arrived in Antwerp for Christmas. I followed, for a friend of mine was very ill. I was at sea on New Year's Day. The seas were stormy, the boats, poor sailers, tossed but the company of two or three refugees returning to Europe was interesting, an Antwerp Jew, a Dutch agricultural student. Alfred was going to re-open the Grain-Union and we were, this time, going to live in his house near the Bourse.

Something intervened. The manager of Alfred's grain firm, a thin, lively dark man had become communist Minister for Food in the new Belgian Government and Alfred himself decided to retire. The Government was paying compensation to firms which had been taken over by the German invaders; and again, though he liked his former manager, he had made his own way and his own fortune and was fearful of Communist rule. From a distance, and seeing how merchants made money out of food, he admired the Communists but he was afraid of their policy.

We went to England, which was then in a very bad way. I had a serious illness, and we returned to Brussels where an old friend of ours and of Alfred's, Mary, had a house divided into apartments: we stayed there two months. I could then only move from chair to chair, but I began typing again; and housekeeping was very easy, the house was charming, well-kept and we were able to buy the hundreds of little made dishes they have in Belgium. When I was fit, we walked about. We had noticed a little white hotel, modest, appealing, on the other side of Brussels, a toecap hotel, situated between two streets coming to a blunted angle, the streets flowing into a cobbled square.

One day Bill returned to say, 'It looks nice, the rooms look out over the street, there are food shops just across the road; there is even a shop where you can buy sparrows, larks, blackbirds and thrushes to eat, though that doesn't interest us; and downstairs in the hotel is a lovely little café quiet and really pretty, you would like it.

I went in for a cup of coffee, good coffee; and you can get snacks. It would suit us. I never noticed that café before.'

In the evening we went over to see it. He said, on the way, 'There is one thing you may not like. The street door into the hotel, at the side, has Pallas Athene in leaded lights.'

'Well, that is just the Belgian manner.'

We had an apéritif in the small café, which had dark blue leather seats, palms between them and a short polished bar at the back. Beside it was a door and the barman told us we could enter the hotel through this side-door: the office was on the first floor – there were no rooms downstairs. Upstairs in the office, was a middle-aged couple, fair large Flemings, the man older than the woman and looking like a country man. Walking along the corridor was a dark woman of thirty, black dress, white apron and cuffs, and carrying a tray.

The Flemish woman spoke French and showed us a room, well kept, light, large, occupying the space of the café beneath. The fittings were sumptuous, in the Belgian style, a deep bed with curtains, porcelain basins, a Brussels carpet shining with health, Brussels lace curtains, light wallpaper and childish pictures on the walls.

'You will have to share the bathroom with only one person, a student who lives here and has a room on the other side.' She showed us that room, a small place like a cloakroom – indeed, there was a row of pegs on the wall.

'We are writers,' said Bill. This is a profession which makes a good impression on people on the Continent. We said we would take the room and come in two days.

'In two days? Not now?'

We said we were with friends and had to tell them. In the office again, she asked for our passports, the usual thing and after looking at them, she gave us a curious glance and said to Bill, *'Alors, c'est Madame?'* (Then, it's your wife?) 'Yes,' we both said with bright faces; we were proud of each other, and always glad we had met. After pondering for a moment, the woman gave us back our passports and we parted with the usual compliments. When we were down a few steps, the maid called us back and the copperhaired manager, Madame Wepf said,

'Excuse me, the room's for you?'

'Yes.'

'For you yourselves – not for a friend?'

'For us.'

'How long do you think you'll stay?'

Bill said cheerily, 'It depends. It's very nice here. For a week, for a month, or a year: that is, if you have the room vacant for so long.'

'Certainly.'

When we arrived two days later, they again asked for our passports for the official record. Madame asked, 'Have you registered with the police?'

'No. Is it necessary?'

'It is the rule; but never mind; we'll count it from today and the police will take our word.'

It was true, we agreed, that after the German occupation, there would be different rules.

Louise, the maid in black and white, took us along and showed us the extraordinary advantages of the room, the feather pillows, the quality of the linen; and she said, 'We change all the linen, everything, every day.'

Every day for a year? I said, 'It isn't necessary: think of the cost.'

'It's our custom here,' said Louise.

Well, it is true, that whatever the Dutch may say (for the Dutch are vain of their domestic arrangements and are flattered by foreigners, too), the Belgians have a very old tradition of housekeeping. This room became our home and there we talked freely. Weeks later, we found that Louise, who had duties around us all day, in the rooms, in the hall, knew not only French and Flemish, but German, Polish and English; a natural linguist. She became very friendly, no doubt after she had learned a good deal about us from our own talk; and then she told us her own story.

She was a Polish Jewess. She had married a Fleming, who deserted her when the Germans entered Belgium. Belgium is a country bitterly divided in language and loyalties; many of the Flemish sided with the Germans out of hatred for the French-speaking Walloons. I have seen a great packed meeting of socialists in Antwerp addressed by a socialist leader (the Food Minister mentioned before) who spoke, of course, both French and Flemish and addressed the audience in both languages. But because he started with French, half the men, men of Flemish cut, walked out. Louise had given her four-year-old daughter to the nuns and consented to her becoming a Catholic; the nuns concealed her half-Jewish origin and saved her from the invaders. Louise herself had been protected by M. and Mme. Wepf and also undoubtedly by the police, who had no reason to love the German authority.

Perhaps she told us her story to find out our leanings. Later, however, on a Jewish holiday, she gave us for a present, a whole salami. 'No, it's too much, Louise.' 'It's the season for doing good deeds,' she said firmly. I cannot think how we found out. I think Louise dropped a hint. She asked us if we slept well, if we were ever disturbed.

'In such fine fresh linen, of course we sleep well.'

No footsteps, no talking? No. All we saw was the oldish student, who said good-day and looked at us irritably.

'I suppose Louise means the people in the café.'

A few days later, Louise said to us,

'This hotel has a very good reputation, the highest: the Princess N. comes here every week and so do members of the Government.'

This was a puzzle, too, for good as it was, it was nothing but a little hotel, off the beaten track and one never saw outside the outsize American cars which were then the rage in Brussels.

'Louise is very loyal.'

We had two close friends in Brussels, one Mary, a Viennese society woman who had married and divorced a Belgian, the other Marian, an English woman who moved in diplomatic society. When at tea with them in Mary's house, we mentioned this business of the Princess N. at the Hotel Athene.

'Oh, yes, she has a famous long-standing love affair with Monsieur A., all Brussels knows,' said Mary.

'So that's where it is,' said Marian.

'It's perfectly well known that they meet once a week,' said Mary.

'Poor lovers, so well known and with only the little hotel,' said I.

'Oh, it's common knowledge,' said Marian indifferently. A middle-aged thickset countrified English woman, she had just had to renounce a lover of her own, because his daughter was to marry an athlete in the news; the love affairs of this Traviata had been common knowledge in Brussels society.

Madame Wepf began to speak to us, discreetly but affectionately, of her clients or visitors; she called them by only one name, *les amoureux*. She had chosen the pictures on the walls, tricksy little water-colours sold by the thousands in tourists' shops, hence seen everywhere in the West; one was the little girl watching her brother make water and exclaiming, 'How practical it is for men!' and another, the little dog observing the wet umbrella trickling from the umbrella stand and saying anxiously, 'They'll certainly blame me!'

Arnold, an old friend, came to see us, sent by Mary, perhaps. A successful Berlin grain merchant, he had fled from the Nazis to Paris where we met him in the early years. During the occupation of Belgium he had been kept alive, for five years, by Mary in the attic of her house in Brussels; and meanwhile she had got a bad reputation for hobnobbing with the Germans. She did it to get food for Arnold. They were severely rationed and she had one extra to feed. She feared her butler, a tall, reticent, and altogether strange person. He was a homosexual and she thought his vice inclination might lead him to the Nazis. Though he kept away from the attic, he treated her superciliously, she felt maliciously; and she slept badly thinking he would denounce them. But he did not denounce and Arnold survived.

Arnold said he had come to see the place we had found, the Hotel Athene. 'Mary says it is very nice. So it is, remarkable, fine and wonderfully cheap, I ought to move here myself.' The next day when we met him in a nearby café, he suggested that we should go to Holland, to The Hague, where he had close friends who would be our friends. The Hague would be much cheaper. He had already telephoned, and his friends had already found us a place, two rooms, bath, verandah facing the Peace Palace, in a street with embassies – full pension, no housework.

We went to The Hague. Bill, who studied every town, every country, before going there, and walked all day satisfying himself with names, dates, history, manners, and who knew Brussels well, had seen all he wanted by then. It made no difference to me.

We went to the pension and lived there. It was opposite the police station. We had, indeed, a wide verandah, almost a room, facing the Peace Palace and looking over the back garden, kept perfectly in the Dutch fashion, by the Tuinman, or gardener. Our rooms were first floor and attic. We could not have the front room on our floor, for it had been the home for many years of a couple of German refugees, a Saxon married to a Jewish woman, who had had to fly from Hitler. The Dutch couple who ran the pension had saved them from the Germans, in conjunction, no doubt, with the police opposite. It was a good place, a narrow white house with a narrow staircase carpeted, the wall decorated with a long stepped series of Dutch prints, the furniture almost too comfortable, at least for typing. Perhaps Arnold and Mary had been shocked by our stay at the Hotel Athene – innocents abroad. In reply to a greeting card sent to M. and Mme. Wepf, we received a postcard for Bill's birthday, a Raphael Tuck card showing a house made of pansies, roses, violets, beside a blue river bordered with lupins, the romantic picture of the rubicund fat Flemish hotel-keeper who was tender to her *amoureux*.

Bill now set out again on his daily travels in The Hague. There we both did better than in Brussels. I had written every day at the Hotel Athene, but had got nowhere, perhaps that luxurious room was too crowded. In The Hague, though obliged to support myself with cushions and books on the downy overstuffed armchair, I wrote in three months, a novella called *Uncle Syme,* which later became *Cotters' England (Dark Places of the Heart* in the USA) while Corrie, the eighteen-year-old little maid did all the work of the house. She was in love with the Tuinman. Before we left, with all this work, she had a heart attack and was away for three weeks.

Bill, who had begun his great outpouring *The World is Mine,* a tremendous work containing much of himself, his mannerisms, and style, on a café table in Antwerp, over a glass of Madeira, in handwriting, now, in The Hague laid the foundations of his novel of love in old age, published in Eastern Germany as *Späte Liebe;* rejected in the USA with the complaint that 'no one is interested in old people'. He was inspired by the old German classics, translated into Dutch, which stood along the mantelpiece in our sitting rooms; and by the picture hats and long dresses of the society women who met in a café near us. In parts of Europe, of course, it is quite correct for women of class to meet in certain cafés, and this one, near the Royal Palace, was one. In this elegant place, Bill saw ladies costumed as had been his own old European aunts, and as, before the war, in the early thirties, we saw the ladies dressed in Baden-Baden. When Bill was a child in New York, his gossipy elders, laughed spitefully at the love between an elderly German doctor and a middle aged Viennese lady, living in Brooklyn. They courted, married and his aunts coarsely scoffed, 'And now she will be a legitimate widow!' Bill never forgot this cruelty. Nearly sixty years later he wrote the story of these lovers.

Afterwards, we returned to England. We never thought of having a home: home was where the other was.

Another View of the Homestead

All night the sleeper sleeps close to a board, irons rattle, a violin played aft vibrates along the side, the body of the ship rises and falls, the engines beat on through seven hundred sleeps. The first day, yellow cliffs, blue coasts, next day, the steep green island south; a new world. Homeward bound on that ship in 1928, a Lithuanian woman in grey knitted skullcap, fifty-five, short, sour, salty; a tall English woman, eighty-four in black, small hat and scarf, who stands for hours by the lounge wall waiting for the Great Bear to rise; a missionary woman, thirty-nine invalided home, worn by tropical disease, her soft dark skin like old chamois; she is going back to the town, street, church she left eighteen years before, because of a painful love-affair with the pastor: his wife now dead, he has just married a girl from the choir, 'Just as I was then,' she says. There's an Australian girl, lively, thin, black hair flying, doing tricks with a glass of water, by the big hold aft, and around her her new nation, Sicilians, her husband one – they are playing the fiddle.

There's a redgold girlish mother from the Northern Rivers, scurrying, chattering, collecting cronies. Three times she booked for England, twice cancelled; the third time, her youngest daughter brought her to the boat in Sydney. Three unmarried daughters, 'Oh, but we are not like other families; we cannot bear to part.' Before Hobart, she telegraphs that she will land at Melbourne, go home by train; but they telegraph, 'Go on, Mother, please.' 'They don't say how they are!' She is faded, sleepless, 'What are they doing now?' At Melbourne, the women dissuade her and she goes on. Across the surly Bight they make her laugh at herself; she laughs and turns away, aggrieved. As we approach Fremantle, she is dreadfully disturbed; the ship may dock in the night and leave before morning. She sends a message to the Captain. At Fremantle, she telegraphs, disembarks, her rose color all back. 'I'm going home! They'll be getting ready! Oh, what a party we'll have!' 'What about the presents?' 'I'll give them back; I did before.'

There's a country minister and his wife, two dusty black bundles who conduct services in the cabin before a number of meek, coloured bundles in Sunday hats. The couple gain in stature the farther they travel, until in the Red Sea, having lost all provincial glumness, the minister shouldering tall against the railing, arm and finger stretched, explains the texts, the riddle of the Pyramids, the meaning of Revelations.

For years, I thought hazily about returning; and like that, it would be, in just such a varied society, myself unhampered, landing unknown, 'Poor amongst the poor' (a line of Kate Brown's I always liked) and would see for myself. After I had looked round lower Sydney where I walked every morning and evening of my highschool, college and work life, I would go out and stand in front of

Lydham Hill, the old sandstone cottage on a ridge which, from a distance looks east over Botany Bay, straight between Cape Banks and Cape Solander, to the Pacific; and the other way, due west, over a grass patch and the yellow road to Stoney Creek, to the Blue Mountains. That is how it was when my cousin and I lived there with other little ones and played in the long grass and under the old pines.

I knew all that was gone; they had driven surveyors' pegs into the gardens, the neglected orchard, before we left for Watson's Bay; and a friend in the Mitchell Library archives some years ago sent me coloured slides of the house that is. But still I would go and look at the homestead.

The other place – 'Watson's'? By a magic that I came by by accident, I was able to transport Watson's noiselessly and as if it were an emulsion or a streak of mist to the Chesapeake; and truly, the other place is not there for me anymore; the magician must believe in himself. And then for long years I had a nightmare, that I was back at Watson's, without a penny saved for my trip abroad, my heart like a stone. It was otherwise. I came by air, the sailor dropped by a roc, Ulysses home without all that reconnoitering of coasts, a temporary citizen of a flying village with fiery windows, creaking and crashing across the star-splattered dark; and looking down on the horizontal rainbows which lie at dawn around Athens, around Darwin.

Unlike the ship, though close-packed as a crate of eggs, we travel with people we may hear but never see. There is only one street in the flying village and in it you mainly see children conducted up and down. Beside me, is a Greek-born mother with her Australian-born son, aged seven, she talking across the alley in English to her

Greek-born neighbours, about the good life in Australia, the peace, the prospects, the education. What you hear in her tones is the good news, the rich boast delivered somewhere outside Athens to the grandparents; it is a wonderful country, we are lucky to be there, no social struggle, plenty of work, success ahead, money everywhere, no coloured people. (It turns out she thinks this.) Standing now in the alley stretching, a tall Italian proud that he has been in the country forty-two years (a year longer than my absence). There are fourteen children of all ages, three high-stomached young women hurrying out to give birth in the lucky place. Few get much sleep but all are goodtempered, it does not matter; their urge and hope is on, on. 'Are you an Australian?' 'Yes.' I am looked at with consideration.

We are a day late, mysteriously stalled at Bangkok: and the talk is of husbands, friends waiting. It is a neighbourly climate – our friendships are nearly three days old; but there is no time for histories and secrets to come out. They will be met soon, go off by plane, train and car, I will never know them.

As for me, high up, almost lunar, I could not take my eyes from the distant earth, every spine and wrinkle visible in the dry air. There did not seem to be a cloud between Darwin and Sydney. Our firebird lazily paddled (so it seemed against the motionless rush of greater vessels up there) under the broad overhang and what a sight all night! – the downpour of stars into the gulf that is not a gulf. In Australia I never lived in suburban or city streets, but with wide waters and skies and this life expanded was coming home to me; you are nearer there (in Australia) to the planets. Even more now – when we have all got a bit of the astronaut in us.

At earliest dawn, the scored and plaited land, water-rivers like trickles of mercury, sand-rivers, the olive furred hide of the red eucalypt land sprawling.

Before that, at Darwin, an airfield in reconstruction. After turnstiles and a forbidding yellow plank staircase, at the top we find a large lounge and in the centre, a small trellissed horseshoe bar, a Chinese gentleman presiding. What good sense, the Australians, what humanity! It is 3:15 a.m. and we are exhausted.

It was there, over the walls, through partitions, in the women's rooms, that there came in high, tired, bangslapping voices, 'Isn't it good to be home?' 'Yes, what a relief!' 'Better than Europe!' 'Oh, yes, I had enough of Europe.' And carolling the gladness like magpies singing with parrots, strangers behind doors, 'Yes, it is good to be home.' (One comes out.) 'How long were you in Europe?' 'Three weeks – three long weeks. And you?' 'Two months.' 'How did you stand it?' (Forty years of Europe! – I left quietly.)

Novalis said, my friend Dorothy Green remarks, that you must know many lands to be at home on earth; perhaps it is that you must be at home on earth to know many lands. A child in Australia, in the home of an active naturalist who loved the country and knew scientists, nature-lovers, all kinds of keen stirring men and women who found their home on earth, I hearing of them, felt at home; this was my first, strongest feeling in babyhood. I have had many homes, am easily at home, requiring very little. My first novel (before *Seven Poor Men of Sydney*) was to be called *The Young Man Will Go Far* and then, *The Wraith and the Wanderer,* two different novels. (I still have part MSS.) The Wanderer, once he has started out in company of the Wraith, the tramp and his whisperer, does not look over his shoulder. He does not think of where to live, somewhere, anywhere; anything may happen, awkward and shameful things do happen; he does not believe it when life is good; by thirty all is not done, neither the shames nor the lucky strikes. He takes no notice, it is his equal but different fate, he marries a stranger, loves an outlaw, neighbours with many, speaks with tongues. So that if he should cross the high bridge of air sometime, going homewards, he is also on the outward path.

Now I am back in shadowy England whose pale streams are sometimes 'gilded by heavenly alchemy', they speak of 'hot summers' but there is not the pour of gold nor the fire from the open hearth. Here are white cliffs and mornings, white horses on the downs, topheavy summer trees, King Arthur in his mound, gods and Herne the Hunter in woods, green folk, little folk, squirrel-faced elves; and stranger creatures still, Langland, Wyatt, Chaucer, Ford and their pursuit of comets, the English splendour; and all this is in the people, their unconscious thoughts and their language.

Under the soft spotted skies of the countries round the North Sea I had forgotten the Australian splendour, the marvellous light; the 'other country' which I always had in me, to which I wrote letters and meant one day to return, it had softened, even the hills outlined in bushfire (which we used to see over Clovelly from Watson's Bay) were paler. The most exquisite thing in my recent life was a giant eucalypt on the North Shore as we turned downhill, the downward leaves so clear, the bark rags, so precise, the patched trunk, so bright. 'Look at that tree!' It was outlined in light. It was scarcely spring, but the lawn outside the house was crowded with camellias, magnolias in bloom, even falling; at both dawn and dusk the kookaburras thrilling high in the trees, the magpies – I had quite forgotten those musicians and their audacity –

and there was even a scary fiendish cry in the bush early; it came nearer, but remained distant. It was just a bantam cockerel – I had one myself years ago in Santa Fe and had forgotten the little dawn-demon with his one-string violin. Too long in London! Everything was like ringing and bright fire and all sharpness. I was at dinner the other night, when someone said, 'What was Australia like?' 'It's the wonderful light, Bill,' I said to the Texan next to me. 'Yes,' affirmed he; and the Indian lady murmured, 'Yes.' Three exiles. No more was said; and the others, Londoners, did not even know what we had understood. It is at least the light. When people ask, I feel like saying, 'It's a brilliant country; they're a brilliant people, just at the beginning of the leaps.' I think this is true, but it may be in part the light, the broad skies, the crowded stars, that red hide stretched out so far to cover so much land; and I do not say, because I don't really understand it, 'And there is the melancholy.' I knew as a girl that looking backward was not joy; I thought it was the waterlessness, the twenty year droughts, the people dead of thirst, again the hatred of England, of the hulks, our black legend. But is it like the uneasiness and loneliness felt by Russians, US Americans, Brazilians, who with, at their backs, the spaces and untamed land, seek Paris, the Riviera and New York?

This brilliance one feels is not related to the present sunnyside air common to countries having a stock exchange and business boom and with money flowing into (and out of) the country; at best, an uncritical supping of splurge and at lowest, baldly expressed, 'It doesn't matter who makes us rich, as long as we get rich.' There are people in Australia who no longer believe in poverty. It has happened elsewhere; and been followed by – but we know that.

I was not long enough there to have an opinion about many things. I know about Canberra, beautiful, desolate, inspiriting Erewhon, where one can feel 'I have awakened into the future of the world'; freer because it is unfinished and all its components not yet joined; and apart, more appealing in its upland, than Washington, D.C. in its swamp; younger, closer at the twenty-first century. I don't understand the settled sadness of some intellectuals, artists and academics. The heat mystery, black shadows in the tropics, the long bright road ending in a mirage? Deserts? Not belonging to ourselves? Not united with our nearest neighbours? Smalltowners in the USA leave farm for town, town for Chicago and New York, the capitals for Paris and London. Perhaps it is just *The Beckoning Fair One* singing her faint irresistible 'very oald tune' (Oliver Onions). Well, let us be discontented then; it has never hurt art.

A SHORT PLAY
DID IT SELL? (or, WAS IT HELL)
By The Wandering Minstrel

DRAMATIS PERSONAE

The Wandering Minstrel.

The Fiends.

A Girl in the Oklahoma Case.

A Boat.

Sc.: Hell and its Environs

The Wandering Minstrel (playing on a squidger):

I have dived as a swimmer swimming underwater in
    the floodtides
        at full moon,
    to the silver bottoms and weedy beds of his soul and
            come up shining and phosphorescent:
I have lived in the full moon of his lusty season,
fished by the light of his lantern
and caught fish in the grottoes of his shore.

The Fiends (a roar):

How much did it sell? How many copies? How many
    editions?

The Minstrel (waking from a dream): Eh? What did you
    say?

The Fiends:

If you're embarrassed, don't tell us. Only one edition
eh?

The Minstrel (ignoring them):

A flake of air fell past my ear sighing, 'Gone!'
At my side was nothing but a violin planted in the sand.
'Look yonder!' said the air and the air became full of
sounds,

thicker and thicker,
and the air began to roar and the sand to whirl
and we were again in the full blast of the sirocco . . .
I thought of the sea-mist that crawls like this,
that crawls over the gunners' tents with sudden drops
and on the leaves of the valley and on my pillow . . .
Why is there so much darkness in the world
that even the sun can only illuminate a small part of our
day, at noon?

There is dewy darkness in the forenoon and dry radiant
shadows at midday

and dusk pregnant with imaginatory forms in the
evening,

but all through the day, thus, the kingdom of dark
remains

and lies in a guet-apens for the time it shall reign.
Also in the mind there are few things which are bright
and clear

but the greater part of our day is spent in internal dark
and what of the inenarrable night sessions of dreams?

The Fiends (solemnly chanting):

THIS SOLD LEAST OF ALL, NO DOUBT THIS
WAS THE WORST.

The Minstrel: (is silent).

The Fiends (a noble chant):

BUT SURELY YOU ADMIT, SOME ARE BETTER

AND SOME NOT SO GOOD? YOU SURELY
FEEL VOX POPULI VOX DEI: THE SALES FIG-
URES ARE AN INDEX. QUESTION YOURSELF!
PERHAPS YOU HAVE FAILED. WHY BLAME IT
ON THE PUBLIC?

The Minstrel (forgetting about them):

You are the cold fire in my polar season –

The Fiends (more sweetly and deceptively):

The beauties and furies referred to are surely those of
SEX: the Minstrel thinks a good deal about SEX.
HOW MUCH DID THIS ONE SELL?

The Minstrel:

I don't know.

The Fiends:

A flop, well, we won't press you.

The Minstrel:

NO ONE EVER MADE ENOUGH MONEY. I say it
in the HARLOT'S HOUSE.

The Fiends (a wild dance):

That was a best-seller, wasn't it? I KNOW you wrote
the HARLOT'S HOUSE. Why everyone has read the
HARLOT'S HOUSE. How many did it sell?

The Minstrel:

I don't know.

The Fiends (anxious):

It WAS a best-seller wasn't it? Because we all read it
under the impression that it was a best-seller. It WAS a
best-seller wasn't it?

The Minstrel: I don't give a damn.

The Fiends: I KNOW it was a best-seller. (But they are
anxious.)

The Minstrel: He saw the stars and the heads of the
woods,
he saw the dim shine of water,

> he saw the track very pale snaking it into
> the woods,
> he saw the lamplight falling through the
> window,
> and he heard the frizzling and frying but he
> didn't see Peaslop.

THE OKLAHOMA GIRL: When we were waiting for trial and my husband was in jail, it kept my mind off my troubles to read your book THE FATHER.

The Minstrel: (blushes).

The Fiends: That didn't sell so well, did it? Or did it?

The Minstrel: It sold one copy to an Oklahoma Girl, for 40¢.

The Fiends: Yes, but come, now, what was the edition? How many copies? I saw it being sold for 40¢. You got nothing out of that did you?

The Minstrel: She merely sat there smiling to herself, looking with rapture at the people who rode in the tram. If they looked well and happy, she understood how they felt! If they looked sad and peaked, she wanted to nudge them and say, 'Rejoice, you are riding! Ride, ride, people can't ride every day! I myself know someone for example – but never mind that, just enjoy yourselves!'

The Fiends: But did ALL FOR LOVE have any sale? Of course, about a girl of almost repellent physique and a poor girl – but did it sell at all? No American girl would have been such a fool nor could she have been so ugly, nor so poor! Did it sell at all?

The Minstrel: Not bad.

The Fiends (anxious to make up for this mistake): Oh! Really! Oh – did it? Oh! Really! Oh – Oh, I'm very pleased for you of course. You say it sold? How many did it sell?

The Minstrel (with an unpleasant expression): 'My darling LETTY, married at last!'

The Fiends: It's a natural best-seller! How's it going? You're not at your sales peak yet. You're a comer? How much did it sell?

Minstrel: Thank you very much.

The Fiends: Everyone says it's selling. It's selling. It's a seller. Everyone's talking about it! It wasn't like that with any of your other books. You've got something better this time. The other books don't hold a candle to this –

The Minstrel: Go and sit on a tack.

The Fiends (delirious): It's selling! It's a seller. It's every-where. If they haven't read it, they're going to read it because EVERYONE KNOWS IT'S A SELLER. It's selling, it's SELLING, it's SELLING!

(The Fiends take gins-and-tonic out of emotion. The Minstrel bursts into a flood of tears.)

Fiends: What's the matter? Isn't it selling? Did they let you down? Poor Minstrel? It isn't selling?

Minstrel: You ins-s-sult my s-s-soul!

Fiends: You mean it ISN'T selling.

Minstrel: (firmly): I mean you insult my soul.

Fiends: Why, I only meant, why, what we mean is – we didn't mean – why be anti-social? We didn't mean that at all – when we said Did it sell, we meant, did it sell, we didn't mean anything except for your interests. Why, if you don't write to sell, why don't you put it in the garbage can once it's written, if it's only for you? Why that's to say you live in an ivory tower. Isn't it? Don't you care for the people at all? The people are reached through SELLING! I don't see – I only said –

The Boat: Ugh! - Ugh! - Ugh! - U-u-g-h! U-G-H!

The Fiends: Wait till you're a BEST-SELLER!

The Boat: Z-z-z-z-z-z-z! U-gh!

The Fiends: Then you'll understand what it is TO SELL!

The Minstrel: Farewell, my own! (He goes to the ticket-window.)

The Fiends (to each other): The Minstrel is quite right: the Minstrel will sell even better when he is abroad: because he will be exotic as well, then. Mark my words, he's a comer – He will S-S-S-SELL! (A bell.) It must be the cash-register. Oh, delight!

The Minstrel: It is a boat! (A bell!)

The Boat: B-E-R-G-E-N-O-P-Z-O-O-O-O-M-M!

The Minstrel: You're right!

_____

Sent by me, with heartfelt appreciation, to those of my friends, not fiends, who never asked me, DID IT SELL?

The Magic Woman and Other Stories

'There are many things science has not explained,' we say, and 'There are powers it is better not to go into too deeply' — probably with the idea that to look too closely and too long (as the poet Ettore Rella says) is to make things disappear. Is that true of feminine intuition?

It is possible that women have something like the cat's whiskers or the snake's tongue, which puts them in possession of certain knowledge immediately: not knowledge of the multiplication table, which must be learned along with the boys, or the next turn of the stock exchange which no one knows, but of what it is necessary in daily life to know. A girl does not get a job in a shop, factory, clinic or library because she has feminine intuition; she does not use it when driving, sitting as magistrate, or when her child has diphtheria: she works, studies, observes street signals, sends for the doctor. In fact, women are never tested for it and the stories about it are usually trifles and trash too feeble for a coffee morning; yet, in a way, people believe in it.

George Sand says 'There is nothing less logical than daily life.' Facts roll in which do not fit our facts; to accept them or reject must be done at once, so that we feel comfortable or know what to do: we need a handy instrument. Instant judgment, immediate deduction is usually absolutely necessary to us, and for it we are obliged to rely on our intuition, a sort of ready reckoner. We do it, we are used to it and think nothing of it. So do men. This is true of teachers, lawyers, doctors, people in critical situations, the pursuer and the pursued. Rapid or instant decisions are needed and may be fatal: and what we then have, the guess, the half-formed notion, the hunch, the intimation, the divination, we call intuition. All these exist.

It is likely that the more we know, the better our intuitions. Yet, strangely enough, we also retain quite superstitiously belief in the untaught intuitions of children, dogs (cats are left out, I don't know why), 'sacred imbeciles', grandmother's mumbling, mother's sour shrewdness; and though the child goes to its murderer for a chocolate or a car-ride, the dog deserts its fond owner for a chop (as its owner sadly knows) and the woman soaked in home-truths is deluded by a coaxing salesman, we like to believe in their illogic; and are much embarrassed if a child, dog or crone turns against us. Do they perceive the essential bad in us? Our friends are embarrassed too, and hastily recall our weaknesses — in 1960 (or 1961?) we did not send them a Christmas card.

For all this is based on a simplehearted belief in a truth, a good and bad, to which local conditions, sickness, temperament, hypocrisy are irrelevant. There is a truth and the dog knows it. At any rate, there must be someone who knows, some brighteyes who can take us through the confusion; and so we go to the crystal-gazer, herb woman, white Rabbi, sackcloth saint; and even lose sleep over a teacup sibyl and her equally implausible brother, the psycho-analyst. There is a truth if we could spot it: there must be a litmus-paper for people.

This natural longing leads to fictions and interesting daydreams, and probably blinds us to the real nature of intuition. About women's insight, there is a sort of folk-lore we inherit. Many women and more men believe in women's peculiar gifts of divination: our husbands, brothers, lovers, sons believe it; more male writers than female refer to it; a sort of shorthand for saying 'she was truly feminine, more sensitive and so saw it all differently,' a careless gallantry. It is something, we infer, left out of male make-up. Women have benefited and suffered from this, which is related to the sex tabus and mysteries, to the white goddesses, to the wicked hag of the gingerbread house, 'the noonday witch', Goethe's 'eternal feminine which leads us forward' (a nauseating sentimentality, but related to the concept of Penelope, Solveig, Deirdre and how many other legends), to mari-olatry, matriolatry and the lover's dream.

Some of this enchantment, foul and fair, comes from our early days when the woman in the home, so weak and ailing, often moneyless, powerless, often anxious, dis-turbed, wretched, with no status to speak of, no trades-union, yet has the awful power of hunger and suck, gives life and holds off death, sets out her law, defies *their* law for our sake; from whom we obtain cure of night-terrors and the milk of paradise, a magic woman sheltering this small creature, ourselves, obliged to live in the country of the giants. Mothers and fathers can and do maim and kill; and children have their moments of fear with even the kindest of parents. But the man's power is evident: the woman's is stranger. Carried further, later, it is the poor muttering woman on the street, conducting a dialogue with the invisible, that we fear: and perhaps what we fear is what we now know to be, in our sensible youth, the insulted, beaten creature, the angry slave, resentful deprivation in skirts, which goes its own way to hidden ends. Behind the concept of woman's strangeness is the idea that a woman may do anything: she is below society, not bound by its law, unpredictable; an attribute given to every member of the league of the unfortunate. To make a small payment for their disability, we endow the slave, the woman, the dark skinned alien with unusual interior vision. We make ourselves inferior to them, not in intellect of course, but in some mysterious psychic gift. It is perhaps our way of recognising that they are thinking inadmissible thoughts. Their angle of seeing is different: it is from underneath, for one thing; not to mention other differences, national, local, personal. But that women's intuition may be a fable, a pretty package handed to the socially disabled, something to hold off the evil eye, does not mean there is no intuition; it does not even mean there is no feminine intuition. We all know it and have felt the quick stick in the ribs of instant knowing, the pleasure or fear and with it the feeling of certainty. There are the whiffs and gleams which are only guesses, instinct hovering here and there; and there are intuitions of various degrees, which appear to be the truth. For to say, as I just read (in a good author), 'She had the wrong intuition,' is to spoil the story. Intuition seems to imply awareness of something hidden but real.

The author was not wrong, however. Intuition is not infallible; it only seems to be the truth. It is a message which we may interpret wrongly. A man enters, you never look him in the eye, you see him fixing something, side-on and he does not say five words; yet you have a very strong conviction about that man — he is a chestnut-skinned, gay and sensual Lothario, that is your impression; though he is of pale skin and silent. Aunt Rose who loves doilies and cream cakes is introduced to a professor of anthropology, who has dirty fingernails and does not pay her comments sufficient respect. 'Don't trust him,' she says; and when six years later he makes off with one of his girl-students, she feels great satisfaction; she was right! Yet, she was not wholly wrong; a professor with dirty fingernails is entirely opposed to the spirit of doilies and cream-cakes which broods over her life. A man you have known for years is alone in the room with you and you suddenly fear him; something wicked hovers here. But you are wrong. He is experiencing something you cannot experience, one of the numerous fits of temper that accompany love; you have received but misunderstood the message. Just the same, you get a message. (This situation is remarkably expressed in the third love-scene between Bazarov and Madame Odinstev, in *Fathers and Sons*, by Turgenev; with just the awkwardness and dryness needed.)

In The Cage by Henry James gives the whole life-atmosphere of a young girl, a tissue of intimations, romantic guesses, mistaken perceptions, springing from her pathetic needs; and though she is never far out in her guesses, her whole interpretation is wrong because she is in 'the cage' (she is a counter-clerk in a telegraph office).

These are all intuitions of different kinds and of common experience. There is the sharp sudden insight which gives the pleasure of the kaleidoscope falling into pattern; there is the lightning-stroke, one of various kinds of electrifying intimations often described as if they were electrical phenomena, 'There was a flash between us;' and the feeling of an unseen but intense beam as in instant hate or love or fear, and there is the divination or sensing that is the result of much forgotten experience. There are pre-conditions and conditions for this immediate knowledge; to begin with, careful observation. I never forgot a dog I met in Bleecker Street, New York, the companion of Tillie a friend of ours, living alone. Emma, the dog, unhandsome, unfriendly, was a patched white mongrel, probably half pit-bull and half fox-terrier. She sat between us the whole afternoon, without a smile or tailwag, turning her head from one to the other, taking in every gesture and tone, forming an opinion of Tillie's opinion of me and by no means relying on my modest behaviour. She was a serious student who knew relations could be subtle.

We are such observers, too. We have never lived alone, from the cradle till now and our senses have taken in many thousand impressions, which have formed our opinions, even our personality. We are unaware of most of them and think we can take a straight impartial view of things; and there they are, unrecognised, waiting to aid us in a crisis. Meeting a person for the first time, is for us, as for Emma, a crisis. We are like the dog, apprehensive, a word with two common meanings.

We are cautioned by sight, sound, touch perhaps, sensations of balance and inharmony, embarrassment, ease and also a powerful sense, often neglected for politeness' sake, smell. I mean not only tobacco-reek, wet raincoats, new-polished leather, but natural hair and skin oils, the smell of flesh, dry clothing, many lesser odours. We may be moved in our judgment by too much cleanliness (conveying sterility, aridity), by a mattress of body-hair, unseen, unguessed-at, but interfering with some sort of signals and I mean nothing mystic. Walking, we move through crowds without jostling and without thinking — we are noting a hundred details of behaviour as we walk. Living in a cellar, we get to judge people's characters by their legs seen up to their knees; driving we know a man's character by his driving: if we shut our eyes and move about, we instantly become aware of signals from the other senses which, open-eyed, we have not been conscious of.

I have observed that the eldest of a family and the youngest of a family convey to others (who know nothing of their history), this part of their make-up and actually form life relationships on this basis. I am certain we must convey many other things about ourselves immediately in this way, conveyed unconsciously and accepted unconsciously (because we cannot be conscious of everything at once); and that all these things are around us when we have an intuition. There is the instant flash and round it these particles gather and cling, the whole bringing us a message.

What is more, our senses, though dulled by habit and conformity, are often finer than we think. There is the true story of the man good at word games who when sent out of the room, was believed to guess by telepathy the words chosen. It was found that he had exceptionally keen hearing; when the tap was turned on in the kitchen his 'telepathy' did not operate. That is, we have an extensive elaborate set of clues which instantly come to us; we are Sherlock Holmes in our own way; it is probably the central truth of Sherlock's method which so long has fascinated us.

It would be interesting to test intuition: perhaps tests could be devised more fascinating (my dear Watson) and useful than those that discover whether or not a housewife's eyelids flicker when she sees a dazzle-jacket on the soap-flakes. But is there *feminine* intuition? Who denies that a walking telegraph-pole, a thick chested stub, a man with jaundice, a cosmonaut, an Arab, a Jew, a coalminer, a housewife, will each see the same event differently? So it is likely that a woman, most women, will see things differently from a man, most men. Not all, but some or most. A friend of ours brought to see us in our little den in Fleet Street, the English physiologist, J.B.S. Haldane, many years ago. He happened to say that in his laboratory at that time, were 'three technicians, two males and one female.' When asked if he noticed any difference between the work of the male and female technicians, he said, Yes, there was a difference. 'They have different viewpoints and may get different solutions. For me science will never be satisfactory until there are male and female technicians in equal numbers.' That may be the answer.

Afterword

By R. G. Geering

Christina Stead knew from childhood that she would be a writer. In the autobiographical piece 'A Writer's Friends' she tells of her early excursions into verse and prose even in primary school. While a pupil at Sydney Girls' High School, where she contributed to the school magazine, a footnote she found in a history text book referring to the Lives of Obscure Men was the seed from which sprang her first novel, *Seven Poor Men of Sydney*, written some ten years later. Throughout life she thought of herself simply as a writer – 'I write because I can', shunning the terms 'career' and 'profession', because they did not fit her view and practice. She never set out to make money from her writing, she never courted popularity and, despite her political radicalism, she never became an apologist for any political group, never compromised her art by writing propaganda. She began and ended her writing life as an individual artist – an amateur in the best sense of the word.

She used to say that she was a naturalist like her father

David Stead, the ichthyologist, an observer who recorded what she saw wherever she happened to be. Such a description does not, in fact, take account of her personal angle of vision, but even *The Salzburg Tales* is not the exception it may appear to be. This collection was, in the first place, inspired by a visit to the Salzburg Festival in 1931; it was, furthermore, a product of her early experience, her reading which took her while in Australia into the world of European folk lore and legend.

Christina Stead's books were written out of the times and places she lived in. Her writings followed her around the world. *The Man Who Loved Children*, her best and best-known book, is a special case, a kind of double-write in which she drew upon her family life in Australia and on locales in the United States where she and William Blake had been living in the late 1930s.

This volume, *Ocean of Story*, brings together for the first time most of the short prose writings that appeared in various places (journals, magazines, and newspapers) outside the thirteen volumes of fiction published during her own life, along with other unpublished pieces found among her personal papers after her death. It omits, in the interests of unity, the rather disjointed early article 'The Writers Take Sides', published in *Left Review* 1935, a report she wrote after attending the First International Congress of Writers for the Defence of Culture in Paris, June 1935 as a member of the British delegation. It omits 'What Goal in Mind?', (an article on the Vietnam war) contributed to *We Took their Orders and are Dead*, 1971. It omits 'Some Deep Spell — A View of Stanley Burnshaw' (a tribute to the friend, American man of letters, who brought about the re-issue in the United States of *The Man Who Loved Children* in 1965) published posthumously in the special Stanley Burnshaw issue of the magazine *Agenda*, Winter-Spring 1983-84. Finally, this volume omits short reviews Christina Stead wrote for periodicals and papers such as *New Masses, New York Times Book Review, Times Literary Supplement* and *National Times*, Sydney.

It seemed best to group the writings for this volume according to their settings and contents rather than chronologically. In this way the book may be seen to follow the contours of Christina Stead's somewhat wandering life and, in its different sections, serve to gloss or supplement her main works.

The main works, with dates of first publication, are: *The Salzburg Tales*, 1934; *Seven Poor Men of Sydney*, 1934; *The Beauties and Furies*, 1936; *House of All Nations*, 1938; *The Man Who Loved Children*, 1940; *For Love Alone*, 1944; *Letty Fox; Her Luck*, 1946; *A Little Tea, A Little Chat*, 1948; *The People with the Dogs*, 1952; *Dark Places of the Heart* (United States) 1966 and as *Cotters' England* (England) 1967; *The Puzzleheaded Girl*, 1967; *The Little Hotel*, 1973; *Miss Herbert*, 1976.

Christina Stead was born on 17 July 1902 in Rockdale, NSW. Her mother died in 1904. Her father, David Stead, remarried and the family moved to Lydham Hill (now Lydham Hall), Bexley in 1907. Christina was a pupil at St George High School and, later, Sydney Girls' High School, when in 1917 the family moved to Watson's Bay. She completed a two-year training course at Sydney Teachers' College, not (she says) because she wanted to be a teacher but because she wanted to further her education. At the conclusion of the course she was awarded a scholarship and became a demonstrator in Experimental Psychology at the College. She suffered voice strain when she went teaching, transferred to the Correspondence School of the Department of Education and then undertook psychological testing in schools. In 1924 she left the Department, learnt typing and short-hand and took up clerical work before sailing for England in 1928.

Section 1 of *Ocean of Story* draws upon early experi-ences in Australia before and after World War I. The three pieces here were, in fact, written late in life. 'The Milk Run' first appeared in the *New Yorker*, 1972; 'A Little Demon' (in an almost identical version) as 'Fairy Child' in the *Harvard Advocate*, 1973; and 'The Old School' (one of the few things Christina Stead worked on in the last three or four years of her life) in *Southerly*, 1984.

Section 2 opens with 'A Night in the Indian Ocean'. Christina sailed for London by S S *Oronsay* in March 1928, travelling Third Class, volunteering for the job Stella does in this story, looking after a well-to-do young woman alcoholic in First Class. This piece, incorporating earlier revisions, was written probably in the late 1920s in London (where she worked as a grain company clerk and first met William Blake) or the early 1930s in Paris (where she worked as a bank clerk in the Rue de la Paix until 1935). She took with her to Paris the manuscript of *Seven Poor Men of Sydney*, written in London in the winter of 1928-29. Peter Davies ultimately came by the manu-script and was prepared to publish it but asked for something else first. Christina Stead then wrote *The Salzburg Tales*, which Peter Davies brought out in January 1934. *Seven Poor Men of Sydney* followed in October 1934. She contributed to another Peter Davies publication in November 1934, *The Fairies Return* or *New Tales For Old By Several Hands*, described as 'a collection of well-known Fairy Stories retold for grown-ups in a modern setting'. (The reader of *The Salzburg Tales* may recall the Philosopher, who says: 'I only tell fairy-tales for I would rather be seen in their sober vestments than in the prismatic unlikelihood of reality. Besides, every fairy-tale has a modern instance'.)

Christina's 'O, If I Could But Shiver!', a modern version of the Grimms' story, 'The Youth Who Could not Shiver and Shake', gives its hero, the dull son, the appropriately Nordic-sounding name, Llud, and would have fitted readily into *The Salzburg Tales* if necessary. One of the Centenarist's brief stories in *The Salzburg Tales*, about Albert Magnus, the alchemist, is a shivering story. So too, in a different way, is the superb 'Hawkins', the North Wind, a bedtime story Louisa makes up for the youngsters in *The Man Who Loved Children*.

Two versions of 'About the House' were among Christina Stead's personal papers, the earlier carrying the heading 'Origin of TMWLC'. These almost certainly date from the 1930s and both fade out after a few pages. It was not unusual for her to take up jottings or sketches years after they were first made and work on them again. Sometimes a book or story came to completion in this way. Occasionally some years intervened even between a more or less finished manuscript and the book in its final, published form. *Cotters' England*, set in working class areas in the England of the early 1950s, was in all essentials complete by 1953; *Miss Herbert*, not published till 1976, likewise goes back to the 1950s. 'Uncle Morgan at the Nats' is an obvious spin-off from *The Man Who Loved Children* and, though probably not an early piece, is accordingly bracketed here with 'About the House'. (It was not published till 1976).

The pieces grouped in Section 3 are set, mainly, in pre-war Europe, though 'The Azhdanov Tailors' and 'Lost American' end with their main characters in the United

States after the war.

Sections 4 brings us to the United States proper. Christina's husband William J. Blake, an unusual combination of Marxian economist, banker, editor and novelist, was an American citizen, who lived a large part of his life outside the United States. Christina paid her first visit to the States with him in 1935 but was soon back in Europe again. *House of All Nations*, her massive novel of the banks and stock exchanges of Paris in the 1930s, was written largely in Spain and France in 1936-37. Later in 1937 the Blakes had settled, more or less, in the United States and were to remain there until World War II was over. This decade of her life saw the publication of *The Man Who Loved Children*, *For Love Alone*, and *Letty Fox. A Little Tea, A Little Chat*, set in New York of the war years, came out in 1948 after her return to Europe. *The People with the Dogs*, her last American novel, did not appear till 1952.

The years in the United States are represented here by the group of stories set, mainly, in New York in the 1930s and 1940s. Most of these seem to have been written (or received the finished touches) considerably later. 'My Friend, Lafe Tilly' (in an earlier version titled 'The Contract') was intended for a volume of short stories, which never eventuated, to be called *The Talking Ghost*. All her life Christina Stead was fascinated with dreams and ghost stories. The mysterious, the bizarre and the grotesque, notable elements in her first three books, surface again even in those later works which seem concerned primarily with aspects of social and political life. The novellas, 'The Puzzleheaded Girl' and 'The Rightangled Creek' are, in their different ways, both stories of hauntings. The most memorable scenes in *Cotters' England* are, without doubt, the bizarre ones –

Nellie and Tom as they dance in the distorting Palace of Mirrors, and the nightmarish scene in which Nellie, dressed in Tom's old airman's suit, forces her victim Caroline to look down from the attic upon the grotesque moonlight dance of the lesbians in the backyard below.

Two pieces in Section 4 of particular interest to students of Stead's work are 'A Harmless Affair' and 'UNO 1945'. The former reworks the rather strange series of events towards the end of *For Love Alone*, which dramatises the triangular relationship between Teresa, Quick and Harry Girton. The notion of the twin self, represented by the pairing of characters, occurs in Catherine and Michael (*Seven Poor Men of Sydney*) and Nellie and Tom (*Cotters' England*) and is associated in both these novels, as here and as in *For Love Alone*, with mirror imagery. 'UNO 1945' first appeared in *Southerly* 1962 with the sub-heading 'Chapter One of an unpublished novel *I'm Dying Laughing*'. Christina Stead worked on this novel of the McCarthy years in the United States over a period of three decades. It has yet to be published.

Section 5 is Europe again, in the late 1940s and early 1950s, when the Blakes lived in the Netherlands, France and Switzerland. Paris is the setting (in part) for the two novellas, in the volume *The Puzzleheaded Girl*, 'The Dianas' and 'Girl from the Beach', studies of American girls, innocents abroad and at home in the immediate post-war years. This section opens with 'The Captain's House', a story set in the old town of St Germaine-en-Laye near Paris in the late 1940s. 'Yac, Yac', the story of the dog, has either developed out of or grown into the longer tale. 'The Hotel-Keeper's Story' was originally intended as the opening chapter of a novel *Mrs Trollope and Madame Blaise* and will be recognised by readers of Stead as the basis for the much longer opening chapter of the novel that finally appeared in 1973 as *The Little Hotel*.

'A Household' written in Basle in 1952 is set in the Rhineland and was meant for a collection of short stories to be called *The Traveller's Bed and Breakfast*, a project never completed. The sinister French pair, the Leglands, have their parallel in *The Little Hotel* in the Blaises, the husband there replacing the wife as the monster in the partnership.

'The Woman in the Bed' is a rewriting of those parts of *The Little Hotel* in which the character Miss Chillard appears as just one of the guest establishment. 'The Boy', which depicts a curious son-and-lover relationship between Fifi Mercier, in her fifties and Paul Bernard, aged thirty-three, a guest in her boarding house, is another of the tales once intended for the volume *The Traveller's Bed and Breakfast.*

The Blakes went to live in England in 1953. They had various addresses in London, Newcastle and Surrey before settling in the London suburb of Surbiton. The longest gap in publication dates between any two of Christina Stead's books occurs now – 1952 (*The People with the Dogs*) and 1966 (*Dark Places of the Heart*). During this period Christina finished *Cotters' England*, rewrote the long novel *I'm Dying Laughing*, brought out translations of three French books, *Colour of Asia* by Fernand Gigon, *The Candid Killer* by Jean Giltène and *In Balloon and Bathyscaphe* by Auguste Piccard, edited an anthology, *Great Stories of the South Sea Islands*, and did some reviewing, mainly for the *Times Literary Supplement*.

Section 6 contains three stories set in London of the 1950s and 1960s – 'Street Idyll', 'A Routine' and 'Accents'. ('Accents' was written, or finished, as late as 1968.) '1954: Days of the Roomers', an autobiographical piece, is included here for its picture of boarding-house life in London in the early 1950s. It first appeared in *Overland* in 1975 and was written to commemorate the birth of that magazine in the year 1954.

'1954: Days of the Roomers' could just as easily have been included in Section 7, which assembles the biographical and autobiographical articles. 'A Writer's Friends', which first appeared as Number 2 of a series Australian Writers in Profile in *Southerly* 1968, describes Christina's earliest ventures in writing and deals in some detail with the fortunes of the manuscript of *Seven Poor Men of Sydney* leading to its publication in 1934. In 'A Waker and Dreamer' Christina writes of her father David Stead, the naturalist. This portrait is clear-eyed and affectionate and should be compulsory reading for would-be biographers of Christina Stead herself and all those simplifiers of that masterpiece *The Man Who Loved Children* who stick labels like male chauvinist or political fascist on Sam Pollit, reducing a richly complex novel to the level of an exposure.

William Blake died in February 1968 and in 1969 Christina Stead paid a short visit to Australia on a Visiting Fellowship to the Australian National University. It was over forty years since she left her home country as a young woman with the vague idea of studying at the Sorbonne and visiting Weimar (she was from early days an admirer of Goethe). 'Another View of the Homestead' published in *Hemisphere* 1970 (later reprinted in the *Paris Review* as 'A View of the Homestead') juxtaposes her arrival in England by ship in 1928 and her return to Australia by plane in 1969. Written in 'shadowy England' after her return, it is a series of reflections by a wanderer fascinated to re-discover the splendour of the Australian light.

The short play entitled 'Did It Sell? (or, Was It Hell)',

a light-hearted piece was intended for circulation (if at all) only among friends. It is published here because it expresses an attitude towards her writing that Christina Stead held throughout her life — that she would never write for money, never aim for a best-seller; she would write simply because she enjoyed writing. In private conversation she was usually reluctant to discuss her own books – if she did happen to speak of them it was, more often than not, slightingly. She seemed not to care what happened once they were published , though she cared greatly during the writing itself. She used to say that her books were her children and that she was not really a good mother. She sent them out into the world and they had to fend for themselves. This unusual detachment, which interviewers often found hard to understand, was perfectly genuine. As a writer she was intensely personal and detached at the same time, like James Joyce. She has been misread by some people, biographical beavers, political pushers, various kinds of social activists, all those whose own commitments and beliefs will not (perhaps cannot) allow Stead the creative artist the advantage of her double vision. Her detachment finds expression in this squib in a form of self-mockery through quotation. It is composed of quotations from each of her books from *The Salzburg Tales* to *Letty Fox*. (For details see *Southerly*, Number One, 1984). The final reference to 'A natural best-seller' is ironical, as *Letty Fox* (which, in fact, neither uses any taboo words nor offers any explicit description of sexual activity) was banned in Australia and denounced in the United States by some reviewers for its alleged salaciousness and its insult to American women.

This collection concludes with a contribution to a Symposium on Women's Intuition published in *Vogue* (U.S.) in 1971 as 'About Women's Insight, There is a

Sort of Folklore We Inherit'. This title is a quotation from the article. Christina Stead's own title was, more characteristically, the one given here, 'The Magic Woman and Other Stories'. In a series of notes written in August 1961 to a woman in Prague, who had applied for information about her books and her viewpoint, Christina Stead wrote thus: 'No doubt because I was brought up by a naturalist, I have always felt an irresistible urge to paint true pictures of society as I have seen it. I often felt that quite well known writings lacked truth, and this was particularly so of the pictures of women, I felt, not only because women took their complete part in society but were not represented as doing so, but because the long literary tradition, thousands of years old, had enabled men completely to express themselves, while women feared to do so. However, my object was by no means to write for women, or to discuss feminine problems, but to depict society as it was; indeed, I felt, I understood men better, having been early introduced to the various colleagues, visitors and others my father met. Naturally, I wished to understand men and women equally.' 'The Magic Woman and Other Stories', which questions certain beliefs (not all popular) about female intuition, may be read as a supplement to these remarks and as a pointer to Christina Stead's practice as a novelist.

The piece used as the introduction to this book and which provides its title is a contribution to 'The International Symposium on the Short Story' in *Kenyon Review*, 1968. This, too, is a highly personal essay rather than a conventional article. 'What is unique about the short story is that we all can tell one, live one, even write one down; that story is steeped in our own view and emotion.' Christina was a listener and a teller of stories as a child, as well as a reader, and this love of story runs throughout her work. *The Salzburg Tales*, the most literary of all her books, makes this clear from the outset. Her novels, too, follow no conventional, predetermined form; they take their shape and direction (some more successfully than others) from her themes and characters. So, as the variety offered by *The Salzburg Tales* attests, she has the freest concept of what constitutes a short story, tying it primarily to life not literature. She puts it well: 'It is the million drops of water that are the looking-glass of all our lives.'

The Salzburg Tales aside, all her fiction derives directly from the places she lives in and people she knew or observed. It would, I believe, be possible to identify all the principal characters and many of the situations in her fiction if we had access to the facts. The strange Benjamin Cullen of 'Lost American' is clearly the real-life Eric of 'A Writer's Friends'; the fantastical Marpurgo of *The Beauties and Furies* is likewise modelled on a man she knew. William Blake, with his encyclopedic knowledge and brilliant conversation, appears as Baruch Mendelssohn in *Seven Poor Men of Sydney*, as Michel Alphendéry in *House of All Nations* and as James Quick in *For Love Alone*. The grain merchant with a genius for money-making, insatiable in his pursuit of women, was an associate of William Blake's, and appears as Henry van Laer in 'The Amenities' (*The Salzburg Tales*), as Henri Léon in *House of All Nations* and again, with certain modifications, as the repulsive Robbie Grant in *A Little Tea, A Little Chat*. In *The Man Who Loved Children* Sam Pollit is based on David Stead, the naturalist, Louisa on Christina herself, as is Teresa in *For Love Alone*. And so we could go on and on, but ultimately none of this really matters. People are used as models for characters and the important thing, the real achievement, is the literary work, the imaginative creation that emerges.

Christina Stead was not always flattered by the attention paid her in later years (by which time her works had become well-known). She certainly believed in what she wrote but was modest, even indifferent, about her achievements. One part of her was quite horrified by the thought that any book of hers should be set for study at a university. She had little time for literary circles, preferring the company of friends from all walks of life to professional writers. She was extremely generous in support of the causes she believed in but as a writer she always preserved her detachment and somewhat prickly individuality.

In the last decade of her life awards and official recognition, which she never sought, came her way. Her Visiting Fellowship to the Australian National University has already been mentioned. She won the Patrick White Award for Australian writers in 1974, the year of her return to Australia. She was visiting writer at Monash and Newcastle Universities. She won the NSW Premier's award for services to Australian literature in 1982. In the same year she was elected to Honorary Membership of the American Academy and Institute of Arts and Letters. In March 1983 the University of New South Wales decided to confer on her the Honorary Degree of Doctor of Letters but her death, on 31 March, occurred before her formal admission to the degree could take place.

The writings collected in this volume vary in quality. This is no matter for surprise, since a little fewer than half of them (some obviously lacking the final polish) were found among her papers after her death. It seemed to me worthwhile putting them together.

Acknowledgements

Places and publication dates of first appearances
'Ocean of Story' ('The Short Story') *Kenyon Review*, 1968
'The Milk Run' *New Yorker*, 9 December, 1972
'O, If I Could But Shiver!' *The Fairies Return*, London, 1934
'Uncle Morgan at the Nats' *Partisan Review*, 1976
'The Azhdanov Tailors' *Commentary*, 1971
'I Live in You' *Sun* (Melbourne), 1973
'An Iced Cake with Cherries' *Meanjin*, 1970
'UNO 1945' *Southerly*, 1962
'The Captain's House' *Courier-Mail* (Brisbane), 1973
'The Hotel-Keeper's Story' *Southerly*, 1952
'A Household' *Southerly*, 1962
'The Woman in the Bed' *Meanjin*, 1968
'The Boy' *Meanjin*, 1973
'Street Idyll' *Sydney Morning Herald*, 3 January, 1972
'1954: Days of the Roomers' *Overland*, 1975
'A Waker and Dreamer' *Overland*, 1972
'A Writer's Friends' *Southerly*, 1968
'Another View of the Homestead' *Hemisphere*, 1970

'The Magic Woman and Other Stories' ('About Women's Insight, There is a Sort of Folklore We Inherit') *Vogue* (US), 1971

All other items (with the exception of 'A Routine' and 'Yac, Yac', which are published here for the first time) in *Southerly*, Numbers 1, 2 and 3, 1984.

R. G. Geering